Achilles
the
Hero

Achilles
the
Hero

Edited and Introduced by
Eirene Allen

General Editor: Jake Jackson

**FLAME TREE
PUBLISHING**

This is a FLAME TREE Book

FLAME TREE PUBLISHING
6 Melbray Mews
Fulham, London SW6 3NS
United Kingdom
www.flametreepublishing.com

Special thanks to Jason Emerson

First published 2023
Copyright © 2023 Flame Tree Publishing Ltd

23 25 27 26 24
1 3 5 7 9 8 6 4 2

ISBN: 978-1-80417-329-9

The classic texts in this book derive from: *The Iliad of Homer*, translated by Samuel
Butler, published by Longmans, Green and Co., New York and Bombay, 1898;
The Odyssey by Homer, translated by Samuel Butler, published by A.C. Fifield,
London, 1900; *The Extant Odes of Pindar*, translated by Ernest Myers, published by
Macmillan and Co., London, 1874; *Hestod, Homeric Hymns, Epic Cycle, Homerica*,
translated by Evelyn-White, H.G. Loeb Classical Library, Volume 57, published by
William Heinemann, London, 1914; *Symposium* and *Apology* by Plato, translated by
Benjamin Jowett, published by C. Scribner's sons, New York, 1871; the *Argonautica*
by Apollonius Rhodius, translated by R.C. Seaton, 1912; *Love Romances* by Parthenius,
translated by J.M. Edmonds and S. Gaselee, published by Harvard University Press,
Cambridge, MA, 1916; the *Metamorphoses* of Ovid, Book 12, translated by Henry
T. Riley, published by George Bell & Sons, London, 1893; the *Achilleid* by Statius,
translated by Mozley, published by Harvard University Press, Cambridge, MA and
William Heinemann Ltd, London, 1928; *The Library* [*Biblioteca*] by Apollodorus,
Volume 2, translated by Sir James George Frazer, published by William Heinemann,
London and G.P. Putnam's Son, New York, 1921; *The Fall of Troy* [*Posthomerica*] by
Quintus Smyrnaeus, translated by A.S. Way, published by William Heinemann, London,
1913; *History of the Fall of Troy* from *The Trojan War: The Chronicles of Dictys of
Crete and Dares the Phrygian*, translated by R.M. Frazer (Jr.), published by Indiana
University Press, 1966; and *Life Stories for Young People: Achilles*, translated and
abridged from the German of Carl Friedrich Becker by George P. Upton, published by
A.C. McClurg & Co., Chicago, 1912.

Printed and bound in the UK by Clays Ltd, Elcograf S.p.A

Contents

Series Foreword

STRETCHING BACK to the oral traditions of thousands of years ago, tales of heroes and disaster, creation and conquest have been told by many different civilizations in many different ways. Their impact sits deep within our culture even though the detail in the tales themselves are a loose mix of historical record, transformed narrative and the distortions of hundreds of storytellers.

Today the language of mythology lives with us: our mood is jovial, our countenance is saturnine, we are narcissistic and our modern life is hermetically sealed from others. The nuances of myths and legends form part of our daily routines and help us navigate the world around us, with its half truths and biased reported facts.

The nature of a myth is that its story is already known by most of those who hear it, or read it. Every generation brings a new emphasis, but the fundamentals remain the same: a desire to understand and describe the events and relationships of the world. Many of the great stories are archetypes that help us find our own place, equipping us with tools for self-understanding, both individually and as part of a broader culture.

For Western societies it is Greek mythology that speaks to us most clearly. It greatly influenced the mythological heritage of the ancient Roman civilization and is the lens through which we still see the Celts, the Norse and many of the other great peoples and religions. The Greeks themselves learned much from their neighbours, the Egyptians, an older culture that became weak with age and incestuous leadership.

It is important to understand that what we perceive now as mythology had its own origins in perceptions of the divine and the rituals of the sacred. The earliest civilizations, in the crucible of the Middle East, in the Sumer of the third millennium BCE, are the source to which many of the mythic archetypes can be traced. As humankind collected together in cities for the first time, developed writing and industrial scale agriculture, started to irrigate the rivers and attempted to control rather than be at the mercy of its environment, humanity began to write down its tentative explanations of natural events, of floods and plagues, of disease.

Early stories tell of Gods (or god-like animals in the case of tribal societies such as African, Native American or Aboriginal cultures) who are crafty and use their wits to survive, and it is reasonable to suggest that these were the first rulers of the gathering peoples of the earth, later elevated to god-like status with the distance of time. Such tales became more political as cities vied with each other for supremacy, creating new Gods, new hierarchies for their pantheons. The older Gods took on primordial roles and became the preserve of creation and destruction, leaving the new gods to deal with more current, everyday affairs. Empires rose and fell, with Babylon assuming the mantle from Sumeria in the 1800s BCE, then in turn to be swept away by the Assyrians of the 1200s BCE; then the Assyrians and the Egyptians were subjugated by the Greeks, the Greeks by the Romans and so on, leading to the spread and assimilation of common themes, ideas and stories throughout the world.

The survival of history is dependent on the telling of good tales, but each one must have the 'feeling' of truth, otherwise it will be ignored. Around the firesides, or embedded in a book or a computer, the myths and legends of the past are still the living materials of retold myth, not restricted to an exploration of origins. Now we have devices and global communications that give us unparalleled access to a diversity of traditions. We can find out about Indigenous American, Indian, Chinese and tribal African mythology in a way that was denied to our ancestors, we can find connections, match the archaeology, religion and the mythologies of the world to build a comprehensive image of the human adventure.

The great leaders of history and heroes of literature have also adopted the mantle of mythic experience, because the stories of historical figures – Cyrus the Great, Alexander, Genghis Khan – and mytho-poetic warriors such as Beowulf achieve a cultural significance that transcends their moment in the chronicles of humankind. Myth, history and literature have become powerful, intwined instruments of perception, with echoes of reported fact and symbolic truths that convey the sweep of human experience. In this series of books we are glad to share with you the wonderful traditions of the past.

Jake Jackson
General Editor

Introduction to Achilles the Hero

IN THE OLDEST WRITTEN SOURCES **through which Achilles'
story reaches us, he is an angry young man doomed to die. His
journey in these ancient poems is to reconcile himself with his
mortal fate and to claim his place in the pantheon of heroes. The
son of a nymph, Thetis, and a mortal king, Peleus, Achilles inherits
his father's mortality, but his mother's divine status offers him a
form of immortalization: in the eternal fame of epic song and as a
hero who is worshipped in cult. According to the scholar Gregory
Nagy, in the ancient Greek world that created and preserved stories
about Achilles, and revisited and reshaped his story in a variety of
visual and verbal media, these two forms of immortalization, one
in myth, one in ritual, inform each other.**

The intense, youthful hero of myth is swift-footed Achilles, the best of the
Achaeans (the archaic term for the Greek speakers who fought at Troy).
Preeminent in martial skills and imbued with superhuman strength, he is
driven to excess, whether for good or ill. He is willing to die to avenge his
beloved companion, Patroclus, but this drive for vengeance also provokes
him to commit outrages that lead to mass destruction and his own death.
Yet after his mortal body dies, his essence is presumed to transition through
Hades and ascend to a divine realm, and he remains a superhuman force
that can be invoked through ritual observances. Propitiating him, and other
heroes, was a way to harness his superhuman power for the benefit of those
who worshipped him.

Achilles' mortal journey, his process of reconciling with his fate, is known
to us today through Homer's epic poems, which were part of a series of
narratives that make up what we call Trojan War mythology. This series
of nested stories is believed to have been passed down orally for perhaps
hundreds of years before being written down in approximately the middle

of the seventh century BCE, being institutionalized in classical Athens, and becoming a cornerstone of Greek identity.

It is in these contexts that the figure of Achilles took shape and the legacy with which the texts in this volume engage.

Oral Culture and the Transition to Written Language

Before there was an alphabet in which Achilles' story could be written down, it was passed from one generation to the next in songs. Though the contexts in which they were experienced cannot be reconstructed with precision and are broadly debated, they may have been sung by bards, possibly accompanied by music and dance. Bards were potentially figures of divine authority believed to have received their stories from the Muses, conceived of as the daughters of Zeus and the goddess of memory, Mnemosyne. In this sense, the songs of bards, composed in the act of performing them, could be thought of as utterances of sacred significance. The range of stories that were recorded, and their at times conflicting details, suggest that what mattered was not so much consistency in the telling, but of remembering and recounting the stories of heroes, whose presence and power continued to be felt by the generations who worshipped them.

Thousands of hero cults existed across the diffuse, decentralized archaic and classical Greek world, specific to the local communities that instituted them. Some are attested in written sources, others in archaeological finds. Still others may remain unknown to us, time having washed away traces of their existence. As the 'best of the Achaeans', Achilles can be thought of as a model on which any hero's journey from myth to cult could be mapped. As Nagy proposes, Achilles' story in Homer's *Iliad*, combined with Odysseus's in the *Odyssey*, communicated everything that was important for ancient Greek speakers to remember about heroes, wherever they were located in the Greek world.

That our Homeric epics have their origins in oral composition only came to light in the last 100 years through the research of American classicists Millman Parry and Albert Lord. Their interdisciplinary approach combined methodical analysis of language and ethnographic study of living Serbo-Croatian bards. From this process, Parry and Lord proposed that the Homeric 'texts' contain features associated with oral composition in performance. Among the evidence for this compositional form is the prevalence across the epics of formulae that can be applied and adapted to a variety of contexts. This repeated patterning can occur at the levels of language, scene or plot. Formulae provided bards with the tools to meet metric demands in the moment while also being flexible enough to adapt to thematic needs. Language analysis has also revealed that the Homeric epics contain a mix of Greek dialects, geographically and across time. Some phrases are believed to be quite ancient, perhaps inherited from Bronze Age Greece, while other usages and references belong to later periods, suggesting an accumulating storytelling tradition that was preserved, paradoxically, through innovation.

Once the stories were written down, however, they became fixed texts. While they may have been edited in some way during the classical period and later, scholars generally believe that the epics' language and references place them no later than approximately 700 BCE. References to these epics as the works of Homer began to appear in the sixth century, but as the scholar Barbara Graziosi has discussed, the earliest mentions of Homeric epics in ancient sources refer to songs rather than texts. Ancient sources portray these songs as passing from the bard to those closely associated with him to leaders who brought them back to their cities. Whatever texts of the epics existed, they seem to have been treated more as scripts to aid memorization for public performance than as documents to be read in isolation. The epics themselves continued to be experienced aurally and communally. Homer's name was initially associated with all the epics about the Trojan War, but by the fourth century came to be associated with the two preeminent among them, the *Iliad* and *Odyssey*.

Also in the sixth century, evidence suggests that the Homeric epics were recited at festivals in honour of the gods and heroes associated with a city (each would have had their own, though they were part of the interconnected whole). The best-known example is their inclusion at Athens' most important festival, the Panathenaea. In addition to being recited at sacred rituals, events from Trojan War myth, and Homer's versions in particular, decorated pottery, statuary and possibly woven garments. The myths were also referenced in histories, philosophical texts and court speeches, and they inspired the plots of tragedies, which were also performed at various ritual events. This suggests that, while the texts of the *Iliad* and *Odyssey* were fixed, how Trojan War mythology was told in other contexts continued to be reshaped and adapted by poets, thinkers and speakers as relevant to their occasions.

When these epics were committed to text, by whom, and under what circumstances, continues to be shrouded in mystery and will likely remain so. It is generally believed that the creation of texts of these oral stories coincided with or followed shortly after the invention of the Greek alphabet, sometime near the beginning of the eighth century BCE. The only texts of these Trojan War stories that have survived mostly complete are the *Iliad* and *Odyssey*, both of which feature Achilles. But they were not the only versions to have circulated, to have been written down and to have narrated Achilles' experiences. The *Iliad* and *Odyssey* were two of eight epics composed in dactylic hexameter verse that are collectively known as the Epic Cycle, which explained the origins of, events at and aftermath of the Trojan War.

The Epic Cycle and the Multiverse

The contents of the six lost epics of the Epic Cycle are known through fragments and summaries written of them in later antiquity and the Middle Ages. This has made it difficult to determine when they were composed, why they were written down and in what context they were experienced. Whether they were composed contemporaneously with the two that have survived, or afterwards to supplement them, is debated. What seems evident from the information available is that they provide both alternative and complementary narratives of Achilles' story in the *Iliad* and *Odyssey*, which impact how it can be interpreted.

Set in chronological order of the events they cover, the eight epics of the Cycle are the *Cypria, Iliad, Aethiopis, Little Iliad, Iliou Persis, Nostoi,*

Odyssey and *Telegony*. The first four in the series concern events before and during the war, in which Achilles figures prominently, and the final three follow the aftermath of the war, in which the central figure is Odysseus. Achilles and Odysseus can be thought of as foils, offering contrasting methods for achieving eternal fame: Achilles is remembered for how he dies while Odysseus is remembered for how he survives. Achilles can be understood as exemplifying how to face death and Odysseus how to tackle life.

Known through fragments and a prose summary attributed to Greek writer Proclus, the *Cypria* narrates events that led up to the Trojan War, some of which are alluded to or patterned in the *Iliad* and some that are taken up in later ancient myth retellings. Those that are referenced in the *Iliad* include Trojan prince Paris leaving Sparta with King Menelaus's wife Helen (described in terms that conflate her own will with divine intervention) and Achilles being awarded Briseis, widow of King Mynes of Lyrnessus, as a war prize. Events taken up elsewhere include Agamemnon using marriage to Achilles as a ruse to lure his daughter Iphigenia to Aulis, where the Achaean forces have amassed to sail to Troy, then sacrificing her to Artemis. Though the *Iliad* does not reference this episode, it complements the conflict that unfolds across it, adding a potential history of animosity between the leader of the Achaean expedition to Troy, Agamemnon, and its best warrior, Achilles.

Examples of nesting patterns and variations between the *Cypria* and *Iliad* occur in two significant ways that impact the interpretation of Achilles. In the *Iliad*, Agamemnon's appropriation of Briseis sparks the conflict that causes Achilles to remove himself from battle. This internal Achaean conflict between Agamemnon and Achilles mirrors the larger conflict that caused the war between the Greeks and the Trojans referenced in the *Cypria*, Paris's appropriation of Helen. In addition, a 'plan of Zeus' is referenced in both the *Cypria* and the *Iliad*. That plan differs in each epic, but the two versions are complementary. In the *Cypria*, Zeus plans the Trojan War to relieve Earth of the burden placed on her by the heroes' excesses. Achilles in the *Iliad* exemplifies these excesses but on a local scale: in his murderous rampage, set in motion by the death of Patroclus, Achilles fills the river Scamander with his many victims until it is overflowing with corpses. This episode follows the pattern of events with Earth in the *Cypria*, but on a smaller scale. Repeating patterns, as exemplified in Achilles' actions, illustrate the cyclicality and eternal recurrence of human events and experiences.

The *Aethiopis*, known through ancient synopsis and commentaries, picks up the Trojan War story after the death of Hector, with which the *Iliad* ends. It describes Achilles' death at the hands of Paris and Apollo, the funeral games held in his honour and the conflict between Achaean warriors Ajax and Odysseus for Achilles' armour. Again, patterning is evident across the *Aeithiopis* and the *Iliad*. In the *Iliad*, Achilles' companion Patroclus dies at the hands of Apollo and another Trojan prince, Hector, and funeral games are held in his honour. At Patroclus's funeral games, numerous conflicts threaten to break out but are smoothly resolved under Achilles' skilful guidance. If the *Iliad* is understood to provide ancient Greek speakers with a template explaining their ritual honouring of heroes, then the variations of the patterns are telling. Patroclus serves as Achilles' ritual double in the *Iliad*, and the ideal resolution of conflict at his funeral games may reflect the intention of ritual: when executed properly, it achieves balance and harmony which 'corrects' the excesses of myth. The magnanimous and calm Achilles who presides over Patroclus's funeral games exemplifies an ideal hero of ritual – skilled, powerful and capable of achieving balance when events threaten to teeter out of control.

Each epic in the Cycle tells a 'complete' story, with its own beginning, middle and end, but the stories together make up a tapestry of pattern and variation, fixed and adapted elements, tradition and innovation. Importantly, ancient listeners of the poems – and their subsequent retellings across antiquity – are believed to have been familiar with this tapestry. The ancients likely would have known that the Achaeans travelled to Troy to avenge Menelaus, whose wife Trojan prince Paris took from Sparta (whether willingly or forcibly). They likely would have known that Achilles removed himself from battle over anger at Agamemnon, returned to avenge the death of his dearest companion and died himself shortly thereafter. And they likely would have known that the Achaeans won the war but lost the peace because their outrages offended the gods. In short, the Trojan War stories functioned as a multiverse of interconnected narratives, with which ancient audiences were intimately acquainted.

What they listened for, then, was perhaps how the familiar stories would be reshaped to speak to the present moment.

The Changing World

In archaic and classical Greece, where heroes of myth and heroes of ritual were inextricably connected, heroes can be understood as belonging to an earlier age of mortals who were descended from the gods and in direct contact with them. Leaders of cities and other prominent families might claim descent from heroes. Poets like Pindar, who wrote victory odes for the winners of athletic games incorporated in ritual worship of the gods, might compare victors to heroes. Philosophers like Plato and tragedians like Euripides might invoke the heroes to explain human nature as it affected people in the present. But a divide seems to have existed between the mortals of the historical present who worshipped heroes, attempting to harness their powers for the benefit of their cities, and the age of heroes that belonged in the mythical past. Over time in antiquity, that distance seems to have gradually diminished. As the divide seems to have become blurred, the meaning of hero stories and the way they were told shifted, as the texts in this collection attest in their transformation of Achilles' meaning and story.

While changes tend to be more gradual and subtle than can be fully tracked, Alexander the Great seems to represent a turning point. Alexander's father, Philip of Macedon, conquered the Greek-speaking world, and his son expanded the empire he inherited, conquering territories in Asia and North Africa. Among Alexander's companions on his campaigns was a copy of the *Iliad*, legendarily annotated by Aristotle, Alexander's tutor. One theory holds that the young leader modelled himself on Achilles. Roman sources who write of the connection between the conqueror and the 'best of the Achaeans' are offered in support. Alexander's mother claimed to be descended from Achilles, and he visited the hero's tomb at Troy before launching his campaign against Persia.

Achilles' actions in the *Iliad* – notably his relationship with Briseis and his desecration of Hector's body – provided a pretext for Alexander to behave likewise. These represent a sample of many associations ancient sources draw between the two figures, one of myth, one of history.

Though the extent of the connection is debated, Alexander's purported emulation of and desire to supplant Achilles may reflect larger socio-political shifts taking place during his conquests. The highly decentralized ancient Greek-speaking world of the archaic and classical periods had been brought under the control of a single ruler for the first time. That this ruler could have been associated with the heroes of excess seems fitting for the moment.

After Alexander's death, his empire fractured into smaller succession empires, the Ptolemies in Egypt, the Seleucids in the East and the Antigonids in Greece. The Ptolemies were based in Alexandria, the city Alexander founded and that was named for him. Unlike the cities of the Greek mainland, Alexandria did not boast an ancient mythic past. It was founded during the historical present and needed to invent its own institutions that brought together the cultures of immigrant Greeks with those of the indigenous Egyptian population, including heroes for worship. One hero became Alexander himself, the 'new' Achilles. The Ptolemies instituted a cult of Alexander in 323 BCE that persisted until the city fell to Octavian, future Roman Emperor Caesar Augustus, in 31 BCE.

Greek cultures, including their poetic traditions, had begun influencing Rome well before the Roman conquest of Greece, but the conquest inevitably changed the dynamic. A paradox presented itself that called for resolution: to paraphrase the Roman poet Horace, Rome had conquered Greece, but Greek culture had conquered Rome. To correct the 'imbalance', and celebrate the new Caesar, Roman poets would need to create an epic to rival and supersede Homer's. Virgil's *Aeneid* capitalized on the *Iliad*'s references to Trojan prince Aeneas being fated to survive the war and fashioned him as the founder of Rome. In doing so, Virgil simultaneously paid homage to Homer, created a 'national' epic for Rome and provided an origin story for its conquest of Greece – as vengeance for the Achaeans' sack of Troy. Achilles as a character does not appear in Virgil's Roman epic, but his presence can be felt in Aeneas's references to escaping the carnage and destruction at Troy and the crude brutality he attributes to 'Greek' heroes.

Later Roman poets, writing at a time when emperors were directly associated with gods and heroes and worshipped in cult, engaged the story of Achilles more directly. Like Virgil and the Greek poets before him, they revisited and reshaped his story to speak to their own times and purposes. As the texts in this collection attest, whether as a figure of worship for his superhuman strength or an object of censure for his violent excesses, Achilles remained, and remains, a fascinating figure for poets and writers. What each retelling reveals is not only the many meanings that Achilles can hold but the culture of the poets and writers who chose to take on and reshape his story.

Eirene Allen holds a PhD from New York University and is the director of the Institute for Classics Education, a US-based nonprofit dedicated to supporting educators who teach Homer and ancient Greek texts in English classrooms. Her writing and research focus on Homer and classical Greek texts. Her publications include study guides for the *Iliad*, *Odyssey*, *Argonautica*, and numerous plays by Sophocles and Euripides.

Achilles in Archaic and Classical Greece

THE COLLECTION OF TEXTS in this section ranges from the earliest written sources of the archaic period, the epics of Homer and the Epic Cycle, to among the latest of the classical period, Plato's dialogues. By the fourth century BCE, the *Iliad* and *Odyssey* had achieved preeminence and become the only epics from the Cycle attributed to Homer. Perhaps as a result, they are the only two to survive complete. Together, they can be understood to tell the story of a cosmic transition, from the Age of Heroes, who were descended from and in close contact with the gods, to the Age of Man, the historical present of the archaic and classical periods. Within this 'present', Achilles can function as an exemplar of the hero's journey from myth to cult.

The *Iliad*'s Book I portrays Achilles as an ambivalent figure, whose drive for honour renders him unstable. It leads to conflict with his expedition leader (Agamemnon) and, eventually, to the death of his dearest companion (Patroclus). In Book XVIII, Achilles begins to face the consequences of his extreme drive and seeks to correct it by avenging Patroclus, even if it means his own death. His corrective action in Book XXIV extends not only to his dearest friend but also to his perceived enemy. Achilles' ability to balance his own needs with the needs of his enemy's may signify his transition from mythic figure to cult hero, a superhuman force who is capable of achieving balance. His appearance in the *Odyssey* suggests that, despite its many hardships, mortal life is worth living: Even Achilles, among the most revered heroes, would prefer to suffer among the living than to be revered among the dead.

Surviving summaries and fragments of the remaining epics in the Cycle fill out the story of the Trojan War and the exploits that poets believed made Achilles worth remembering. Revealed in these are both his positive and destructive qualities: his outstanding martial skill, his drive for honour, his devotion to Patroclus and finally his acceptance of the need to balance his divine and mortal portions. These stories provided the raw material for poets, philosophers and tragedians to rethink his function and reshape his story. The works of Pindar and Plato inaugurate that process, which continues to this day. They revisit the story of Achilles as a way to understand the successes, challenges and debates of their times, always with an emphasis on his sacred status.

Pindar, who lived from 518 to at least 446 BCE, was an acclaimed composer of victory odes for winners at festival games. Held in honour of gods and heroes, the sacred context of these events shaped the significance of stories like Achilles', invoked to praise victors who may have claimed heroic ancestry. Mythological heroes frequently feature as points of comparison, tying their excellence to that of the victor. In the extract from the *Nemean* 3, Pindar's description of young Achilles chasing down deer provides an origin story for his epithet in Homer, 'swift-footed Achilles'. In addition, it establishes him as destined for heroism via his inborn excellence, a quality he shares with the subject of the ode.

Similarly, the dialogues of Athenian philosopher Plato (approximately 427–347 BCE) draw on Achilles as an exemplar of heroic self-sacrifice. The *Symposium* is a collection of speeches in praise of love. The extract features the first speaker, Phaedrus, using Achilles as an example of the way love can fuel acts of outstanding courage. His love for his companion inspired him to sacrifice his own life for no other reason than to avenge him. In the *Apology of Socrates*, Achilles, the hero *par excellence*, merges with Socrates, Plato's 'hero' of philosophy. In both cases, Achilles serves as an example of proper conduct, behaving only with regard for what is right rather than for personal gain.

The Iliad

Book I

The Quarrel Between Agamemnon and Achilles – Achilles Withdraws from the War and Sends His Mother Thetis to Ask Jove to Help the Trojans – Scene Between Jove and Juno on Olympus

SING, O GODDESS, the anger of Achilles son of Peleus, that brought countless ills upon the Achaeans. Many a brave soul did it send hurrying down to Hades, and many a hero did it yield a prey to dogs and vultures, for so were the counsels of Jove fulfilled from the day on which the son of Atreus, king of men, and great Achilles, first fell out with one another.

And which of the gods was it that set them on to quarrel? It was the son of Jove and Leto; for he was angry with the king and sent a pestilence upon the host to plague the people, because the son of Atreus had dishonoured Chryses his priest. Now Chryses had come to the ships of the Achaeans to free his daughter, and had brought with him a great ransom: moreover, he bore in his hand the sceptre of Apollo wreathed with a suppliant's wreath, and he besought the Achaeans, but most of all the two sons of Atreus, who were their chiefs.

"Sons of Atreus," he cried, "and all other Achaeans, may the gods who dwell in Olympus grant you to sack the city of Priam, and to reach your homes in safety; but free my daughter, and accept a ransom for her, in reverence to Apollo, son of Jove."

On this the rest of the Achaeans with one voice were for respecting the priest and taking the ransom that he offered; but not so Agamemnon, who spoke fiercely to him and sent him roughly away. "Old man," said he, "let me not find you tarrying about our ships, nor yet coming hereafter. Your sceptre of the god and your wreath shall profit you nothing. I will not free her. She shall grow old in my house at Argos far from her own home, busying herself with her loom and visiting my couch; so go, and do not provoke me or it shall be the worse for you."

The old man feared him and obeyed. Not a word he spoke, but went by the shore of the sounding sea and prayed apart to King Apollo whom lovely Leto had borne. "Hear me," he cried, "O god of the silver bow, that protectest Chryse and holy Cilla and rulest Tenedos with thy might, hear me oh thou of Sminthe. If I have ever decked your temple with garlands, or burned your thigh-bones in fat of bulls or goats, grant my prayer, and let your arrows avenge these my tears upon the Danaans."

Thus did he pray, and Apollo heard his prayer. He came down furious from the summits of Olympus, with his bow and his quiver upon his shoulder, and the arrows rattled on his back with the rage that trembled within him. He sat himself down away from the ships with a face as dark as night, and his silver bow rang death as he shot his arrow in the midst of them. First he smote their mules and their hounds, but presently he aimed his shafts at the people themselves, and all day long the pyres of the dead were burning.

For nine whole days he shot his arrows among the people, but upon the tenth day Achilles called them in assembly – moved thereto by Juno, who saw the Achaeans in their death-throes and had compassion upon them. Then, when they were got together, he rose and spoke among them.

"Son of Atreus," said he, "I deem that we should now turn roving home if we would escape destruction, for we are being cut down by war and pestilence at once. Let us ask some priest or prophet, or some reader of dreams (for dreams, too, are of Jove) who can tell us why Phoebus Apollo is so angry, and say whether it is for some vow that we have broken, or hecatomb that we have not offered, and whether he will accept the savour of lambs and goats without blemish, so as to take away the plague from us."

With these words he sat down, and Calchas son of Thestor, wisest of augurs, who knew things past present and to come, rose to speak. He it was who had guided the Achaeans with their fleet to Ilius, through the prophesyings with which Phoebus Apollo had inspired him. With all sincerity and goodwill he addressed them thus: – "Achilles, loved of heaven, you bid me tell you about the anger of King Apollo, I will therefore do so; but consider first and swear that you will stand by me heartily in word and deed, for I know that I shall offend one who rules the Argives with might, to whom all the Achaeans are in subjection. A plain man cannot stand against the anger of a king, who if he swallow his displeasure now, will yet nurse revenge till he has wreaked it. Consider, therefore, whether or no you will protect me."

And Achilles answered, "Fear not, but speak as it is borne in upon you from heaven, for by Apollo, Calchas, to whom you pray, and whose oracles you reveal to us, not a Danaan at our ships shall lay his hand upon you, while I yet live to look upon the face of the earth – no, not though you name Agamemnon himself, who is by far the foremost of the Achaeans."

Thereon the seer spoke boldly. "The god," he said, "is angry neither about vow nor hecatomb, but for his priest's sake, whom Agamemnon has dishonoured, in that he would not free his daughter nor take a ransom for her; therefore has he sent these evils upon us, and will yet send others. He will not deliver the Danaans from this pestilence till Agamemnon has restored the girl without fee or ransom to her father, and has sent a holy hecatomb to Chryse. Thus, we may perhaps appease him."

With these words he sat down, and Agamemnon rose in anger. His heart was black with rage, and his eyes flashed fire as he scowled on Calchas and said, "Seer of evil, you never yet prophesied smooth things concerning me, but have ever loved to foretell that which was evil. You have brought me neither comfort nor performance; and now you come seeing among Danaans, and saying that Apollo has plagued us because I would not take a ransom for this girl, the daughter of Chryses. I have set my heart on keeping her in my own house, for I love her better even than my own wife Clytemnestra, whose peer she is alike in form and feature, in understanding and accomplishments. Still, I will give her up if I must, for I would have the people live, not die; but you must find me a prize instead, or I alone among the Argives shall be without one. This is not well; for you behold, all of you, that my prize is to go elsewhither."

And Achilles answered, "Most noble son of Atreus, covetous beyond all mankind, how shall the Achaeans find you another prize? We have no common store from which to take one. Those we took from the cities have been awarded; we cannot disallow the awards that have been made already. Give this girl, therefore, to the god, and if ever Jove grants us to sack the city of Troy we will requite you three and fourfold."

Then Agamemnon said, "Achilles, valiant though you be, you shall not thus outwit me. You shall not overreach, and you shall not persuade me. Are you to keep your own prize, while I sit tamely under my loss and give up the girl at your bidding? Let the Achaeans find me a prize in fair exchange to my liking, or I will come and take your own, or that of Ajax or of Ulysses; and he to whomsoever I may come shall rue my coming. But of this we will take thought hereafter; for the present, let us draw a ship into the sea, and find a crew for her expressly; let us put a hecatomb on board, and let us send Chryseis also; further, let some chief man among us be in command, either Ajax, or Idomeneus, or yourself, son of Peleus, mighty warrior that you are, that we may offer sacrifice and appease the anger of the god."

Achilles scowled at him and answered, "You are steeped in insolence and lust of gain. With what heart can any of the Achaeans do your bidding, either on foray or in open fighting? I came not warring here for any ill the Trojans had done me. I have no quarrel with them. They have not raided my cattle nor my horses, nor cut down my harvests on the rich plains of Phthia; for between me and them there is a great space, both mountain and sounding sea. We have followed you, Sir Insolence! for your pleasure, not ours – to gain satisfaction from the Trojans for your shameless self and for Menelaus. You forget this and threaten to rob me of the prize for which I have toiled, and which the sons of the Achaeans have given me. Never when the Achaeans sack any rich city of the Trojans do I receive so good a prize as you do, though it is my hands that do the better part of the fighting. When the sharing comes, your share is far the largest, and I, forsooth, must go back to my ships, take what I can get and be thankful, when my labour of fighting is done. Now, therefore, I shall go back to Phthia; it will be much better for me to return home with my ships, for I will not stay here dishonoured to gather gold and substance for you."

And Agamemnon answered, "Fly if you will, I shall make you no prayers to stay you. I have others here who will do me honour, and above all Jove, the lord of counsel. There is no king here so hateful to me as you are, for you are ever quarrelsome and ill-affected. What though you be brave? Was it not heaven that made you so? Go home, then, with your ships and comrades to lord it over the Myrmidons. I care neither for you nor for your anger; and thus will I do: since

Phoebus Apollo is taking Chryseis from me, I shall send her with my ship and my followers, but I shall come to your tent and take your own prize Briseis, that you may learn how much stronger I am than you are, and that another may fear to set himself up as equal or comparable with me."

The son of Peleus was furious, and his heart within his shaggy breast was divided whether to draw his sword, push the others aside, and kill the son of Atreus, or to restrain himself and check his anger. While he was thus in two minds, and was drawing his mighty sword from its scabbard, Minerva came down from heaven (for Juno had sent her in the love she bore to them both) and seized the son of Peleus by his yellow hair, visible to him alone, for of the others no man could see her. Achilles turned in amaze, and by the fire that flashed from her eyes at once knew that she was Minerva. "Why are you here," said he, "daughter of aegis-bearing Jove? To see the pride of Agamemnon, son of Atreus? Let me tell you – and it shall surely be – he shall pay for this insolence with his life."

And Minerva said, "I come from heaven, if you will hear me, to bid you stay your anger. Juno has sent me, who cares for both of you alike. Cease, then, this brawling, and do not draw your sword; rail at him if you will, and your railing will not be vain, for I tell you – and it shall surely be – that you shall hereafter receive gifts three times as splendid by reason of this present insult. Hold, therefore, and obey."

"Goddess," answered Achilles, "however angry a man may be, he must do as you two command him. This will be best, for the gods ever hear the prayers of him who has obeyed them."

He stayed his hand on the silver hilt of his sword and thrust it back into the scabbard as Minerva bade him. Then she went back to Olympus among the other gods, and to the house of aegis-bearing Jove.

But the son of Peleus again began railing at the son of Atreus, for he was still in a rage. "Wine-bibber," he cried, "with the face of a dog and the heart of a hind, you never dare to go out with the host in fight, nor yet with our chosen men in ambuscade. You shun this as you do death itself. You had rather go round and rob his prizes from any man who contradicts you. You devour your people, for you are king over a feeble folk; otherwise, son of Atreus, henceforward you would insult no man. Therefore I say, and swear it with a great oath – nay, by this my sceptre which shalt sprout neither leaf nor shoot, nor bud anew from the day on which it left its parent stem upon the mountains – for the axe stripped it of leaf and bark, and now the sons of the Achaeans bear it as judges and guardians of the decrees of heaven – so surely and solemnly do I swear that hereafter they shall look fondly for Achilles and shall not find him. In the day of your distress, when your men fall dying by the murderous hand of Hector, you shall not know how to help them, and shall rend your heart with rage for the hour when you offered insult to the bravest of the Achaeans."

With this the son of Peleus dashed his gold-bestudded sceptre on the ground and took his seat, while the son of Atreus was beginning fiercely from his place upon the other side. Then uprose smooth-tongued Nestor, the facile speaker of the Pylians, and the words fell from his lips sweeter than honey. Two generations of men born and bred in Pylos had passed away under his rule, and he was now reigning over the third. With all sincerity and goodwill, therefore, he addressed them thus: – "Of a truth," he said, "a great sorrow has befallen the Achaean land. Surely Priam with his sons would rejoice, and the Trojans be glad at heart if they could hear this quarrel between you two, who are so excellent in fight and counsel. I am older than either of you; therefore be guided by me. Moreover, I have been the familiar friend of men even greater than you are, and they did not disregard my counsels. Never again can I behold such men as Pirithous and Dryas shepherd of his people, or as Caeneus, Exadius, godlike Polyphemus, and Theseus son of Aegeus, peer of the immortals. These were the mightiest men ever born upon this earth: mightiest were they, and when they fought the fiercest tribes of mountain savages they utterly overthrew them. I came from distant Pylos, and went about among them, for they would have me come, and I fought as it was in me to do. Not a man now living could withstand them, but they heard my words, and were persuaded by them. So be it also with yourselves, for this is the more excellent way. Therefore, Agamemnon, though you be strong, take not this girl away, for the sons of the Achaeans have already given her to Achilles; and you, Achilles, strive not further with the king, for no man who by the grace of Jove wields a sceptre has like honour with Agamemnon. You are strong, and have a goddess for your mother; but Agamemnon is stronger than you, for he has more people under him. Son of Atreus, check your anger, I implore you; end this quarrel with Achilles, who in the day of battle is a tower of strength to the Achaeans."

And Agamemnon answered, "Sir, all that you have said is true, but this fellow must needs become our lord and master: he must be lord of all, king of all, and captain of all, and this shall hardly be. Granted that the gods have made him a great warrior, have they also given him the right to speak with railing?"

Achilles interrupted him. "I should be a mean coward," he cried, "were I to give in to you in all things. Order other people about, not me, for I shall obey no longer. Furthermore I say – and lay my saying to your heart – I shall fight neither you nor any man about this girl, for those that take were those also that gave. But of all else that is at my ship you shall carry away nothing by force. Try, that others may see; if you do, my spear shall be reddened with your blood."

When they had quarrelled thus angrily, they rose, and broke up the assembly at the ships of the Achaeans. The son of Peleus went back to his tents and ships with the son of Menoetius and his company, while Agamemnon drew a vessel into the water and chose a crew of twenty oarsmen. He escorted Chryseis on board and sent moreover a hecatomb for the god. And Ulysses went as captain.

These, then, went on board and sailed their ways over the sea. But the son of Atreus bade the people purify themselves; so they purified themselves and cast their filth into the sea. Then they offered hecatombs of bulls and goats without blemish on the seashore, and the smoke with the savour of their sacrifice rose curling up towards heaven.

Thus did they busy themselves throughout the host. But Agamemnon did not forget the threat that he had made Achilles, and called his trusty messengers and squires Talthybius and Eurybates. "Go," said he, "to the tent of Achilles, son of Peleus; take Briseis by the hand and bring her hither; if he will not give her I shall come with others and take her – which will press him harder."

He charged them straightly further and dismissed them, whereon they went their way sorrowfully by the seaside, till they came to the tents and ships of the Myrmidons. They found Achilles sitting by his tent and his ships, and ill-pleased he was when he beheld them. They stood fearfully and reverently before him, and never a word did they speak, but he knew them and said, "Welcome, heralds, messengers of gods and men; draw near; my quarrel is not with you but with Agamemnon who has sent you for the girl Briseis. Therefore, Patroclus, bring her and give her to them, but let them be witnesses by the blessed gods, by mortal men, and by the fierceness of Agamemnon's anger, that if ever again there be need of me to save the people from ruin, they shall seek and they shall not find. Agamemnon is mad with rage and knows not how to look before and after that the Achaeans may fight by their ships in safety."

Patroclus did as his dear comrade had bidden him. He brought Briseis from the tent and gave her over to the heralds, who took her with them to the ships of the Achaeans – and the woman was loth to go. Then Achilles went all alone by the side of the hoar sea, weeping and looking out upon the boundless waste of waters. He raised his hands in prayer to his immortal mother, "Mother," he cried, "you bore me doomed to live but for a little season; surely Jove, who thunders from Olympus, might have made that little glorious. It is not so. Agamemnon, son of Atreus, has done me dishonour, and has robbed me of my prize by force."

As he spoke he wept aloud, and his mother heard him where she was sitting in the depths of the sea hard by the old man her father. Forthwith she rose as it were a grey mist out of the waves, sat down before him as he stood weeping, caressed him with her hand, and said, "My son, why are you weeping? What is it that grieves you? Keep it not from me, but tell me, that we may know it together."

Achilles drew a deep sigh and said, "You know it; why tell you what you know well already? We went to Thebe the strong city of Eetion, sacked it, and brought hither the spoil. The sons of the Achaeans shared it duly among themselves, and chose lovely Chryseis as the meed of Agamemnon; but Chryses, priest of Apollo, came to the ships of the Achaeans to free his daughter, and brought with him a great ransom: moreover he bore in his hand the sceptre of Apollo, wreathed with a suppliant's wreath, and he besought the Achaeans, but most of all the two sons of Atreus who were their chiefs.

"On this the rest of the Achaeans with one voice were for respecting the priest and taking the ransom that he offered; but not so Agamemnon, who spoke fiercely to him and sent him roughly away. So he went back in anger, and Apollo, who loved him dearly, heard his prayer. Then the god sent a deadly dart upon the Argives, and the people died thick on one another, for the arrows went everywhither among the wide host of the Achaeans. At last a seer in the fulness of his knowledge declared to us the oracles of Apollo, and I was myself first to say that we should appease him. Whereon the son of Atreus rose in anger, and threatened that which he has since done. The

Achaeans are now taking the girl in a ship to Chryse, and sending gifts of sacrifice to the god; but the heralds have just taken from my tent the daughter of Briseus, whom the Achaeans had awarded to myself.

"Help your brave son, therefore, if you are able. Go to Olympus, and if you have ever done him service in word or deed, implore the aid of Jove. Ofttimes in my father's house have I heard you glory in that you alone of the immortals saved the son of Saturn from ruin, when the others, with Juno, Neptune, and Pallas Minerva would have put him in bonds. It was you, goddess, who delivered him by calling to Olympus the hundred-handed monster whom gods call Briareus, but men Aegaeon, for he is stronger even than his father; when therefore he took his seat all-glorious beside the son of Saturn, the other gods were afraid, and did not bind him. Go, then, to him, remind him of all this, clasp his knees, and bid him give succour to the Trojans. Let the Achaeans be hemmed in at the sterns of their ships, and perish on the seashore, that they may reap what joy they may of their king, and that Agamemnon may rue his blindness in offering insult to the foremost of the Achaeans."

Thetis wept and answered, "My son, woe is me that I should have borne or suckled you. Would indeed that you had lived your span free from all sorrow at your ships, for it is all too brief; alas, that you should be at once short of life and long of sorrow above your peers: woe, therefore, was the hour in which I bore you; nevertheless I will go to the snowy heights of Olympus, and tell this tale to Jove, if he will hear our prayer: meanwhile stay where you are with your ships, nurse your anger against the Achaeans, and hold aloof from fight. For Jove went yesterday to Oceanus, to a feast among the Ethiopians, and the other gods went with him. He will return to Olympus twelve days hence; I will then go to his mansion paved with bronze and will beseech him; nor do I doubt that I shall be able to persuade him."

On this she left him, still furious at the loss of her that had been taken from him. Meanwhile Ulysses reached Chryse with the hecatomb. When they had come inside the harbour they furled the sails and laid them in the ship's hold; they slackened the forestays, lowered the mast into its place, and rowed the ship to the place where they would have her lie; there they cast out their mooring-stones and made fast the hawsers. They then got out upon the seashore and landed the hecatomb for Apollo; Chryseis also left the ship, and Ulysses led her to the altar to deliver her into the hands of her father. "Chryses," said he, "King

Agamemnon has sent me to bring you back your child, and to offer sacrifice to Apollo on behalf of the Danaans, that we may propitiate the god, who has now brought sorrow upon the Argives."

So saying he gave the girl over to her father, who received her gladly, and they ranged the holy hecatomb all orderly round the altar of the god. They washed their hands and took up the barley-meal to sprinkle over the victims, while Chryses lifted up his hands and prayed aloud on their behalf. "Hear me," he cried, "O god of the silver bow, that protectest Chryse and holy Cilla, and rulest Tenedos with thy might. Even as thou didst hear me aforetime when I prayed, and didst press hardly upon the Achaeans, so hear me yet again, and stay this fearful pestilence from the Danaans."

Thus did he pray, and Apollo heard his prayer. When they had done praying and sprinkling the barley-meal, they drew back the heads of the victims and killed and flayed them. They cut out the thighbones, wrapped them round in two layers of fat, set some pieces of raw meat on the top of them, and then Chryses laid them on the wood fire and poured wine over them, while the young men stood near him with five-pronged spits in their hands. When the thighbones were burned and they had tasted the inward meats, they cut the rest up small, put the pieces upon the spits, roasted them till they were done, and drew them off: then, when they had finished their work and the feast was ready, they ate it, and every man had his full share, so that all were satisfied. As soon as they had had enough to eat and drink, pages filled the mixing-bowl with wine and water and handed it round, after giving every man his drink-offering.

Thus all day long the young men worshipped the god with song, hymning him and chaunting the joyous paean, and the god took pleasure in their voices; but when the sun went down, and it came on dark, they laid themselves down to sleep by the stern cables of the ship, and when the child of morning, rosy-fingered Dawn, appeared they again set sail for the host of the Achaeans. Apollo sent them a fair wind, so they raised their mast and hoisted their white sails aloft. As the sail bellied with the wind the ship flew through the deep blue water, and the foam hissed against her bows as she sped onward. When they reached the wide-stretching host of the Achaeans, they drew the vessel ashore, high and dry upon the sands, set her strong props beneath her, and went their ways to their own tents and ships.

But Achilles abode at his ships and nursed his anger. He went not to the honourable assembly, and sallied not forth to fight, but gnawed at his own heart, pining for battle and the war cry.

Now after twelve days the immortal gods came back in a body to Olympus, and Jove led the way. Thetis was not unmindful of the charge her son had laid upon her, so she rose from under the sea and went through great heaven with early morning to Olympus, where she found the mighty son of Saturn sitting all alone upon its topmost ridges. She sat herself down before him, and with her left hand seized his knees, while with her right she caught him under the chin, and besought him, saying: – "Father Jove, if I ever did you service in word or deed among the immortals, hear my prayer, and do honour to my son, whose life is to be cut short so early. King Agamemnon has dishonoured him by taking his prize and keeping her. Honour him then yourself, Olympian lord of counsel, and grant victory to the Trojans, till the Achaeans give my son his due and load him with riches in requital."

Jove sat for a while silent, and without a word, but Thetis still kept firm hold of his knees, and besought him a second time. "Incline your head," said she, "and promise me surely, or else deny me – for you have nothing to fear – that I may learn how greatly you disdain me."

At this Jove was much troubled and answered, "I shall have trouble if you set me quarrelling with Juno, for she will provoke me with her taunting speeches; even now she is always railing at me before the other gods and accusing me of giving aid to the Trojans. Go back now, lest she should find out. I will consider the matter, and will bring it about as you wish. See, I incline my head that you may believe me. This is the most solemn promise that I can give to any god. I never recall my word, or deceive, or fail to do what I say, when I have nodded my head."

As he spoke the son of Saturn bowed his dark brows, and the ambrosial locks swayed on his immortal head, till vast Olympus reeled.

When the pair had thus laid their plans, they parted – Jove to his house, while the goddess quitted the splendour of Olympus, and plunged into the depths of the sea. The gods rose from their seats, before the coming of their sire. Not one of them dared to remain sitting, but all stood up as he came among them. There, then, he took his seat. But Juno, when she saw him, knew that he and the old merman's daughter, silver-footed Thetis, had been hatching mischief, so she at once began to upbraid him. "Trickster," she cried, "which of the gods have you been taking into your counsels now? You are always settling matters in secret behind my back, and have never yet told me, if you could help it, one word of your intentions."

"Juno," replied the sire of gods and men, "you must not expect to be informed of all my counsels. You are my wife, but you would find it hard to understand them. When it is proper for you to hear, there is no one, god or man, who will be told sooner, but when I mean to keep a matter to myself, you must not pry nor ask questions."

"Dread son of Saturn," answered Juno, "what are you talking about? I? Pry and ask questions? Never. I let you have your own way in everything. Still, I have a strong misgiving that the old merman's daughter Thetis has been talking you over, for she was with you and had hold of your knees this self-same morning. I believe, therefore, that you have been promising her to give glory to Achilles, and to kill much people at the ships of the Achaeans."

"Wife," said Jove, "I can do nothing but you suspect me and find it out. You will take nothing by it, for I shall only dislike you the more, and it will go harder with you. Granted that it is as you say; I mean to have it so; sit down and hold your tongue as I bid you for if I once begin to lay my hands about you, though all heaven were on your side it would profit you nothing."

On this Juno was frightened, so she curbed her stubborn will and sat down in silence. But the heavenly beings were disquieted throughout the house of Jove, till the cunning workman Vulcan began to try and pacify his mother Juno. "It will be intolerable," said he, "if you two fall to wrangling and setting heaven in an uproar about a pack of mortals. If such ill counsels are to prevail, we shall have no pleasure at our banquet. Let me then advise my mother – and she must herself know that it will be better – to make friends with my dear father Jove, lest he again scold her and disturb our feast. If the Olympian Thunderer wants to hurl us all from our seats, he can do so, for he is far the strongest, so give him fair words, and he will then soon be in a good humour with us."

As he spoke, he took a double cup of nectar, and placed it in his mother's hand. "Cheer up, my dear mother," said he, "and make the best of it. I love you dearly, and should be very sorry to see you get a thrashing; however grieved I might be, I could not help, for there is no standing against Jove. Once before when I was trying to help you, he caught me by the foot and flung me from the heavenly threshold. All day long from morn till eve, was I falling, till at sunset I came to ground in the island of Lemnos, and there I lay, with very little life left in me, till the Sintians came and tended me."

Juno smiled at this, and as she smiled she took the cup from her son's hands. Then Vulcan drew sweet nectar from the mixing-bowl, and served it round among the gods, going from left to right; and the blessed gods laughed out a loud applause as they saw him bustling about the heavenly mansion.

Thus, through the livelong day to the going down of the sun they feasted, and everyone had his full share, so that all were satisfied. Apollo struck his lyre, and the Muses lifted up their sweet voices, calling and answering one another. But when the sun's glorious light had faded, they went home to bed, each in his own abode, which lame Vulcan with his consummate skill had fashioned for them. So Jove, the Olympian Lord of Thunder, hied him to the bed in which he always slept; and when he had got on to it he went to sleep, with Juno of the golden throne by his side.

Book XVIII

The Grief of Achilles Over Patroclus – The Visit of Thetis to Vulcan and the Armour That He Made for Achilles

THUS THEN DID THEY fight as it were a flaming fire. Meanwhile the fleet runner Antilochus, who had been sent as messenger, reached Achilles, and found him sitting by his tall ships and boding that which was indeed too surely true. "Alas," said he to himself in the heaviness of his heart, "why are the Achaeans again scouring the plain and flocking towards the ships? Heaven grant the gods be not now bringing that sorrow upon me of which my mother Thetis spoke, saying that while I was yet alive the bravest of the Myrmidons should fall before the Trojans, and see the light

of the sun no longer. I fear the brave son of Menoetius has fallen through his own daring and yet I bade him return to the ships as soon as he had driven back those that were bringing fire against them, and not join battle with Hector."

As he was thus pondering, the son of Nestor came up to him and told his sad tale, weeping bitterly the while. "Alas," he cried, "son of noble Peleus, I bring you bad tidings, would indeed that they were untrue. Patroclus has fallen, and a fight is raging about his naked body – for Hector holds his armour."

A dark cloud of grief fell upon Achilles as he listened. He filled both hands with dust from off the ground, and poured it over his head, disfiguring his comely face, and letting the refuse settle over his shirt so fair and new. He flung himself down all huge and hugely at full length, and tore his hair with his hands. The bondswomen whom Achilles and Patroclus had taken captive screamed aloud for grief, beating their breasts, and with their limbs failing them for sorrow. Antilochus bent over him the while, weeping and holding both his hands as he lay groaning for he feared that he might plunge a knife into his own throat. Then Achilles gave a loud cry and his mother heard him as she was sitting in the depths of the sea by the old man her father, whereon she screamed, and all the goddesses daughters of Nereus that dwelt at the bottom of the sea, came gathering round her. There were Glauce, Thalia and Cymodoce, Nesaia, Speo, Thoe and dark-eyed Halie, Cymothoe, Actaea and Limnorea, Melite, Iaera, Amphithoe and Agave, Doto and Proto, Pherusa and Dynamene, Dexamene, Amphinome and Callianeira, Doris, Panope, and the famous sea-nymph Galatea, Nemertes, Apseudes and Callianassa. There were also Clymene, Ianeira and Ianassa, Maera, Oreithuia and Amatheia of the lovely locks, with other Nereids who dwell in the depths of the sea. The crystal cave was filled with their multitude, and they all beat their breasts while Thetis led them in their lament.

"Listen," she cried, "sisters, daughters of Nereus, that you may hear the burden of my sorrows. Alas, woe is me, woe in that I have borne the most glorious of offspring. I bore him fair and strong, hero among heroes, and he shot up as a sapling; I tended him as a plant in a goodly garden, and sent him with his ships to Ilius to fight the Trojans, but never shall I welcome him back to the house of Peleus. So long as he lives to look upon the light of the sun he is in heaviness, and though I go to him I cannot help him. Nevertheless I will go, that I may see my dear son and learn what sorrow has befallen him though he is still holding aloof from battle."

She left the cave as she spoke, while the others followed weeping after, and the waves opened a path before them. When they reached the rich plain of Troy, they came up out of the sea in a long line on to the sands, at the place where the ships of the Myrmidons were drawn up in close order round the tents of Achilles. His mother went up to him as he lay groaning; she laid her hand upon his head and spoke piteously, saying, "My son, why are you thus weeping? What sorrow has now befallen you? Tell me; hide it not from me. Surely Jove has granted you the prayer you made him, when you lifted up your hands and besought him that the Achaeans might all of them be pent up at their ships, and rue it bitterly in that you were no longer with them."

Achilles groaned and answered, "Mother, Olympian Jove has indeed vouchsafed me the fulfilment of my prayer, but what boots it to me, seeing that my dear comrade Patroclus has fallen – he whom I valued more than all others, and loved as dearly as my own life? I have lost him; aye, and Hector when he had killed him stripped the wondrous armour, so glorious to behold, which the gods gave to Peleus when they laid you in the couch of a mortal man. Would that you were still dwelling among the immortal sea-nymphs, and that Peleus had taken to himself some mortal bride. For now you shall have grief infinite by reason of the death of that son whom you can never welcome home – nay, I will not live nor go about among mankind unless Hector fall by my spear, and thus pay me for having slain Patroclus son of Menoetius."

Thetis wept and answered, "Then, my son, is your end near at hand – for your own death awaits you full soon after that of Hector."

Then said Achilles in his great grief, "I would die here and now, in that I could not save my comrade. He has fallen far from home, and in his hour of need my hand was not there to help him. What is there for me? Return to my own land I shall not, and I have brought no saving neither to Patroclus nor to my other comrades of whom so many have been slain by mighty Hector; I stay here by my ships a bootless burden upon the earth, I, who in fight have no peer among the Achaeans, though in council there are better than I.

Therefore, perish strife both from among gods and men, and anger, wherein even a righteous man will harden his heart – which rises up in the soul of a man like smoke, and the taste thereof is sweeter than drops of honey. Even so has Agamemnon angered me. And yet – so be it, for it is over; I will force my soul into subjection as I needs must; I will go; I will pursue Hector who has slain him whom I loved so dearly, and will then abide my doom when it may please Jove and the other gods to send it. Even Hercules, the best beloved of Jove – even he could not escape the hand of death, but fate and Juno's fierce anger laid him low, as I too shall lie when I am dead if a like doom awaits me. Till then I will win fame, and will bid Trojan and Dardanian women wring tears from their tender cheeks with both their hands in the grievousness of their great sorrow; thus shall they know that he who has held aloof so long will hold aloof no longer. Hold me not back, therefore, in the love you bear me, for you shall not move me."

Then silver-footed Thetis answered, "My son, what you have said is true. It is well to save your comrades from destruction, but your armour is in the hands of the Trojans; Hector bears it in triumph upon his own shoulders. Full well I know that his vaunt shall not be lasting, for his end is close at hand; go not, however, into the press of battle till you see me return hither; tomorrow at break of day I shall be here, and will bring you goodly armour from King Vulcan."

On this she left her brave son, and as she turned away she said to the sea nymphs her sisters, "Dive into the bosom of the sea and go to the house of the old sea-god my father. Tell him everything; as for me, I will go to the cunning workman Vulcan on high Olympus, and ask him to provide my son with a suit of splendid armour."

When she had so said, they dived forthwith beneath the waves, while silver-footed Thetis went her way that she might bring the armour for her son.

Thus, then, did her feet bear the goddess to Olympus, and meanwhile the Achaeans were flying with loud cries before murderous Hector till they reached the ships and the Hellespont, and they could not draw the body of Mars's servant Patroclus out of reach of the weapons that were showered upon him, for Hector son of Priam with his host and horsemen had again caught up to him like the flame of a fiery furnace; thrice did brave Hector seize him by the feet, striving with might and main to draw him away and calling loudly on the Trojans, and thrice did the two Ajaxes, clothed in valour as with a garment, beat him from off the body; but all undaunted he would now charge into the thick of the fight, and now again he would stand still and cry aloud, but he would give no ground. As upland shepherds that cannot chase some famished lion from a carcase, even so could not the two Ajaxes scare Hector son of Priam from the body of Patroclus.

And now he would even have dragged it off and have won imperishable glory, had not Iris fleet as the wind, winged her way as messenger from Olympus to the son of Peleus and bidden him arm. She came secretly without the knowledge of Jove and of the other gods, for Juno sent her, and when she had got close to him she said, "Up, son of Peleus, mightiest of all mankind; rescue Patroclus about whom this fearful fight is now raging by the ships. Men are killing one another, the Danaans in defence of the dead body, while the Trojans are trying to hale it away, and take it to windy Ilius: Hector is the most furious of them all; he is for cutting the head from the body and fixing it on the stakes of the wall. Up, then, and bide here no longer; shrink from the thought that Patroclus may become meat for the dogs of Troy. Shame on you, should his body suffer any kind of outrage."

And Achilles said, "Iris, which of the gods was it that sent you to me?"

Iris answered, "It was Juno the royal spouse of Jove, but the son of Saturn does not know of my coming, nor yet does any other of the immortals who dwell on the snowy summits of Olympus."

Then fleet Achilles answered her saying, "How can I go up into the battle? They have my armour. My mother forbade me to arm till I should see her come, for she promised to bring me goodly armour from Vulcan; I know no man whose arms I can put on, save only the shield of Ajax son of Telamon, and he surely must be fighting in the front rank and wielding his spear about the body of dead Patroclus."

Iris said, "We know that your armour has been taken, but go as you are; go to the deep trench and show yourself before the Trojans, that they may fear you and cease fighting. Thus will the fainting sons of the Achaeans gain some brief breathing-time, which in battle may hardly be."

Iris left him when she had so spoken. But Achilles dear to Jove arose, and Minerva flung her tasselled aegis round his strong shoulders; she crowned his head with a halo of golden cloud from which she kindled a glow of gleaming fire. As the smoke that goes up into heaven from some city that is being beleaguered on an island far out at sea – all day long do men sally from the city and fight their hardest, and at the going down of the sun the line of beacon-fires blazes forth, flaring high for those that dwell near them to behold, if so be that they may come with their ships and succour them – even so did the light flare from the head of Achilles, as he stood by the trench, going beyond the wall – but he did not join the Achaeans for he heeded the charge which his mother laid upon him.

There did he stand and shout aloud. Minerva also raised her voice from afar, and spread terror unspeakable among the Trojans. Ringing as the note of a trumpet that sounds alarm then the foe is at the gates of a city, even so brazen was the voice of the son of Aeacus, and when the Trojans heard its clarion tones they were dismayed; the horses turned back with their chariots for they boded mischief, and their drivers were awe-struck by the steady flame which the grey-eyed goddess had kindled above the head of the great son of Peleus.

Thrice did Achilles raise his loud cry as he stood by the trench, and thrice were the Trojans and their brave allies thrown into confusion; whereon twelve of their noblest champions fell beneath the wheels of their chariots and perished by their own spears. The Achaeans to their great joy then drew Patroclus out of reach of the weapons, and laid him on a litter: his comrades stood mourning round him, and among them fleet Achilles who wept bitterly as he saw his true comrade lying dead upon his bier. He had sent him out with horses and chariots into battle, but his return he was not to welcome.

Then Juno sent the busy sun, loth though he was, into the waters of Oceanus; so he set, and the Achaeans had rest from the tug and turmoil of war.

Now the Trojans when they had come out of the fight, unyoked their horses and gathered in assembly before preparing their supper. They kept their feet, nor would any dare to sit down, for fear had fallen upon them all because Achilles had shown himself after having held aloof so long from battle. Polydamas son of Panthous was first to speak, a man of judgement, who alone among them could look both before and after. He was comrade to Hector, and they had been born upon the same night; with all sincerity and goodwill, therefore, he addressed them thus: –

"Look to it well, my friends; I would urge you to go back now to your city and not wait here by the ships till morning, for we are far from our walls. So long as this man was at enmity with Agamemnon the Achaeans were easier to deal with, and I would have gladly camped by the ships in the hope of taking them; but now I go in great fear of the fleet son of Peleus; he is so daring that he will never bide here on the plain whereon the Trojans and Achaeans fight with equal valour, but he will try to storm our city and carry off our women. Do then as I say, and let us retreat. For this is what will happen. The darkness of night will for a time stay the son of Peleus, but if he find us here in the morning when he sallies forth in full armour, we shall have knowledge of him in good earnest. Glad indeed will he be who can escape and get back to Ilius, and many a Trojan will become meat for dogs and vultures may I never live to hear it. If we do as I say, little though we may like it, we shall have strength in counsel during the night, and the great gates with the doors that close them will protect the city. At dawn we can arm and take our stand on the walls; he will then rue it if he sallies from the ships to fight us. He will go back when he has given his horses their fill of being driven all whithers under our walls, and will be in no mind to try and force his way into the city. Neither will he ever sack it, dogs shall devour him ere he do so."

Hector looked fiercely at him and answered, "Polydamas, your words are not to my liking in that you bid us go back and be pent within the city. Have you not had enough of being cooped up behind walls? In the old days the city of Priam was famous the whole world over for its wealth of gold and bronze, but our treasures are wasted out of our houses, and much goods have been sold away to Phrygia and fair Meonia, for the hand of Jove has been laid heavily upon us. Now, therefore, that the son of scheming Saturn has vouchsafed me to win glory here and to hem the Achaeans in at their ships, prate no more in this fool's wise among the people. You will have no man with you; it shall not be; do all of you as I now say; – take your suppers in your companies throughout the host, and keep your watches and be wakeful every man of you. If any Trojan is uneasy about his possessions, let him gather them and give them out among the people. Better let these, rather than the Achaeans, have them. At daybreak we will arm and fight about the ships; granted that Achilles has again come forward to defend them, let it be as he will, but it shall go hard with him. I shall not shun him, but will fight him, to fall or conquer. The god of war deals out like measure to all, and the slayer may yet be slain."

Thus spoke Hector; and the Trojans, fools that they were, shouted in applause, for Pallas Minerva had robbed them of their understanding. They gave ear to Hector with his evil counsel, but the wise words of Polydamas no man would heed. They took their supper throughout the host, and meanwhile through the whole night the Achaeans mourned Patroclus, and the son of Peleus led them in their lament. He laid his murderous hands upon the breast of his comrade, groaning again and again as a bearded lion when a man who was chasing deer has robbed him of his young in some dense forest; when the lion comes back he is furious, and searches dingle and dell to track the hunter if he can find him, for he is mad with rage – even so with many a sigh did Achilles speak among the Myrmidons saying, "Alas! vain were the words with which I cheered the hero Menoetius in his own house; I said that I would bring his brave son back again to Opoeis after he had sacked Ilius and taken his share of the spoils – but Jove does not give all men their heart's desire. The same soil shall be reddened here at Troy by the blood of us both, for I too shall never be welcomed home by the old knight Peleus, nor by my mother Thetis, but even in this place shall the earth cover me. Nevertheless, O Patroclus, now that I am left behind you, I will not bury you, till I have brought hither the head and armour of mighty Hector who has slain you. Twelve noble sons of Trojans will I behead before your bier to avenge you; till I have done so you shall lie as you are by the ships, and fair women of Troy and Dardanus, whom we have taken with spear and strength of arm when we sacked men's goodly cities, shall weep over you both night and day."

Then Achilles told his men to set a large tripod upon the fire that they might wash the clotted gore from off Patroclus. Thereon they set a tripod full of bath water on to a clear fire: they threw sticks on to it to make it blaze, and the water became hot as the flame played about the belly of the tripod. When the water in the cauldron was boiling they washed the body, anointed it with oil, and closed its wounds with ointment that had been kept nine years. Then they laid it on a bier and covered it with a linen cloth from head to foot, and over this they laid a fair white robe. Thus all night long did the Myrmidons gather round Achilles to mourn Patroclus.

Then Jove said to Juno his sister-wife, "So, Queen Juno, you have gained your end, and have roused fleet Achilles. One would think that the Achaeans were of your own flesh and blood."

And Juno answered, "Dread son of Saturn, why should you say this thing? May not a man though he be only mortal and knows less than we do, do what he can for another person? And shall not I – foremost of all goddesses both by descent and as wife to you who reign in heaven – devise evil for the Trojans if I am angry with them?"

Thus did they converse. Meanwhile Thetis came to the house of Vulcan, imperishable, star-bespangled, fairest of the abodes in heaven, a house of bronze wrought by the lame god's own hands. She found him busy with his bellows, sweating and hard at work, for he was making twenty tripods that were to stand by the wall of his house, and he set wheels of gold under them all that they might go of their own selves to the assemblies of the gods, and come back again – marvels indeed to see. They were finished all but the ears of cunning workmanship which yet remained to be fixed to them: these he was now fixing, and he was hammering at the rivets. While he was thus at work silver-footed Thetis came to the house. Charis, of graceful head-dress, wife to the far-famed lame god, came towards her as soon as she saw her, and took her hand in her own, saying, "Why have you come to our house, Thetis, honoured and ever welcome – for you do not visit us often? Come inside and let me set refreshment before you."

The goddess led the way as she spoke, and bade Thetis sit on a richly decorated seat inlaid with silver; there was a footstool also under her feet. Then she called Vulcan and said, "Vulcan, come here, Thetis wants you;" and the far-famed lame god answered, "Then it is indeed an august and honoured goddess who has come here; she it was that took care of me when I was suffering from the heavy fall which I had through my cruel mother's anger – for she would have got rid of me because I was lame. It would have gone hardly with me had not Eurynome, daughter of the ever-encircling waters of Oceanus, and Thetis, taken me to their bosom. Nine years did I stay with them, and many beautiful works in bronze, brooches, spiral armlets, cups, and chains, did I make for them in their cave, with the roaring waters of Oceanus foaming as they rushed ever past it; and no one knew, neither of gods nor men, save only Thetis and Eurynome who took care of me. If, then, Thetis has come to my house I must make her due requital for having saved me; entertain her, therefore, with all hospitality, while I put by my bellows and all my tools."

On this the mighty monster hobbled off from his anvil, his thin legs plying lustily under him. He set the bellows away from the fire, and gathered his tools into a silver chest. Then he took a sponge and washed his face and hands, his shaggy chest and brawny neck; he donned his shirt, grasped his strong staff, and limped towards the door. There were golden handmaids also who worked for him, and were like real young women, with sense and reason, voice also and strength, and all the learning of the immortals; these busied themselves as the king bade them, while he drew near to Thetis, seated her upon a goodly seat, and took her hand in his own, saying, "Why have you come to our house, Thetis honoured and ever welcome – for you do not visit us often? Say what you want, and I will do it for you at once if I can, and if it can be done at all."

Thetis wept and answered, "Vulcan, is there another goddess in Olympus whom the son of Saturn has been pleased to try with so much affliction as he has me? Me alone of the marine goddesses did he make subject to a mortal husband, Peleus son of Aeacus, and sorely against my will did I submit to the embraces of one who was but mortal, and who now stays at home worn out with age. Neither is this all. Heaven vouchsafed me a son, hero among heroes, and he shot up as a sapling. I tended him as a plant in a goodly garden and sent him with his ships to Ilius to fight the Trojans, but never shall I welcome him back to the house of Peleus. So long as he lives to look upon the light of the sun, he is in heaviness, and though I go to him I cannot help him; King Agamemnon has made him give up the maiden whom the sons of the Achaeans had awarded him, and he wastes with sorrow for her sake. Then the Trojans hemmed the Achaeans in at their ships' sterns and would not let them come forth; the elders, therefore, of the Argives besought Achilles and offered him great treasure, whereon he refused to bring deliverance to them himself, but put his own armour on Patroclus and sent him into the fight with much people after him. All day long they fought by the Scaean gates and would have taken the city there and then, had not

Apollo vouchsafed glory to Hector and slain the valiant son of Menoetius after he had done the Trojans much evil. Therefore I am suppliant at your knees if haply you may be pleased to provide my son, whose end is near at hand, with helmet and shield, with goodly greaves fitted with ancle-clasps, and with a breastplate, for he lost his own when his true comrade fell at the hands of the Trojans, and he now lies stretched on earth in the bitterness of his soul."

And Vulcan answered, "Take heart, and be no more disquieted about this matter; would that I could hide him from death's sight when his hour is come, so surely as I can find him armour that shall amaze the eyes of all who behold it."

When he had so said he left her and went to his bellows, turning them towards the fire and bidding them do their office. Twenty bellows blew upon the melting-pots, and they blew blasts of every kind, some fierce to help him when he had need of them, and others less strong as Vulcan willed it in the course of his work. He threw tough copper into the fire, and tin, with silver and gold; he set his great anvil on its block, and with one hand grasped his mighty hammer while he took the tongs in the other.

First he shaped the shield so great and strong, adorning it all over and binding it round with a gleaming circuit in three layers; and the baldric was made of silver. He made the shield in five thicknesses, and with many a wonder did his cunning hand enrich it.

He wrought the earth, the heavens, and the sea; the moon also at her full and the untiring sun, with all the signs that glorify the face of heaven – the Pleiads, the Hyads, huge Orion and the Bear, which men also call the Wain and which turns round ever in one place, facing Orion, and alone never dips into the stream of Oceanus.

He wrought also two cities, fair to see and busy with the hum of men. In the one were weddings and wedding feasts, and they were going about the city with brides whom they were escorting by torchlight from their chambers. Loud rose the cry of Hymen, and the youths danced to the music of flute and lyre, while the women stood each at her house door to see them.

Meanwhile the people were gathered in assembly, for there was a quarrel, and two men were wrangling about the blood-money for a man who had been killed, the one saying before the people that he had paid damages in full, and the other that he had not been paid. Each was trying to make his own case good, and the people took sides, each man backing the side that he had taken; but the heralds kept them back, and the elders sate on their seats of stone in a solemn circle, holding the staves which the heralds had put into their hands. Then they rose and each in his turn gave judgement, and there were two talents laid down, to be given to him whose judgement should be deemed the fairest.

About the other city there lay encamped two hosts in gleaming armour, and they were divided whether to sack it, or to spare it and accept the half of what it contained. But the men of the city would not yet consent, and armed themselves for a surprise; their wives and little children kept guard upon the walls, and with them were the men who were past fighting through age; but the others sallied forth with Mars and Pallas Minerva at their head – both of them wrought in gold and clad in golden raiment, great and fair with their armour as befitting gods, while they that followed were smaller. When they reached the place where they would lay their ambush, it was on a riverbed to which livestock of all kinds would come from far and near to water; here, then, they lay concealed, clad in full armour. Some way off them there were two scouts who were on the look-out for the coming of sheep or cattle, which presently came, followed by two shepherds who were playing on their pipes, and had not so much as a thought of danger. When those who were in ambush saw this, they cut off the flocks and herds and killed the shepherds. Meanwhile the besiegers, when they heard much noise among the cattle as they sat in council, sprang to their horses, and made with all speed towards them; when they reached them they set battle in array by the banks of the river, and the hosts aimed their bronze-shod spears at one another. With them were Strife and Riot, and fell Fate who was dragging three men after her, one with a fresh wound, and the other unwounded, while the third was dead, and she was dragging him along by his heel: and her robe was bedrabbled in men's blood. They went in and out with one another and fought as though they were living people hauling away one another's dead.

He wrought also a fair fallow field, large and thrice ploughed already. Many men were working at the plough within it, turning their oxen to and fro, furrow after furrow. Each time that they turned on reaching the headland a man would come up to them and give them a cup of wine, and they would go back to their furrows looking forward to the time when they should again reach the headland. The part that they had ploughed was dark behind them, so that the field, though it was of gold, still looked as if it were being ploughed – very curious to behold.

He wrought also a field of harvest corn, and the reapers were reaping with sharp sickles in their hands. Swathe after swathe fell to the ground in a straight line behind them, and the binders bound them in bands of twisted straw. There were three binders, and behind them there were boys who gathered the cut corn in armfuls and kept on bringing them to be bound: among them all the owner of the land stood by in silence and was glad. The servants were getting a meal ready under an oak, for they had sacrificed a great ox, and were busy cutting him up, while the women were making a porridge of much white barley for the labourers' dinner.

He wrought also a vineyard, golden and fair to see, and the vines were loaded with grapes. The bunches overhead were black, but the vines were trained on poles of silver. He ran a ditch of dark metal all round it, and fenced it with a fence of tin; there was only one path to it, and by this the vintagers went when they would gather the vintage. Youths and maidens all blithe and full of glee, carried the luscious fruit in plaited baskets; and with them there went a boy who made sweet music with his lyre, and sang the Linos-song with his clear boyish voice.

He wrought also a herd of horned cattle. He made the cows of gold and tin, and they lowed as they came full speed out of the yards to go and feed among the waving reeds that grow by the banks of the river. Along with the cattle there went four shepherds, all of them in gold, and their nine fleet dogs went with them. Two terrible lions had fastened on a bellowing bull that was with the foremost cows, and bellow as he might they dragged him, while the dogs and men gave chase: the lions tore through the bull's thick hide and were gorging on his blood and bowels, but the herdsmen were afraid to do anything, and only hounded on their dogs; the dogs dared not fasten on the lions but stood by barking and keeping out of harm's way.

The god wrought also a pasture in a fair mountain dell, and a large flock of sheep, with a homestead and huts, and sheltered sheepfolds.

Furthermore he wrought a green, like that which Daedalus once made in Cnossus for lovely Ariadne. Hereon there danced youths and maidens whom all would woo, with their hands on one another's wrists. The maidens wore robes of light linen, and the youths well woven shirts that were slightly oiled. The girls were crowned with garlands, while the young men had daggers of gold that hung by silver baldrics; sometimes they would dance deftly in a ring with merry twinkling feet, as it were a potter sitting at his work and making trial of his wheel to see whether it will run, and sometimes they would go all in line with one another, and much people was gathered joyously about the green. There was a bard also to sing to them and play his lyre, while two tumblers went about performing in the midst of them when the man struck up with his tune.

All round the outermost rim of the shield he set the mighty stream of the river Oceanus.

Then when he had fashioned the shield so great and strong, he made a breastplate also that shone brighter than fire. He made a helmet, close fitting to the brow, and richly worked, with a golden plume overhanging it; and he made greaves also of beaten tin.

Lastly, when the famed lame god had made all the armour, he took it and set it before the mother of Achilles; whereon she darted like a falcon from the snowy summits of Olympus and bore away the gleaming armour from the house of Vulcan.

Book XXIV

Priam Ransoms the Body of Hector
– Hector's Funeral

THE ASSEMBLY NOW BROKE UP and the people went their ways each to his own ship. There they made ready their supper, and then bethought them of the blessed boon of sleep; but Achilles still wept for thinking of his dear comrade, and sleep, before whom all things bow, could take no hold upon him. This way and that did

he turn as he yearned after the might and manfulness of Patroclus; he thought of all they had done together, and all they had gone through both on the field of battle and on the waves of the weary sea. As he dwelt on these things he wept bitterly and lay now on his side, now on his back, and now face downwards, till at last he rose and went out as one distraught to wander upon the seashore.

Then, when he saw dawn breaking over beach and sea, he yoked his horses to his chariot, and bound the body of Hector behind it that he might drag it about. Thrice did he drag it round the tomb of the son of Menoetius, and then went back into his tent, leaving the body on the ground full length and with its face downwards. But Apollo would not suffer it to be disfigured, for he pitied the man, dead though he now was; therefore he shielded him with his golden aegis continually, that he might take no hurt while Achilles was dragging him.

Thus shamefully did Achilles in his fury dishonour Hector; but the blessed gods looked down in pity from heaven, and urged Mercury, slayer of Argus, to steal the body. All were of this mind save only Juno, Neptune, and Jove's grey-eyed daughter, who persisted in the hate which they had ever borne towards Ilius with Priam and his people; for they forgave not the wrong done them by Alexandrus in disdaining the goddesses who came to him when he was in his sheepyards, and preferring her who had offered him a wanton to his ruin.

When, therefore, the morning of the twelfth day had now come, Phoebus Apollo spoke among the immortals saying, "You gods ought to be ashamed of yourselves; you are cruel and hard-hearted. Did not Hector burn you thighbones of heifers and of unblemished goats? And now dare you not rescue even his dead body, for his wife to look upon, with his mother and child, his father Priam, and his people, who would forthwith commit him to the flames, and give him his due funeral rites? So, then, you would all be on the side of mad Achilles, who knows neither right nor ruth? He is like some savage lion that in the pride of his great strength and daring springs upon men's flocks and gorges on them. Even so has Achilles flung aside all pity, and all that conscience which at once so greatly banes yet greatly boons him that will heed it. A man may lose one far dearer than Achilles has lost – a son, it may be, or a brother born from his own mother's womb; yet when he has mourned him and wept over him he will let him bide, for it takes much sorrow to kill a man; whereas Achilles, now that he has slain noble Hector, drags him behind his chariot round the tomb of his comrade. It were better of him, and for him, that he should not do so, for brave though he be we gods may take it ill that he should vent his fury upon dead clay."

Juno spoke up in a rage. "This were well," she cried, "O lord of the silver bow, if you would give like honour to Hector and to Achilles; but Hector was mortal and suckled at a woman's breast, whereas Achilles is the offspring of a goddess whom I myself reared and brought up. I married her to Peleus, who is above measure dear to the immortals; you gods came all of you to her wedding; you feasted along with them yourself and brought your lyre – false, and fond of low company, that you have ever been."

Then said Jove, "Juno, be not so bitter. Their honour shall not be equal, but of all that dwell in Ilius, Hector was dearest to the gods, as also to myself, for his offerings never failed me. Never was my altar stinted of its dues, nor of the drink-offerings and savour of sacrifice which we claim of right. I shall therefore permit the body of mighty Hector to be stolen; and yet this may hardly be without Achilles coming to know it, for his mother keeps night and day beside him. Let some one of you, therefore, send Thetis to me, and I will impart my counsel to her, namely that Achilles is to accept a ransom from Priam, and give up the body."

On this Iris fleet as the wind went forth to carry his message. Down she plunged into the dark sea midway between Samos and rocky Imbrus; the waters hissed as they closed over her, and she sank into the bottom as the lead at the end of an ox-horn, that is sped to carry death to fishes. She found Thetis sitting in a great cave with the other sea goddesses gathered round her; there she sat in the midst of them weeping for her noble son who was to fall far from his own land, on the rich plains of Troy. Iris went up to her and said, "Rise Thetis; Jove, whose counsels fail not, bids you come to him." And Thetis answered, "Why does the mighty god so bid me? I am in great grief, and shrink from going in and out among the immortals. Still, I will go, and the word that he may speak shall not be spoken in vain."

The goddess took her dark veil, than which there can be no robe more sombre, and went forth with fleet Iris leading the way before her. The waves of the sea opened them a path, and when they reached the shore they flew up into the heavens, where they found the all-seeing son of Saturn with the blessed gods that live for ever assembled near him. Minerva gave up her seat to her, and she sat down by the side of father Jove. Juno then placed a fair golden cup in her hand, and spoke to her in words of comfort, whereon Thetis drank and gave her back the cup; and the sire of gods and men was the first to speak.

"So, goddess," said he, "for all your sorrow, and the grief that I well know reigns ever in your heart, you have come hither to Olympus, and I will tell you why I have sent for you. This nine days past the immortals have been quarrelling about Achilles waster of cities and the body of Hector. The gods would have Mercury slayer of Argus steal the body, but in furtherance of our peace and amity henceforward, I will concede such honour to your son as I will now tell you. Go, then, to the host and lay these commands upon him; say that the gods are angry with him, and that I am myself more angry than them all, in that he keeps Hector at the ships and will not give him up. He may thus fear me and let the body go. At the same time I will send Iris to great Priam to bid him go to the ships of the Achaeans, and ransom his son, taking with him such gifts for Achilles as may give him satisfaction."

Silver-footed Thetis did as the god had told her, and forthwith down she darted from the topmost summits of Olympus. She went to her son's tents where she found him grieving bitterly, while his trusty comrades round him were busy preparing their morning meal, for which they had killed a great woolly sheep. His mother sat down beside him and caressed him with her hand saying, "My son, how long will you keep on thus grieving and making moan? You are gnawing at your own heart, and think neither of food nor of woman's embraces; and yet these too were well, for you have no long time to live, and death with the strong hand of fate are already close beside you. Now, therefore, heed what I say, for I come as a messenger from Jove; he says that the gods are angry with you, and himself angrier than them all, in that you keep Hector at the ships and will not give him up. Therefore let him go, and accept a ransom for his body."

And Achilles answered, "So be it. If Olympian Jove of his own motion thus commands me, let him that brings the ransom bear the body away."

Thus did mother and son talk together at the ships in long discourse with one another. Meanwhile the son of Saturn sent Iris to the strong city of Ilius. "Go," said he, "fleet Iris, from the mansions of Olympus, and tell King Priam in Ilius, that he is to go to the ships of the Achaeans and free the body of his dear son. He is to take such gifts with him as shall give satisfaction to Achilles, and he is to go alone, with no other Trojan, save only some honoured servant who may drive his mules and waggon, and bring back the body of him whom noble Achilles has slain. Let him have no thought nor fear of death in his heart, for we will send the slayer of Argus to escort him, and bring him within the tent of Achilles. Achilles will not kill him nor let another do so, for he will take heed to his ways and sin not, and he will entreat a suppliant with all honourable courtesy."

On this Iris, fleet as the wind, sped forth to deliver her message. She went to Priam's house, and found weeping and lamentation therein. His sons were seated round their father in the outer courtyard, and their raiment was wet with tears: the old man sat in the midst of them with his mantle wrapped close about his body, and his head and neck all covered with the filth which he had clutched as he lay grovelling in the mire. His daughters and his sons' wives went wailing about the house, as they thought of the many and brave men who lay dead, slain by the Argives. The messenger of Jove stood by Priam and spoke softly to him, but fear fell upon him as she did so. "Take heart," she said, "Priam offspring of Dardanus, take heart and fear not. I bring no evil tidings, but am minded well towards you. I come as a messenger from Jove, who though he be not near, takes thought for you and pities you. The lord of Olympus bids you go and ransom noble Hector, and take with you such gifts as shall give satisfaction to Achilles. You are to go alone, with no Trojan, save only some honoured servant who may drive your mules and waggon, and bring back to the city the body of him whom noble Achilles has slain. You are to have no thought, nor fear of death, for Jove will send the slayer of Argus to escort you. When he has brought you within Achilles' tent, Achilles will not kill you nor let another do so, for he will take heed to his ways and sin not, and he will entreat a suppliant with all honourable courtesy."

Iris went her way when she had thus spoken, and Priam told his sons to get a mule-waggon ready, and to make the body of the waggon fast upon the top of its bed. Then he went down into his fragrant storeroom, high-vaulted, and made of cedar-wood, where his many treasures were kept, and he called Hecuba his wife. "Wife," said he, "a messenger has come to me from Olympus, and has told me to go to the ships of the Achaeans to ransom my dear son, taking with me such gifts as shall give satisfaction to Achilles. What think you of this matter? for my own part I am greatly moved to pass through the camps of the Achaeans and go to their ships."

His wife cried aloud as she heard him, and said, "Alas, what has become of that judgement for which you have been ever famous both among strangers and your own people? How can you venture alone to the ships of the Achaeans, and look into the face of him who has slain so many of your brave sons? You must have iron courage, for if the cruel savage sees you and lays hold on you, he will know neither respect nor pity. Let us then weep Hector from afar here in our own house, for when I gave him birth the threads of overruling fate were spun for him that dogs should eat his flesh far from his parents, in the house of that terrible man on whose liver I would fain fasten and devour it. Thus would I avenge my son, who showed no cowardice when Achilles slew him, and thought neither of flight nor of avoiding battle as he stood in defence of Trojan men and Trojan women."

Then Priam said, "I would go, do not therefore stay me nor be as a bird of ill omen in my house, for you will not move me. Had it been some mortal man who had sent me some prophet or priest who divines from sacrifice – I should have deemed him false and have given him no heed; but now I have heard the goddess and seen her face to face, therefore I will go and her saying shall not be in vain. If it be my fate to die at the ships of the Achaeans even so would I have it; let Achilles slay me, if I may but first have taken my son in my arms and mourned him to my heart's comforting."

So saying he lifted the lids of his chests, and took out 12 goodly vestments. He took also 12 cloaks of single fold, 12 rugs, 12 fair mantles and an equal number of shirts. He weighed out 10 talents of gold, and brought moreover two burnished tripods, four cauldrons and a very beautiful cup which the Thracians had given him when he had gone to them on an embassy; it was very precious, but he grudged not even this, so eager was he to ransom the body of his son. Then he chased all the Trojans from the court and rebuked them with words of anger. "Out," he cried, "shame and disgrace to me that you are. Have you no grief in your own homes that you are come to plague me here? Is it a small thing, think you, that the son of Saturn has sent this sorrow upon me, to lose the bravest of my sons? Nay, you shall prove it in person, for now he is gone the Achaeans will have easier work in killing you. As for me, let me go down within the house of Hades, ere mine eyes behold the sacking and wasting of the city."

He drove the men away with his staff, and they went forth as the old man sped them. Then he called to his sons, upbraiding Helenus, Paris, noble Agathon, Pammon, Antiphonus, Polites of the loud battle cry, Deiphobus, Hippothous and Dius. These nine did the old man call near him. "Come to me at once," he cried, "worthless sons who do me shame; would that you had all been killed at the ships rather than Hector. Miserable man that I am, I have had the bravest sons in all Troy – noble Nestor, Troilus the dauntless charioteer, and Hector who was a god among men, so that one would have thought he was son to an immortal – yet there is not one of them left. Mars has slain them and those of whom I am ashamed are alone left me. Liars, and light of foot, heroes of the dance, robbers of lambs and kids from your own people, why do you not get a waggon ready for me at once, and put all these things upon it that I may set out on my way?"

Thus did he speak, and they feared the rebuke of their father. They brought out a strong mule waggon, newly made, and set the body of the waggon fast on its bed. They took the mule yoke from the peg on which it hung, a yoke of boxwood with a knob on the top of it and rings for the reins to go through. Then they brought a yoke band 11 cubits long, to bind the yoke to the pole; they bound it on at the far end of the pole, and put the ring over the upright pin making it fast with three turns of the band on either side the knob, and bending the thong of the yoke beneath it. This done, they brought from the store chamber the rich ransom that was to purchase the body of Hector, and they set it all orderly on the waggon; then they yoked the strong harness mules which the Mysians had on a time given as a goodly present to Priam; but for Priam himself they yoked horses which the old king had bred, and kept for his own use.

Thus heedfully did Priam and his servant see to the yoking of their cars at the palace. Then Hecuba came to them all sorrowful, with a golden goblet of wine in her right hand, that they might make a drink offering before they set out. She stood in front of the horses and said, "Take this, make a drink offering to father Jove, and since you are minded to go to the ships in spite of me, pray that you may come safely back from the hands of your enemies. Pray to the son of Saturn lord of the whirlwind, who sits on Ida and looks down over all Troy, pray him to send his swift messenger on your right hand, the bird of omen which is strongest and most dear to him of all birds, that you may see it with your own eyes and trust it as you go forth to the ships of the Danaans. If all-seeing Jove will not send you this messenger, however set upon it you may be, I would not have you go to the ships of the Argives."

And Priam answered, "Wife, I will do as you desire me; it is well to lift hands in prayer to Jove, if so be he may have mercy upon me."

With this the old man bade the serving-woman pour pure water over his hands, and the woman came, bearing the water in a bowl. He washed his hands and took the cup from his wife; then he made the drink-offering and prayed, standing in the middle of the courtyard and turning his eyes to heaven. "Father Jove," he said, "that rulest from Ida, most glorious and most great, grant that I may be received kindly and compassionately in the tents of Achilles; and send your swift messenger upon my right hand, the bird of omen which is strongest and most dear to you of all birds, that I may see it with my own eyes and trust it as I go forth to the ships of the Danaans."

So did he pray, and Jove the lord of counsel heard his prayer. Forthwith he sent an eagle, the most unerring portent of all birds that fly, the dusky hunter that men also call the Black Eagle. His wings were spread abroad on either side as wide as the well-made and well-bolted door of a rich man's chamber. He came to them flying over the city upon their right hands, and when they saw him they were glad and their hearts took comfort within them. The old man made haste to mount his chariot, and drove out through the inner gateway and under the echoing gatehouse of the outer court. Before him went the mules drawing the four-wheeled waggon, and driven by wise Idaeus; behind these were the horses, which the old man lashed with his whip and drove swiftly through the city, while his friends followed after, wailing and lamenting for him as though he were on his road to death. As soon as they had come down from the city and had reached the plain, his sons and sons-in-law who had followed him went back to Ilius.

But Priam and Idaeus as they showed out upon the plain did not escape the ken of all-seeing Jove, who looked down upon the old man and pitied him; then he spoke to his son Mercury and said, "Mercury, for it is you who are the most disposed to escort men on their way, and to hear those whom you will hear, go, and so conduct Priam to the ships of the Achaeans that no other of the Danaans shall see him nor take note of him until he reach the son of Peleus."

Thus he spoke and Mercury, guide and guardian, slayer of Argus, did as he was told. Forthwith he bound on his glittering golden sandals with which he could fly like the wind over land and sea; he took the wand with which he seals men's eyes in sleep, or wakes them just as he pleases, and flew holding it in his hand till he came to Troy and to the Hellespont. To look at, he was like a young man of noble birth in the hey-day of his youth and beauty with the down just coming upon his face.

Now when Priam and Idaeus had driven past the great tomb of Ilius, they stayed their mules and horses that they might drink in the river, for the shades of night were falling, when, therefore, Idaeus saw Mercury standing near them he said to Priam, "Take heed, descendant of Dardanus; here is matter which demands consideration. I see a man who I think will presently fall upon us; let us fly with our horses, or at least embrace his knees and implore him to take compassion upon us?"

When he heard this the old man's heart failed him, and he was in great fear; he stayed where he was as one dazed, and the hair stood on end over his whole body; but the bringer of good luck came up to him and took him by the hand, saying, "Whither, father, are you thus driving your mules and horses in the dead of night when other men are asleep? Are you not afraid of the fierce Achaeans who are hard by you, so cruel and relentless? Should some one of them see you bearing so much treasure through the darkness of the flying night, what would not your state then be? You are no longer young, and he who is with you is too old to protect you from those who would attack you. For myself, I will do you no harm, and I will defend you from anyone else, for you remind me of my own father."

And Priam answered, "It is indeed as you say, my dear son; nevertheless, some god has held his hand over me, in that he has sent such a wayfarer as yourself to meet me so opportunely; you are so comely in mien and figure, and your judgement is so excellent that you must come of blessed parents."

Then said the slayer of Argus, guide and guardian, "Sir, all that you have said is right; but tell me and tell me true, are you taking this rich treasure to send it to a foreign people where it may be safe, or are you all leaving strong Ilius in dismay now that your son has fallen who was the bravest man among you and was never lacking in battle with the Achaeans?"

And Priam said, "Who are you, my friend, and who are your parents, that you speak so truly about the fate of my unhappy son?"

The slayer of Argus, guide and guardian, answered him, "Sir, you would prove me, that you question me about noble Hector. Many a time have I set eyes upon him in battle when he was driving the Argives to their ships and putting them to the sword. We stood still and marvelled, for Achilles in his anger with the son of Atreus suffered us not to fight. I am his squire, and came with him in the same ship. I am a Myrmidon, and my father's name is Polyctor: he is a rich man and about as old as you are; he has six sons besides myself, and I am the seventh. We cast lots, and it fell upon me to sail hither with Achilles. I am now come from the ships on to the plain, for with daybreak the Achaeans will set battle in array about the city. They chafe at doing nothing, and are so eager that their princes cannot hold them back."

Then answered Priam, "If you are indeed the squire of Achilles son of Peleus, tell me now the whole truth. Is my son still at the ships, or has Achilles hewn him limb from limb, and given him to his hounds?"

"Sir," replied the slayer of Argus, guide and guardian, "neither hounds nor vultures have yet devoured him; he is still just lying at the tents by the ship of Achilles, and though it is now twelve days that he has lain there, his flesh is not wasted nor have the worms eaten him although they feed on warriors. At daybreak Achilles drags him cruelly round the sepulchre of his dear comrade, but it does him no hurt. You should come yourself and see how he lies fresh as dew, with the blood all washed away, and his wounds every one of them closed though many pierced him with their spears. Such care have the blessed gods taken of your brave son, for he was dear to them beyond all measure."

The old man was comforted as he heard him and said, "My son, see what a good thing it is to have made due offerings to the immortals; for as sure as that he was born my son never forgot the gods that hold Olympus, and now they requite it to him even in death. Accept therefore at my hands this goodly chalice; guard me and with heaven's help guide me till I come to the tent of the son of Peleus."

Then answered the slayer of Argus, guide and guardian, "Sir, you are tempting me and playing upon my youth, but you shall not move me, for you are offering me presents without the knowledge of Achilles whom I fear and hold it great guilt to defraud, lest some evil presently befall me; but as your guide I would go with you even to Argos itself, and would guard you so carefully whether by sea or land, that no one should attack you through making light of him who was with you."

The bringer of good luck then sprang on to the chariot, and seizing the whip and reins he breathed fresh spirit into the mules and horses. When they reached the trench and the wall that was before the ships, those who were on guard had just been getting their suppers, and the slayer of Argus threw them all into a deep sleep. Then he drew back the bolts to open the gates, and took Priam inside with the treasure he had upon his waggon. Ere long they came to the lofty dwelling of the son of Peleus for which the Myrmidons had cut pine and which they had built for their king; when they had built it they thatched it with coarse tussock-grass which they had mown out on the plain, and all round it they made a large courtyard, which was fenced with stakes set close together. The gate was barred with a single bolt of pine which it took three men to force into its place, and three to draw back so as to open the gate, but Achilles could draw it by himself. Mercury opened the gate for the old man, and brought in the treasure that he was taking with him for the son of Peleus. Then he sprang from the chariot on to the ground and said, "Sir, it is I, immortal Mercury, that am come with you, for my father sent me to escort you. I will now leave you, and will not enter into the presence of Achilles, for it might anger him that a god should befriend mortal men thus openly. Go you within, and embrace the knees of the son of Peleus: beseech him by his father, his lovely mother, and his son; thus you may move him."

With these words Mercury went back to high Olympus. Priam sprang from his chariot to the ground, leaving Idaeus where he was, in charge of the mules and horses. The old man went straight into the house where Achilles, loved of the gods, was sitting. There he found him with his men seated at a distance from him: only two, the hero Automedon, and Alcimus of the race of Mars, were busy in attendance about his person, for he had but just done eating and drinking, and the table was still there. King Priam entered without their seeing him, and going right up to Achilles he clasped his knees and kissed the dread murderous hands that had slain so many of his sons.

As when some cruel spite has befallen a man that he should have killed someone in his own country, and must fly to a great man's protection in a land of strangers, and all marvel who see him, even so did Achilles marvel as he beheld Priam. The others looked one to another and marvelled also, but Priam besought Achilles saying, "Think of your father, O Achilles like unto the gods, who is such even as I am, on the sad threshold of old age. It may be that those who dwell near him harass him, and there is none to keep war and ruin from him. Yet when he hears of you being still alive, he is glad, and his days are full of hope that he shall see his dear son come home to him from Troy; but I, wretched man that I am, had the bravest in all Troy for my sons, and there is not one of them left. I had fifty sons when the Achaeans came here; nineteen of them were from a single womb, and the others were borne to me by the women of my household. The greater part of them has fierce Mars laid low, and Hector, him who was alone left, him who was the guardian of the city and ourselves, him have you lately slain; therefore I am now come to the ships of the Achaeans to ransom his body from you with a great ransom. Fear, O Achilles, the wrath of heaven; think on your own father and have compassion upon me, who am the more pitiable, for I have steeled myself as no man yet has ever steeled himself before me, and have raised to my lips the hand of him who slew my son."

Thus spoke Priam, and the heart of Achilles yearned as he bethought him of his father. He took the old man's hand and moved him gently away. The two wept bitterly – Priam, as he lay at Achilles' feet, weeping for Hector, and Achilles now for his father and now for Patroclus, till the house was filled with their lamentation. But when Achilles was now sated with grief and had unburthened the bitterness of his sorrow, he left his seat and raised the old man by the hand, in pity for his white hair and beard; then he said, "Unhappy man, you have indeed been greatly daring; how could you venture to come alone to the ships of the Achaeans, and enter the presence of him who has slain so many of your brave sons? You must have iron courage: sit now upon this seat, and for all our grief we will hide our sorrows in our hearts, for weeping will not avail us. The immortals know no care, yet the lot they spin for man is full of sorrow; on the floor of Jove's palace there stand two urns, the one filled with evil gifts, and the other with good ones. He for whom Jove the lord of thunder mixes the gifts he sends, will meet now with good and now with evil fortune; but he to whom Jove sends none but evil gifts will be pointed at by the finger of scorn, the hand of famine will pursue him to the ends of the world, and he will go up and down the face of the earth, respected neither by gods nor men. Even so did it befall Peleus; the gods endowed him with all good things from his birth upwards, for he reigned over the Myrmidons excelling all men in prosperity and wealth, and mortal though he was they gave him a goddess for his bride. But even on him too did heaven send misfortune, for there is no race of royal children born to him in his house, save one son who is doomed to die all untimely; nor may I take care of him now that he is growing old, for I must stay here at Troy to be the bane of you and your children. And you too, O Priam, I have heard that you were aforetime happy. They say that in wealth and plenitude of offspring you surpassed all that is in Lesbos, the realm of Makar to the northward, Phrygia that is more inland, and those that dwell upon the great Hellespont; but from the day when the dwellers in heaven sent this evil upon you, war and slaughter have been about your city continually. Bear up against it, and let there be some intervals in your sorrow. Mourn as you may for your brave son, you will take nothing by it. You cannot raise him from the dead, ere you do so yet another sorrow shall befall you."

And Priam answered, "O king, bid me not be seated, while Hector is still lying uncared for in your tents, but accept the great ransom which I have brought you, and give him to me at once that I may look upon him. May you prosper with the ransom and reach your own land in safety, seeing that you have suffered me to live and to look upon the light of the sun."

Achilles looked at him sternly and said, "Vex me, sir, no longer; I am of myself minded to give up the body of Hector. My mother, daughter of the old man of the sea, came to me from Jove to bid me deliver it to you. Moreover I know well, O Priam, and you cannot hide it, that some god has brought you to the ships of the Achaeans, for else, no man however strong and in his prime would dare to come to our host; he could neither pass our guard unseen, nor draw the bolt of my gates thus easily; therefore, provoke me no further, lest I sin against the word of Jove, and suffer you not, suppliant though you are, within my tents."

The old man feared him and obeyed. Then the son of Peleus sprang like a lion through the door of his house, not alone, but with him went his two squires Automedon and Alcimus who were closer to him than any others of his comrades now that Patroclus was no more. These unyoked the horses and mules, and bade Priam's herald and attendant be seated within the house. They lifted the ransom for Hector's body from the waggon, but they left two mantles and a goodly shirt, that Achilles might wrap the body in them when he gave it to be taken home. Then he called to his servants and ordered them to wash the body and anoint it, but he first took it to a place where Priam should not see it, lest if he did so, he should break out in the bitterness of his grief, and enrage Achilles, who might then kill him and sin against the word of Jove. When the servants had washed the body and anointed it, and had wrapped it in a fair shirt and mantle, Achilles himself lifted it on to a bier, and he and his men then laid it on the waggon. He cried aloud as he did so and called on the name of his dear comrade, "Be not angry with me, Patroclus," he said, "if you hear even in the house of Hades that I have given Hector to his father for a ransom. It has been no unworthy one, and I will share it equitably with you."

Achilles then went back into the tent and took his place on the richly inlaid seat from which he had risen, by the wall that was at right angles to the one against which Priam was sitting. "Sir," he said, "your son is now laid upon his bier and is ransomed according to desire; you shall look upon him when you take him away at daybreak; for the present let us prepare our supper. Even lovely Niobe had to think about eating, though her twelve children – six daughters and six lusty sons – had been all slain in her house. Apollo killed the sons with arrows from his silver bow, to punish Niobe, and Diana slew the daughters, because Niobe had vaunted herself against Leto; she said Leto had borne two children only, whereas she had herself borne many – whereon the two killed the many. Nine days did they lie weltering, and there was none to bury them, for the son of Saturn turned the people into stone; but on the tenth day the gods in heaven themselves buried them, and Niobe then took food, being worn out with weeping. They say that somewhere among the rocks on the mountain pastures of Sipylus, where the nymphs live that haunt the river Achelous, there, they say, she lives in stone and still nurses the sorrows sent upon her by the hand of heaven. Therefore, noble sir, let us two now take food; you can weep for your dear son hereafter as you are bearing him back to Ilius – and many a tear will he cost you."

With this Achilles sprang from his seat and killed a sheep of silvery whiteness, which his followers skinned and made ready all in due order. They cut the meat carefully up into smaller pieces, spitted them, and drew them off again when they were well roasted. Automedon brought bread in fair baskets and served it round the table, while Achilles dealt out the meat, and they laid their hands on the good things that were before them. As soon as they had had enough to eat and drink, Priam, descendant of Dardanus, marvelled at the strength and beauty of Achilles for he was as a god to see, and Achilles marvelled at Priam as he listened to him and looked upon his noble presence. When they had gazed their fill Priam spoke first. "And now, O king," he said, "take me to my couch that we may lie down and enjoy the blessed boon of sleep. Never once have my eyes been closed from the day your hands took the life of my son; I have grovelled without ceasing in the mire of my stable yard, making moan and brooding over my countless sorrows. Now, moreover, I have eaten bread and drunk wine; hitherto I have tasted nothing."

As he spoke Achilles told his men and the women-servants to set beds in the room that was in the gatehouse, and make them with good red rugs, and spread coverlets on the top of them with woollen cloaks for Priam and Idaeus to wear. So the maids went out carrying a torch and got the two beds ready in all haste. Then Achilles said laughingly to Priam, "Dear sir, you shall lie outside, lest some counsellor of those who in due course keep coming to advise with me should see you here in the darkness of the flying night, and tell it to Agamemnon. This might cause delay in the delivery of the body. And now tell me and tell me true, for how many days would you celebrate the funeral rites of noble Hector? Tell me, that I may hold aloof from war and restrain the host."

And Priam answered, "Since, then, you suffer me to bury my noble son with all due rites, do thus, Achilles, and I shall be grateful. You know how we are pent up within our city; it is far for us to fetch wood from the mountain, and the people live in fear. Nine days, therefore, will we mourn Hector in my house; on the tenth day we will bury him and there shall be a public feast in his honour; on the eleventh we will build a mound over his ashes, and on the twelfth, if there be need, we will fight."

And Achilles answered, "All, King Priam, shall be as you have said. I will stay our fighting for as long a time as you have named."

As he spoke he laid his hand on the old man's right wrist, in token that he should have no fear; thus then did Priam and his attendant sleep there in the forecourt, full of thought, while Achilles lay in an inner room of the house, with fair Briseis by his side.

And now both gods and mortals were fast asleep through the livelong night, but upon Mercury alone, the bringer of good luck, sleep could take no hold for he was thinking all the time how to get King Priam away from the ships without his being seen by the strong force of sentinels. He hovered therefore over Priam's head and said, "Sir, now that Achilles has spared your life, you seem to have no fear about sleeping in the thick of your foes. You have paid a great ransom, and have received the body of your son; were you still alive and a prisoner the sons whom you have left at home would have to give three times as much to free you; and so it would be if Agamemnon and the other Achaeans were to know of your being here."

When he heard this the old man was afraid and roused his servant. Mercury then yoked their horses and mules, and drove them quickly through the host so that no man perceived them. When they came to the ford of eddying Xanthus, begotten of immortal Jove, Mercury went back to high Olympus, and dawn in robe of saffron began to break over all the land. Priam and Idaeus then drove on toward the city lamenting and making moan, and the mules drew the body of Hector. No one neither man nor woman saw them, till Cassandra, fair as golden Venus standing on Pergamus, caught sight of her dear father in his chariot, and his servant that was the city's herald with him. Then she saw him that was lying upon the bier, drawn by the mules, and with a loud cry she went about the city saying, "Come hither Trojans, men and women, and look on Hector; if ever you rejoiced to see him coming from battle when he was alive, look now on him that was the glory of our city and all our people."

At this there was not man nor woman left in the city, so great a sorrow had possessed them. Hard by the gates they met Priam as he was bringing in the body. Hector's wife and his mother were the first to mourn him: they flew towards the waggon and laid their hands upon his head, while the crowd stood weeping round them. They would have stayed before the gates, weeping and lamenting the livelong day to the going down of the sun, had not Priam spoken to them from the chariot and said, "Make way for the mules to pass you. Afterwards when I have taken the body home you shall have your fill of weeping."

On this the people stood asunder, and made a way for the waggon. When they had borne the body within the house they laid it upon a bed and seated minstrels round it to lead the dirge, whereon the women joined in the sad music of their lament. Foremost among them all Andromache led their wailing as she clasped the head of mighty Hector in her embrace. "Husband," she cried, "you have died young, and leave me in your house a widow; he of whom we are the ill-starred parents is still a mere child, and I fear he may not reach manhood. Ere he can do so our city will be razed and overthrown, for you who watched over it are no more – you who were its saviour, the guardian of our wives and children. Our women will be carried away captives to the ships, and I among them; while you, my child, who will be with me will be put to some unseemly tasks, working for a cruel master. Or, may be, some Achaean will hurl you (O miserable death) from our walls, to avenge some brother, son, or father whom Hector slew; many of them have indeed bitten the dust at his hands, for your father's hand in battle was no light one. Therefore do the people mourn him. You have left, O Hector, sorrow unutterable to your parents, and my own grief is greatest of all, for you did not stretch forth your arms and embrace me as you lay dying, nor say to me any words that might have lived with me in my tears night and day for evermore."

Bitterly did she weep the while, and the women joined in her lament. Hecuba in her turn took up the strains of woe. "Hector," she cried, "dearest to me of all my children. So long as you were alive the gods loved you well, and even in death they have not been utterly unmindful of you; for when Achilles took any other of my sons, he would sell him beyond the seas, to Samos Imbrus or rugged Lemnos; and when he had slain you too with his sword, many a time did he drag you round the sepulchre of his comrade

– though this could not give him life – yet here you lie all fresh as dew, and comely as one whom Apollo has slain with his painless shafts."

Thus did she too speak through her tears with bitter moan, and then Helen for a third time took up the strain of lamentation. "Hector," said she, "dearest of all my brothers-in-law – for I am wife to Alexandrus who brought me hither to Troy – would that I had died ere he did so – twenty years are come and gone since I left my home and came from over the sea, but I have never heard one word of insult or unkindness from you. When another would chide with me, as it might be one of your brothers or sisters or of your brothers' wives, or my mother-in-law – for Priam was as kind to me as though he were my own father – you would rebuke and check them with words of gentleness and goodwill. Therefore my tears flow both for you and for my unhappy self, for there is no one else in Troy who is kind to me, but all shrink and shudder as they go by me."

She wept as she spoke and the vast crowd that was gathered round her joined in her lament. Then King Priam spoke to them saying, "Bring wood, O Trojans, to the city, and fear no cunning ambush of the Argives, for Achilles when he dismissed me from the ships gave me his word that they should not attack us until the morning of the twelfth day."

Forthwith they yoked their oxen and mules and gathered together before the city. Nine days long did they bring in great heaps of wood, and on the morning of the tenth day with many tears they took brave Hector forth, laid his dead body upon the summit of the pile, and set the fire thereto. Then when the child of morning, rosy-fingered dawn, appeared on the eleventh day, the people again assembled, round the pyre of mighty Hector. When they were got together, they first quenched the fire with wine wherever it was burning, and then his brothers and comrades with many a bitter tear gathered his white bones, wrapped them in soft robes of purple, and laid them in a golden urn, which they placed in a grave and covered over with large stones set close together. Then they built a barrow hurriedly over it keeping guard on every side lest the Achaeans should attack them before they had finished. When they had heaped up the barrow they went back again into the city, and being well assembled they held high feast in the house of Priam their king.

Thus, then, did they celebrate the funeral of Hector tamer of horses.

The Odyssey

Fragments from Book XI

♞

"AND I SAID, 'Achilles, son of Peleus, foremost champion of the Achaeans, I came to consult Teiresias, and see if he could advise me about my return home to Ithaca, for I have never yet been able to get near the Achaean land, nor to set foot in my own country, but have been in trouble all the time. As for you, Achilles, no one was ever yet so fortunate as you have been, nor ever will be, for you were adored by all us Argives as long as you were alive, and now that you are here you are a great prince among the dead. Do not, therefore, take it so much to heart even if you are dead.'

"'Say not a word,' he answered, 'in death's favour; I would rather be a paid servant in a poor man's house and be above ground than king of kings among the dead. But give me news about son; is he gone to the wars and will he be a great soldier, or is this not so? Tell me also if you have heard anything about my father Peleus – does he still rule among the Myrmidons, or do they show him no respect throughout Hellas and Phthia now that he is old and his limbs fail him? Could I but stand by his side, in the light of day, with the same strength that I had when I killed the bravest of our foes upon the plain of Troy- could I but be as I then was and go even for a short time to my father's house, anyone who tried to do him violence or supersede him would soon me it.'

"'I have heard nothing,' I answered, 'of Peleus, but I can tell you all about your son Neoptolemus, for I took him in my own ship from Scyros with the Achaeans. In our councils of war before Troy he was always first to speak, and his judgement was unerring. Nestor and I were the only two who could surpass him; and when it came to fighting on the plain of Troy, he would never remain with the body of his men, but would dash on far in front, foremost of them all in valour. Many a man did he kill in battle – I cannot name every single one of those whom he slew while fighting on the side of the Argives, but will only say how he killed that valiant hero Eurypylus son of Telephus, who was the handsomest man I ever saw except Memnon; many others also of the Ceteians fell around him by reason of a woman's bribes. Moreover, when all the bravest of the Argives went inside the horse that Epeus had made, and it was left to me to settle when we should either open the door of our ambuscade, or close it, though all the other leaders and chief men among the Danaans were drying their eyes and quaking in every limb, I never once saw him turn pale nor wipe a tear from his cheek; he was all the time urging me to break out from the horse – grasping the handle of his sword and his bronze-shod spear, and breathing fury against the foe. Yet when we had sacked the city of Priam he got his handsome share of the prize money and went on board (such is the fortune of war) without a wound upon him, neither from a thrown spear nor in close combat, for the rage of Mars is a matter of great chance.'"

Nemean Odes

Book III

BUT TO WHAT HEADLAND of a strange shore, O my soul, art thou carrying aside the course of my ship? To Aiakos and to his race I charge thee bring the Muse. Herein is perfect justice, to speak the praise of good men: neither are desires for things alien the best for men to cherish: search first at home: a fitting glory for thy sweet song hast thou gotten there in deeds of ancient valour.

Glad was King Peleus when he cut him his gigantic spear, he who took Iolkos by his single arm without help of any host, he who held firm in the struggle Thetis the daughter of the sea.

Also the city of Laomedon did mighty Telamon sack, when he fought with Iolaos by his side, and again to the war of the Amazons with brazen bows he followed him; neither at any time did man-subduing terror abate the vigour of his soul.

By inborn worth doth one prevail mightily; but whoso hath but precepts is a vain man and is fain now for this thing and now again for that, but a sure step planteth he not at any time, but handleth countless enterprises with a purpose that achieveth naught.

Now Achilles of the yellow hair, while he dwelt in the house of Philyra, being yet a child made mighty deeds his play; and brandishing many a time his little javelin in his hands, swift as the wind he dealt death to wild lions in the fight, and boars he slew also and dragged their heaving bodies to the Centaur, son of Kronos, a six years' child when he began, and thenceforward continually. And Artemis marvelled at him, and brave Athene, when he slew deer without dogs or device of nets; for by fleetness of foot he overcame them.

The Cypria

Fragments

Fragment I – Synopsis
Proclus, Chrestomathia, i

THIS IS CONTINUED by the epic called Cypria which is current is 11 books. Its contents are as follows. Zeus plans with Themis to bring about the Trojan war. Strife arrives while the gods are feasting at the marriage of Peleus and starts a dispute between Hera, Athena and Aphrodite as to which of them is fairest. The three are led by Hermes at the command of Zeus to Alexandrus on Mount Ida for his decision, and Alexandrus, lured by his promised marriage with Helen, decides in favour of Aphrodite. Then Alexandrus builds his ships at Aphrodite's suggestion, and

Helenus foretells the future to him, and Aphrodite order Aeneas to sail with him, while Cassandra prophesies as to what will happen afterwards.

Alexandrus next lands in Lacedaemon and is entertained by the sons of Tyndareus, and afterwards by Menelaus in Sparta, where in the course of a feast he gives gifts to Helen. After this, Menelaus sets sail for Crete, ordering Helen to furnish the guests with all they require until they depart. Meanwhile, Aphrodite brings Helen and Alexandrus together, and they, after their union, put very great treasures on board and sail away by night. Hera stirs up a storm against them and they are carried to Sidon, where Alexandrus takes the city. From there he sailed to Troy and celebrated his marriage with Helen.

In the meantime Castor and Polydeuces, while stealing the cattle of Idas and Lynceus, were caught in the act, and Castor was killed by Idas, and Lynceus and Idas by Polydeuces. Zeus gave them immortality every other day. Iris next informs Menelaus of what has happened at his home. Menelaus returns and plans an expedition against Ilium with his brother, and then goes on to Nestor. Nestor in a digression tells him how Epopeus was utterly destroyed after seducing the daughter of Lycus, and the story of Oedipus, the madness of Heracles and the story of Theseus and Ariadne. Then they travel over Hellas and gather the leaders, detecting Odysseus when he pretends to be mad, not wishing to join the expedition, by seizing his son Telemachus for punishment at the suggestion of Palamedes. All the leaders then meet together at Aulis and sacrifice. The incident of the serpent and the sparrows takes place before them, and Calchas foretells what is going to befall. After this, they put out to sea, and reach Teuthrania and sack it, taking it for Ilium. Telephus comes out to the rescue and kills Thersander and son of Polyneices, and is himself wounded by Achilles. As they put out from Mysia a storm comes on them and scatters them, and Achilles first puts in at Scyros and marries Deidameia, the daughter of Lycomedes, and then heals Telephus, who had been led by an oracle to go to Argos, so that he might be their guide on the voyage to Ilium. When the expedition had mustered a second time at Aulis, Agamemnon, while at the chase, shot a stag and boasted that he surpassed even Artemis. At this the goddess was so angry that she sent stormy winds and prevented them from sailing. Calchas then told them of the anger of the goddess and bade them sacrifice Iphigenia [Agamemnon's daughter] to Artemis. This they attempt to do, sending to fetch Iphigenia as though for marriage with Achilles. Artemis, however, snatched her away and transported her to the Tauri, making her immortal, and putting a stag in place of the girl upon the altar.

Next they sail as far as Tenedos: and while they are feasting, Philoctetes is bitten by a snake and is left behind in Lemnos because of the stench of his sore. Here, too, Achilles quarrels with Agamemnon because he is invited late. Then the Greeks tried to land at Ilium, but the Trojans prevent them, and Protesilaus is killed by Hector. Achilles then kills Cycnus, the son of Poseidon, and drives the Trojans back. The Greeks take up their dead and send envoys to the Trojans demanding the surrender of Helen and the treasure with her. The Trojans refusing, they first assault the city, and then go out and lay waste the country and cities round about. After this, Achilles desires to see Helen, and Aphrodite and Thetis contrive a meeting between them. The Achaeans next desire to return home, but are restrained by Achilles, who afterwards drives off the cattle of Aeneas, and sacks Lyrnessus and Pedasus and many of the neighbouring cities, and kills Troilus. Patroclus carries away Lycaon to Lemnos and sells him as a slave, and out of the spoils Achilles receives Briseis as a prize, and Agamemnon Chryseis. Then follows the death of Palamedes, the plan of Zeus to relieve the Trojans by detaching Achilles from the Hellenic confederacy, and a catalogue of the Trojan allies.

Fragment III – The Plan of Zeus
Scholiast on Homer, Il. i. 5

"There was a time when the countless tribes of men, though wide-dispersed, oppressed the surface of the deep-bosomed earth, and Zeus saw it and had pity and in his wise heart resolved to relieve the all-nurturing earth of men by causing the great struggle of the Ilian war, that the load of death might empty the world. And so the heroes were slain in Troy, and the plan of Zeus came to pass."

Fragment IV – Thetis and Zeus
Volumina Herculan, II. viii. 105

The author of the *Cypria* says that Thetis, to please Hera, avoided union with Zeus, at which he was enraged and swore that she should be the wife of a mortal.

Fragment V – Peleus and Thetis
Scholiast on Homer, Il. xvii. 140

For at the marriage of Peleus and Thetis, the gods gathered together on Pelion to feast and brought Peleus gifts. Cheiron gave him a stout ashen shaft which he had cut for a spear, and Athena, it is said, polished it, and Hephaestus fitted it with a head. The story is given by the author of the *Cypria*.

The Aethiopis

Fragment I – Synopsis
Proclus, Chrestomathia, ii

THE CYPRIA, described in the preceding book, has its sequel in the Iliad of Homer, which is followed in turn by the five books of the Aethiopis, the work of Arctinus of Miletus. Their contents are as follows.

The Amazon Penthesileia, the daughter of Ares and of Thracian race, comes to aid the Trojans, and after showing great prowess, is killed by Achilles and buried by the Trojans. Achilles then slays Thersites for abusing and reviling him for his supposed love for Penthesileia. As a result, a dispute arises amongst the Achaeans over the killing of Thersites, and Achilles sails to Lesbos and after sacrificing Artemis and Leto to Apollo, is purified by Odysseus from bloodshed.

Then Memnon, the son of Eos, wearing armour made by Hephaestus, comes to help the Trojans, and Thetis tells her son about Memnon. A battle takes place in which Antilochus is slain by Memnon and Memnon by Achilles. Eos then obtains of Zeus and bestows upon her son immortality; but Achilles routs the Trojans and, rushing into the city with them, is killed by Paris and Apollo.

A great struggle for the body then follows, Aias taking up the body and carrying it to the ships, while Odysseus drives off the Trojans behind. The Achaeans then bury Antilochus and lay out the body of Achilles, while Thetis, arriving with the Muses and her sisters, bewails her son, whom she afterwards catches away from the pyre and transports to the White Island. After this, the Achaeans pile him a cairn and hold games in his honour. Lastly a dispute arises between Odysseus and Aias over the arms of Achilles.

The Little Iliad

Fragment I – Synopsis
Proclus, Chrestomathia, ii

NEXT COMES the Little Iliad in four books by Lesches of Mitylene: its contents are as follows.

The adjudging of the arms of Achilles takes place, and Odysseus, by the contriving of Athena, gains them. Aias then becomes mad and destroys the herd of the Achaeans and kills himself. Next Odysseus lies in wait and catches Helenus, who prophesies as to the taking of Troy, and Diomede accordingly brings Philoctetes from Lemnos. Philoctetes is healed by Machaon, fights in single combat with Alexandrus and kills him: the dead body is outraged by Menelaus, but the Trojans recover and bury it.

After this Deiphobus marries Helen, Odysseus brings Neoptolemus from Scyros and gives him his father's arms, and the ghost of Achilles appears to him. Eurypylus the son of Telephus arrives to aid the Trojans, shows his prowess and is killed by Neoptolemus. The Trojans are now closely besieged, and Epeius, by Athena's instruction, builds the wooden horse. Odysseus disfigures himself and goes into Ilium as a spy, and there being recognized by Helen, plots with her for the taking of the city; after killing certain of the Trojans, he returns to the ships. Next he carries the Palladium out of Troy with help of Diomedes. Then after putting their best men in the wooden horse and burning their huts, the main body of the Hellenes sail to Tenedos. The Trojans, supposing their troubles over, destroy a part of their city wall and take the wooden horse into their city and feast as though they had conquered the Hellenes.

Symposium

Excerpt from Phaedrus' Speech

LOVE WILL MAKE MEN dare to die for their beloved – love alone; and women as well as men. Of this, Alcestis, the daughter of Pelias, is a monument to all Hellas; for she was willing to lay down her life on behalf of her husband, when no one else would, although he had a father and mother; but the tenderness of her love so far exceeded theirs, that she made them seem to be strangers in blood to their own son, and in name only related to him; and so noble did this action of hers appear to the gods, as well as to men, that among the many who have done virtuously she is one of the very few to whom, in admiration of her noble action, they have granted the privilege of returning alive to earth; such exceeding honour is paid by the gods to the devotion and virtue of love.

But Orpheus, the son of Oeagrus, the harper, they sent empty away, and presented to him an apparition only of her whom he sought, but herself they would not give up, because he showed no spirit; he was only a harp player, and did not dare like Alcestis to die for love, but was contriving how he might enter Hades alive; moreover, they afterwards caused him to suffer death at the hands of women, as the punishment of his cowardliness.

Very different was the reward of the true love of Achilles towards his lover Patroclus – his lover and not his love (the notion that Patroclus was the beloved one is a foolish error into which Aeschylus has fallen, for Achilles was surely the fairer of the two, fairer also than all the other heroes; and, as Homer informs us, he was still beardless, and younger far). And greatly as the gods honour the virtue of love, still the return of love on the part of the beloved to the lover is more admired and valued and rewarded by them, for the lover is more divine, because he is inspired by God. Now Achilles was quite aware, for he had been told by his mother, that he might avoid death and return home, and live to a good old age, if he abstained from slaying Hector. Nevertheless, he gave his life to revenge his friend, and dared to die, not only in his defence, but after he was dead. Wherefore the gods honoured him even above Alcestis, and sent him to the Islands of the Blest.

These are my reasons for affirming that Love is the eldest and noblest and mightiest of the gods; and the chiefest author and giver of virtue in life, and of happiness after death.

Apology of Socrates

Excerpt

SOMEONE WILL SAY: And are you not ashamed, Socrates, of a course of life which is likely to bring you to an untimely end? To him I may fairly answer: There you are mistaken: a man who is good for anything ought not to calculate the chance of living or

dying; he ought only to consider whether in doing anything he is doing right or wrong – acting the part of a good man or of a bad.

Whereas, according to your view, the heroes who fell at Troy were not good for much, and the son of Thetis above all, who altogether despised danger in comparison with disgrace; and when his goddess mother said to him, in his eagerness to slay Hector, that if he avenged his companion Patroclus, and slew Hector, he would die himself – "Fate," as she said, "waits upon you next after Hector"; he, hearing this, utterly despised danger and death, and instead of fearing them, feared rather to live in dishonour, and not to avenge his friend. "Let me die next," he replies, "and be avenged of my enemy, rather than abide here by the beaked ships, a scorn and a burden of the earth."

Had Achilles any thought of death and danger? For wherever a man's place is, whether the place which he has chosen or that in which he has been placed by a commander, there he ought to remain in the hour of danger; he should not think of death or of anything, but of disgrace. And this, O men of Athens, is a true saying.

Achilles in the Hellenistic Period

IN HELLENISTIC ALEXANDRIA, the mythical Achilles became an object of study for the increasingly literary scholars of the city's celebrated museum and library of Alexandria, established by the Ptolemies to study and preserve the Greek past. One of its head librarians may have been Apollonius of Rhodes (active in the third century BCE). Though the *Argonautica* is his only surviving work, he is also believed to have composed commentaries on Homer (among others), but his epic draws its plot from earlier myths. In the *Argonautica*, Achilles appears not yet as a hero in his own right but as the son of a hero, Peleus. The story Apollonius recounts of Thetis attempting to immortalize Achilles is not narrated in the epic material that has survived, but it has a parallel in the Homeric *Hymn to Demeter*. Like Thetis, Demeter attempts to burn away a child's mortal portion but is interrupted by his parent. To honour the attempt, she establishes rituals in the child's honour. By replicating the story, Apollonius offers a complementary origin story for the cult of Achilles, a hero special to the founder of the poet's city, Alexander.

Parthenius (active in the first century BCE) was a Greek grammarian and poet from Asia Minor. He is believed to have been captured in the Mithridatic wars between Rome and the Kingdom of Pontus. Brought to Rome, sources report, he eventually became the Greek tutor of Roman poet Virgil. The *Love Romances,* his only surviving work, brings together Greek texts of classical and Hellenistic origin. The two stories that feature Achilles portray him as single-mindedly focused on martial excess. In 'The Story of Pisidice', Aphrodite inspires a young woman to fall in love with Achilles so that she will betray her city for him, a recurring theme in mythic narratives. But Achilles only has eyes for conquest. This portrait is mirrored in 'The Story of Apriate', in which Achilles is so focused on warfare that he unknowingly murders the son of his friend, fellow Trojan war hero Ajax Telamon.

The Argonautica

From Book IV

SHE SPAKE, and vanished into the depths of the sea; but sharp pain smote Peleus, for never before had he seen her come, since first she left her bridal chamber and bed in anger, on account of noble Achilles, then a babe. For she ever encompassed the child's mortal flesh in the night with the flame of fire; and day by day she anointed with ambrosia his tender frame, so that he might become immortal and that she might keep off from his body loathsome old age.

But Peleus leapt up from his bed and saw his dear son gasping in the flame; and at the sight he uttered a terrible cry, fool that he was; and she heard it, and catching up the child threw him screaming to the ground, and herself like a breath of wind passed swiftly from the hall as a dream and leapt into the sea, exceeding wroth, and thereafter returned not again.

Love Romances

Preface
Parthenius to Cornelius Gallus, Greeting

I THOUGHT, my dear Cornelius Gallus, that to you above all men there would be something particularly agreeable in this collection of romances of love, and I have put them together and set them out in the shortest possible form.

The stories, as they are found in the poets who treat this class of subject, are not usually related with sufficient simplicity; I hope that, in the way I have treated them, you will have the summary of each: and you will thus have at hand a storehouse from which to draw material, as may seem best to you, for either epic or elegiac verse. I am sure that you will not think the worse of them because they have not that polish of which you are yourself such a master: I have only put them together as aids to memory, and that is the sole purpose for which they are meant to be of service to you.

Story 21
The Story of Pisidice

THERE IS A STORY that Achilles, when he was sailing along and laying waste the islands close to the mainland, arrived at Lesbos, and there attacked each of its cities in turn and plundered it. But the inhabitants of Methymna held out against him very valiantly, and he was in great straits because he was unable to take the city, when a girl of Methymna named Pisidice, a daughter of the king, saw him from the walls and fell in love with him.

Accordingly, she sent him her nurse, and promised to put the town into his possession if he would take her to wife. At the moment, indeed, he consented to her terms; but when the town was now in his power he felt the utmost loathing for what she had done, and bade his soldiers stone her. The poet of 'The Founding of Lesbos' relates this tragedy in these words:

> *Achilles slew the hero Lampetus and Hicetaon (of Methymna son*
> *And Lepteymnus, born of noble sires) and Helicaon's brother,*
>   *bold like him,*
> *Hypsipylus, the strongest man alive. But lady Cypris laid great*
>   *wait for him:*

> For she set poor Pisidice's young heart a-fluttering with love for
>   him, when as
> She saw him reveling in battle's lust amid the Achaean champions;
>   and full oft
> Into the buxom air her arms she flung in craving for his love.

Then, a little further down, he goes on: –

> Within the city straight the maiden brought the whole Achaean
>   hosts, the city gates
> Unbarring stealthily; yea, she endured with her own eyes to see
>   her aged sires
> Put to the sword, the chains of slavery about the women whom
>   Achilles dragged
> – So had he sworn – down to his ships: and all that she might sea-
>   born Thetis' daughter be,
> The sons of Aeacus her kin, and dwell at Phthia, royal husband's
>   goodly spouse.
> But it was not to be: he but rejoiced to see her city's doom, while her befell
> A sorry marriage with great Peleus' son, poor wretch, at Argive
>   hands; for her they slew,
> Casting great stones upon her, one and all.

Story 26
The Story of Apriate from the
Thrax of Euphorion

TRAMBELUS, THE SON of Telamon, fell in love with a girl
named Apriate in Lesbos. He used every effort to gain her:
but, as she showed no signs at all of relenting, he determined
to win her by strategy and guile.

She was walking one day with her attendant handmaids to one of her father's domains which was by the seashore, and there he laid an ambush for her and made her captive; but she struggled with the greatest violence to protect her virginity, and at last Trambelus in fury threw her into the sea, which happened at that point to be deep inshore. Thus did she perish; the story has, however, been related by others in the sense that she threw herself in while fleeing from his pursuit.

It was not long before divine vengeance fell upon Trambelus: Achilles was ravaging Lesbos and carrying away great quantities of booty, and Trambelus got together a company of the inhabitants of the island, and went out to meet him in battle. In the course of it he received a wound in the breast and instantly fell to the ground; while he was still breathing, Achilles, who had admired his valour, inquired of his name and origin. When he was told that he was the son of Telamon, he bewailed him long and deeply, and piled up a great barrow for him on the beach: it is still called 'the hero Trambelus' mound'.

Achilles in the Roman Empire

FOR POETS writing in the Roman Empire, both Greek and Roman, Achilles effectively becomes a character in a story. That story continues to be reshaped, but the sacred associations with him that existed during the archaic and classical periods, and which echoed in Alexandria during the Hellenistic age, seem to fall away, perhaps to make space for new or different heroes, including, in the case of the Roman Empire, the emperors themselves. The extracts in this section highlight both Achilles' demotion from cult hero to mythic character and the malleability of his myth.

In compendia, which were popular in the empire period, Greek and Roman poets feature Achilles' story as one among many, none taking particular precedence or connected to a sacred context. The most celebrated and influential of these compendia in the modern day is arguably the *Metamorphoses* by Ovid (43 BCE–17 CE), who wrote during the reign of Caesar Augustus and was exiled from Rome in 8 CE for reasons that continue to be debated. The *Metamorphoses* is acutely aware of power dynamics, in particular on the violence of power and of the fatal cost of mortal mistakes, experiences of which Ovid himself may have been acutely aware. Achilles appears in a comparatively brief section in which Ovid presents a truncated synopsis of the Trojan War. Ovid steers clear of Homer's treatment of Achilles, choosing instead to retell an incident from the Epic Cycle known today only through summary: Achilles' relentless pursuit and killing of Cycnus (often anglicized to 'Cygnus'). In Ovid, Achilles is a brash young warrior, almost humorously confident in his primacy, but for his brutality.

The *Achilleid* is an unfinished biographical poem of Achilles by Roman poet Statius (45–96 CE). His portrait of Achilles infuses lesser-revisited events from the hero's early life with wit and whimsy but without entirely abandoning the reckless anger and violence the hero is known for in earlier poetry. Statius crafts an Achilles who treads a fine line between the chilling humour of Ovid's portrait and the gravity of Homer's. Though it exerted considerable influence in late antiquity and the Middle Ages, the *Achilleid*'s influence in the modern day has receded. Despite this, Statius is the earliest source to provide the story with which Achilles is arguably most associated: his legendary vulnerable heel. This anecdote touches on Achilles' semi-divine status, but in a way that differentiates him from cult hero associations inherent in Apollonius (and the *Hymn to Demeter*).

The *Biblioteca* is effectively an encyclopedia of Greek myths collected from earlier Greek sources, covering everything from the origins of the gods through the end of Odysseus's story and noting the existence of multiple variants attributed to different poets. Though it seems to have been influential and well-read in ancient and medieval times, nothing is known about its author, other than that the text was written in Greek and excludes Italian myths. Initially mistakenly attributed to an Apollodorus, the author is now often cited as Pseudo-Apollodorous. Language analysis has dated its composition to no earlier than the first century CE, possibly later. As with the other myths in the collection, Achilles' experiences are reported without embellishment or commentary and seem to be reconstructed largely from epic material. The reportorial tone perhaps reflects its function to bring together in one collection the mythological canon as the heritage of Greek speakers. In this, it is an invaluable resource for readers who wish to acquaint themselves with features of Achilles' story in early Greek sources that are otherwise lost.

The Metamorphoses

Book XI

Fables V and VI

FOR THE AGED PROTEUS had said to Thetis, "Goddess of the waves, conceive; thou shalt be the mother of a youth, who by his gallant actions shall surpass the deeds of his father, and shall be called greater than he." Therefore, lest the world might contain something greater than Jove, although he had felt no gentle flame in his breast, Jupiter avoided the embraces of Thetis, the Goddess of the sea, and commanded his grandson, the son of Aeacus, to succeed to his own pretensions, and rush into the embraces of the ocean maid.

There is a bay of Haemonia, curved into a bending arch; its arms project out; there, were the water *but* deeper, there would be a harbour, *but* the sea is *just* covering the surface of the sand. It has a firm shore, which retains not the impression of the foot, nor delays the step *of the traveller*, nor is covered with seaweeds. There is a grove of myrtle at hand, planted with parti-coloured berries. In the middle there is a cave, whether formed by nature or art, it is doubtful; still, by art rather. To this, Thetis, thou wast wont often to come naked, seated on thy harnessed dolphin. There Peleus seized upon thee, as thou wast lying fast bound in sleep; and because, being tried by entreaties, thou didst resist, he resolved upon violence, clasping thy neck with both his arms. And, unless thou hadst had recourse to thy wonted arts, by frequently changing thy shape, he would have succeeded in his attempt. But, at one moment, thou wast a bird (still, as a bird he held thee fast); at another time a large tree: to *that* tree did Peleus cling. Thy third form was that of a spotted tiger; frightened by that, the son of Aeacus loosened his arms from thy body.

Then pouring wine upon its waters, he worshipped the Gods of the sea, both with the entrails of sheep and with the smoke of frankincense; until the Carpathian prophet said, from the middle of the waves, "Son of Aeacus, thou shalt gain the alliance desired by thee. Do thou only, when she shall be resting fast asleep in the cool cave, bind her unawares with cords and tenacious bonds. And let her not deceive thee, by imitating a hundred forms; but hold her fast, whatever she shall be, until she shall reassume the form which she had before." Proteus said this, and hid his face in the sea, and received his own waves at his closing words. Titan was *now* descending, and, with the pole of his chariot bent downward, was taking possession of the Hesperian main; when the beautiful Nereid, leaving the deep, entered her wonted place of repose. Hardly had Peleus well seized the virgin's limbs, *when* she changed her shape, until she perceived her limbs to be held fast, and her arms to be extended different ways. Then, at last, she sighed, and said, "Not without *the aid of* a Divinity, dost thou overcome me;" and then she appeared *as* Thetis *again.* The hero embraced her *thus* revealed, and enjoyed his wish, and by her was the father of great Achilles.

Book XII

Fables I and II

HIS FATHER PRIAM mourned him, not knowing that Aeacus, having assumed wings, was still living; Hector, too, with his brothers, made unavailing offerings at a tomb, that bore his name on it. The presence of Paris was wanting, at this mournful office: who, soon after, brought into his country a lengthened war, together with a ravished wife; and 1,000 ships uniting together, followed him, and, together with them, the whole body of the Pelasgian nation.

Nor would vengeance have been delayed, had not the raging winds made the seas impassable, and the Boeotian land detained in fishy Aulis the ships ready to depart. Here, when they had prepared a sacrifice to Jupiter, after the manner of their country, as the ancient altar was heated with kindled fires, the Greeks beheld an azure-coloured serpent creep into a plane tree, which was standing near the sacrifice they had begun. There was on the top of the tree a nest of twice four birds, which the serpent seized together, and the dam as she fluttered around *the scene of* her loss, and he buried them in his greedy maw. All stood amazed. But *Calchas*, the son of Thestor, a soothsayer, foreseeing the truth, says, "Rejoice, Pelasgians, we shall conquer. Troy will fall, but the continuance of our toil will be long"; and he allots the nine birds to the years of the war. *The serpent*, just as he is, coiling around the green branches in the tree, becomes a stone, and, under the form of a serpent, retains that stone *form*.

Nereus continued boisterous in the Ionian waves, and did not impel the sails onwards; and there are some who think that Neptune favoured Troy, because he made the walls of the city. But not *so* the son of Thestor. For neither was he ignorant, nor did he conceal, that the wrath of the virgin Goddess must be appeased by the blood of a virgin. After the public good had prevailed over affection, and the king over the father, and Iphigenia, ready to offer her chaste blood, stood before the altar, while the priests were weeping; the Goddess was appeased, and cast a mist before their eyes, and, amid the service and the hurry of the rites, and the voices of the suppliants, is said to have changed Iphigenia, the Mycenian maiden, for a substituted hind. Wherefore, when the Goddess was appeased by a death which was *more* fitting, and at the same moment the wrath of Phoebe, and of the sea was past, the 1,000 ships received the winds astern, and having suffered much, they gained the Phrygian shore.

There is a spot in the middle of the world, between the land and the sea, and the regions of heaven, the confines of the threefold universe, whence is beheld whatever anywhere exists, although it may be in far *distant* regions, and every sound pierces the hollow ears. *Of this place* Fame is possessed, and chooses for herself a habitation on the top of a tower, and has added innumerable avenues, and 1,000 openings to her house, and has closed the entrances with no gates. Night and day are they open. It is all of sounding brass; it is all resounding, and it re-echoes the voice, and repeats what it hears. Within there is no rest, and silence in no part. Nor yet is there a clamour, but the murmur of a low voice, such as is wont to arise from the waves of the sea, if one listens at a distance, or like the sound which the end of the thundering *makes* when Jupiter has clashed the black clouds together. A crowd occupies the hall; the fickle vulgar come and go; and 1,000 rumours, false mixed with true, wander up and down, and circulate confused words. Of these, some fill the empty ears with conversation; some are carrying elsewhere what is told them; the measure of the fiction is ever on the increase, and each fresh narrator adds something to what he has heard. There, is Credulity, there, rash Mistake, and empty Joy, and alarmed Fears, and sudden Sedition, and Whispers of doubtful origin. She sees what things are done in heaven and on the sea, and on the earth; and she pries into the whole universe.

She has made it known that Grecian ships are on their way, with valiant troops: nor does the enemy appear in arms unlooked for. The Trojans oppose their landing, and defend the shore, and thou, Protesilaus, art, by the decrees of fate, the first to fall by the spear of Hector; and the battles *now* commenced, and the courageous spirits of *the Trojans*, and Hector, *till then* unknown, cost the Greeks dear. Nor do the Phrygians experience at small expense of blood what the Grecian right hand can do. And now the Sigaean shores are red *with blood*: now Cygnus, the son of Neptune, has slain 1,000 men. Now is Achilles pressing on in his chariot, and levelling the Trojan ranks, with the blow of his Peleian spear; and seeking through the lines either Cygnus or Hector, he engages with Cygnus: Hector is reserved for the 10th year. Then animating the horses, having their white necks pressed with the yoke, he directed his chariot against the enemy, and brandishing his quivering spear with his arm, he said, "O youth, whoever thou art, take this consolation in thy death, that thou art slain by the Haemonian Achilles."

Thus far the grandson of Aeacus. His heavy lance followed his words. But, although there was no missing in the unerring lance, yet it availed nothing, by the sharpness of its point, *thus* discharged; and as it only bruised his breast with a blunt stroke, *the other* said, "Thou son of a Goddess, (for by report have we known of thee beforehand) why art thou surprised that wounds are warded off from me? (for *Achilles* was surprised); not this helmet that thou seest tawny with the horse's mane, nor the hollowed shield, the burden of my left arm, are assistant to me; from them ornament *alone* is sought; for this cause, too, Mars is wont to take up arms. All the assistance of defensive armour shall be removed, *and* yet I shall come off unhurt. It is something to be born, not of a Nereid, but *of one* who rules both Nereus and his daughter, and the whole ocean."

Thus he spoke; and he hurled against the descendant of Aeacus his dart, destined to stick in the rim of his shield; it broke through both the brass and the next nine folds of bull's hide; but stopping in the 10th circle *of the hide*, the hero wrenched it out, and again hurled the quivering weapon with a strong hand; again his body was without a wound, and unharmed, nor was a third spear able *even* to graze Cygnus, unprotected, and exposing himself. Achilles raged no otherwise than as a bull, in the open Circus, when with his dreadful horns he butts against the purple-coloured garments, used as the means of provoking him, and perceives that his wounds are evaded. Still, he examines whether the point has chanced to fall from off the spear. It is *still* adhering to the shaft. "My hand then is weak," says he, "and it has spent *all* the strength it had before, upon one man. For decidedly it was strong enough, both when at first I overthrew the walls of Lyrnessus, or when I filled both Tenedos and Eetionian Thebes with their own blood. Or when Caÿcus flowed empurpled with the slaughter of its people: and Telephus was twice sensible of the virtue of my spear. Here, too, where so many have been slain, heaps of whom I both have made along this shore, and I *now* behold, my right hand has proved mighty, and is mighty."

Thus he spoke; and as if he distrusted what he had done before, he hurled his spear against Menoetes, one of the Lycian multitude, who *was* standing opposite, and he tore asunder both his coat of mail, and his breast beneath it. He, beating the solid earth with his dying head, he drew the same weapon from out of the reeking wound, and said, "This is the hand, this the lance, with which I conquered but now. The same will I use against him; in his *case*, I pray that the event may prove the same." Thus he said, and he hurled it at Cygnus, nor did the ashen lance miss him; and, not escaped *by him*, it resounded on his left shoulder: thence it was repelled, as though by a wall, or a solid rock. Yet Achilles saw Cygnus marked with blood, where he had been struck, and he rejoiced, *but in vain.* There was no wound; that was the blood of Menoetes.

Then indeed, raging, he leaps headlong from his lofty chariot, and hand to hand, with his gleaming sword striking at his fearless foe, he perceives that the shield and the helmet are pierced with his sword, and that his weapon, too, is blunted upon his hard body. He endures it no longer; and drawing back his shield, he three or four times strikes the face of the hero, and his hollow temples, with the hilt of the sword; and following, he presses onward as the other gives ground, and confounds him, and drives him on, and gives him no respite in his confusion. Horror seizes on him, and darkness swims before his eyes; and as he moves backwards his retreating steps, a stone in the middle of the field stands in his way. Impelled over this, with his breast upwards, Achilles throws Cygnus with great violence, and dashes him to the earth. Then, pressing down his breast with his shield and his hard knees, he draws tight the straps of his helmet, which, fastened beneath his pressed chin, squeeze close his throat, and take away his respiration and the passage of his breath.

He is preparing to strip his vanquished *foe;* he sees *nothing but* his armour, left behind. The God of the Ocean changed his body into a white bird, of which he *so* lately bore the name.

Fables III and IV

This toil and this combat brought on a cessation for many days; and both sides rested, laying aside their arms. And while a watchful guard was keeping the Phrygian walls, and a watchful guard was keeping the Argive trenches, a festive day had arrived, on which Achilles, the conqueror of Cygnus, appeased Pallas with the blood of a heifer, adorned with fillets.

As soon as he had placed its entrails upon the glowing altars, and the smell, acceptable to the Deities, mounted up to the skies, the sacred rites had their share, the other part was served up at the table. The chiefs reclined on couches, and sated their bodies with roasted flesh, and banished both their cares and their thirst with wine. No harps, no melody of voices, no long pipe of boxwood pierced with many a hole, delights them; but in discourse they pass the night, and valour is the subject matter of their conversation.

They relate the combats of the enemy and their own; and often do they delight to recount, in turn, both the dangers that they have encountered and that they have surmounted. For of what *else* should Achilles speak? or of what, in preference, should they speak before the great Achilles? *But* especially the recent victory over the conquered Cygnus was the subject of discourse. It seemed wonderful to them all, that the body of the youth was penetrable by no weapon, and was susceptible of no wounds, and that it blunted the steel itself. This same thing, the grandson of Aeacus, this, the Greeks wondered at.

When thus Nestor says *to them*: "Cygnus has been the only despiser of weapons in your time, and penetrable by no blows. But I myself formerly saw the Perrhaebean Caeneus bear a thousand blows with his body unhurt; Caeneus the Perrhaebean, *I say*, who, famous for his achievements, inhabited Othrys. And that this, too, might be the more wondrous in him, he was born a woman." They are surprised, whoever are present, at the singular nature of this prodigy, and they beg him to tell the story. Among them, Achilles says, "Pray tell us, (for we all have the same desire to hear it,) O eloquent old man, the wisdom of our age; who was *this* Caeneus, *and* why changed to the opposite sex? in what war, and in the engagements of what contest was he known to thee? by whom was he conquered, if he was conquered by anyone?"

Then the aged man *replied*: "Although tardy old age is a disadvantage to me, and many things which I saw in my early years escape me *now*, yet I remember most *of them*; and there is nothing, amid so many transactions of war and peace, that is more firmly fixed in my mind than that circumstance. And if extended age could make anyone a witness of many deeds, I have lived two hundred years, *and* now my third century is being passed *by me*. Caenis, the daughter of Elatus, was remarkable for her charms; the most beauteous virgin among the Thessalian maids, and one sighed for in vain by the wishes of many wooers through the neighbouring *cities*, and through thy cities, Achilles, for she was thy countrywoman. Perhaps, too, Peleus would have attempted that alliance; but at that time the marriage of thy mother had either befallen him, or had been promised him. Caenis did not enter into any nuptial ties; and as she was walking along the lonely shore, she suffered violence from the God of the ocean. 'Twas thus that report stated;

and when Neptune had experienced the pleasures of this new amour, he said, 'Be thy wishes secure from all repulse; choose whatever thou mayst desire.' The same report has related this too; Caenis replied, 'This mishap makes my desire extreme, that I may not be in a condition to suffer any such thing *in future*. Grant that I be no *longer* a woman, *and* thou wilt have granted me all.' She spoke these last words with a hoarser tone, and the voice might seem to be that of a man, as *indeed* it was.

"For now the God of the deep ocean had consented to her wish; and had granted moreover that he should not be able to be pierced by any wounds, or to fall by *any* steel. Exulting in his privilege, the Atracian departed; and *now* spent his time in manly exercises, and roamed over the Peneïan plains. *Pirithous*, the son of the bold Ixion, had married Hippodame, and had bidden the cloud-born monsters to sit down at the tables ranged in order, in a cave shaded with trees. The Haemonian nobles were there; I, too, was there, and the festive palace resounded with the confused rout. Lo! they sing the marriage song, and the halls smoke with the fires; the maiden, too, is there, remarkable for her beauty, surrounded by a crowd of matrons and newly married women. We *all* pronounce Pirithous fortunate in her for a wife; an omen which we had well nigh falsified. For thy breast, Eurytus, most savage of the savage Centaurs, is inflamed as much with wine as with seeing the maiden; and drunkenness, redoubled by lust, holds sway *over thee*. On the sudden the tables being overset, disturb the feast, and the bride is violently dragged away by her seized hair. Eurytus snatches up Hippodame, *and* the others such as each one fancies, or is able *to seize*; and there is *all* the appearance of a captured city. The house rings with the cries of women. Quickly we all rise; and first, Theseus says, 'What madness, Eurytus, is impelling thee, who, while I *still* live, dost provoke Pirithous, and, in thy ignorance, in one dost injure two?' And that the valiant hero may not say these things in vain, he pushes them off as they are pressing on, and takes her whom they have seized away from them as they grow furious.

"He says nothing in answer, nor, indeed, can he defend such actions by words; but he attacks the face of her protector with insolent hands, and strikes his generous breast. By chance, there is near at hand an ancient bowl, rough with projecting figures, which, huge as it is, the son of Aegeus, himself huger *still*, takes up and hurls full in his face. He, vomiting both from his wounds and his mouth clots of blood, and brains and wine together, lying on his back, kicks on the soaking sand. *The double-limbed centaurs* are inflamed at the death of their brother; and all vying, with one voice exclaim, 'To arms! to arms!' Wine gives them courage, and, in the first onset, cups hurled are flying about, and shattered casks and hollow cauldrons; things before adapted for a banquet, now for war and slaughter. First, the son of Ophion, Amycus, did not hesitate to spoil the interior of the house of its ornaments; and first, from the shrine he tore up a chandelier, thick set with blazing lamps; and lifting it on high, like him who attempts to break the white neck of the bull with sacrificial axe, he dashed it against the forehead of Celadon the Lapithean, and left his skull mashed into his face, no *longer* to be recognized. His eyes started out, and the bones of his face being dashed to pieces, his nose was driven back, and was fixed in the middle of his palate. Him, Belates the Pellaean, having torn away the foot of a maple table, laid flat on the ground, with his chin sunk upon his breast, and vomiting forth his teeth mixed with blood; and sent him, by a twofold wound, to the shades of Tartarus.

"As Gryneus stood next, looking at the smoking altar with a grim look, he said, '*And* why do we not make use of this?' and *then* he raised an immense altar, together with its fire; and hurled it into the midst of the throng of the Lapithae, and struck down two *of them*, Broteus and Orius. The mother of Orius was Mycale, who was known by her incantations to have often drawn down the horns of the struggling moon. *On this* Exadius says, 'Thou shalt not go unpunished, if only the opportunity of getting a weapon is given me'; and, as his weapon, he wields the antlers of a votive stag, which were upon a lofty pine tree. With the double branches of these, Gryneus is pierced through the eyes, and has those eyes scooped out. A part of them adheres to the antlers, a part runs down his beard, and hangs down clotted with gore. Lo! Rhoetus snatches up an immense flaming brand, from the middle of the altar, and on the right side breaks through the temples of Charaxus, covered with yellow hair. His locks, seized by the violent flames, burn like dry corn, and the blood seared in the wound emits a terrific noise in its hissing, such as the iron glowing in the flames is often wont to emit, which, when the smith has drawn it out with the crooked pincers, he plunges into the trough; whereon it whizzes, and, sinking in the bubbling water, hisses. Wounded, he shakes the devouring fire from his locks, and takes upon his shoulders the threshold, torn up out of the ground, a *whole* wagonload, which its very weight hinders him from throwing full against the foe. The stony mass, too, bears down Cometes, a friend, who is standing at a short distance; nor does Rhoetus *then* restrain his joy, *and* he says, 'In such manner do I pray that the rest of the throng of thy party may be brave'; and *then* he increases the wound, redoubled with the half-burnt stake, and three or four times he breaks the sutures of his head with heavy blows, and its bones sink within the oozing brains.

"Victorious, he passes on to Evagrus, and Corythus, and Dryas; of which *number*, when Corythus, having his cheeks covered with their first down, has fallen, Evagrus says, 'What glory has been acquired by thee, in killing a boy?' Rhoetus permits him to say no more, and fiercely thrusts the glowing flames into the open mouth of the hero, as he is speaking, and through the mouth into the breast. Thee, too, cruel Dryas, he pursues, whirling the fire around his head, but the same issue does not await thee as well. Thou piercest him with a stake burnt at the end, while triumphing in the success of an uninterrupted slaughter, in the spot where the neck is united to the shoulder. Rhoetus groans aloud, and with difficulty wrenches the stake out of the hard bone, and, drenched in his own blood, he flies. Orneus flies, too, and Lycabas, and Medon, wounded in his right shoulder blade, and Thaumas with Pisenor; Mermerus, too, who lately excelled all in speed of foot, *but* now goes more slowly from the wound he has received; Pholus, too, and Melaneus, and Abas a hunter of boars, and Astylos the augur, who has in vain dissuaded his own party from this warfare. He also says to Nessus, as he dreads the wounds, 'Fly not! *for* thou shalt be reserved for the bow of Hercules.' But Eurynomus and Lycidas, and Areos, and Imbreus did not escape death, all of whom the right hand of Dryas pierced right through. Thou, too, Crenaeus, didst receive a wound in front, although thou didst turn thy back in flight; for looking back, thou didst receive the fatal steel between thy two eyes, where the nose is joined to the lower part of the forehead. In the midst of so much noise, Aphidas was lying fast asleep from the wine which he had drunk incessantly, and was not aroused, and in his languid hand was grasping the mixed bowl, stretched at full length upon the shaggy skin of a bear of Ossa. Soon as Phorbas beheld him from afar, wielding no arms, he inserted his fingers in the strap of his lance, and said, 'Drink thy wine mingled with *the water of Styx*;' and, delaying no longer, he hurled his javelin against the youth, and the ash pointed with steel was driven into his neck, as, by chance, he lay *there* on his back. His death happened without his being sensible of it; and the blood flowed from his full throat, both upon the couch and into the bowl itself.

"I saw Petraeus endeavouring to tear up an acorn-bearing oak from the earth; *and*, as he was grasping it in his embrace, and was shaking it on this side and that, and was moving about the loosened tree, the lance of Pirithous hurled at the ribs of Petraeus, transfixed his struggling breast together with the tough oak. They said, *too*, that Lycus fell by the valour of Pirithous, *and* that Chromis fell *by the hand* of Pirithous. But each of them *gave* less glory to the conqueror, than Dictys and Helops gave. Helops was transfixed by the javelin, which passed right through his temples, and, hurled from the right side, penetrated to his left ear. Dictys, slipping from the steep point of a rock, while, in his fear, he is flying from the pursuing son of Ixion, falls down headlong, and, by the weight of his body, breaks a huge ash tree, and spits his own entrails upon it, *thus* broken. Aphareus advances *as* his avenger, and endeavours to hurl a stone torn away from the mountain. As he is endeavouring *to do so*, the son of Aegeus attacks him with an oaken club, and breaks the huge bones of his arm, and has neither leisure, nor, *indeed*, does he care to put his useless body to death; and he leaps upon the back of the tall Bianor, not used to bear any other than himself; and he fixes his knees in his ribs, and holding his long hair, seized with his left hand, shatters his face, and his threatening features, and his very hard temples, with the knotty oak. With his oak, *too*, he levels Nedymnus, and Lycotas the darter, and Hippasus having his breast covered with his flowing beard, and Ripheus, who towered above the topmost woods, and Tereus, who used to carry home the bears, caught in the Haemonian mountains, alive and raging.

"Demoleon could not any longer endure Theseus enjoying this success in the combat, and he tried with vast efforts to tear up from the thick-set wood an aged pine; because he could not affect this, he hurled it, broken short, against his foe. But Theseus withdrew afar from the approaching missile, through the warning of Pallas; so *at least* he himself wished it to be thought. Yet the tree did not fall without effect: for it struck off from the throat of the tall Crantor, both his breast and his left shoulder. He, Achilles, had been the armour-bearer of thy father: him Amyntor, king of the Dolopians, when conquered in war, had given to the son of Aeacus, as a pledge and confirmation of peace. When Peleus saw him at a distance, mangled with a foul wound, he said, 'Accept however, Crantor, most beloved of youths, this sacrifice'; and, with a strong arm, and energy of intention, he hurled his ashen lance against Demoleon, which broke through the enclosures of his ribs, and quivered, sticking amid the bones. He draws out with his hand the shaft without the point; even that follows, with much difficulty; the point is retained within his lungs. The very pain gives vigour to his resolution; *though* wounded, he rears against the enemy, and tramples upon the hero with his horse's feet. The other receives the re-echoing strokes upon his helmet and his shield, and defends his shoulders, and holds his arms extended before him, and through the shoulder blades he pierces two breasts at one stroke. But first, from afar, he had consigned to death Phlegraeus, and Hyles; in closer combat, Hiphinous and Clanis. To these is added Dorylas, who had his temples covered with a wolf's skin, and the real horns of oxen reddened with much blood, that performed the duty of a cruel weapon.

"To him I said, for courage gave me strength, 'Behold, how much thy horns are inferior to my steel'; and *then* I threw my javelin. When he could not avoid this, he held up his right hand before his forehead, about to receive the blow; *and* to his forehead his hand was pinned. A shout arose; but Peleus struck him delaying, and overpowered by the painful wound, (for he was standing next to him) with his sword beneath the middle of his belly. He leaped forth, and fiercely dragged his own bowels on the ground, and trod on them *thus* dragged, and burst them *thus* trodden; and he entangled his legs, as well in them, and fell down, with his belly emptied *of its inner parts*. Nor did thy beauty, Cyllarus, save thee while fighting, if only we allow beauty to that *monstrous* nature *of thine*. His beard was beginning *to grow*; the colour of his beard was that of gold; and golden-coloured hair was hanging from his shoulders to the middle of his shoulder blades. In his face there was a pleasing briskness; his neck, and his shoulders, and his hands and his breast *were* resembling the applauded statues of the artists, and *so* in those parts in which he was a man; nor was the shape of the horse beneath that *shape*, faulty and inferior to *that of* the man. Give him *but* the neck and the head *of a horse, and* he would be worthy of Castor. So fit is his back to be sat upon, so stands his breast erect with muscle; *he is* all over blacker than black pitch; yet his tail is white; the colour, too, of his legs is white. Many a female of his own kind longed for him; but Hylonome alone gained him, than whom no female more handsome lived in the lofty woods, among the half beasts. She alone attaches Cyllarus, both by her blandishments, and by loving, and by confessing that she loves him. Her care, too, of her person is as great as can be in those limbs: so that her hair is smoothed with a comb; so that she now decks herself with rosemary, now with violets or roses, *and* sometimes she wears white lilies; and twice a day she washes her face with streams that fall from the height of the Pagasaean wood; *and* twice she dips her body in the stream: and she throws over her shoulder or her left side no skins but what are becoming, and are those of choice beasts.

"Their love was equal: together they wandered upon the mountains; together they entered the caves; and then, too, together had they entered the Lapithaean house; together were they waging the fierce warfare. The author *of the deed* is unknown: *but* a javelin came from the left side, and pierced thee, Cyllarus, below *the spot* where the breast is joined to the neck. The heart, being pierced with a small wound, grew cold, together with the whole body, after the weapon was drawn out. Immediately, Hylonome receives his dying limbs, and cherishes the wound, by laying her hand on it, and places her mouth on his, and strives to stop the fleeting life. When she sees him dead, having uttered what the clamour hinders from reaching my ears, she falls upon the weapon that has pierced him, and as she dies, embraces her husband. He, too, *now* stands before my eyes, Phaeocomes, *namely*, who had bound six lions' skins together with connecting knots; covered all over, both horse and man. He, having discharged the trunk of a tree, which two yokes of oxen joined together could hardly have moved, battered the son of Phonolenus on the top of his head. The very broad round form of his skull was broken; and through his mouth, and through his hollow nostrils, and his eyes, and his ears, his softened brains poured down; just as curdled milk is wont through the oaken twigs, or as *any* liquor flows under the weight of a well-pierced sieve, and is squeezed out thick through the numerous holes. But I, while he was preparing to strip him of his arms as he lay, (this thy sire knows,) plunged my sword into the lower part of his belly, as he was spoiling him. Chthonius, too, and Teleboas, lay *pierced* by my sword. The former was bearing a two-forked bough *as his weapon*, the latter a javelin; with his javelin he gave me a wound. You see the marks; look! the old scar is still visible.

"Then ought I to have been sent to the taking of Troy; then I might, if not have overcome, *still* have stayed the arms of the mighty Hector. But at that time Hector was not existing, or *but* a boy; *and* now my age is failing. Why tell thee of Periphas, the conqueror of the two-formed Pyretus? Why of Ampyx, who fixed his cornel-wood spear, without a point, full in the face of the four-footed Oëclus? Macareus, struck down the Pelethronian Erigdupus, by driving a crowbar into his breast. I remember, too, that a hunting spear, hurled by the hand of Nessus, was buried in the groin of Cymelus. And do not believe that Mopsus, the son of Ampycus, only foretold things to come; a two-formed *monster* was slain by Mopsus, darting *at him*, and Odites in vain attempted to speak, his tongue being nailed to his chin, and his chin to his throat. Caeneus had put five to death, Stiphelus, and Bromus, and Antimachus, and Helimus, and Pyracmos, wielding the axe. I do not remember *their respective* wounds, *but* I marked their numbers, and their names. Latreus, most huge both in his limbs and his body, sallied forth, armed with the spoils of Emathian Halesus, whom he had consigned to death. His age was between that of a youth, and an old man; his vigour that of a youth; grey hairs variegated his temples. Conspicuous by his buckler, and his helmet, and his Macedonian pike; and turning his face towards both sides, he brandished his arms, and rode in one same round, and vaunting, poured forth thus many words into the yielding air: –

"'And shall I put up with thee, too, Caenis? for to me thou shalt ever be a woman, to me always Caenis. Does not thy natal origin lower thy *spirit*? And does it not occur to thy mind for what *foul* deed thou didst get thy reward, and at what price the false resemblance to a man? Consider both what thou wast born, as well as what thou hast submitted to: go, and take up a distaff together with thy baskets, and twist the threads with thy thumb; leave warfare to men.' As he is vaunting in such terms, Caeneus pierces his side, stretched in running, with a lance hurled at him, just where the man is joined to the horse. He raves with pain, and strikes at the exposed face of the Phylleian youth with his pike. It bounds back no otherwise than hail from the roof of a house; or than if any one were to beat a hollow drum with a little pebble. Hand to hand he encounters him, and strives to plunge his sword into his tough side; *but* the parts are impervious to his sword. 'Yet,' says he, 'thou shalt not escape me; with the middle of the sword shalt thou be slain, since the point is blunt;' and *then* he slants the sword against his side, and grasps his stomach with his long right arm. The blow produces an echo, as on a body of marble when struck; and the shivered blade flies different ways, upon striking his neck.

"After Caeneus had enough exposed his unhurt limbs to him in his amazement, 'Come now,' said he, 'let us try thy body with my steel'; and up to the hilt he plunged his fatal sword into his shoulder blade, and extended his hand unseen into his entrails, and worked it about, and in the wound made a *fresh* wound. Lo! the double-limbed *monsters,* enraged, rush on in an impetuous manner, and all of them hurl and thrust their weapons at him alone. Their weapons fall blunted. Unstabbed and bloodless the Elateïan Caeneus remains from each blow. This strange thing makes them astonished. 'Oh great disgrace!' cries Monychus; 'a *whole* people, we are overcome by one, and that hardly a man; although, *indeed*, he is a man; and we by our dastardly actions, are what he *once* was. What signify our huge limbs? What our twofold strength? What that our twofold nature has united in us the stoutest animals in existence? I neither believe that we are born of a goddess for our mother, nor of Ixion, who was so great a person, that he conceived hopes of *even* the supreme Juno. By a half male foe are we baffled. Heap upon him stones and beams, and entire mountains, and dash out his long-lived breath, by throwing *whole* woods *upon him*. Let a *whole* wood press on his jaws; and weight shall be in the place of wounds.'

"*Thus* he said; and by chance having got a tree, thrown down by the power of the boisterous south wind, he threw it against the powerful foe: and he was an example *to the rest*; and in a short time, Othrys, thou wast bare of trees, and Pelion had no shades. Overwhelmed by this huge heap, Caeneus swelters beneath the weight of the trees, and bears on his brawny shoulders the piled-up oaks. But after the load has increased upon his face and his head, and his breath has no air to draw; at one moment he faints, at another he endeavours, in vain, to raise himself into the *open* air, and to throw off the wood cast *upon him*: and sometimes he moves it. Just as lo! we see, if lofty Ida is convulsed with earthquakes. The event is doubtful. Some gave out that his body was hurled to roomy Tartarus by the weight of the wood. The son of Ampycus denied this, and saw go forth into the liquid air, from amid the pile, a bird with tawny wings; which then was beheld by me for the first time, then, *too*, for the last. When Mopsus saw it with gentle flight surveying his camp, and making a noise around it with a vast clamour, following him both with his eyes and his feelings, he said, 'Hail! thou glory of the Lapithaean race, once the greatest of men, but now the only bird *of thy kind*, Caeneus.' This thing was credited from its assertor. Grief added resentment, and we bore it with disgust, that one was overpowered by foes so many. Nor did we cease to exercise our weapons, in *shedding their* blood, before a part of them was put to death, and flight and the night dispersed the rest."

Fables V and VI

As the Pylian related this fight between the Lapithae and the Centaurs, but half human, Tlepolemus could not endure his sorrow for Alcides being passed by with silent lips, and said, "It is strange, old man, that thou shouldst have a forgetfulness of the exploits of Hercules; at least, my father himself used often to relate to me, that these cloud-begotten monsters were conquered by him."

The Pylian, sad at this, said, "Why dost thou force me to call to mind my misfortunes, and to rip up my sorrows, concealed beneath years, and to confess my hatred of, and disgust at, thy father? He, indeed, ye Gods! performed things beyond all belief, and filled the world with his services; which I could rather wish could be denied; but we are in the habit of praising neither Deiphobus nor Polydamas, nor Hector himself: for who would commend an enemy? That father of thine once overthrew the walls of Messene, and demolished guiltless cities, Elis and Pylos, and carried the sword and flames into my abode. And, that I may say nothing of others whom he slew, we were twice six sons of Neleus, goodly youths; the twice six fell by the might of Hercules, myself alone excepted. And that the others were vanquished might have been endured; *but* the death of Periclymenus is wonderful; to whom Neptune, the founder of the Neleian family, had granted to be able to assume whatever shapes he might choose, and again, when assumed, to lay them aside. He, after he had in vain been turned into all other shapes, was turned into the form of the bird that is wont to carry the lightnings in his crooked talons, the most acceptable to the king of the Gods. Using the strength of *that* bird, his wings, and his crooked bill, together with his hooked talons, he tore the face of the hero. The Tirynthian hero aims at him his bow, too unerring, and hits him, as he moves his limbs aloft amid the clouds, and hovering *in the air*, just where the wing is joined to the side.

"Nor is the wound a great one, but his sinews, cut by the wound, fail him, and deny him motion and strength for flying. He fell down to the earth, his weakened pinions not catching the air; and where the smooth arrow had stuck in his wing, it was pressed *still further* by the weight of his pierced body, and it was driven, through the upper side, into the left part of the neck. Do I seem to be owing encomiums to the exploits of thy *father* Hercules, most graceful leader of the Rhodian fleet? Yet I will no further avenge my brothers, than by being silent on his brave deeds: with thyself I have a firm friendship." After the son of Neleus had said these things with his honied tongue, the gifts of Bacchus being resumed after the discourse of the aged man, they arose from their couches: the rest of the night was given to sleep.

But the God who commands the waters of the sea with his trident, laments, with the affection of a father, the body of his son, changed into the bird of the son of Sthenelus; and abhorring the ruthless Achilles, pursues his resentful wrath in more than an ordinary manner. And now, the war having been protracted for almost twice five years, with such words as these he addresses the unshorn Smintheus: "O thou, most acceptable to me, by far, of the sons of my brother, who, together with me, didst build the walls of Troy in vain; and dost thou not grieve when thou lookest upon these towers so soon to fall? or dost thou not lament that so many thousands are slain in defending these walls? and (not to recount them all) does not the ghost of Hector, dragged around his Pergamus, recur to thee? Though still the fierce Achilles, more blood-stained than war itself, lives on, the destroyer of our toil, let him but put himself in my power, I will make him feel what I can do with my triple spear. But since it is not allowed us to encounter the enemy in close fight, destroy him, when off his guard, with a secret shaft."

He nodded his assent; and the Delian *God*, indulging together both his own resentment and that of his uncle, veiled in a cloud, comes to the Trojan army, and in the midst of the slaughter of the men, he sees Paris, at intervals, scattering his darts among the ignoble Greeks; and, discovering himself to be a Divinity, he says, "Why dost thou waste thy arrows upon the blood of the vulgar? If thou hast any concern for thy friends, turn upon the grandson of Aeacus, and avenge thy slaughtered brothers." *Thus* he said; and pointing at the son of Peleus, mowing down the bodies of the Trojans with the sword, he turned his bow towards him, and directed his unerring arrow with a fatal right hand. This was *the only thing* at which, after *the death of* Hector, the aged Priam could rejoice. And art thou then, Achilles, the conqueror of men so great, conquered by the cowardly ravisher of a Grecian wife? But if it had been fated for thee to fall by the hand of a woman, thou wouldst rather have fallen by the Thermodontean battle-axe.

Now that dread of the Phrygians, the glory and defence of the Pelasgian name, the grandson of Aeacus, a head invincible in war, had been burnt: the same Divinity had armed him, and had burned him. He is now *but* ashes; and there remains of Achilles, so renowned, I know not what; that which will not well fill a little urn. But his glory lives, which can fill the whole world: this allowance is befitting that hero, and in this the son of Peleus is equal to himself, and knows not the empty Tartarus. Even his very shield gives occasion for war, that you may know to whom it belongs; and arms are wielded for arms. The son of Tydeus does not dare to claim them, nor Ajax, the son of Oileus, nor the younger son of Atreus, nor he who is his superior both in war and age, nor *any* others; the hope of so much glory exists only in him begotten by Telamon and *the son* of Laertes. The descendant of Tantalus removes from himself the burden and the odium *of a decision*, and orders the Argive leaders to sit in the midst of the camp, and transfers the judgment of the dispute to them all.

Achilleid

Book I

ELL, O GODDESS, of great-hearted Aeacides and of the progeny
that the Thunderer feared and forbade to inherit his father's
heaven. Highly renowned are the warrior's deeds in Maeonian
song, but more remains untold: suffer me – for such is my desire –
to recount the whole story of the hero, to summon him forth from
his hiding place in Scyros with the Dulichian trumpet, and not to
stop short at the dragging of Hector, but to lead the youth through
the whole tale of Troy. Only do thou, O Phoebus, if with a worthy
draught I drained the former fount, vouchsafe new springs and
weave my hair with propitious chaplets; for not as a newcomer do
I seek entrance to the Aonian grove, nor are these the first fillets
that magnify my brow. The fields of Dirce know it, and Thebes
counts my name among her forefathers of old time and with her
own Amphion.

But thou whom far before all others the pride of Italy and Greece regards
with reverent awe, for whom the laurels twain of poet and warrior-chief
flourish in mutual rivalry – already one of them grieves to be surpassed –
grant pardon, and allow me anxiously to toil in this dust awhile. Thine is the
theme whereat with long nor yet confident preparation I am labouring, and
great Achilles plays the prelude unto thee.

The Dardan shepherd had set sail from the Oebalian shore, having
wrought sweet havoc in thoughtless Amyclae, and fulfilling the presage of
his mother's dream was retracing his guilty way, where Helle deep sunk
below the sea and now a Nereid holds sway over the detested waves: when
Thetis – ah! never vain are a parent's auguries! – started with terror beneath
the glassy flood at the Idaean oars. Without delay she sprang forth from her

watery bower, accompanied by her train of sisters: the narrowing shores of Phrixus swam, and the straitened sea had not room for its mistresses.

As soon as she had shaken the brine from off her, and entered the air of heaven: "There is danger to me," said she, "in yonder fleet, and threat of deadly harm; I recognize the truth of Proteus' warnings. Lo! Bellona brings from the vessel amid uplifted torches a new daughter-in-law to Priam; already I see the Ionian and Aegean seas pressed by a thousand keels; nor does it suffice that all the country of the Grecians conspires with the proud sons of Atreus, soon will my Achilles be sought for by land and sea, ay, and himself will wish to follow them. Why indeed did I suffer Pelion and the stern master's cave to cradle his infant years? There, if I mistake not, he plays, the rogue, at the battle of the Lapiths, and already takes his measure with his father's spear. O sorrow! O fears that came to late to a mother's heart! Could I not, unhappy that I am, when first the timber of Rhoeteum was launched upon my flood, have raised a mighty sea and pursued with a tempest on the deep the adulterous robber's sails and led on all my sisters against him? Even now – but 'tis too late, the outrage hath been wrought in full. Yet will I go, and clinging to the gods of ocean and the right hand of second Jove – nought else remains – entreat him in piteous supplication by the years of Tethys and his aged sire for one single storm."

She spoke, and opportunely beheld the mighty monarch; he was coming from Oceanus his host, gladdened by the banquet, and his countenance suffused with the nectar of the deep: wherefore the winds and tempests are silent and with tranquil song proceed the Tritons who bear his armour and the rock-like sea monsters and the Tyrrhenian herds, and gambol around and below him, saluting their king; he towers on high above the peaceful waves, urging on his team with his three-pronged spear: front wise they run at furious speed amid showers of foam, behind they swim and blot out their footprints with their tails:– when Thetis: "O sire and ruler of the mighty deep, seest thou to what uses thou hast made a way o'er the hapless ocean? The crimes of the nations pass by with unmolested sails, since the Pagasaean bark broke through the sanctions of the waters and profaned their hallowed majesty on Jason's quest of plunder. Lo! freighted with another wicked theft, the spoils of hospitality, sails the daring arbiter of unjust Ida, destined to cause what sorrow alas! to heaven and earth, and what to me! Is it thus we requite the joy of the Phrygian triumph, is this the way of Venus, is this her gift to her dear ward? These ships at least – no demigods nor our own Theseus do they carry home – overwhelm, if thou still hast any regard for the waters, or give the sea into my power; no cruelty do I purpose; suffer me to fear for my own son. Grant me to drive away my sorrow, nor let it be thy pleasure that out of all the seas I find a home in but a single coast and the rocks of an Ilian tomb."

With torn cheeks she made her prayer, and with bare bosom would fain hinder the cerulean steeds. But the ruler of the seas invites her into his chariot, and soothes her thus with friendly words: "Seek not in vain, Thetis, to sink the Dardanian fleet: the fates forbid it, 'tis the sure ordinance of heaven that Europe and Asia should join in bloody conflict, and Jupiter hath issued his decree of war and appointed years of dreary carnage. What prowess of thy son in the Sigean dust, what vast funeral trains of Phrygian matrons shalt thou victoriously behold, when thy Aeacides shall flood the Trojan fields with streaming blood, and anon forbid the choked rivers to flow and check his chariot's speed with Hector's corpse and mightily overthrow my walls, my useless toil! Cease now to complain of Peleus and thy inferior wedlock: thy child shall be deemed begotten of Jove; nor shalt thou suffer unavenged, but shalt use thy kindred seas: I will grant thee to raise the billows, when the Danaans return and Caphareus shows forth his nightly signals and we search together for the terrible Ulysses."

He spoke; but she, downcast at the stern refusal, for but now she was preparing to stir up the waters and make war upon the Ilian craft, devised in her mind another plan, and sadly turned her strokes toward the Haemonian land. Thrice strove she with her arms, thrice spurned the clear water with her feet, and the Thessalian waves are washing her snow-white ankles. The mountains rejoice, the marriage-bowers fling open their recesses, and Spercheus in wide, abundant streams flows to meet the goddess and laps her footsteps with his fresh water. She delights not in the scene, but wearies her mind with schemes essayed, and taught cunning by her devoted love seeks out the aged Chiron. His lofty home bores deep into the mountain, beneath the long, overarching vault of Pelion; part had been hollowed out by toil, part worn away by its own age. Yet the images and couches of the gods are shown, and the places that each had sanctified by his reclining and his sacred presence; within are the centaur's wide and lofty stalls, far different from those of his wicked brethren. Here are no spears that have tasted human blood, nor ashen clubs broken in festal conflict, nor mixing bowls shattered upon kindred foemen, but innocent quivers and mighty hides of beasts. These did he take while yet in the prime of age; but now, a warrior no more, his only toil was to learn herbs that bring health to creatures doubting of their lives, or to describe to his pupil upon his lyre the heroes of old time.

On the threshold's edge he awaited his return from hunting, and was urging the laying of the feast and brightening his abode with lavish fire: when far off the Nereid was seen climbing upward from the shore; he burst forth from the forests – joy speeds his going – and the well-known hoof-beat of the sage rang on the now unwonted plain. Then bowing down to his horse's shoulders he leads her with courtly hand within his humble dwelling and warns her of the cave.

Long time has Thetis been scanning every corner with silent glance: then, impatient of delay, she cries: "Tell me, Chiron, where is my darling? Why spends the boy any time apart from thee? Is it not with reason that my sleep is troubled, and terrible portents from the gods and fearful panics – would they were false! – afflict his mother's heart? For now I behold swords that threaten to pierce my womb, now my arms are bruised with lamentation, now savage beasts assail my breasts; often – ah, horror! – I seem to take my son down to the void of Tartarus, and dip him a second time in the springs of Styx. The Carpathian seer bids me banish these terrors by the ordinance of a magic rite, and purify the lad in secret waters beyond the bound of heaven's vault, where is the farthest shore of ocean and father Pontus is warmed by the ingliding stars. There awful sacrifices and gifts to gods unknown – but 'tis long to recount all, and I am forbidden; give him to me rather."

Thus spoke his mother in lying speech – nor would he have given him up, had she dared to confess to the old man the soft raiment and dishonourable garb. Then he replies: "Take him, I pray, O best of parents, take him, and assuage the gods with humble entreaty. For thy hopes are pitched too high, and envy needs much appeasing. I add not to thy fears, but will confess the truth: some swift and violent deed – the forebodings of a sire deceive me not – is preparing, far beyond his tender years. Formerly he was wont to endure my anger, and listen eagerly to my commands nor wander far from my cave: now Ossa cannot contain him, nor mighty Pelion and all the snows of Thessaly. Even the centaurs often complain to me of plundered homes and herds stolen before their eyes, and that they themselves are driven from field and river; they devise violence and fraud, and utter angry threats. Once when the Thessalian pine bore hither the princes of Argos, I saw the young Alcides and Theseus – but I say no more."

Cold pallor seized the daughter of Nereus: lo! he was come, made larger by much dust and sweat, and yet for all his weapons and hastened labours still pleasant to the sight; a radiant glow shimmers on his snow-white countenance, and his locks shine more comely than tawny gold. The bloom of youth is not yet changed by new-springing down, a tranquil flame burns in his glance, and there is much of his mother in his look: even as when the hunter Apollo returns from Lycia and exchanges his fierce quiver for the quill. By chance too he is in joyful mood – ah, how joy enhances beauty! –; beneath Pholoe's cliff he had stricken a lioness lately delivered and had left her in the empty lair, but had brought the cubs and was making them show their claws. Yet when he sees his mother on the well-known threshold, away he throws them, catches her up and binds her in his longing arms, already violent in his embrace and equal to her in height. Patroclus follows him, bound to him even then by a strong affection, and strains to rival all his mighty doings, well-matched in the pursuits and ways of youth, but far behind in strength, and yet to pass to Pergamum with equal fate.

Straightway with rapid bound he hies him to the nearest river, and freshens in its waters his steaming face and hair: just as Castor enters the shallows of Eurotas on his panting steed, and tricks out anew the weary splendours of his star. The old man marvels as he adorns him, caressing now his breast, now his strong shoulders: her very joy pierces his mother's heart. Then Chiron prays her to taste the banquet and the gifts of Bacchus, and contriving various amusements for her beguiling at last brings forth the lyre and moves the care-consoling strings, and trying the chords lightly with his finger gives them to the boy. Gladly he sings of the mighty causes of noble deeds: how many behests of his haughty stepmother the son of Amphitryon performed, how Pollux with his glove smote down the cruel Bebryx, with what a grip the son of Aegeus enfolded and crushed the limbs of the Minoan bull, lastly his own mother's marriage feast and Pelion trodden by the gods.

Then Thetis relaxed her anxious countenance and smiled. Night draws them on to slumber: the huge centaur lays him down on a stony couch, and Achilles lovingly twines his arms about his shoulders – though his faithful parent is there – and prefers the wonted breast.

But Thetis, standing by night upon the sea-echoing rocks, this way and that divides her purpose, and ponders in what hiding place she will set her son, in what country she shall choose to conceal him. Nearest is Thrace, but steeped in the passionate love of war; nor does the hardy folk of Macedon please her, nor the sons of Cecrops, sure to excite to noble deeds, nor Sestos and the bay of Abydos, too opportune for ships; she decides to roam the lofty Cyclades. Of these she spurns Myconos and humble Seriphos, and Lemnos cruel to its men, and Delos, that gives all the world a welcome. Of late from the unwarlike palace of Lycomedes had she heard the sound of maiden bands and the echo of their sport along the shore, what time she was sent to follow Aegaeon freed from his stubborn bonds and to count the hundred fetters of the god. This land finds favour, and seems safest to the timid mother. Even so a bird already taking anxious thought, as her deliver draws nigh, on what branch to hang her empty home, here foresees winds, there bethinks her fearfully of snakes, and there of men; at last in her doubt a shady spot finds favour; scarce has she alighted on the boughs, and straightway loves the tree.

One more care abides in her mind and troubles the sad goddess, whether she shall carry her son in her own bosom over the waves, or use great Triton's aid, whether she shall summon the swift winds to help her, or the Thaumantian that is wont to drink the main. Then she calls out from the waves and bridles with a sharp-edged shell her team of dolphins twain, which Tethys, mighty queen, had nourished for her in an echoing vale beneath the sea; – none throughout all Neptune's watery realm had such renown for their sea-green beauty, nor greater speed of swimming, nor more of human sense; – these she halts in the deep shore water, lest they take harm from the touch of naked earth. Then in her own arms she carries Achilles, his body utterly relaxed in a boy's slumber, from the rocks of the Haemonian cave down to the placid waters and the beach that she had bidden be silent; Cynthia lights her way and shines out with full orb. Chiron escorts the goddess, and careless of the sea entreats her speedy return, and hides his moistened eyes and high upon his horse's body gazes out towards them as suddenly they are whirled away, and now – and now are lost to view, where for a short while the foamy marks of their going gleam white and the wake dies away into the watery main. Him destined never more to return to Thessalian Tempe now mournful Pholoe bewails, now cloudy Othrys, and Spercheos with diminished flood and the silent grotto of the sage; the fauns listen for his boyish songs in vain, and the nymphs bemoan their long-hoped-for nuptials.

Now day overwhelms the stars, and from the low and level main Titan wheels heavenward his dripping steeds, and down from the expanse of air falls the sea that the chariot bore up; but long since had the mother traversed the waves and gained the Scyrian shores, and the weary dolphins had been loosed from their mistress' yoke: when the boy's sleep was stirred, and his opening eyes grew conscious of the inpouring day. In amaze at the light that greets him he asks, where is he, what are these waves, where is Pelion? All he beholds is different and unknown, and he hesitates to recognize his mother. Quickly she caresses him and soothes his fear: "If, dear lad, a kindly lot had brought me the wedlock that it offered, in the fields of heaven should I be holding thee, a glorious star, in my embrace, nor a celestial mother should I fear the lowly Fates or the destinies of earth. But now unequal is they birth, my son, and only on thy mother's side is the way of death barred for thee; moreover, times of terror draw nigh, and peril hovers about the utmost goal. Retire we then, relax awhile they mighty spirit, and scorn not this raiment of mine. If the Tirynthian took in his rough hand Lydian wool and women's wands, if it becomes Bacchus to trail a gold-embroidered robe behind him, if Jupiter put on a woman's form, and doubtful sex weakened not the mighty Caeneus, this way, I entreat thee, suffer me to escape the threatening, baleful cloud. Soon will I restore the plains and the fields where the centaurs roam: by this beauty of thine and the coming joys of youth I pray thee, if for thy sake I endured the earth and an inglorious mate, if at thy birth I fortified thee with the stern waters of Styx – ay, would I had wholly! – take these safe robes awhile, they will in no wise harm thy valour. Why doest thou turn away? What means that glance? Art thou ashamed to soften thee in this garb? Dear lad, I swear it by my kindred waters, Chiron shall know nought of this."

So doth she work on his rough heart, vainly cajoling; the thought of his sire and his great teacher oppose her prayer and the rude beginnings of his mighty spirit. Even so, should one try to subdue with earliest rein a horse full of the mettlesome fire of ungoverned youth, he having long delighted in stream and meadow and his own proud beauty, gives not his neck to the yoke, nor his fierce mouth to the bridle, and snorts with rage at passing beneath a master's sway and marvels that he learns another gait.

What god endued the despairing mother with fraud and cunning? What device drew Achilles from his stubborn purpose? It chanced that Scyros was keeping festal day in honour of Pallas, guardian of the shore, and that the sisters, offspring of peace-loving Lycomedes, had on this sacred morn gone forth from their native town – a licence rarely given – to pay tribute of the spring, and bind their grave tresses with the leaf of the goddess and scatter flowers upon her spear. All were of rarest beauty, all clad alike and all in lusty youth, their years of girlish modesty now ended, and maidenhood ripe for the marriage-couch. But as far as Venus by comparison doth surpass the green nymphs of the sea, or as Diana rises taller by head and shoulders than the naiads, so doth Deidamia, queen of the lovely choir, outshine and dazzle her fair sisters. The bright colour flames upon her rosy countenance, a more brilliant light is in her jewels, the gold has a more alluring gleam; as beauteous were the goddess herself, would she but lay aside the serpents on her breast, and doff her helm and pacify her brow. When he beheld her far in advance of her attendant train, the lad, ungentle as he was and heart-whole from any touch of passion, stood spellbound and drank in strange fire through all his frame. Nor does the love he has imbibed lie hidden, but the flame pulsating in his inmost being returns to his face and colours the glow upon his cheeks, and as he feels its power runs over his body with a light sweat. As when the Massagetae darken milk-white bowls with blood-red dye, or ivory is stained with purple, so by varying signs of blush and pallor does the sudden fire betray its presence. He would rush forward and unprovoked fiercely break up the ceremonies of his hosts, reckless of the crowd and forgetful of his years, did not shame restrain him and awe of the mother by his side. As when a bullock, soon to be the sire and leader of a herd, though his horns have not yet come full circle, perceives a heifer of snowy whiteness, the comrade of his pasture, his spirit takes fire, and he foams at the mouth with his first passion; glad at heart the herdsmen watch him and check his fury.

Seizing the moment his mother purposely accosts him: "Is it too hard a thing, my son, to make pretence of dancing and join hands in sport among these maidens? Hast thou aught such 'neath Ossa and the crags of Pelion? O, if it were my lot to match two loving hearts, and to bear another Achilles in my arms!"

He is softened, and blushes for joy, and with sly and sidelong glance repels the robes less certainly. His mother sees him in doubt and willing to be compelled, and casts the raiment over him; then she softens his stalwart neck and bows his strong shoulders, and relaxes the muscles of his arms, and tames and orders duly his uncombed tresses, and sets her own necklace about the neck she loves; then keeping his step within the embroidered skirt she teaches him gait and motion and modesty of speech. Even as the waxen images that the artist's thumb will make to live take form and follow the fire and the hand that carves them, such was the picture of the goddess as she transformed her son. Nor did she struggle long; for plenteous charm remains to him though his manhood brook it not, and he baffles beholders by the puzzle of his sex that by a narrow margin hides its secret.

They go forward, and Thetis unsparingly plies her counsels and persuasive words: "Thus then, my son, must thou manage thy gait, thus thy features and thy hands, and imitate thy comrades and counterfeit their ways, lest the king suspect thee and admit thee not to the women's chambers, and the crafty cunning of our enterprise be lost." So speaking she delays not to put correcting touches to his attire. Thus when Hecate returns wearied to her sire and brother from Therapnae, haunt of maidens, her mother bears her company as she goes, and with her own hand covers her shoulders and bared arms, herself arranges the bow and quiver, and pulls down the girt-up robe, and is proud to trim the disordered tresses.

Straightway she accosts the monarch, and there in the presence of the altars: "Here, O king," she says, "I present to thee the sister of my Achilles – seest thou not how proud her glance and like her brother's? – so high her spirit, she begged for arms and a bow to carry on her shoulders, and like an Amazon to spurn the thought of wedlock. But my son is enough care for me; let her carry the baskets at the sacrifice, do thou control and tame her wilfulness, and keep her to her sex, till the time for marriage come and the end of her maiden modesty; nor suffer her to engage in wanton wrestling matches, nor to frequent the woodland haunts. Bring her up indoors, in seclusion among girls of her own age; above all remember to keep her from the harbour and the shore. Lately thou sawest the Phrygian sails: already ships that have crossed the sea have learnt treason to mutual loyalties."

The sire accedes to her words, and receives the disguised Achilles by his mother's ruse – who can resist when gods deceive? Nay more, he venerates her with a suppliant's hand, and gives thanks that he was chosen; nor is the band of duteous Scyrian maidens slow to dart keen glances at the face of their new comrade, how she overtops them by head and neck, how broad her expanse of breast and shoulders; then they invite her to join the dance and approach the holy rites, and make room for her in their ranks and rejoice to be near her. Just as Idalian birds, cleaving the soft clouds and long since gathered in the sky or in their homes, if a strange bird from some distant region has joined them wing to wing, are at first all filled with amaze and fear; then nearer and nearer they fly, and while yet in the air have made him one of them and hover joyfully around with favouring beat of pinions and lead him to their lofty resting places.

Long, ere she departs, lingers the mother at the gate, while she repeats advice and implants whispered secrets in his ear and in hushed tones gives her last counsels. Then she plunges into the main, and gazing back swims far away, and entreats with flattering prayers the island shore: "O land that I love, to whom by timid cunning I have committed the pledge of my anxious care, a trust that is great indeed, mayst thou prosper and be silent, I beg, as Crete was silent for Rhea; enduring honour and everlasting shrines shall gird thee, nor shalt thou be surpassed by unstable Delos; sacred alike to wind and wave shalt thou be, and clam abode of Nereids among the shallows of the Cyclades, where the rocks are shattered by Aegean storms, an isle that sailors swear by – only admit no Danaan keels, I beg! Here are only the wands of Bacchus, nought that avails for war; that tale bid rumour spread, and while the Dorian armaments make ready and Mavors rages from world to world – he may, for aught I care – let Achilles be the maiden daughter of good Lycomedes."

Meanwhile avenging Europe, inflamed by war's sweet frenzy and the monarchs' complaining entreaties, excites her righteous ire; more earnestly pleads that son of Atreus whose spouse abides at home, and by his telling makes the Ilian crime more grievous: how without aid of Mars or force of arms the daughter of heaven and child of mighty Sparta was taken, and justice, good faith and the gods spurned by one deed of rapine. Is this then Phrygian honour? Is this the intercourse of land with land? What awaits the common folk, when wrong so deadly attacks the foremost chieftains? All races, all ages flock together: nor are they only aroused whom the Isthmian barrier with its rampart fronting on two seas encloses and Malea's wave-resounding promontory, but where afar the strait of Phrixus sunders Europe and Asia; and the peoples that fringe Abydos' shore, bound fast by the waters of the upper sea.

The war fever rises high, thrilling the agitated cities. Temese tames her bronze, the Euboean coast shakes with its dockyards, Mycenae echoes with innumerable forges, Pisa makes new chariots, Nemea gives the skins of wild beasts, Cirrha vies in packing tight the arrow-bearing quivers, Lerna in covering heavy shields with the hides of slaughtered bullocks. Aetolia and fierce Acarnania send infantry to war, Argos collects her squadrons, the pasture lands of rich Arcadia are emptied, Epiros bridles her swift-footed nurslings, ye shades of Phocis and Aonia grow scant by reason of the javelins, Pylos and Messene strain their fortress engines. No land but bears its burden; ancestral weapons long renounced are torn from lofty portals, gifts to the gods melt in the flame; gold reft from divine keeping Mars turns to fiercer use. Nowhere are the shady haunts of old: Othrys is lesser grown, lofty Taygetus sinks low, the shorn hills see the light of day. Now the whole forest is afloat: oaks are hewn to make a fleet, the woods are diminished for oars. Iron is forced into countless uses, for riveting prows, for armour of defence, for bridling chargers, for knitting rough coats of mail by a thousand links, to smoke with blood, to drink deep of wounds, to drive death home in conspiracy with poison; they make the dripping whetstones thin with grinding, and add wrath to sluggish sword points. No limit is there to the shaping of bows or heaping up of bullets or the charring of stakes or the heightening of helms with crests. Amid such commotion Thessaly alone bewails her indolent repose, and brings a twofold complaint against the Fates, that Peleus is too old and Achilles not yet ripe of age.

Already the lord of war had drained the land of Pelops and the Grecian world, madly flinging aboard both men and horses. All aswarm are the harbours and the bays invisible for shipping, and the moving fleet stirs its own storms and billows; the sea itself fails the vessels, and their canvas swallows up every breath of wind.

Aulis, sacred to Hecate, first gathers together the Danaan fleet, Aulis, whose exposed cliff and long-projecting ridge climb the Euboean sea, coast beloved by the mountain-wandering goddess, and Caphereus, that raises his head hard by against the barking waves. He, when he beheld the Pelasgian ships sail by, thrice thundered from peak to wave, and gave presage of a night of fury. There assembles the armament for Troy's undoing, there the vast array is sworn, while the sun completes an annual course. Then first did Greece behold her own might; then a scattered, dissonant mass took form and feature, and was marshalled under one single lord. Even so does the round hunting-net confine the hidden beasts, and gradually hem them in as the toils are drawn close. They in panic of the torches and the shouting leave their wide pathless haunts, and marvel that their own mountain is shrinking, till from every side they pour into the narrow vale; the herds startle each other, and are tamed by mutual fear; bristly boar and bear and wolf are driven together, and the hind despises the captured lions.

But although the twain Atridae make war in their own cause together, though Sthenelus and Tydeus' son surpass in eager valour their fathers' fame, and Antilochus heeds not his years, and Ajax shakes upon his arm the seven leaders of the herd and the circle vast as a city wall, though Ulysses, sleepless in counsel and deeds of arms, joins in the quarrel, yet all the host yearns ardently for the absent Achilles, lovingly they dwell upon Achilles' name, Achilles alone is called for against Hector, him and none other do they speak of as the doom of Priam and of Troy. For who else grew up from infancy crawling on fresh-dug snow in the Haemonian valleys? Whom else did the centaur take in hand and shape his rude beginnings and tender years? Whose line of ancestry runs nearer heaven? Whom else did a Nereid take by stealth through the Stygian waters and make his fair limbs impenetrable to steel? Such talk do the Grecian cohorts repeat and interchange. The band of chieftains yields before him and gladly owns defeat. So when the pale denizens of heaven flocked into the Phlegraean camp, and already Gradivus was towering to the height of his Odrysian spear and Tritonia raised her Libyan snakes and the Delian strongly bent his mighty bow, Nature in breathless terror stood looking to the Thunderer alone – when would *he* summon the lightnings and the tempests from the clouds, how many thunderbolts would he ask of fiery Aetna?

There, while the princes, surrounded by the mingled multitudes of their folk, hold counsel of times for sailing and for war, Protesilaus amid great tumult rebukes the prophet Calchas and cries – for to him was given the keenest desire to fight, and the glory even then of suffering death the first: "O son of Thestor, forgetful of Phoebus and thy own tripods, when wilt thou open thy god-possessed lips more surely, or why dost thou hide the secret things of Fate? Seest thou how all are amazed at the unknown Aeacides and clamour for him? The Calydonian hero seems nought in the people's eyes, and so too Ajax born of mighty Telamon and lesser Ajax, so do we also: but Mars and the capture of Troy will prove the truth. Slighting their leaders – for shame! – they all love him as a deity of war. Quickly speak, or why are thy locks enwreathed and held in honour? In what coasts lies he hidden? In what land must we seek him? For report has it that he is living neither in Chiron's cave nor in the halls of Peleus his sire. Come, break in upon the gods, harry the fates that lie concealed! Quaff greedily, if ever thou dost, thy draughts of laurelled fire! We have relieved thee of dread arms and cruel swords, and never shall a helm profane thy unwarlike locks, yet blest shalt thou be and foremost of our chiefs, if of thyself thou doest find great Achilles for the Danaans."

Long since has the son of Thestor been glancing round about him with excited movements, and by his first pallor betrayed the incoming of the god; soon he rolls fiery, bloodshot eyes, seeing neither his comrades nor the camp, but blind and absent from the scene he now overhears the mighty councils of gods in the upper air, now accosts the prescient birds, now the stern sisters' threads, now anxiously consults the incense-laden altars, and quickly scans the shooting flames and feeds upon the sacred vapours. His hair streams out, and the fillet totters on his stiffened locks, his head rolls and he staggers in his gait. At last trembling he looses his weary lips from their long bellowings, and his voice has struggled free from the resisting frenzy: "Whither bearest thou, O Nereid, by thy woman's guile great Chiron's mighty pupil? Send him hither: why dost thou carry him away? I will not suffer it: mine is he, mine! Thou art a goddess of the deep, but I too am inspired by Phoebus. In what hiding-places triest thou to conceal the destroyer of Asia? I see her all bewildered among the Cyclades, in base stealth seeking out the coast. We are ruined! The accomplice land of Lycomedes finds favour. Ah! horrid deed! see, flowing garments drape his breast. Rend them, boy, rend them, and yield not to thy timid mother. Woe, woe! he is rapt away and is gone! Who is that wicked maiden yonder?"

Here tottering he ceased, the madness lost its force, and with a shudder he collapsed and fell before the altar. Then the Calydonian hero accosts the hesitating Ithacan: "Tis us that task summons; for I could not refuse to bear thee company, should thy thought so lead thee. Though he be sunk in the echoing caves of Tethys far removed and in the bosom of watery Nereus, thou wilt find him. Do thou but keep alert the cunning and foresight of thy watchful mind, and arouse thy fertile craft: no prophet, methinks, would make bold in perplexity to see the truth before thee."

Ulysses in joy makes answer: "So may almighty God bring it to pass, and the virgin guardian of thy sire grant to thee! But fickle hope gives me pause; a great enterprise is it indeed to bring Achilles and his arms to our camp, but should the fates say nay, how woeful a disgrace were it to return! Yet will I not leave unventured the fulfilment of the Danaans' desire. Ay, verily, either the Pelean hero shall accompany me hither, or the truth lies deep indeed and Calchas hath not spoken by Apollo."

The Danai shout applause, and Agamemnon urges on the willing pair; the gathering breaks up, and the dispersing ranks depart with joyful murmurs, even as at nightfall the birds wing their way homeward from the pastures, or kindly Hybla sees the swarms returning laden with fresh honey to their cells. Without delay the canvas of the Ithacan is already calling for a favouring breeze, and the merry crew are seated at the oars.

But far away Deidamia – and she alone – had learnt in stolen secrecy the manhood of Aeacides, that lay hid beneath the show of a feigned sex; conscious of guilt concealed there is nought she does not fear, and thinks that her sisters know, but hold their peace. For when Achilles, rough as he was, stood amid the maiden company, and the departure of his mother rid him of his artless bashfulness, straightway although the whole band gathers round him, he chose her as his comrade and assails with new and winning wiles her unsuspecting innocence; her he follows, and persistently besets, toward her he ever and again directs his gaze. Now too zealously he clings to her side, nor does she avoid him, now he pelts her with light garlands, now with baskets that let their burden fall, now with the thyrsus that harms her not, or again he shows her the sweet strings of the lyre he knows so well, and the gentle measures and songs of Chiron's teaching, and guides her hand and makes her fingers strike the sounding harp, now as she sings he makes a conquest of her lips, and binds her in his embrace, and praises her amid a thousand kisses. With pleasure does she learn of Pelion's summit and of Aeacides, and hearing the name and exploits of the youth is spellbound in constant wonder, and sings of Achilles in his very presence.

She in her turn teaches him to move his strong limbs with more modest grace and to spin out the unwrought wool by rubbing with his thumb, and repairs the distaff and the skeins that his rough hand has damaged; she marvels at the deep tones of his voice, how he shuns all her fellows and pierces her with too-attentive gaze and at all times hangs breathless on her words; and now he prepares to reveal the fraud, but she like a fickle girl avoids him, and will not allow him to confess. Even so beneath his mother Rhea's rule the young prince of Olympus gave treacherous kisses to his sister; he was still her brother and she thought no harm, until the reverence for their common blood gave way, and the sister feared a lover's passion.

At length the timorous Nereid's cunning was laid bare. There stood a lofty grove, scene of the rites of Agenorean Bacchus, a grove that reached to heaven; within its shade the pious matrons were wont to renew the recurrent three-yearly festival, and to bring torn animals of the herd and uprooted saplings, and to offer to the god the frenzy wherein he took delight. The law bade males keep far away; the reverend monarch repeats the command, and makes proclamation that no man may draw nigh the sacred haunt. Nor is that enough; a venerable priestess stands at the appointed limit and scans the approaches, lest any defiler come near in the train of women; Achilles laughed silently to himself. His comrades wonder at him as he leads the band of virgins and moves his mighty arms with awkward motion – his own sex and his mother's counterfeit alike become him. No more is Deidamia the fairest of her company, and as she surpasses her own sisters, so does she herself own defeat compared with proud Aeacides. But when he let the fawn skin hang from his shapely neck, and with ivy gathered up its flowing folds, and bound the purple fillet high upon his flaxen temples, and with powerful hand made the enwreathed missile quiver, the crowd stood awestruck, and leaving the sacred rites are fain to throng about him, uplifting their bowed heads to gaze. Even so Euhius, what time he has relaxed at Thebes his martial spirit and frowning brow, and sated his soul with the luxury of his native land, takes chaplet and mitre from his locks, and arms the green thyrsus for the fray, and in more martial guise sets out to meet his Indian foes.

The moon in her rosy chariot was climbing to the height of mid-heaven, when drowsy sleep glided down with full sweep of his pinions to earth and gathered a silent world to his embrace: the choirs reposed, the stricken bronze awhile was mute, when Achilles, parted in solitude from the virgin train, thus spoke with himself: "How long wilt thou endure the precepts of thy anxious mother, and waste the first flower of thy manhood in this soft imprisonment? No weapons of war mayst thou brandish, no beasts mayst thou pursue. Oh! for the plains and valleys of Haemonia! Lookest thou in vain, Spercheus, for my swimming, and for my promised tresses? Or hast thou no regard for the foster-child that has deserted thee? Am I already spoken of as borne to the Stygian shades afar, and does Chiron in solitude bewail my death? Thou, O Patroclus, now does aim my darts, dost bend my bow and mount the team that was nourished for me; but I have learnt to fling wide my arms as I grasp the vine-wands, and to spin the distaff-thread – ah! shame and vexation to confess it! Nay more, night and day thou dost dissemble the love that holds thee, and thy passion for the maid of equal years. How long wilt thou conceal the wound that galls thy heart, nor even in love – for shame! – prove thy own manhood?"

So he speaks; and in the thick darkness of the night, rejoicing that the unstirring silence gives timely aid to his secret deeds, he gains by force his desire, and with all his vigour strains her in a real embrace; the whole choir of stars beheld from on high, and the horns of the young moon blushed red. She indeed filled the grove and mountain with her cries, but the train of Bacchus, dispelling slumber's cloud, deemed it the signal for the dance; on every side the familiar shout arises, and Achilles once more brandishes the thyrsus; yet first with friendly speech he solaces the anxious maid: "I am he – why fearest thou? – whom my cerulean mother bore wellnigh to Jove, and sent to find my nurture in the woods and snows of Thessaly. Nor had I endured this dress and shameful garb, had I not seen thee on the seashore; 'twas for thee I did submit, for thee I carry skeins and bear the womanly timbrel. Why dost thou weep who art made daughter-in-law of mighty ocean? Why does thou moan who shalt bear valiant grandsons to Olympus? But thy father – Scyros shall be destroyed by fire and sword and these walls shall be in ruins and the sport of wanton winds, ere thou pay by cruel death for my embraces: not so utterly am I subject to my mother."

Horror-struck was the princess at such dark happenings, albeit long since she had suspected his good faith, and shuddered at his presence, and his countenance was changed as he made confession. What is she to do? Shall she bear the tale of her misfortune to her father, and ruin both herself and her lover, who perchance would suffer untimely death? And still there abode within her breast the love so long deceived. Silent is she in her grief, and dissembles the crime that both now share alike; her nurse alone she resolves to make a partner in deceit, and she, yielding to the prayers of both, assents. With secret cunning she conceals the rape and the swelling womb and the burden of the months of ailing, till Lucina brought round by token the appointed season, her course now fully run, and gave deliverance of her child.

And now the Laertian bark was threading the winding ways of the Aegean, while the breezes changed one for another the countless Cyclades; already Paros and Olearos are hid, now they skirt lofty Lemnos and behind them Bacchic Naxos is lost to view, while Samos grows before them; now Delos darkens the deep, and there from the tall stern they pour cups of libation, and pray that he oracle be true and Calchas undeceived. The Wielder of the Bow heard them, and from the top of Cynthus sent a zephyr flying and gave the doubting ones the good omen of a bellying sail. The ship sails over the sea untroubled; for the Thunderer's high commands suffered not Thetis to overturn the sure decrees of Fate, faint as he was with tears, and foreboding much because she could not excite the main and straightway pursue the hated Ulysses with all her winds and waves.

Already Phoebus, stooping low upon the verge of Olympus, was sending forth broken rays, and promising to his panting steeds the yielding shore of ocean, when rocky Scyros rose aloft; the Laertian chieftain from the stern let out all sail to make it, and bade his crew resume the deep and with their oars supply the failing zephyrs. Nearer they draw, and more undoubtedly, more surely was it Scyros, and Tritonia above, the guardian of the tranquil shore. They disembark, and venerate the power of the friendly goddess, Aetolian and Ithacan alike. Then the prudent hero, lest they should frighten the hospitable walls with sudden throng, bids his crew remain upon the ship; he himself with trusty Diomede ascends the heights. But already Abas, keeper of the coastal tower, had gone before them and given tidings to the king, that unknown sails, though Greek, were drawing nigh to land. Forward they go, like two wolves leagued together on a winter's night: though their cubs' hunger and their own assails them, yet do they utterly dissemble ravening rage, and go slinking on their way, lest the alertness of dogs announce a foe and warn the anxious herdsmen to keep vigil.

So with slow pace the heroes move, and with mutual converse tread the open plain that lies between the harbour and the high citadel; first keen Tydides speaks: "By what means now are we preparing to search out the truth? For in perplexity of mind have I long been pondering why thou didst buy those unwarlike wands and cymbals in the city marts, and didst bring hither Bacchic hides and turbans, and fawn-skins decked with patterns of gold. Is it with these thou wilt arm Achilles to be the doom of Priam and the Phrygians?"

To him with a smile and somewhat less stern of look the Ithacan replied: "These things, I tell thee, if only he be lurking among the maidens in Lycomedes' palace, shall draw the son of Peleus to the fight, ay, self-confessed! Remember thou to bring them all quickly from the ship, when it is time, and to join to these gifts a shield that is beautiful with carving and rough with work of gold; this spear will suffice; let the good trumpeter Agyrtes be with thee, and let him bring a hidden bugle for a secret purpose."

He spoke and spied the king in the very threshold of the gate, and displaying the olive first announced his peaceful purpose: "Loud report, I ween, hath long since reached thy ears, O gentle monarch, of that fierce war which now is shaking both Europe and Asia. If perchance the chieftains' names have been borne hither, in whom the avenging son of Atreus trusts, here beholdest thou him whom great-hearted Tydeus begot, mightier even than so great a sire, and I am Ulysses the Ithacan chief. The cause of our voyage – for why should I fear to confess all to thee, who art a Greek and of all men most renowned by sure report? – is to spy out the approaches to Troy and her hated shores, and what their schemes may be."

Ere he had finished the other broke in upon him: "May Fortune assist thee, I pray, and propitious gods prosper that enterprise! Now honour my roof and pious home by being my guests." Therewith he leads them within the gate. Straightway numerous attendants prepare the couches and the tables. Meanwhile Ulysses scans and searches the palace with his gaze, if anywhere he can find trace of a tall maiden or a face suspect for its doubtful features; uncertainly he wanders idly in the galleries and, as though in wonder, roams the whole house through; just as yon hunter, having come upon his prey's undoubted haunts, scours the fields with his silent Molossian hound, till he behold his foe stretched out in slumber 'neath the leaves and his jaws resting on the turf.

Long since has a rumour been noised throughout the secret chamber where the maidens had their safe abode, that Pelasgian chiefs are come, and a Grecian ship and its mariners have been made welcome. With good reason are the rest affrighted; but Pelides scarce conceals his sudden joy, and eagerly desires even as he is to see the newly arrived heroes and their arms. Already the noise of princely trains fills the palace, and the guests are reclining on gold-embroidered couches, when at their sire's command his daughters and their chaste companions join the banquet; they approach, like unto Amazons on the Maeotid shore, when, having made plunder of Scythian homesteads and captured strongholds of the Getae, they lay aside their arms and feast. Then indeed does Ulysses with intent gaze ponder carefully both forms and features, but night and the lamps that are brought in deceive him, and their stature is hidden as soon as they recline. One nevertheless with head erect and wandering gaze, one who preserves no sign of virgin modesty, he marks, and with sidelong glance points out to his companion. But if Deidamia, to warn the hasty youth, had not clasped him to her soft bosom, and ever covered with her own robe his bare breast and naked arms and shoulders, and many a time forbidden him to start up from the couch and ask for wine, and replaced the golden hairband on his brow, Achilles had even then been revealed to the Argive chieftains.

When hunger was assuaged and the banquet had twice and three times been renewed, the monarch first addresses the Achaeans, and pledges them with the wine cup: "Ye famous heroes of the Argolic race, I envy, I confess, your enterprise; would that I too were of more valiant years, as when I utterly subdued the Dolopes who attacked the shores of Scyros, and shattered on the sea those keels that ye beheld on the forefront of my lofty walls, tokens of my triumph! At least if I had offspring that I would send to war, – but now ye see for yourselves my feeble strength and my dear children: ah, when will these numerous daughters give me grandsons?"

He spoke, and seizing the moment crafty Ulysses made reply: "Worthy indeed is the object of thy desire; for who would not burn to see the countless peoples of the world and various chieftains and princes with their trains? All the might and glory of powerful Europe hath sworn together willing allegiance to our righteous arms. Cities and fields alike are empty, we have spoiled the lofty mountains, the whole sea lies hidden beneath the far-spread shadow of our sails; fathers give weapons, youths snatch them and are gone beyond recall. Never was offered to the brave such an opportunity for high renown, never had valour so wide a field of exercise."

He sees him all attentive and drinking in his words with vigilant ear, though the rest are alarmed and turn aside their downcast eyes, and he repeats: "Whoever hath pride of race and ancestry, whoever hath sure javelin and valiant steed, or skill of bow, all honour there awaits him, there is the strife of mighty names: scarce do timorous mothers hold back or troops of maids; ah! doomed to barren years and hated of the gods is he whom this new chance of glory passes by in idle sloth."

Up from the couches had he sprung, had not Deidamia, watchfully giving the sign to summon all her sisters, left the banquet clasping him in her arms; yet still he lingers looking back at the Ithacan, and goes out from the company the last of all. Ulysses indeed leaves unsaid somewhat of his purposed speech, yet adds a few words: "But do thou abide in deep and tranquil peace, and find husbands for thy beloved daughters, whom fortune has given thee, goddess-like in their starry countenances. What awe touched me anon and holds me silent? Such charm and beauty joined to manliness of form!"

The sire replies: "What if thou couldst see them performing the rites of Bacchus, or about the altars of Pallas? Ay, and thou shalt, if perchance the rising south wind prove a laggard." They eagerly accept his promise, and hope inspires their silent prayers. All else in Lycomedes' palace are at rest in peaceful quiet, their troubles laid aside, but to the cunning Ithacan the night is long; he yearns for the day and brooks not slumber.

Scarce had day dawned, and already the son of Tydeus accompanied by Agyrtes was present bringing the appointed gifts. The maids of Scyros too went forth from their chamber and advanced to display their dances and promised rites to the honoured strangers. Brilliant before the rest is the princess with Pelides her companion: even as beneath the rocks of Aetna in Sicily Diana and bold Pallas and the consort of the Elysian monarch shine forth among the nymphs of Enna. Already they begin to move, and the Ismenian pipe gives signal to the dancers; four times they beat the cymbals of Rhea, four times the maddening drums, four times they trace their manifold windings. Then together they raise and lower their wands, and complicate their steps, now in such fashion as the Curetes and devout Samothracians use, now turning to face each other in the Amazonian comb, now in the ring wherein the Delian sets the Laconian girls a-dancing, and whirls them shouting her praises into her own Amyclae. Then indeed, then above all is Achilles manifest, caring neither to keep his turn nor to join arms; then more than ever does he scorn the delicate step, the womanly attire, and breaks the dance and mightily disturbs the scene. Even so did Thebes already sorrowing behold Pentheus spurning the wands and the timbrels that his mother welcomed.

The troop disperses amid applause, and they seek again their father's threshold, where in the central chamber of the palace the son of Tydeus had long since set out gifts that should attract maidens' eyes, the mark of kindly welcome and the guerdon of their toil; he bids them choose, nor does the peaceful monarch say them nay. Alas! how simple and untaught, who knew not the cunning of the gifts nor Grecian fraud nor Ulysses' many wiles! Thereupon the others, prompted by nature and their ease-loving sex, try the shapely wands or the timbrels that answer to the blow, and fasten jewelled band around their temples; the weapons they behold, but think them a gift to their mighty sire. But the bold son of Aeacus no sooner saw before him the gleaming shield enchased with battle scenes – by chance too it shone red with the fierce stains of war – and leaning against the spear, than he shouted loud and rolled his eyes, and his hair rose up from his brow; forgotten were his mother's words, forgotten his secret love, and Troy fills all his breast. As a lion, torn from his mother's dugs, submits to be tamed and lets his mane be combed, and learns to have awe of man and not to fly into a rage save when bidden, yet if but once the steel has glittered in his sight, his fealty is forsworn, and his tamer becomes his foe: against him he first ravens, and feels shame to have served a timid lord. But when he came nearer, and the emulous brightness gave back his features and he saw himself mirrored in the reflecting gold, he thrilled and blushed together.

Then quickly went Ulysses to his side and whispered: "Why dost thou hesitate? We know thee, thou art the pupil of the half-beast Chiron, thou art the grandson of the sky and sea; thee the Dorian fleet, thee thy own Greece awaits with standards uplifted for the march, and the very walls of Pergamum totter and sway for thee to overturn. Up! delay no more! Let perfidious Ida grow pale, let they father delight to hear these tidings, and guileful Thetis feel shame to have so feared for thee."

Already was he stripping his body of the robes, when Agyrtes, so commanded, blew a great blast upon the trumpet: the gifts are scattered, and they flee and fall with prayers before their sire and believe that battle is joined. But from his breast the raiment fell without his touching, already the shield and puny spear are lost in the grasp of his hand – marvellous to believe! – and he seemed to surpass by head and shoulders the Ithacan and the Aetolian chief: with a sheen so awful does the sudden blaze of arms and the martial fire dazzle the palace hall. Mighty of limb, as though forthwith summoning Hector to the fray, he stands in the midst of the panic-stricken house: and the daughter of Peleus is sought in vain.

But Deidamia in another chamber bewailed the discovery of the fraud, and as soon as he heard her loud lament and recognized the voice that he knew so well, he quailed and his spirit was broken by his hidden passion. He dropped the shield, and turning to the monarch's face, while Lycomedes is dazed by the scene and distraught by the strange portent, just as he was, in naked panoply of arms, he thus bespeaks him: "'Twas I, dear father, I whom bounteous Thetis gave thee – dismiss thy anxious fears! – long since did this high renown await thee; 'tis thou who wilt send Achilles, long sought for, to the Greeks, more welcome to me than my might sire – if it is right so to speak – and than beloved Chiron. But, if thou wilt, give me thy mind awhile, and of thy favour hear these words: Peleus and Thetis thy guest make thee the father-in-law of their son, and recount their kindred deities on either side; they demand one of thy train of virgin daughters: doest thou give her? or seem we a mean and coward race? Thou dost not refuse. Join then our hands, and make the treaty, and pardon thy own kin. Already hath Deidamia been known to me in stolen secrecy; for how could she have resisted these arms of mine, how once in my embrace repel my might? Bid me atone that deed: I lay down these weapons and restore them to the Pelasgians, and I remain here. Why these angry cries? Why is thy aspect changed? Already art thou my father-in-law" – he placed the child before his feet, and added: "and already a grandsire! How often shall the pitiless sword be plied! We are a multitude!"

Then the Greeks too and Ulysses with his persuasive prayer entreat by the holy rites and the sworn word of hospitality. He, though moved by the discovery of his dear daughter's wrong and the command of Thetis, though seeming to betray the goddess and so grave a trust, yet fears to oppose so many destinies and delay the Argive war – even were he fain, Achilles had spurned even his mother then. Nor is he unwilling to take unto himself so great a son-in-law: he is won. Deidamia comes shamefast from her dark privacy, nor in her despair believes at first his pardon, and puts forward Achilles to appease her sire.

A messenger is sent to Haemonia to give Peleus full tidings of these great events, and to demand ships and comrades for the war. Moreover, the Scyrian prince launches two vessels for his son-in-law, and makes excuse to the Achaeans for so poor a show of strength. Then the day was brought to its end with feasting, and at last the bond was made known to all, and conscious night joined the now fearless lovers.

Before her eyes new wars and Xanthus and Ida pass, and the Argolis fleet, and she imagines the very waves and fears the coming of the dawn; she flings herself about her new lord's beloved neck, and at last clasping his limbs gives way to tears: 'Shall I see thee again, and lay myself on this breast of thine, O son of Aeacus? Wilt thou deign once more to look upon thy offspring? Or wilt thou proudly bring back spoils of captured Pergamum and

Teucrian homes and wish to forget where thou didst hide thee as a maid? What should I entreat, or alas! what rather fear? How can I in my anxiety lay a behest on thee, who have scarce time to weep? One single night has given and grudged thee to me! Is this the season for our espousals? Is this free wedlock? Ah! those stolen sweets! that cunning fraud! Ah! how I fear! Achilles is given to me only to be torn away. Go! for I would not dare to stay such mighty preparations; go, and be cautious, and remember that the fears of Thetis were not vain; go, and good luck be with thee, and come back mine!

"Yes too bold is my request: soon the fair Trojan dames will sigh for thee with tears and beat their breasts, and pray that they may offer their necks to thy fetters, and weigh thy couch against their homes, or Tyndaris herself will please thee, too much belauded for her incestuous rape. But I shall be a story to thy henchmen, the tale of a lad's first fault, or I shall be disowned and forgotten. Nay, come, take me as thy comrade; why should I not carry the standards of Mars with thee? Thou dist carry with me the wands and holy things of Bacchus, though ill-fated Troy believe it not. Yet this babe, whom thou dost leave as my sad solace – keep him at least within thy heart, and grant this one request, that no foreign wife bear thee a child, that no captive woman give unworthy grandsons to Thetis."

As thus she speaks, Achilles, moved to compassion himself, comforts her, and gives her his sworn oath, and pledges it with tears, and promises her on his return tall handmaidens and spoils of Ilium and gifts of Phrygian treasure. The fickle breezes swept his words unfulfilled away.

Book II

DAY ARISING from ocean set free the world from dank enfolding shades, and the father of the flashing light upraised his torch still dimmed by the neighbouring gloom and moist with sea water not yet shaken off.

And now all behold Aeacides, his shoulders stripped of the scarlet robe, and glorious in those very arms he first had seized – for the wind is calling and his kindred seas are urging him – and quake before the youthful chieftain, not daring to remember aught; so wholly changed to the sight hath he come back, as though he had never experienced the shores of Scyros, but were embarking from the Pelian cave. Then duly – for so Ulysses counselled – he does sacrifice to the gods and the waters and south winds, and venerates with a bull the cerulean king below the waves and Nereus his grandsire: his mother is appeased with garlanded heifer. Thereupon casting the swollen entrails on the salt foam he addresses her: "Mother, I have obeyed thee, though thy commands were hard to bear; too obedient have I been: now they demand me, and I go to the Trojan war and the Argolic fleet." So speaking he leapt into the bark, and was swept away far from the neighbourhood of land by the whistling south wind; already lofty Scyros beings to gather mist about her, and to fade from sight over the long expanse of sea.

Far away on the summit of a tower with weeping sisters round her his wife leaned forth, holding her precious charge, who bore the name of Pyrrhus, and with her eyes fixed on the canvas sailed herself upon the sea, and all alone still saw the vessel. He too turned his gaze aside to the walls he held dear, he thinks upon the widowed home and the sobs of her he had left: the hidden passion glows again within his heart, and martial ire gives place. The Laertian hero perceives him sorrowing, and draws nigh to influence him with gentle words: "Was it thou, O destined destroyer of great Troy, whom Danaan fleets and divine oracles are demanding, and War aroused is awaiting with unbarred portals – was it thou whom a crafty mother profaned with feminine robes, and trusted yonder hiding-place with so great a secret, and hoped the trust was sure? O too anxious, O too true a mother! Could such valour lie inert and hidden, that scarce hearing the trumpet-blast fled from Thetis and companions and the heart's unspoken passion? Nor is it due to us that thou comest to the war, and compliest with our prayers; thou wouldst have come."

He spoke, and thus the Aeacian hero takes up the word: "'Twere long to set forth the causes of my tarrying and my mother's crime; this sword shall make excuse for Scyros and my dishonourable garb, the reproach of destiny. Do thou rather, while the sea is peaceful and the sails enjoy the zephyr, tell how the Danaans began so great a war: I would fain draw straightway from thy words a righteous anger."

Then the Ithacan, tracing far back the beginning of the tale: "A shepherd, they say – if we believe such things – was chosen in Hector's domain of Ida to end a strife of beauty, and while he kept the goddesses anxious doubt looked not with friendly eye upon Minerva's frowning countenance nor on the consort of the heavenly ruler, but gazed overmuch on Dione alone. And verily that quarrel arose in thy own glades, at a gathering of the gods, when pleasant Pelion made marriage-feast for Peleus, and thou even then wert promised to our armament. Wrath thrills the vanquished ones: the judge demands his fateful reward, and compliant Amyclae is shown to the ravisher. He cuts down the Phrygian groves, the secret haunts of the turret-crowned mother, and flings down pines that fear to fall to earth, and borne over the sea to Achaean lands he plunders the marriage chamber of his host the son of Atreus – ah! shame and pity on proud Europe! – and exulting in Helen puts to sea and brings home to Pergamum the spoils of Argos. Then, as the rumours spread far and wide through the cities, of our own will, none urging us, we gather, who could endure the unlawful, crafty breaking of the marriage bond, or a consort carried off in unresisted rape, as though a beast of the flock or herd, would shake even a valiant heart. Masterful Agenor endured not the treachery of the gods, but went in quest of sacred lowings and Europa riding on a mighty god, and scorned the Thunderer as a son-in-law; Aeetes endured not the rape of his daughter from the Scythian shore, but with ships and steel pursued the princes and the vessel fated to join the stars: shall we endure a Phrygian eunuch hovering about the coasts and harbours of Argos with his incestuous bark? Are our horses and men so utterly vanished? Are the seas so impassable to Greeks? What if someone now were to carry of Deidamia from her native shores, and tear her from her lonely chamber in dire dismay and crying on the name of great Achilles?"

His hand flew to the sword hilt, and a dark flush surged over his face: Ulysses was silent and content.

Then spoke Oenides: "Nay, O thou worthiest progeny of heaven, tell us, thy admiring friends, of the ways in which thy spirit first was trained, and as the vigour of thy youth increased what stirring themes of glory Chiron was wont to recount to thee, and how thy valour grew, by what arts he made strong thy limbs or fired thy courage; let it be worthy while to have sought Scyros over long leagues of sea, and to have first shown weapons to those arms of thine."

Who would find it hard to tell of his own deeds? Yet he begins modestly, somewhat uncertain and more like one compelled: "Even in my years of crawling infancy, when the Thessalian sage received me on his stark mountainside, I am said to have devoured no wonted food, nor to have sated my hunger at the nourishing breast, but to have gnawed the tough entrails of lions and the bowels of a half-slain she-wolf. That was my first bread, that the bounty of joyous Bacchus, in such wise did that father of mine feed me. Then he taught me to go with him through pathless deserts, dragging me on with mighty stride, and to laugh at sight of the wild beasts, nor tremble at the shattering rocks by rushing torrents or at the silence of the lonely forest. Already at that time weapons were in my hand and quivers on my shoulders, the love of steel grew apace within me, and my skin was hardened by much sun and frost; nor were my limbs weakened by soft couches, but I shared the hard rock with my master's mighty frame.

"Scarce had my raw youth turned the wheel of twice six years, when already he made me outpace swift hinds and Lapith steeds and running overtake the flung dart; often Chiron himself, while yet he was swift of foot, chased me at full gallop with headlong speed over all the plains, and when I was exhausted by roaming over the meads he praised my joyously and hoisted me upon his back. Often too in the first freezing of the streams he would bid me go upon them with light step nor break the ice. These were my boyhood glories. Why now should I tell thee of the woodland battles and of the glades that know my fierce shout no more? Never would he suffer me to follow unwarlike does through the pathless glens of Ossa, or lay low timid lynxes with my spear, but only to drive angry bears from their resting-places, and boars with lightning thrust; or if anywhere a mighty tiger lurked or a lioness with her cubs in some secret lair upon the mountain-side, he himself, seated in his vast cave, awaited my exploits, if perchance I should return bespattered with dark blood; nor did he admit me to his embrace before he had scanned my weapons.

"And already I was being prepared for the armed tumults of the neighbouring folk, and no fashion of savage warfare passed me by. I learnt how the Paeonians whirl and fling their darts and the Macetae their javelins, with how fierce a rush the Sarmatian plies his pike and the Getan his falchion, how the Gelonian draws his bow, and how the Balearic wielder of the pliant thong keeps the missile swinging round with balanced motion, and as he swings it marks out a circle in the air. Scarce could I recount all my doings, successful though they were; now he instructs me to span huge dykes by leaping, now to climb and grasp the airy mountain peak, with what stride to run upon the level, how to catch flung stones in mimic battle on my shielded arm, to pass through burning houses, and to check flying four-horse teams on foot.

"Spercheus, I remember was flowing with rapid current, fed full with constant rains and melted snows and carrying on its flood boulders and living trees, when he sent me in, there were the waves rolled fiercest, and bade me stand against them and hurl back the swelling billows that he himself could scarce have borne, though he stood to face them with so many a limb. I strove to stand, but the violence of the stream and the dizzy panic of the broad spate forced me to give ground; he loomed o'er me from above and fiercely threatened, and flung taunts to shame me. Nor did I depart till he gave me word, so far did the lofty love of fame constrain me, and my toils were not too hard with such a witness. For to fling the Oebalian quoit far out of sight into the clouds, or to practise the holds of the sleek wrestling bout, and to scatter blows with the boxing gloves were sport and rest to me: nor laboured I more therein that when I struck with my quill the sounding strings, or told the wondrous fame of heroes of old.

"Also did he teach me of juices and the grasses that succour disease, what remedy will staunch too fast a flow of blood, what will lull to sleep, what will close gaping wounds; what plague should be checked by the knife, what will yield to herbs; and he implanted deep within my heart the precepts of divine justice, whereby he was wont to give revered laws to the tribes that dwelt on Pelion, and tame his own two-formed folk. So much do I remember, friends, of the training of my earliest years, and sweet is their remembrance; the rest my mother knows."

Biblioteca

Book III, Section XIII Continued

♟

PELEUS MARRIED POLYDORA, daughter of Perieres, by whom he had a putative son Menesthius, though in fact Menesthius was the son of the river Sperchius. Afterwards he married Thetis, daughter of Nereus, for whose hand Zeus and Poseidon had been rivals; but when Themis prophesied that the son born of Thetis would be mightier than his father, they withdrew. But some say that when Zeus was bent on gratifying his passion for her, Prometheus declared that the son borne to him by her would be lord of heaven; and others affirm that Thetis would not consort with Zeus because she had been brought up by Hera, and that Zeus in anger would marry her to a mortal.

Chiron, therefore, having advised Peleus to seize her and hold her fast in spite of her shapeshifting, he watched his chance and carried her off, and though she turned, now into fire, now into water, and now into a beast, he did not let her go till he saw that she had resumed her former shape. And he married her on Pelion, and there the gods celebrated the marriage with feast and song. And Chiron gave Peleus an ashen spear, and Poseidon gave him horses, Balius and Xanthus, and these were immortal.

When Thetis had got a babe by Peleus, she wished to make it immortal, and unknown to Peleus she used to hide it in the fire by night in order to destroy the mortal element which the child inherited from its father, but by day she anointed him with ambrosia. But Peleus watched her, and, seeing the child writhing on the fire, he cried out; and Thetis, thus prevented from accomplishing her purpose, forsook her infant son and departed to the Nereids. Peleus brought the child to Chiron, who received him and fed him on the inwards of lions and wild swine and the marrows of bears, and named him **Achilles**, because he had not put his lips to the breast; but before that time his name was Ligyron.

After that Peleus, with Jason and the Dioscuri, laid waste Tolcus; and he slaughtered Astydamia, wife of Acastus, and, having divided her limb from limb, he led the army through her into the city. When **Achilles** was nine years old, Calchas declared that Troy could not be taken without him; so Thetis, foreseeing that it was fated he should perish if he went to the war, disguised him in female garb and entrusted him as a maiden to Lycomedes. Bred at his court, Achilles had an intrigue with Deidamia, daughter of Lycomedes, and a son Pyrrhus was born to him, who was afterwards called Neoptolemus. But the secret of **Achilles** was betrayed, and Ulysses, seeking him at the court of Lycomedes, discovered him by the blast of a trumpet. And in that way Achilles went to Troy. He was accompanied by Phoenix, son of Amyntor. This Phoenix had been blinded by his father on the strength of à false accusation of seduction preferred against him by his father's concubine Phthia.

But Peleus brought him to Chiron, who restored his sight, and thereupon Peleus made him king of the Dolopians. Achilles was also accompanied by Patroclus, son of Menoetius and Sthenele, daughter of Acastus; or the mother of Patroclus was Periopis, daughter of Pheres, or, as Philocrates says, she was Polymele, daughter of Peleus.

At Opus, in a quarrel over a game of dice, Patroclus killed the boy Clitonymus, son of Amphidamas, and flying with his father he dwelt at the house of Peleus and became a minion of Achilles.[...]

[...]When the armament was in Aulis, after a sacrifice to Apollo, a serpent darted from the altar beside the neighbouring plane tree, in which there was a nest; and having consumed the eight sparrows in the nest, together with the mother bird, which made the ninth, it was turned to stone. Calchas said that this sign was given them by the will of Zeus, and he inferred from what had happened that Troy was destined to be taken in a period of 10 years. And they made ready to sail against Troy. So Agamemnon in person was in command of the whole army, and Achilles was admiral, being 15 years old.

But not knowing the course to steer for Troy, they put in to Mysia and ravaged it, supposing it to be Troy. Now Telephus son of Hercules, was king of the Mysians, and seeing the country pillaged, he armed the Mysians, chased the Greeks in a crowd to the ships, and killed many, among them Thersander, son of Polynices, who had made stand. But when Achilles rushed at him, Telephus did not abide the onset and was pursued, and in the pursuit he was entangled in a vine branch and wounded with a spear in the thigh. Departing from Mysia, the Greeks put to sea, and a violent storm coming on, they were separated from each other and landed in their own countries. So the Greeks returned at that time, and it is said that the war lasted 20 years. For it was in the second year after the rape of Helen that the Greeks, having completed their preparations, set out on the expedition and after their retirement from Mysia to Greece eight years elapsed before they again returned to Argos and came to Aulis.

Having again assembled at Aulis after the aforesaid interval of eight years, they were in great perplexity about the voyage, because they had no leader who could show them the way to Troy. But Telephus, because his wound was unhealed, and Apollo had told him that he would be cured when the one who wounded him should turn physician, came from Mysia to Argos, clad in rags, and begged the help of Achilles, promising to show the course to steer for Troy. So Achilles healed him by scraping off the rust of his Pelian spear. Accordingly, on being healed, Telephus showed the course to steer, and the accuracy of his information was confirmed by Calchas by means of his own art of divination. But when they had put to sea from Argos and arrived for the second time at Aulis, the fleet was windbound, and Calchas said that they could not sail unless the fairest of Agamemnon's daughters were presented as a sacrifice to Artemis; for the goddess was angry with Agamemnon, both because, on shooting a deer, he had said, "Artemis herself could not (do it better)," and because Atreus had not sacrificed to her the golden lamb. On receipt of this oracle, Agamemnon sent Ulysses and Talthybius to Clytaemnestra and asked for Iphigenia, alleging a promise of his to give her to Achilles to wife in reward for his military service. So Clytaemnestra sent her, and Agamemnon set her beside the altar, and was about to slaughter her, when Artemis carried her off to the Taurians and appointed her to be her priestess, substituting a deer for her at the altar; but some say that Artemis made her immortal.

After putting to sea from Aulis they touched at Tenedos. It was ruled by Tenes, son of Cycnus and Proclia, but according to some, he was a son of Apollo. He dwelt there because he had been banished by his father. For Cycnus had a son Tenes and a daughter Hemithea by Proclia, daughter of Laomedon, but he afterwards married Philonome, daughter of Tragasus; and she fell in love with Tenes, and, failing to seduce him, falsely accused him to Cycnus of attempting to debauch her, and in witness of it she produced a flute player, by name Eumolpus.

Cycnus believed her, and putting him and his sister in a chest he set them adrift on the sea. The chest was washed up on the island of Leucophrys, and Tenes landed and settled in the island, and called it Tenedos after himself. But Cycnus afterwards learning the truth, stoned the flute player to death and buried his wife alive in the earth.

So when the Greeks were standing in for Tenedos, Tenes saw them and tried to keep them off by throwing stones, but was killed by Achilles with a sword cut in the breast, though Thetis had forewarned Achilles not to kill Tenes, because he himself would die by the hand of Apollo if he slew Tenes. And as they were offering a sacrifice to Apollo, a water snake approached from the altar and bit Philoctetes; and as the sore did not heal and grew noisome, the army could not endure the stench, and Ulysses, by the orders of Agamemnon, put him ashore on the island of Lemnos, with the bow of Hercules which he had in his possession; and there, by shooting birds with the bow, he subsisted in the wilderness.

Putting to sea from Tenedos they made sail for Troy, and sent Ulysses and Menelaus to demand the restoration of Helen and the property. But the Trojans, having summoned an assembly, not only refused to restore Helen, but threatened to kill the envoys. These were, however, saved by Antenor; but the Greeks, exasperated at the insolence of the barbarians, stood to arms and made sail against them. Now Thetis charged Achilles not to be the first to land from the ships, because the first to land would be the first to die. Being apprised of the hostile approach of the fleet, the barbarians marched in arms to the sea, and endeavoured by throwing stones to prevent the landing. Of the Greeks the first to land from his ship was Protesilaus, and having slain not a few of the barbarians, he fell by the hand of Hector. His wife Laodamia loved him even after his death, and she made an image of him and consorted with it. The gods had pity on her, and Hermes brought up Protesilaus from Hades. On seeing him, Laodamia thought it was himself returned from Troy, and she was glad; but when he was carried back to Hades, she stabbed herself to death.

On the death of Protesilaus, Achilles landed with the Myrmidons, and throwing a stone at the head of Cycnus, killed him. When the barbarians saw him dead, they fled to the city, and the Greeks, leaping from their ships, filled the plain with bodies. And having shut up the Trojans, they besieged them; and they drew up the ships. The barbarians showing no courage, Achilles waylaid Troilus and slaughtered him in the sanctuary of Thymbraean Apollo, and coming by night to the city he captured Lycaon. Moreover, taking some of the chiefs with him, Achilles laid waste the country, and made his way to Ida to lift the cows of Aeneas. But Aeneas fled, and Achilles killed the cowherds and Mestor, son of Priam, and drove away the cows. He also took Lesbos and Phocaea, then Colophon, and Smyrna, and Clazomenae, and Cyme; and afterwards Aegialus and Tenos, the so called Hundred Cities; then, in order, Adramytium and Side; then Endium, and Linaeum and Colone. He took also Hypoplacian Thebes and Lyrnessus, and further Antandrus, and many other cities.

A period of nine years having elapsed, allies came to join the Trojans: from the surrounding cities, Aeneas, son of Anchises, and with him Archelochus and Acamas, sons of Antenor, and Theanus, leaders of the Dardanians; of the Thracians, Acamas, son of Eusorus; of the Cicones, Euphemus, son of Troezenus; of the Paeonians, Pyraechmes; of the Paphlagonians, Pylaemenes, son of Bilsates; from Zelia, Pandarus, son of Lycaon; from Adrastia, Adrastus and Amphius, sons of Merops; from Arisbe, Asius, son of Hyrtacus; from Larissa, Hippothous, son of Pelasgus ; from Mysia, Chromius and Ennomus, sons of Arsinous; of the Alizones, Odius and Epistrophus, sons of Mecisteus; of the Phrygians, Phorcys and Ascanius, sons of Aretaon; of the Maeonians, Mesthles and Antiphus, sons of Talaemenes; of the Carians, Nastes and Amphimachus, sons of Nomion; of the Lycians, Sarpedon, son of Zeus, and Glaucus, son of Hippolochus.

Epitome, Section IV

ACHILLES DID NOT go forth to the war, because he was angry on account of Briseis, the daughter of Chryses the priest. Therefore the barbarians took heart of grace and sallied out of the city. And Alexander fought a single combat with Menelaus; and when Alexander got the worst of it, Aphrodite carried him off. And Pandarus, by shooting an arrow at Menelaus, broke the truce. Diomedes, doing doughty deeds, wounded Aphrodite when she came to the help of Aeneas; and encountering Glaucus, he recalled the friendship of their fathers and exchanged arms. And Hector having challenged the bravest to single combat, many came forward, but the lot fell on Ajax, and he did doughty deeds; but night coming on, the heralds parted them.

The Greeks made a wall and a ditch to protect the roadstead, and a battle taking place in the plain, the Trojans chased the Greeks within the wall. But the Greeks sent Ulysses, Phoenix and Ajax as ambassadors to Achilles, begging him to fight for them, and promising Briseis and other gifts. And night coming on, they sent Ulysses and Diomedes as spies; and these killed Dolon, son of Eumelus, and Rhesus, the Thracian (who had arrived the day before as an ally of the Trojans, and having not yet engaged in the battle was encamped at some distance from the Trojan force and apart from Hector); they also slew the 12 men that were sleeping around him, and drove the horses to the ships. But by day a fierce fight took place; Agamemnon and Diomedes, Ulysses, Eurypylus and Machaon were wounded, the Greeks were put to flight, Hector made a breach in the wall and entered and, Ajax having retreated, he set fire to the ships.

But when Achilles saw the ship of Protesilaus burning, he sent out Patroclus with the Myrmidons, after arming him with his own arms and giving him the horses. Seeing him the Trojans thought that he was Achilles and turned to flee. And having chased them within the wall, he killed many, amongst them Sarpedon, son of Zeus, and was himself killed by Hector, after being first wounded by Euphorbus. And a fierce fight taking place for the corpse, Ajax with difficulty, by performing feats of valour, rescued the body. And Achilles laid aside his anger and recovered Briseis. And a suit of armour having been brought him from Hephaestus, he donned the armour and went forth to the war, and chased the Trojans in a crowd to the Scamander, and there killed many, and amongst them Asteropaeus, son of Pelegon, son of the river Axius; and the river rushed at him in fury. But Hephaestus dried up the streams of the river, after chasing them with a mighty flame. And Achilles slew Hector in single combat, and fastening his ankles to his chariot dragged him to the ships. And having buried Patroclus, he celebrated games in his honour, at which Diomedes was victorious in the chariot race, Epeus in boxing, and Ajax and Ulysses in wrestling. And after the games Priam came to Achilles and ransomed the body of Hector, and buried it.

Epitome, Section V

PENTHESILIA, daughter of Otrere and Ares, accidentally killed Hippolyte and was purified by Priam. In battle she slew many, and Machaon, and was afterwards herself killed by Achilles, who fell in love with the Amazon after her death and slew Thersites for jeering at him. Hippolyte was the mother of Hippolytus; she also goes by the names of Glauce and Melanippe. For when the marriage of Phaedra was being celebrated, Hippolyte appeared in arms with her Amazons, and said that she would slay the guests of Theseus. So a battle took place, and she was killed, whether in voluntarily by her ally Penthesilia, or by Theseus, or because his men, seeing the threatening attitude of the Amazons, hastily closed the doors and so intercepted and slew her.

Memnon, the son of Tithonus and the Dawn, came with a great force of Ethiopians to Troy against the Greeks, and having slain many of the Greeks, including Antilochus, he was himself slain by Achilles. Having chased the

Trojans also, Achilles was shot with an arrow in the ankle by Alexander and Apollo at the Scaean gate. A fight taking place for the corpse, Ajax killed Glaucus, and gave the arms to be conveyed to the ships, but the body he carried, in a shower of darts, through the midst of the enemy, while Ulysses fought his assailants.

The death of Achilles filled the army with dismay, and they buried him with Patroclus in the White Isle, mixing the bones of the two together. It is said that after death Achilles consorts with Medea in the Isles of the Blest. And they held games in his honour, at which Eumelus won the chariot race, Diomedes the foot race, Ajax the quoit match and Teucer the competition in archery. Also his arms were offered as a prize to the bravest, and Ajax and Ulysses came forward as competitors. The judges were the Trojans or, according to some, the allies, and Ulysses was preferred.

Disordered by chagrin, Ajax planned a nocturnal attack on the army. And Athena drove him mad, and turned him, sword in hand, among the cattle, and in his frenzy he slaughtered the cattle with the herdsmen, taking them for the Achaeans. But afterwards he came to his senses and slew also himself. And Agamemnon forbade his body to be burnt; and he alone of all who fell at Ilium is buried in a coffin. His grave is at Rhoeteum.

Achilles in Late Antiquity

THE POSTHOMERICA is attributed to Quintus of Smyrna, who is generally believed to have been active in the late third century BCE, though some date his work later. Not much is known about the author, other than that he was from Asia Minor and wrote in Greek. His 14-book epic can be characterized as a sequel to Homer's *Iliad* and a prequel to his *Odyssey*. The first five books recount events connected to Achilles, including his duels with Amazon warrior Penthesilea and Aethiopian king Memnon, from both of which Achilles emerges the victor, as well as his death, the funeral games in his honour and the conflict over his armour.

Like the work of Hellenistic poet Apollodorus, Quintus engages with what by then were the literary traditions of prior works composed in Greek. As in other post-Homeric texts that engage with the myth of Achilles, the *Posthomerica* shapes the story of Achilles, and the larger Trojan War conflict, in moral allegorical terms: Virtue and Excellence require toil and sacrifice but, if achieved, are rewarded in the afterlife.

Dated to the fifth century CE, *History of the Fall of Troy* is a prose work composed in Latin that presents itself as eyewitness testimony to the fall of Troy. Its purported author, Dares of Phrygia, is named in the *Iliad* book five as a priest of Hephaestus, and it is under this pseudonym that the work first appeared. After the fall of Rome in the fifth century, knowledge of Greek was lost in the West, and *History of the Fall of Troy* became an important source of Trojan War mythology.

In the mythological canon, the Phrygians were allied with the Trojans, and Dares' account has accordingly been characterized as more sympathetic to that side. Homer's 'plan of Zeus' that shapes the course of Achilles' narrative arc recedes in Dares, as the focus shifts from divine intention to human motivation. Troy's eventual fall is attributed to betrayal from within, rather than a cosmic plan. Similarly, Achilles' animosity towards Agamemnon finds its origin not in Zeus's design but in a marriage contract thwarted by the failure to make peace.

Posthomerica

Book I

WHEN GODLIKE HECTOR by Peleides slain passed, and the pyre had ravined up his flesh, and earth had veiled his bones, the Trojans then tarried in Priam's city, sore afraid before the might of stout-heart Aeacus's son: as cattle they were, that midst the corpses shrink from faring forth to meet a lion grim, but in dense thickets terror-huddled cower; so in their fortress shivered these to see that mighty man. Of those already dead they thought of all whose lives he reft away as by Scamander's outfall on he rushed, and all that in mid-flight to that high wall he slew, how he quelled Hector, how he haled his corpse round Troy; – yea, and of all beside laid low by him since that first day whereon over restless seas he brought the Trojans doom. Ay, all these they remembered, while they stayed thus in their town, and over them anguished grief hovered dark-winged, as though that very day all Troy with shrieks were crumbling down in fire.

Then from Thermodon, from broad-sweeping streams, came, clothed upon with beauty of goddesses, Penthesileia – came athirst indeed for groan-resounding battle, but yet more fleeing abhorred reproach and evil fame, lest they of her own folk should rail on her because of her own sister's death, for whom ever her sorrows waxed, Hippolyte, whom she had struck dead with her mighty spear, not of her will – 'twas at a stag she hurled. So came she to the far-famed land of Troy. Yea, and her warrior spirit pricked her on, of murder's dread pollution thus to cleanse her soul, and with such sacrifice to appease the Awful Ones, the Erinnyes, who in wrath for her slain sister straightway haunted her unseen: for ever round the sinner's steps they hover; none may escape those goddesses.

And with her followed 12 beside, each one a princess, hot for war and battle grim, far-famous each, yet handmaids unto her: Penthesileia far outshone them all. As when in the broad sky amidst the stars the moon rides over all preeminent, when through the thunderclouds the cleaving heavens open, when sleep the fury-breathing winds; so peerless was she amid that charging host. Clonie was there, Polemusa, Derinoe, Evandre, and Antandre, and Bremusa, Hippothoe, dark-eyed Harmothoe, Alcibie, Derimacheia, Antibrote and Thermodosa glorying with the spear. All these to battle fared with warrior-souled Penthesileia: even as when descends Dawn from Olympus's crest of adamant, Dawn, heart-exultant in her radiant steeds amidst the bright-haired Hours; and over them all, how flawless-fair soever these may be, her splendour of beauty glows preeminent; so peerless amid all the Amazons unto Troy-town Penthesileia came. To right, to left, from all sides hurrying thronged the Trojans, greatly marvelling, when they saw the tireless war-god's child, the mailed maid, like to the Blessed Gods; for in her face glowed beauty glorious and terrible. Her smile was ravishing: beneath her brows, her love-enkindling eyes shone like to stars, and with the crimson rose of shamefastness bright were her cheeks, and mantled over them unearthly grace with battle-prowess clad.

Then joyed Troy's folk, despite past agonies, as when, far-gazing from a height, the hinds behold a rainbow spanning the wide sea, when they be yearning for the heaven-sent shower, when the parched fields be craving for the rain; then the great sky at last is overgloomed, and men see that fair sign of coming wind and imminent rain, and seeing, they are glad, who for their cornfields' plight sore sighed before; even so the sons of Troy when they beheld there in their land Penthesileia dread afire for battle, were exceeding glad; for when the heart is thrilled with hope of good, all smart of evils past is wiped away. So, after all his sighing and his pain, gladdened a little while was Priam's soul. As when a man who hath suffered many a pang from blinded eyes, sore longing to behold the light, and, if he may not, fain would die, then at the last, by a cunning leech's skill, or by a god's grace, sees the dawn-rose flush, sees the mist rolled back from before his eyes, – yea, though clear vision come not as of old, yet, after all his anguish, joys to have some small relief, albeit the stings of pain prick sharply yet beneath his eyelids; – so joyed the old king to see that terrible queen – the shadowy joy of one in anguish whelmed for slain sons. Into his halls he led the Maid, and with glad welcome honoured her, as one who greets a daughter to her home returned from a far country in the 20th year; and set a feast before her, sumptuous as battle-glorious kings, who have brought low nations of foes, array in splendour of pomp, with hearts in pride of victory triumphing. And gifts he gave her costly and fair to see, and pledged him to give many more, so she would save the Trojans from the imminent doom. And she such deeds she promised as no man had hoped for, even to lay Achilles low, to smite the wide host of the Argive men, and cast the brands red-flaming on the ships. Ah fool! – but little knew she him, the lord of ashen spears, how far Achilles' might in warrior-wasting strife overpassed her own!

But when Andromache, the stately child of king Eetion, heard the wild queen's vaunt, low to her own soul bitterly murmured she: "Ah hapless! why with arrogant heart dost thou speak such great swelling words? No strength is thine to grapple in fight with Peleus' aweless son. Nay, doom and swift death shall he deal to thee. Alas for thee! What madness thrills thy soul? Fate and the end of death stand hard by thee! Hector was mightier far to wield the spear than thou, yet was for all his prowess slain, slain for the bitter grief of Troy, whose folk the city through looked on him as a god. My glory and his noble parents' glory was he while yet he lived – O that the earth over my dead face had been mounded high, or ever through his throat the breath of life followed the cleaving spear! But now have I looked – woe is me! – on grief unutterable, when round the city those fleet-footed steeds haled him, steeds of Achilles, who had made me widowed of mine hero-husband, made my portion bitterness through all my days." So spake Eetion's lovely-ankled child low to her own soul, thinking on her lord. So evermore the faithful-hearted wife nurseth for her lost love undying grief.

Then in swift revolution sweeping round into the ocean's deep stream sank the sun, and daylight died. So when the banqueters ceased from the wine-cup and the goodly feast, then did the handmaids spread in Priam's halls for Penthesileia dauntless-souled the couch heart-cheering, and she laid her down to rest; and slumber mist-like overveiled her eyes depths like sweet dew dropping round. From heavens' blue slid down the might of a deceitful dream at Pallas's hest, that so the warrior-maid might see it, and become a curse to Troy and to herself, when strained her soul to meet;

the whirlwind of the battle. In this wise the Trito-born, the subtle-souled, contrived: Stood over the maiden's head that baleful dream in likeness of her father, kindling her fearlessly front to front to meet in fight fleet-footed Achilles. And she heard the voice, and all her heart exulted, for she imagined that she should on that dawning day achieve a mighty deed in battle's deadly toil. Ah, fool, who trusted for her sorrow a dream out of the sunless land, such as beguiles full oft the travail-burdened tribes of men, whispering mocking lies in sleeping ears, and to the battle's travail lured her then!

But when the Dawn, the rosy-ankled, leapt up from her bed, then, clad in mighty strength of spirit, suddenly from her couch uprose Penthesileia. Then did she array her shoulders in those wondrous-fashioned arms given her of the war-god. First she laid beneath her silver-gleaming knees the greaves fashioned of gold, close-clipping the strong limbs. Her rainbow-radiant corslet clasped she then about her, and around her shoulders slung, with glory in her heart, the massy brand whose shining length was in a scabbard sheathed of ivory and silver. Next, her shield unearthly splendid, caught she up, whose rim swelled like the young moon's arching chariot-rail when high over ocean's fathomless-flowing stream she rises, with the space half filled with light betwixt her bowing horns. So did it shine unutterably fair. Then on her head she settled the bright helmet overstreamed with a wild mane of golden-glistering hairs. So stood she, lapped about with flaming mail, in semblance like the lightning, which the might, the never-wearied might of Zeus, to earth hurleth, what time he showeth forth to men fury of thunderous-roaring rain, or swoop resistless of his shouting host of winds. Then in hot haste forth of her bower to pass caught she two javelins in the hand that grasped her shield-band; but her strong right hand laid hold on a huge halberd, sharp of either blade, which terrible Eris gave to Ares' child to be her Titan weapon in the strife that raveneth souls of men. Laughing for glee thereover, swiftly flashed she forth the ring of towers. Her coming kindled all the sons of Troy to rush into the battle forth which crowneth men with glory. Swiftly all hearkened her gathering, and thronging came, champions, yea, even such as theretofore shrank back from standing in the ranks of war against Achilles the all-ravager. But she in pride of triumph on she rode throned on a goodly steed and fleet, the gift of Oreithyia, the wild North-wind's bride, given to her guest the warrior-maid, what time she came to Thrace, a steed whose flying feet could match the Harpies' wings. Riding thereon Penthesileia in her goodness left the tall palaces of Troy behind. And ever were the ghastly-visaged Fates thrusting her on into the battle, doomed to be her first against the Greeks – and last! To right, to left, with unreturning feet the Trojan thousands followed to the fray, the pitiless fray, that death-doomed warrior-maid, followed in throngs, as follow sheep the ram that by the shepherd's art strides before all. So followed they, with battle-fury filled, strong Trojans and wild-hearted Amazons. And like Tritonis seemed she, as she went to meet the giants, or as flasheth far through war-hosts Eris, waker of onset-shouts. So mighty in the Trojans' midst she seemed, Penthesileia of the flying feet.

Then unto Cronos's son Laomedon's child upraised his hands, his sorrow-burdened hands, turning him toward the sky-encountering fane of Zeus of Ida, who with sleepless eyes looks ever down on Ilium; and he prayed: "Father, give ear! Vouchsafe that on this day Achaea's host may fall before the hands of this our warrior-queen, the war-god's child; and do thou bring her back unscathed again unto mine halls: we pray thee by the love thou bear'st to Ares of the fiery heart thy son, yea, to her also! is she not most wondrous like the heavenly goddesses? And is she not the child of thine own seed? Pity my stricken heart withal! Thou know'st all agonies I have suffered in the deaths of dear sons whom the Fates have torn from me by Argive hands in the devouring fight. Compassionate us, while a remnant yet remains of noble Dardanus's blood, while yet this city stands unwasted! Let us know from ghastly slaughter and strife one breathing space!"

In passionate prayer he spake: – lo, with shrill scream swiftly to left an eagle darted by and in his talons bare a gasping dove. Then round the heart of Priam all the blood was chilled with fear. Low to his soul he said: "Never shall I see return alive from war Penthesileia!" On that self-same day the Fates prepared his boding to fulfil; and his heart brake with anguish of despair.

Marvelled the Argives, far across the plain seeing the hosts of Troy charge down on them, and midst them Penthesileia, Ares' child. These seemed like ravening beasts that mid the hills bring grimly slaughter to the fleecy flocks; and she, as a rushing blast of flame she seemed that maddeneth through the corpses summer-scorched, when the wind drives it on; and in this wise spake one to other in their mustering host: "Who shall this be who thus can rouse to war the Trojans, now that Hector hath been slain – these who, we said, would never more find heart to stand against us? Lo now, suddenly forth are they rushing, madly afire for fight! Sure, in their midst some great one kindleth them to battle's toil! Thou verily wouldst say this were a god, of such great deeds he dreams! Go to, with aweless courage let us arm our own breasts: let us summon up our might in battle-fury. We shall lack not help of Gods this day to close in fight with Troy."

So cried they; and their flashing battle-gear cast they about them: forth the ships they poured clad in the rage of fight as with a cloak. Then front to front their battles closed, like ravenous beasts, locked in tangle of gory strife. Clanged their bright mail together, clashed the spears, the corslets and the stubborn-welded shields and adamant helms. Each stabbed at other's flesh with the fierce brass: was neither ruth nor rest, and all the Trojan soil was crimson red.

Then first Penthesileia smote and slew Molion; now Persinous falls, and now Eilissus; reeled Antitheus beneath her spear the pride of Lernus quelled she: down she bore Hippalmus beneath her horse hoofs; Haemon's son died; withered stalwart Elasippus's strength. And Derinoe laid low Laogonus, and Clonie Menippus, him who sailed long since from Phylace, led by his lord Protesilaus to the war with Troy. Then was Podarces, son of Iphiclus, heart-wrung with grief and wrath to see him lie dead, of all battle comrades best-beloved. Swiftly at Clonie he hurled, the maid fair as a goddess: plunged the unswerving lance 'twixt hip and hip, and rushed the dark blood forth after the spear, and all her bowels gushed out. Then wroth was Penthesileia; through the brawn of his right arm she drove the long spear's point, she shore atwain the great blood-brimming veins, and through the wide gash of the wound the gore spirted, a crimson fountain. With a groan backward he sprang, his courage wholly quelled by bitter pain; and sorrow and dismay thrilled, as he fled, his men of Phylace. A short way from the fight he reeled aside, and in his friends' arms died in little space.

Then with his lance Idomeneus thrust out, and by the right breast stabbed Bremusa. Stilled for ever was the beating of her heart. She fell, as falls a graceful-shafted pine hewn mid the hills by woodmen: heavily, sighing through all its boughs, it crashes down. So with a wailing shriek she fell, and death unstrung her every limb: her breathing soul mingled with multitudinous-sighing winds. Then, as Evandre through the murderous fray with Thermodosa rushed, stood Meriones, a lion in the path, and slew: his spear right to the heart of one he drave, and one stabbed with a lightning sword-thrust 'twixt the hips: leapt through the wounds the life, and fled away. Oileus's fiery son smote Derinoe 'twixt throat and shoulder with his ruthless spear; and on Alcibie Tydeus's terrible son swooped, and on Derimacheia: head with neck clean from the shoulders of these twain he shore with ruin-wreaking brand. Together down fell they, as young calves by the massy axe of brawny flesher felled, that, shearing through the sinews of the neck, lops life away. So, by the hands of Tydeus's son laid low upon the Trojan plain, far, far away from their own highland home, they fell.

Nor these alone died; for the might of Sthenelus down on them hurled Cabeirus's corpse, who came from Sestos, keen to fight the Argive foe, but never saw his fatherland again. Then was the heart of Paris filled with wrath for a friend slain. Full upon Sthenelus aimed he a shaft death-winged, yet touched him not, despite his thirst for vengeance: otherwhere the arrow glanced aside, and carried death whither the stern Fates guided its fierce wing, and slew Evenor brazen-tasleted, who from Dulichium came to war with Troy. For his death fury-kindled was the son of haughty Phyleus: as a lion leaps upon the flock, so swiftly rushed he: all shrank huddling back before that terrible man. Itymoneus he slew, and Hippasus' son Agelaus: from Miletus brought they war against the Danaan men by Nastes led, the god-like, and Amphimachus mighty souled. On Mycale they dwelt; beside their home rose Latmus's snowy crests, stretched the long glens of Branchus, and Panormus's water-meads. Maeander's flood deep-rolling swept thereby, which from the Phrygian uplands, pastured over by myriad flocks, around a thousand forelands curls, swirls and drives his hurrying ripples on down to the vine-clad land of Carian men these mid the storm of battle Meges slew, nor these alone, but whomsoever his lance black-shafted touched, were dead men; for his breast the glorious Trito-born with courage thrilled to bring to all his foes the day of doom.

And Polypoetes, dear to Ares, slew Dresaeus, whom the nymph Neaera bare to passing-wise Theiodamas for these spread was the bed of love beside the foot of Sipylus the Mountain, where the gods made Niobe a stony rock, wherefrom tears ever stream: high up, the rugged crag bows as one weeping, weeping, waterfalls cry from far-echoing Hermus, wailing moan of sympathy: the sky-encountering crests of Sipylus, where always floats a mist hated of shepherds, echo back the cry. Weird marvel seems that Rock of Niobe to men that pass with feet fear-goaded: there they see the likeness of a woman bowed, in depths of anguish sobbing, and her tears drop, as she mourns grief-stricken, endlessly. Yea, thou wouldst say that verily so it was, viewing it from afar; but when hard by thou standest, all the illusion vanishes; and lo, a steep-browed rock, a fragment rent from Sipylus – yet Niobe is there, dreeing her weird, the debt of wrath divine, a broken heart in guise of shattered stone.

All through the tangle of that desperate fray stalked slaughter and doom. The incarnate Onset-shout raved through the rolling battle; at her side paced Death the ruthless, and the fearful Fates, beside them strode, and in red hands bare murder and the groans of dying men. That day the beating of full many a heart, Trojan and Argive, was forever stilled, while roared the battle round them, while the fury of Penthesileia fainted not nor failed; but as amid long ridges of lone hills a lioness, stealing down a deep ravine, springs on the cattle with lightning leap, athirst for blood wherein her fierce heart revelleth; so on the Danaans leapt that warrior-maid.

And they, their souls were cowed: backward they shrank, and fast she followed, as a towering surge chases across the thunder-booming sea a flying bark, whose white sails strain beneath the wind's wild buffering, and all the air maddens with roaring, as the rollers crash on a black foreland looming on the lee where long reefs fringe the surf-tormented shores. So chased she, and so dashed the ranks asunder triumphant-souled, and hurled fierce threats before: "Ye dogs, this day for evil outrage done to Priam shall ye pay! No man of you shall from mine hands deliver his own life, and win back home, to gladden parents' eyes, or comfort wife or children. Ye shall lie dead, ravaged on by vultures and by wolves, and none shall heap the earth-mound over your clay. Where skulketh now the strength of Tydeus's son, and where the might of Aeacus's scion? Where is Aias's bulk? Ye vaunt them mightiest men of all your rabble. Ha! they will not dare with me to close in battle, lest I drag forth from their fainting frames their craven souls!"

Then heart-uplifted leapt she on the foe, resistless as a tigress, crashing through ranks upon ranks of Argives, smiting now with that huge halberd massy-headed, now hurling the keen dart, while her battle horse flashed through the fight, and on his shoulder bare quiver and bow death-speeding, close to her hand, if mid that revel of blood she willed to speed the bitter-biting shaft. Behind her swept the charging lines of men fleet-footed, friends and brethren of the man who never flinched from close death grapple, Hector, panting all the hot breath of the war-god from their breasts, all slaying Danaans with the ashen spear, who fell as frost-touched leaves in autumn fall one after other, or as drops of rain. And aye went up a moaning from earth's breast all blood-bedrenched, and heaped with corpse on corpse. Horses pierced through with arrows, or impaled on spears, were snorting forth their last of strength with screaming neighings. Men, with gnashing teeth biting the dust, lay gasping, while the steeds of Trojan charioteers stormed in pursuit, trampling the dying mingled with the dead as oxen trample corn in threshing floors.

Then one exulting boasted mid the host of Troy, beholding Penthesileia rush on through the foes' array, like the black storm that maddens over the sea, what time the sun allies his might with winter's goat-horned star; and thus, puffed up with vain hope, shouted he: "O friends, in manifest presence down from heaven one of the deathless gods this day hath come to fight the Argives, all of love for us, yea, and with sanction of almighty Zeus, he whose compassion now remembereth haply strong-hearted Priam, who may boast for his a lineage of immortal blood. For this, I believe, no mortal woman seems, who is so aweless-daring, who is clad in splendour-flashing arms: nay, surely she shall be Athene, or the mighty-souled Enyo – haply Eris, or the Child of Leto world-renowned. O yea, I look to see her hurl amid yon Argive men mad-shrieking slaughter, see her set aflame yon ships wherein they came long years agone bringing us many sorrows, yea, they came bringing us woes of war intolerable. Ha! to the homeland Hellas never shall these with joy return, since Gods on our side fight."

In overweening exultation so vaunted a Trojan. Fool! – he had no vision of ruin onward rushing upon himself and Troy, and Penthesileia's self withal. For not as yet had any tidings come of that wild fray to Aias stormy-souled, nor to Achilles, waster of tower and town. But on the gravemound of Menoetius's son they both were lying, with sad memories of a dear comrade crushed, and echoing each one the other's groaning. One it was of the blest gods who still was holding back these from the battle-tumult far away, till many Greeks should fill the measure up of woeful havoc, slain by Trojan foes and glorious Penthesileia, who pursued with murderous intent their rifled ranks, while ever waxed her valour more and more, and waxed her might within her: never in vain she aimed the unswerving spear thrust: aye she pierced the backs of them that fled, the breasts of such as charged to meet her. All the long shaft dripped with steaming blood. Swift were her feet as wind as down she swooped. Her aweless spirit failed for weariness nor fainted, but her might was adamantine.

The impending doom, which roused unto the terrible strife not yet Achilles, clothed her still with glory; still aloof the dread power stood, and still would shed splendour of triumph over the death-ordained but for a little space, ere it should quell that maiden beneath the hands of Aeaeus's son. In darkness ambushed, with invisible hand ever it thrust her on, and drew her feet destruction-ward, and lit her path to death with glory, while she slew foe after foe. As when within a dewy garden-close, longing for its green springtide freshness, leaps a heifer, and there rangeth to and fro, when none is by to stay her, treading down all its green herbs, and all its wealth of bloom, devouring greedily this, and marring that with trampling feet; so ranged she, Ares' child, through reeling squadrons of Achaea's sons, slew these, and hunted those in panic rout.

From Troy afar the women marvelling gazed at the maid's battle-prowess. Suddenly a fiery passion for the fray hath seized Antimachus's daughter, Meneptolemus's wife, Tisiphone. Her heart waxed strong, and filled with lust of fight she cried to her fellows all, with desperate daring words, to spur them on to woeful war, by recklessness made strong. "Friends, let a heart of valour in our breasts awake! Let us be like our lords, who fight with foes for fatherland, for babes, for us, and never pause for breath in that stern strife! Let us too throne war's spirit in our hearts! Let us too face the fight which favoureth none! For we, we women, be not creatures cast in diverse mould from men: to us is given such energy of life as stirs in them. Eyes have we like to theirs, and limbs: throughout fashioned we are alike: one common light we look on, and one common air we breathe: with like food are we nourished – nay, wherein have we been dowered of God more niggardly than men? Then let us shrink not from the fray see ye not yonder a woman far excelling men in the grapple of fight?

"Yet is her blood nowise akin to ours, nor fighteth she for her own city. For an alien king she warreth of her own heart's prompting, fears the face of no man; for her soul is thrilled with valour and with spirit invincible. But we – to right, to left, lie woes on woes about our feet: this mourns beloved sons, and that a husband who for hearth and home hath died; some wail for fathers now no more; some grieve for brethren and for kinsmen lost. Not one but hath some share in sorrow's cup. Behind all this a fearful shadow looms, the day of bondage! Therefore flinch not ye from war, O sorrow-laden! Better far to die in battle now, than afterwards hence to be hauled into captivity to alien folk, we and our little ones, in the stern grip of fate leaving behind a burning city, and our husbands' graves."

So cried she, and with passion for stern war thrilled all those women; and with eager speed they hasted to go forth without the wall mail-clad, afire to battle for their town and people: all their spirit was aflame. As when within a hive, when winter-tide is over and gone, loud hum the swarming bees what time they make them ready forth to fare to bright flower pastures, and no more endure to linger there within, but each to other crieth the challenge-cry to sally forth; even so bestirred themselves the women of Troy, and kindled each her sister to the fray. The weaving wool, the distaff far they flung, and to grim weapons stretched their eager hands.

And now without the city these had died in that wild battle, as their husbands died and the strong Amazons died, had not one voice of wisdom cried to stay their maddened feet, when with dissuading words Theano spake: "Wherefore, ah wherefore for the toil and strain of battle's fearful tumult do ye yearn, infatuate ones? Never your limbs have toiled in conflict yet. In utter ignorance panting for labour unendurable, ye rush on all-unthinking; for your strength can never be as that of Danaan men, men trained in daily battle. Amazons have joyed in ruthless fight, in charging steeds, from the beginning: all the toil of men do they endure; and therefore evermore the spirit of the war-god thrills them through. They fall not short of men in anything: their labour-hardened frames make great their hearts for all achievement: never faint their knees nor tremble. Rumour speaks their queen to be a daughter of the mighty Lord of War. Therefore no woman may compare with her in prowess – if she be a woman, not a god come down in answer to our prayers. Yea, of one blood be all the race of men, yet unto diverse labours still they turn; and that for each is evermore the best whereto he bringeth skill of use and wont. Therefore do ye from tumult of the fray hold you aloof, and in your women's bowers before the loom still pace ye to and fro; and war shall be the business of our lords. Lo, of fair issue is there hope: we see the Achaeans falling fast: we see the might of our men waxing ever: fear is none of evil issue now: the pitiless foe beleaguer not the town: no desperate need there is that women should go forth to war."

So cried she, and they hearkened to the words of her who had garnered wisdom from the years; so from afar they watched the fight. But still Penthesileia brake the ranks, and still before her quailed the Achaeans: still they found nor screen nor hiding place from imminent death. As bleating goats are by the blood-stained jaws of a grim panther torn, so slain were they. In each man's heart all lust of battle died, and fear alone lived. This way, that way fled the panic-stricken: some to earth had flung the armour from their shoulders; some in dust grovelled in terror beneath their shields: the steeds fled through the rout unreined of charioteers. In rapture of triumph charged the Amazons, with groan and scream of agony died the Greeks. Withered their manhood was in that sore strait; brief was the span of all whom that fierce maid mid the grim jaws of battle overtook. As when with mighty roaring bursteth down a storm upon the forest trees, and some uprendeth by the roots, and on the earth dashes them down, the tail stems blossom-crowned, and snappeth some athwart the trunk, and high whirls them through air, till all confused they lie a ruin of splintered stems and shattered sprays; so the great Danaan host lay, dashed to dust by doom of Fate, by Penthesileia's spear.

But when the very ships were now at point to be by hands of Trojans set aflame, then battle-bider Aias heard afar the panic-cries, and spake to Aeacus's son: "Achilles, all the air about mine ears is full of multitudinous cries, is full of thunder of battle rolling nearer aye. Let us go forth then, ere the Trojans win unto the ships, and make great slaughter there of Argive men, and set the ships aflame. Foulest reproach such thing on thee and me should bring; for it beseems not that the seed of mighty Zeus should shame the sacred blood of hero-fathers, who themselves of old with Hercules the battle-eager sailed to Troy, and smote her even at her height of glory, when Laomedon was king. Ay, and I think that our hands even now shall do the like: we too are mighty men."

He spake: the aweless strength of Aeacus's son hearkened thereto, for also to his ears by this the roar of bitter battle came. Then hasted both, and donned their warrior-gear all splendour-gleaming: now, in these arrayed facing that stormy tossing rout they stand. Loud clashed their glorious armour: in their souls a battle fury like the war-god's wrath maddened; such might was breathed into these twain by Atrytone, Shaker of the Shield, as on they pressed. With joy the Argives saw the coming of that mighty twain: they seemed in semblance like Aloeus's giant sons who in the old time made that haughty vaunt of piling on Olympus's brow the height of Ossa steeply-towering, and the crest of sky encountering Pelion, so to rear a mountain stair for their rebellious rage to scale the highest heaven. Huge as these the sons of Aeacus seemed, as forth they strode to stem the tide of war. A gladsome sight to friends who have fainted for their coming, now onward they press to crush triumphant foes. Many they slew with their resistless spears; as when two herd-destroying lions come on sheep amid the corpses feeding, far from help of shepherds, and in heaps on heaps slay them, till they have drunken to the full of blood, and filled their maws insatiate with flesh, so those destroyers twain slew on, spreading wide havoc through the hosts of Troy.

There Deiochus and gallant Hyllus fell by Alas slain, and fell Eurynomus lover of war, and goodly Enyeus died. But Peleus's son burst on the Amazons smiting Antandre, Polemusa then, Antibrote, fierce-souled Hippothoe, hurling Harmothoe down on sisters slain. Then hard on all their reeling ranks he pressed with Telamon's mighty hearted son; and now before their hands battalions dense and strong crumbled as weakly and as suddenly as when in mountain folds the forest brakes shrivel before a tempest-driven fire.

When battle-eager Penthesileia saw these twain, as through the scourging storm of war like ravening beasts they rushed, to meet them there she sped, as when a leopard grim, whose mood is deadly, leaps from forest-coverts forth, lashing her tail, on hunters closing round, while these, in armour clad, and putting trust in their long spears, await her lightning leap; so did those warriors twain with spears upswung wait Penthesileia. Clanged the brazen.

plates about their shoulders as they moved. And first leapt the long-shafted lance sped from the hand of goodly Penthesileia. Straight it flew to the shield of Aeacus's son, but glancing thence this way and that the shivered fragments sprang as from a rock-face: of such temper were the cunning-hearted Fire-god's gifts divine. Then in her hand the warrior-maid swung up a second javelin fury-winged, against Aias, and with fierce words defied the two: "Ha, from mine hand in vain one lance hath leapt! But with this second look I suddenly to quell the strength and courage of two foes, – ay, though ye vaunt you mighty men of war amid your Danaans! Die ye shall, and so lighter shall be the load of war's affliction that lies upon the Trojan chariot-lords. Draw nigh, come through the press to grips with me, so shall ye learn what might wells up in breasts of Amazons. With my blood is mingled war! No mortal man begat me, but the Lord of War, insatiate of the battle cry. Therefore my might is more than any man's."

With scornful laughter spake she: then she hurled her second lance; but they in utter scorn laughed now, as swiftly flew the shaft, and smote the silver greave of Aias, and was foiled thereby, and all its fury could not scar the flesh within; for fate had ordered not that any blade of foes should taste the blood of Aias in the bitter war. But he recked of the Amazon naught, but turned him thence to rush upon the Trojan host, and left Penthesileia unto Peleus's son alone, for well he knew his heart within that she, for all her prowess, none the less would cost Achilles battle-toil as light, as effortless, as doth the dove the hawk.

Then groaned she an angry groan that she had sped her shafts in vain; and now with scoffing speech to her in turn the son of Peleus spake: "Woman, with what vain vauntings triumphing hast thou come forth against us, all athirst to battle with us, who be mightier far than earthborn heroes? We from Cronos' son, the thunder-roller, boast our high descent. Ay, even Hector quailed, the battle-swift, before us, even though far away he saw our onrush to grim battle. Yea, my spear slew him, for all his might. But thou – thine heart is utterly mad, that thou hast greatly dared to threaten us with death this day! On thee thy latest hour shall swiftly come – is come! Thee not thy sire the war-god now shall pluck out of mine hand; but thou the debt shalt pay of a dark doom, as when mid mountain-folds a buck meets a lion, waster of herds. What, woman, hast thou heard not of the heaps of slain, that into Xanthus' rushing stream were thrust by these mine hands? – or hast thou heard in vain, because the Blessed Ones have stolen wit and discretion from thee, to the end that doom's relentless gulf might gape for thee?"

He spake; he swung up in his mighty hand and sped the long spear warrior-slaying, wrought by Chiron, and above the right breast pierced the battle-eager maid. The red blood leapt forth, as a fountain wells, and all at once fainted the strength of Penthesileia's limbs; dropped the great battle axe from her nerveless hand; a mist of darkness overveiled her eyes, and anguish thrilled her soul. Yet even so still drew she difficult breath, still dimly saw the hero, even now in act to drag her from the swift steed's back. Confusedly she thought: "Or shall I draw my mighty sword, and bide Achilles' fiery onrush, or hastily cast me from my fleet horse down to earth, and kneel unto this godlike man, and with wild breath promise for ransoming great heaps of brass and gold, which pacify the hearts of victors never so athirst for blood, if haply so the murderous might of Aeacus's son may hearken and may spare, or peradventure may compassionate my youth, and so vouchsafe me to behold mine home again? – for O, I long to live!"

So surged the wild thoughts in her; but the gods ordained it otherwise. Even now rushed on in terrible anger Peleus' son: he thrust with sudden spear, and on its shaft impaled the body of her tempest-footed steed, even as a man in haste to sup might pierce flesh with the spit, above the glowing hearth to roast it, or as in a mountain-glade a hunter sends the shaft of death clear through the body of a stag with such winged speed that the fierce dart leaps forth beyond, to plunge into the tall stem of an oak or pine. So that death-ravening spear of Peleus's son clear through the goodly steed rushed on, and pierced Penthesileia. Straightway fell she down into the dust of earth, the arms of death, in grace and comeliness fell, for naught of shame dishonoured her fair form. Face down she lay on the long spear gasping her last breath, stretched upon that fleet horse as on a couch; like some tall pine snapped by the icy mace of Boreas, earth's forest-fosterling reared by a spring to stately height, amidst long mountain glens, a glory of mother earth; so from the once fleet steed low fallen lay Penthesileia, all her shattered strength brought down to this, and all her loveliness.

Now when the Trojans saw the warrior queen struck down in battle, ran through all their lines a shiver of panic. Straightway to their walls turned they in flight, heart-agonized with grief. As when on the wide sea, beneath buffetings of storm blasts, castaways whose ship is wrecked escape, a remnant of a crew, forspent with desperate conflict with the cruel sea: late and at last appears the land hard by, appears a city: faint and weary limbed with that grim struggle, through the surf they strain to land, sore grieving for the good ship lost, and shipmates whom the terrible surge dragged down to nether gloom; so, Troyward as they fled from battle, all those Trojans wept for her, the child of the resistless war-god, wept for friends who died in groan-resounding fight.

Then over her with scornful laugh the son of Peleus vaunted: "In the dust lie there a prey to teeth of dogs, to ravens' beaks, thou wretched thing! Who cozened thee to come forth against me? And thoughtest thou to fare home from the war alive, to bear with thee right royal gifts from Priam the old king, thy guerdon for slain Argives? Ha, 'twas not the Immortals who inspired thee with this thought, who know that I of heroes mightiest am, the Danaans' light of safety, but a woe to Trojans and to thee, O evil-starred! Nay, but it was the darkness-shrouded Fates and thine own folly of soul that pricked thee on to leave the works of women, and to fare to war, from which strong men shrink shuddering back."

So spake he, and his ashen spear the son of Peleus drew from that swift horse, and from Penthesileia in death's agony. Then steed and rider gasped their lives away slain by one spear. Now from her head he plucked the helmet splendour-flashing like the beams of the great sun, or Zeus's own glory light. Then, there as fallen in dust and blood she lay, rose, like the breaking of the dawn, to view beneath dainty pencilled brows a lovely face, lovely in death. The Argives thronged around, and all they saw and marvelled, for she seemed like an Immortal. In her armour there upon the earth she lay, and seemed the Child of Zeus, the tireless Huntress Artemis sleeping, what time her feet forwearied are with following lions with her flying shafts over the hills far-stretching. She was made a wonder of beauty even in her death by Aphrodite glorious-crowned, the bride of the strong war-god, to the end that he, the son of noble Peleus, might be pierced with the sharp arrow of repentant love. The warriors gazed, and in their hearts they prayed that fair and sweet like her their wives might seem, laid on the bed of love, when home they won. Yea, and Achilles' very heart was wrung with love's remorse to have slain a thing so sweet, who might have borne her home, his queenly bride, to chariot-glorious Phthia; for she was flawless, a very daughter of the Gods, divinely tall, and most divinely fair.

Then Ares' heart was thrilled with grief and rage for his child slain. Straight from Olympus down he darted, swift and bright as thunderbolt terribly flashing from the mighty hand of Zeus, far leaping over the trackless sea, or flaming over the land, while shuddereth all wide Olympus as it passeth by. So through the quivering air with heart aflame swooped Ares armour-clad, soon as he heard the dread doom of his daughter. For the Gales, the north wind's fleet-winged daughters, bare to him, as through the wide halls of the sky he strode, the tidings of the maiden's woeful end. Soon as he heard it, like a tempest blast down to the ridges of Ida leapt he: quaked under his feet the long glens and ravines deep-scored, all Ida's torrent-beds, and all far-stretching foothills. Now had Ares brought a day of mourning on the Myrmidons, but Zeus himself from far Olympus sent mid shattering thunders terror of lightning bolts which thick and fast leapt through the sky down before his feet, blazing with fearful flames. And Ares saw, and knew the stormy threat of the mighty thundering Father, and he stayed his eager feet, now on the very brink of battle's turmoil. As when some huge crag thrust from a beetling cliff brow by the winds and torrent rains, or lightning-lance of Zeus, leaps like a wild beast, and the mountain glens fling back their crashing echoes as it rolls in mad speed on, as with resistless swoop of bound on bound it rushes down, until it cometh to the levels of the plain, and there perforce its stormy flight is stayed.

So Ares, battle-eager Son of Zeus, was stayed, how loth soever; for all the gods to the Ruler of the Blessed needs must yield, seeing he sits high-throned above them all, clothed in his might unspeakable. Yet still many a wild thought surged through Ares' soul, urging him now to dread the terrible threat of Cronos' wrathful son, and to return heavenward, and now to reck not of his sire, but with Achilles' blood to stain those hands, the battle-tireless. At the last his heart remembered how that many and many a son of Zeus himself in many a war had died, nor in their fall had Zeus availed them aught. Therefore he turned him from the Argives – else, down smitten by the blasting thunderbolt, with Titans in the nether gloom he had lain, who dared defy the eternal will of Zeus.

Then did the warrior sons of Argos strip with eager haste from corpses strown all round the blood-stained spoils. But ever Peleus's son gazed, wild with all regret, still gazed on her, the strong, the beautiful, laid in the dust; and all his heart was wrung, was broken down with sorrowing love, deep, strong as he had known when that beloved friend Patroclus died.

Loud jeered Thersites, mocking to his face: "Thou sorry-souled Achilles! art not shamed to let some evil power beguile thine heart to pity of a pitiful Amazon whose furious spirit purposed naught but ill to us and ours? Ha, woman-mad art thou, and thy soul lusts for this thing, as she were some lady wise in household ways, with gifts and pure intent for honoured wedlock wooed! Good had it been had her spear reached thine heart, the heart that sighs for woman creatures still! Thou carest not, unmanly souled, not thou, for valour's glorious path, when once thine eye lights on a woman! Sorry wretch, where now is all thy goodly prowess? where thy wit? And where the might that should beseem a king all-stainless? Dost not know what misery this self-same woman-madness wrought for Troy? Nothing there is to men more ruinous than lust for woman's beauty; it maketh fools of wise men. But the toil of war attains renown. To him that is a hero indeed glory of victory and the war-god's works are sweet. 'Tis but the battle-blencher craves the beauty and the bed of such as she!"

So railed he long and loud: the mighty heart of Peleus's son leapt into flame of wrath. A sudden buffet of his resistless hand smote beneath the railer's ear, and all his teeth were dashed to the earth: he fell upon his face: forth of his lips the blood in torrent gushed: swift from his body fled the dastard soul of that vile niddering. Achaea's sons rejoiced thereat, for aye he wont to rail on each and all with venomous gibes, himself a scandal and the shame of all the host. Then mid the warrior Argives cried a voice: "Not good it is for baser men to rail on kings, or secretly or openly; for wrathful retribution swiftly comes. The Lady of Justice sits on high; and she who heapeth woe on woe on humankind, even Ate, punisheth the shameless tongue."

So mid the Danaans cried a voice: nor yet within the mighty soul of Peleus's son lulled was the storm of wrath, but fiercely he spake: "Lie there in dust, thy follies all forgot! 'Tis not for knaves to beard their betters: once thou didst provoke Odysseus's steadfast soul, babbling with venomous tongue a thousand gibes, and didst escape with life; but thou hast found the son of Peleus not so patient-souled, who with one only buffet from his hand unkennels thy dog's soul! A bitter doom hath swallowed thee: by thine own rascalry thy life is sped. Hence from Achaean men, and mouth out thy revilings midst the dead!"

So spake the valiant-hearted aweless son of Aeacus. But Tydeus's son alone of all the Argives was with anger stirred against Achilles for Thersites slain, seeing these two were of the self-same blood, the one, proud Tydeus's battle-eager son, the other, seed of godlike Agrius: brother of noble Oeneus Agrius was; and Oeneus in the Danaan land begat Tydeus the battle-eager, son to whom was stalwart Diomedes. Therefore wroth was he for slain Thersites, yea, had raised against the son of Peleus vengeful hands, except the noblest of Aehaea's sons had thronged around him, and besought him sore, and held him back therefrom. With Peleus's son also they pleaded; else those mighty two, the mightiest of all Argives, were at point to close with clash of swords, so stung were they with bitter wrath; yet hearkened they at last to prayers of comrades, and were reconciled.

Then of their pity did the Atreid kings – for these too at the imperial loveliness of Penthesileia marvelled – render up her body to the men of Troy, to bear unto the burg of Ilus far-renowned with all her armour. For a herald came asking this boon for Priam; for the king longed with deep yearning of the heart to lay that battle-eager maiden, with her arms, and with her war horse, in the great earth mound of old Laomedon. And so he heaped a high broad pyre without the city wall: upon the height thereof that warrior queen they laid, and costly treasures did they heap around her, all that well beseems to burn around a mighty queen in battle slain. And so the fire-god's swift-upleaping might, the ravening flame, consumed her. All around the people stood on every hand, and quenched the pyre with odorous wine. Then gathered they the bones, and poured sweet ointment over them, and laid them in a casket: over all shed they the rich fat of a heifer, chief among the herds that grazed on Ida's slope. And, as for a beloved daughter, rang all round the Trojan men's heart-stricken wail, as by the stately wall they buried her on an outstanding tower, beside the bones of old Laomedon, a queen beside a king. This honour for the war-god's sake they rendered, and for Penthesileia's own. And in the plain beside her buried they the Amazons, even all that followed her to battle, and by Argive spears were slain. For

Atreus's sons begrudged not these the boon of tear-besprinkled graves, but let their friends, the warrior Trojans, draw their corpses forth, yea, and their own slain also, from amidst the swath of darts over that grim harvest field. Wrath strikes not at the dead: pitied are foes when life has fled, and left them foes no more.

Far off across the plain the while uprose smoke from the pyres whereon the Argives laid the many heroes overthrown and slain by Trojan hands what time the sword devoured; and multitudinous lamentation wailed over the perished. But above the rest mourned they over brave Podarces, who in fight was no less mighty than his hero brother Protesilaus, he who long ago fell, slain of Hector: so Podarces now, struck down by Penthesileia's spear, hath cast over all Argive hearts the pall of grief. Wherefore apart from him they laid in clay the common throng of slain; but over him toiling they heaped an earth mound far-descried in memory of a warrior aweless-souled. And in a several pit withal they thrust the niddering Thersites' wretched corpse. Then to the ships, acclaiming Aeacus's son, returned they all. But when the radiant day had plunged beneath the ocean stream, and night, the holy, overspread the face of earth, then in the rich king Agamemnon's tent feasted the might of Peleus's son, and there sat at the feast those other mighty ones all through the dark, till rose the dawn divine.

Book III

WHEN SHONE THE LIGHT of dawn the splendour-throned, then to the ships the Pylian spearmen bore Antilochus's corpse, sore sighing for their prince, and by the Hellespont they buried him with aching hearts. Around him groaning stood the battle-eager sons of Argives, all, of love for Nestor, shrouded over with grief. But that grey hero's heart was nowise crushed by sorrow; for the wise man's soul endures bravely, and cowers not under affliction's stroke. But Peleus's son, wroth for Antilochus his dear friend, armed for vengeance terrible upon the Trojans. Yea, and these withal, despite their dread of mighty Achilles' spear, poured battle-eager forth their gates, for now the Fates with

courage filled their breasts, of whom many were doomed to Hades to descend, whence there is no return, thrust down by hands of Aeacus's son, who also was foredoomed to perish that same day by Priam's wall. Swift met the fronts of conflict: all the tribes of Troy's host, and the battle-biding Greeks, afire with that new-kindled fury of war.

Then through the foe the son of Peleus made wide havoc: all around the earth was drenched with gore, and choked with corpses were the streams of Simois and Xanthus. Still he chased, still slaughtered, even to the city's walls; for panic fell on all the host. And now all had he slain, had dashed the gates to earth, rending them from their hinges, or the bolts, hurling himself against them, had he snapped, and for the Danaans into Priam's burg had made a way, had utterly destroyed that goodly town – but now was Phoebus wroth against him with grim fury, when he saw those countless troops of heroes slain of him. Down from Olympus with a lion-leap he came: his quiver on his shoulders lay, and shafts that deal the wounds incurable. Facing Achilles stood he; round him clashed quiver and arrows; blazed with quenchless flame his eyes, and shook the earth beneath his feet. Then with a terrible shout the great god cried, so to turn back from war Achilles awed by the voice divine, and save from death the Trojans: "Back from the Trojans, Peleus's son! Beseems not that longer thou deal death unto thy foes, lest an Olympian god abase thy pride."

But nothing quailed the hero at the voice immortal, for that round him even now hovered the unrelenting Fates. He cared naught of the god, and shouted his defiance. "Phoebus, why dost thou in mine own despite stir me to fight with gods, and wouldst protect the arrogant Trojans? Heretofore hast thou by thy beguiling turned me from the fray, when from destruction thou at the first didst save Hector, whereat the Trojans all through Troy exulted. Nay, thou get thee back: return unto the mansion of the blessed, lest I smite thee – ay, immortal though thou be!"

Then on the god he turned his back, and sped after the Trojans fleeing cityward, and harried still their flight; but wroth at heart thus Phoebus spake to his indignant soul: "Out on this man! he is sense-bereft! But now not Zeus himself nor any other Power shall save this madman who defies the gods!"

From mortal sight he vanished into cloud, and cloaked with mist a baleful shaft he shot which leapt to Achilles' ankle: sudden pangs with mortal sickness made his whole heart faint. He reeled, and like a tower he fell, that falls smit by a whirlwind when an earthquake cleaves a chasm for rushing blasts from underground; so fell the goodly form of Aeacus's son. He glared, a murderous glance, to right, to left, [upon the Trojans, and a terrible threat] shouted, a threat that could not be fulfilled: "Who shot at me a stealthy-smiting shaft? Let him but dare to meet me face to face! So shall his blood and all his bowels gush out about my spear, and he be hellward sped! I know that none can meet me man to man and quell in fight – of earth-born heroes none, though such an one should bear within his breast a heart unquailing, and have sinews of brass. But dastards still in stealthy ambush lurk for lives of heroes. Let him face me then! – ay! though he be a god whose anger burns against the Danaans! Yea, mine heart forebodes that this my smiter was Apollo, cloaked in deadly darkness. So in days gone by my mother told me how that by his shafts I was to die before the Scaean Gates a piteous death. Her words were not vain words."

Then with unflinching hands from out the wound incurable he drew the deadly shaft in agonized pain. Forth gushed the blood; his heart waxed faint beneath the shadow of coming doom. Then in indignant wrath he hurled from him the arrow: a sudden gust of wind swept by, and caught it up, and, even as he trod Zeus's threshold, to Apollo gave it back; for it beseemed not that a shaft divine, sped forth by an Immortal, should be lost. He unto high Olympus swiftly came, to the great gathering of immortal gods, where all assembled watched the war of men, these longing for the Trojans' triumph, those for Danaan victory; so with diverse wills watched they the strife, the slayers and the slain.

Him did the bride of Zeus behold, and straight upbraided with exceeding bitter words: "What deed of outrage, Phoebus, hast thou done this day, forgetful of that day whereon to godlike Peleus's marriage gathered all the Immortals? Yea, amidst the feasters thou sangest how Thetis silver-footed left the sea's abysses to be Peleus's bride; and as thou harpedst all earth's children came to hearken, beasts and birds, high craggy hills, rivers and all deep-shadowed forests came. All this hast thou forgotten, and hast wrought a ruthless deed, hast slain a godlike man, albeit thou with other gods didst pour the nectar, praying that he might be the son by Thetis given to Peleus. But that prayer hast thou forgotten, favouring the folk of tyrannous Laomedon, whose cattle thou keptest. He, a mortal, did despite to thee, the deathless! O, thou art wit-bereft! Thou favourest Troy, thy sufferings all forgot. Thou wretch, and doth thy false heart know not this, what man is an offence, and meriteth suffering, and who is honoured of the gods? Ever Achilles showed us reverence – yea, was of our race. Ha, but the punishment of Troy, I think, shall not be lighter, though Aeacus's son have fallen; for his son right soon shall come from Scyros to the war to help the Argive men, no less in might than was his sire, a bane to many a foe. But thou – thou for the Trojans dost not care, but for his valour envied Peleus's son, seeing he was the mightiest of all men. Thou fool! how wilt thou meet the Nereid's eyes, when she shall stand in Zeus's hall midst the gods, who praised thee once, and loved as her own son?"

So Hera spake, in bitterness of soul upbraiding, but he answered her not a word, of reverence for his mighty father's bride; nor could he lift his eyes to meet her eyes, but sat abashed, aloof from all the gods eternal, while in unforgiving wrath scowled on him all the Immortals who maintained the Danaans' cause; but such as fain would bring triumph to Troy, these with exultant hearts extolled him, hiding it from Hera's eyes, before whose wrath all Heaven-abiders shrank.

But Peleus's son the while forgot not yet war's fury: still in his invincible limbs the hot blood throbbed, and still he longed for fight. Was none of all the Trojans dared draw nigh the stricken hero, but at distance stood, as round a wounded lion hunters stand mid forest brakes afraid, and, though the shaft stands in his heart, yet faileth not in him his royal courage, but with terrible glare roll his fierce eyes, and roar his grimly jaws; so wrath and anguish of his deadly hurt to fury stung Peleides' soul; but aye his strength ebbed through the god-envenomed wound. Yet leapt he up, and rushed upon the foe, and flashed the lightning of his lance; it slew the goodly Orythaon, comrade stout of Hector, through his temples crashing clear: his helm stayed not the long lance fury-sped which leapt therethrough, and won within the bones the heart of the brain, and spilt his lusty life. Then stabbed he beneath the brow Hipponous even to the eye-roots, that the eyeball fell to earth: his soul to Hades flitted forth. Then through the jaw he pierced

Alcathous, and shore away his tongue: in dust he fell gasping his life out, and the spearhead shot out through his ear. These, as they rushed on him, that hero slew; but many a fleer's life he spilt, for in his heart still leapt the blood.

But when his limbs grew chill, and ebbed away his spirit, leaning on his spear he stood, while still the Trojans fled in huddled rout of panic, and he shouted unto them: "Trojan and Dardan cravens, ye shall not even in my death, escape my merciless spear, but unto mine avenging spirits ye shall pay – ay, one and all – destruction's debt!"

He spake; they heard and quailed: as mid the hills fawns tremble at a lion's deep-mouthed roar, and terror-stricken flee the monster, so the ranks of Trojan chariot-lords, the lines of battle-helpers drawn from alien lands, quailed at the last shout of Achilles, deemed that he was woundless yet. But beneath the weight of doom his aweless heart, his mighty limbs, at last were overborne. Down midst the dead he fell, as fails a beetling mountain-cliff. Earth rang beneath him: clanged with a thunder crash his arms, as Peleus's son the princely fell. And still his foes with most exceeding dread stared at him, even as, when some murderous beast lies slain by shepherds, tremble still the sheep eyeing him, as beside the fold he lies, and shrinking, as they pass him, far aloof and, even as he were living, fear him dead; so feared they him, Achilles now no more.

Yet Paris strove to kindle those faint hearts; for his own heart exulted, and he hoped, now Peleus's son, the Danaans' strength, had fallen, wholly to quench the Argive battle-fire: "Friends, if ye help me truly and loyally, let us this day die, slain by Argive men, or live, and hale to Troy with Hector's steeds in triumph Peleus's son thus fallen dead, the steeds that, grieving, yearning for their lord to fight have borne me since my brother died. Might we with these but hale Achilles slain, glory were this for Hector's horses, yea, for Hector – if in Hades men have sense of righteous retribution. This man aye devised but mischief for the sons of Troy; and now Troy's daughters with exultant hearts from all the city streets shall gather round, as pantheresses wroth for stolen cubs, or lionesses might stand around a man whose craft in hunting vexed them while he lived. So round Achilles – a dead corpse at last! – in hurrying throngs Troy's daughters then shall come in unforgiving, unforgetting hate, for parents wroth, for husbands slain, for sons, for noble kinsmen. Most of all shall joy my father, and the ancient men, whose feet unwillingly are chained within the walls by old age, if we shall hale him through our gates, and give our foe to fowls of the air for meat."

Then they, which feared him theretofore, in haste closed round the corpse of strong-heart Aeacus's son, Glaucus, Aeneas, battle-fain Agenor and other cunning men in deadly fight, eager to haul him thence to Ilium the god-built burg. But Aias failed him not. Swiftly that godlike man bestrode the dead: back from the corpse his long lance thrust them all. Yet ceased they not from onslaught; thronging round, still with swift rushes fought they for the prize, one following other, like to long-lipped bees which hover round their hive in swarms on swarms to drive a man thence; but he, recking naught of all their fury, carveth out the combs of nectareous honey: harassed sore are they by smoke-reek and the robber; spite of all ever they dart against him; naught cares he; so naught of all their onsets Aias cared; but first he stabbed Agelaus in the breast, and slew that son of Maion: Thestor next: Ocythous he smote, Agestratus, Aganippus, Zorus, Nessus, Erymas the war-renowned, who came from Lycia-land with mighty hearted Glaucus, from his home in Melanippion on the mountain ridge, Athena's temple, which Massikyton fronts anigh Chelidonia's headland, dreaded sore of scared seafarers, when its lowering crags must needs be doubled. For his death the blood of famed Hippolochus's son was horror-chilled; for this was his dear friend. With one swift thrust he pierced the sevenfold hides of Aias's shield, yet touched his flesh not; stayed the spearhead was by those thick hides and by the corset plate which lapped his battle-tireless limbs. But still from that stern conflict Glaucus drew not back, burning to vanquish Aias, Aeacus's son, and in his folly vaunting threatened him: "Aias, men name thee mightiest man of all the Argives, hold thee in passing-high esteem even as Achilles: therefore thou, I wot, by that dead warrior dead this day shalt lie!"

So hurled he forth a vain word, knowing not how far in might above him was the man whom his spear threatened. Battle-bider Aias darkly and scornfully glaring on him, said "Thou craven wretch, and knowest thou not this, how much was Hector mightier than thou in warcraft? yet before my might, my spear, he shrank. Ay, with his valour was there blent discretion. Thou thy thoughts are deathward set, who dares defy me to the battle, me, a mightier far than thou! Thou canst not say that friendship of our fathers thee shall screen; nor me thy gifts shall wile to let thee pass scatheless from war, as once did Tydeus's son. Though thou didst escape his fury, will not I suffer thee to return alive from war. Ha, in thy many helpers dost thou trust who with thee, like so many worthless flies, flit round the noble Achilles' corpse? To these death and black doom shall my swift onset deal."

Then on the Trojans this way and that he turned, as mid long forest glens a lion turns on hounds, and Trojans many and Lycians slew that came for honour hungry, till he stood mid a wide ring of flinchers; like a shoal of darting fish when sails into their midst dolphin or shark, a huge sea-fosterling; so shrank they from the might of Telamon's son, as aye he charged amidst the rout. But still swarmed fighters up, till round Achilles' corpse to right, to left, lay in the dust the slain countless, as boars around a lion at bay; and evermore the strife waxed deadlier. Then too Hippolochus's war-wise son was slain by Aias of the heart of fire. He fell backward upon Achilles, even as falls a sapling on a sturdy mountain oak; so quelled by the spear on Peleus's son he fell. But for his rescue Anchises' stalwart son strove hard, with all his comrades battle-fain, and haled the corpse forth, and to sorrowing friends gave it, to bear to Ilium's hallowed burg. Himself to spoil Achilles still fought on, till warrior Aias pierced him with the spear through the right forearm. Swiftly leapt he back from murderous war, and hasted thence to Troy. There for his healing cunning leeches wrought, who stanched the blood-rush, and laid on the gash balms, such as salve war-stricken warriors' pangs.

But Aias still fought on: here, there he slew with thrusts like lightning flashes. His great heart ached sorely for his mighty cousin slain. And now the warrior-king Laertes' son fought at his side: before him blenched the foe, as he smote down Peisander's fleet-footed son, the warrior Maenalus, who left his home in far-renowned Abydos: down on him he hurled Atymnius, the goodly son whom Pegasis the bright-haired nymph had borne to strong Emathion by Granicus's stream. Dead by his side he laid Orestius's son, Proteus, who dwelt beneath lofty Ida's folds. Ah, never did his mother welcome home that son from war, Panaceia beauty-famed! He fell by Odysseus's hands, who spilt the lives of many more whom his death-hungering spear reached in that fight around the mighty dead. Yet Alcon, son of Megacles battle-swift, hard by Odysseus's right knee drove the spear home, and about the glittering greave the blood dark-crimson welled. He recked not of the wound, but was unto his smiter sudden death; for clear through his shield he stabbed him with his spear amidst his battle fury: to the earth backward he dashed him by his giant might and strength of hand: clashed round him in the dust his armour, and his corslet was distained with crimson lifeblood.

Forth from flesh and shield the hero plucked the spear of death: the soul followed the lance head from the body forth, and life forsook its mortal mansion. Then rushed on his comrades, in his wound's despite, Odysseus, nor from that stern battle-toil refrained him. And by this a mingled host of Danaans eager-hearted fought around the mighty dead, and many and many a foe slew they with those smooth-shafted ashen spears. Even as the winds strew down upon the ground the flying leaves, when through the forest glades sweep the wild gusts, as waneth autumn-tide, and the old year is dying; so the spears of dauntless Danaans strewed the earth with slain, for loyal to dead Achilles were they all, and loyal to hero Aias to the death.

For like black Doom he blasted the ranks of Troy. Then against Aias Paris strained his bow; but he was ware thereof, and sped a stone swift to the archer's head: that bolt of death crashed through his crested helm, and darkness closed round him. In dust down fell he: naught availed his shafts their eager lord, this way and that scattered in dust: empty his quiver lay, flew from his hand the bow. In haste his friends caught him up from the earth, and Hector's steeds hurried him thence to Troy, scarce drawing breath, and moaning in his pain. Nor left his men the weapons of their lord, but gathered up all from the plain, and bare them to the prince; while Aias after him sent a wrathful shout: "Dog, thou hast escaped the heavy hand of death Today! But swiftly thy last hour shall come by some strong Argive's hands, or by mine own, but now have I a nobler task in hand, from murder's grip to rescue Achilles' corpse."

Then turned he on the foe, hurling swift doom on such as fought around Peleides yet. These saw how many yielded up the ghost beneath his strong hands, and, with hearts failing them for fear, against him could they stand no more. As rascal vultures were they, which the swoop of an eagle, king of birds, scares far away from carcasses of sheep that wolves have torn; so this way, that way scattered they before the hurtling stones, the sword, the might of Aias. In utter panic from the war they fled, in huddled rout, like starlings from the swoop of a death-dealing hawk, when, fleeing bane, one drives against another, as they dart all terror-huddled in tumultuous flight. So from the war to Priam's burg they fled wretchedly clad with terror as a cloak, quailing from mighty Aias's battle-shout, as with hands dripping blood-gouts he pursued.

Yea, all, one after other, had he slain, had they not streamed through city gates flung wide hard-panting, pierced to the very heart with fear. Pent there within he left them, as a shepherd leaves folded sheep, and strode back over the plain; yet never touched he with his feet the ground, but aye he trod on dead men, arms and blood; for countless corpses lay over that wide stretch even from broad-wayed Troy to Hellespont, bodies of strong men slain, the spoil of Doom. As when the dense stalks of sun-ripened corn fall beneath the reapers' hands, and the long swaths, heavy with full ears, overspread the field, and joys the heart of him who oversees the toil, lord of the harvest; even so, by baleful havoc overmastered, lay all round face-downward men remembering not the death-denouncing war shout.

But the sons of fair Achaea left their slaughtered foes in dust and blood unstripped of arms awhile till they should lay upon the pyre the son of Peleus, who in battle-shock had been their banner of victory, charging in his might. So the kings drew him from that stricken field straining beneath the weight of giant limbs, and with all loving care they bore him on, and laid him in his tent before the ships. And round him gathered that great host, and wailed heart-anguished him who had been the Achaeans' strength, and now, forgotten all the splendour of spears, lay mid the tents by moaning Hellespont, in stature more than human, even as lay Tityos, who sought to force Queen Leto, when she fared to Pytho: swiftly in his wrath Apollo shot, and laid him low, who seemed invincible: in a foul lake of gore there lay he, covering many a rood of ground, on the broad earth, his mother; and she moaned over her son, of blessed gods abhorred; but Lady Leto laughed.

So grand of mould there in the foemen's land lay Aeacus's son, for joy to Trojans, but for endless grief to Achaean men lamenting. Moaned the air with sighing from the abysses of the sea; and passing heavy grew the hearts of all, thinking: "Now shall we perish by the hands of Trojans!" Then by those dark ships they thought of white-haired fathers left in halls afar, of wives new-wedded, who by couches cold mourned, waiting, waiting, with their tender babes for husbands unreturning; and they groaned in bitterness of soul. A passion of grief came over their hearts; they fell upon their faces on the deep sand flung down, and wept as men all comfortless round Peleus's mighty son, and clutched and plucked out by the roots their hair, and east upon their heads defiling sand. Their cry was like the cry that goeth up from folk that after battle by their walls are slaughtered, when their maddened foes set fire to a great city, and slay in heaps on heaps her people, and make spoil of all her wealth; so wild and high they wailed beside the sea, because the Danaans' champion, Aeacus's son, lay, grand in death, by a god's arrow slain, as Ares lay, when She of the Mighty Father with that huge stone down dashed him on Troy's plain.

Ceaselessly wailed the Myrmidons Achilles, a ring of mourners round the kingly dead, that kind heart, friend alike to each and all, to no man arrogant nor hard of mood, but ever tempering strength with courtesy.

Then Aias first, deep-groaning, uttered forth his yearning over his father's brother's son god-stricken – ay, no man had smitten him of all upon the wide-wayed earth that dwell! Him glorious Aias heavy-hearted mourned, now wandering to the tent of Peleus's son, now cast down all his length, a giant form, on the sea sands; and thus lamented he: "Achilles, shield and sword of Argive men, thou hast died in Troy, from Phthia's plains afar, smitten unawares by that accursed shaft, such thing as weakling dastards aim in fight! For none who trusts in wielding the great shield, none who for war can skill to set the helm upon his brows, and sway the spear in grip, and cleave the brass about the breasts of foes, warreth with arrows, shrinking from the fray. Not man to man he met thee, whoso smote; else woundless never had he escaped thy lance! But haply Zeus purposed to ruin all, and maketh all our toil and travail vain – ay, now will grant the Trojans victory who from Achaea now hath reft her shield! Ah me! how shall old Peleus in his halls take up the burden of a mighty grief now in his joyless age! His heart shall break at the mere rumour of it. Better so, thus in a moment to forget all pain. But if these evil tidings slay him not, ah, laden with sore sorrow age shall come upon him, eating out his heart with grief by a lone hearth Peleus so passing dear once to the Blessed! But the gods vouchsafe no perfect happiness to hapless men."

So he in grief lamented Peleus's son. Then ancient Phoenix made heart-stricken moan, clasping the noble form of Aeacus's seed, and in wild anguish wailed the wise of heart: "Thou art robbed from me, dear child, and cureless pain hast left to me! Oh that upon my face the veiling earth had fallen, ere I saw thy bitter doom! No pang more terrible hath ever stabbed mine heart no, not that hour of exile, when I fled from fatherland and noble parents, fleeing Hellas through, till Peleus welcomed me with gifts, and lord of his Dolopians made me. In his arms thee through his halls one day he bare, and set upon my knees, and bade me foster thee, his babe, with all love, as mine own dear child: I hearkened to him: blithely didst thou cling about mine heart, and, babbling wordless speech, didst call me 'father' oft, and didst bedew my breast and tunic with thy baby lips. Ofttimes with soul that laughed for glee I held thee in mine arms; for mine heart whispered me 'This fosterling through life shall care for thee, staff of thine age shall be.' And that mine hope was for a little while fulfilled; but now thou hast vanished into darkness, and to me is left long heartache wild with all regret. Ah, might my sorrow slay me, ere the tale to noble Peleus come! When on his ears falleth the heavy tidings, he shall weep and wail without surcease. Most piteous grief we two for thy sake shall inherit aye, thy sire and I, who, ere our day of doom, mourning shall go down to the grave for thee – ay, better this than life unholpen of thee!"

So moaned his ever-swelling tide of grief. And Atreus's son beside him mourned and wept with heart on fire with inly smouldering pain: "Thou hast perished, chiefest of the Danaan men, hast perished, and hast left the Achaean host fenceless! Now thou art fallen, are they left an easier prey to foes. Thou hast given joy to Trojans by thy fall, who dreaded thee as sheep a lion. These with eager hearts even to the ships will bring the battle now. Zeus, Father, thou too with deceitful words beguilest mortals! Thou didst promise me that Priam's burg should be destroyed; but now that promise given dost thou not fulfil, but thou didst cheat mine heart: I shall not win the war's goal, now Achilles is no more."

So did he cry heart-anguished. Mourned all round wails multitudinous for Peleus's son: the dark ships echoed back the voice of grief, and sighed and sobbed the immeasurable air. And as when long sea rollers, onward driven by a great wind, heave up far out at sea, and strandward sweep with terrible rush, and aye headland and beach with shattered spray are scourged, and roar unceasing; so a dread sound rose of moaning of the Danaans round the corpse, ceaselessly wailing Peleus's aweless son.

And on their mourning soon black night had come, but spake unto Atreides Neleus's son, Nestor, whose own heart bare its load of grief remembering his own son Antilochus: "O mighty Agamemnon, sceptre-lord of Argives, from wide-shrilling lamentation refrain we for this day. None shall withhold hereafter these from all their heart's desire of weeping and lamenting many days. But now go to, from aweless Aeacus's son wash we the foul blood-gouts, and lay we him upon a couch: unseemly it is to shame the dead by leaving them untended long."

So counselled Neleus's son, the passing-wise. Then hasted he his men, and bade them set caldrons of cold spring water over the flames, and wash the corpse, and clothe in vesture fair, sea-purple, which his mother gave her son at his first sailing against Troy. With speed they did their lord's command: with loving care, all service meetly rendered, on a couch laid they the mighty fallen, Peleus's son.

The Trito-born, the passing-wise, beheld and pitied him, and showered upon his head ambrosia, which hath virtue aye to keep taintless, men say, the flesh of warriors slain. Like softly breathing sleeper dewy fresh she made him: over that dead face she drew a stern frown, even as when he lay, with wrath darkening his grim face, clasping his slain friend Patroclus; and she made his frame to be more massive, like a war-god to behold. And wonder seized the Argives, as they thronged and saw the image of a living man, where all the stately length of Peleus's son lay on the couch, and seemed as though he slept.

Around him all the woeful captive maids, whom he had taken for a prey, what time he had ravaged hallowed Lemnos, and had scaled the towered crags of Thebes, Eetion's town, wailed, as they stood and rent their fair young flesh, and smote their breasts, and from their hearts bemoaned that lord of gentleness and courtesy, who honoured even the daughters of his foes. And stricken most of all with heart-sick pain Briseis, hero Achilles' couch mate, bowed over the dead, and tore her fair young flesh with ruthless fingers, shrieking: her soft breast was ridged with gory weals, so cruelly she smote it thou hadst said that crimson blood had dripped on milk. Yet, in her griefs despite, her winsome loveliness shone out, and grace hung like a veil about her, as she wailed: "Woe for this grief passing all griefs beside! Never on me came anguish like to this not when my brethren died, my fatherland was wasted – like this anguish for thy death! Thou wast my day, my sunlight, my sweet life, mine hope of good, my strong defence from harm, dearer than all my beauty – yea, more dear than my lost parents! Thou wast all in all to me, thou only, captive though I be. Thou tookest from me every bondmaid's task and like a wife didst hold me. Ah, but now me shall some new Achaean master bear to fertile Sparta, or to thirsty Argos. The bitter cup of thraldom shall I drain, severed, ah me, from thee! Oh that the earth had veiled my dead face ere I saw thy doom!"

So for slain Peleus's son did she lament with woeful handmaids and heart-anguished Greeks, mourning a king, a husband. Never dried her tears were: ever to the earth they streamed like sunless water trickling from a rock while frost and snow yet mantle over the earth above it; yet the frost melts down before the east wind and the flame shafts of the sun.

Now came the sound of that upringing wail to Nereus's daughters, dwellers in the depths unfathomed. With sore anguish all their hearts were smitten: piteously they moaned: their cry shivered along the waves of Hellespont. Then with dark mantles overpalled they sped swiftly to where the Argive men were thronged. As rushed their troop up silver paths of sea, the flood disported round them as they came. With one wild cry they floated up; it rang, a sound as when fleet-flying cranes forebode a great storm. Moaned the monsters of the deep plaintively round that train of mourners. Fast on sped they to their goal, with awesome cry wailing the while their sister's mighty son. Swiftly from Helicon the Muses came heart-burdened with undying grief, for love and honour to the Nereid starry-eyed.

Then Zeus with courage filled the Argive men, that eyes of flesh might undismayed behold that glorious gathering of goddesses. Then those divine ones round Achilles' corpse pealed forth with one voice from immortal lips a lamentation. Rang again the shores of Hellespont. As rain upon the earth their tears fell round the dead man, Aeacus's son; for out of depths of sorrow rose their moan. And all the armour, yea, the tents, the ships of that great sorrowing multitude were wet with tears from ever-welling springs of grief.

His mother cast her on him, clasping him, and kissed her son's lips, crying through her tears: "Now let the rosy vestured Dawn in heaven exult! Now let broad-flowing Axius exult, and for Asteropaeus dead put by his wrath! Let Priam's seed be glad but I unto Olympus will ascend, and at the feet of everlasting Zeus will cast me, bitterly planning that he gave me, an unwilling bride, unto a man – a man whom joyless age soon overtook, to whom the Fates are near, with death for gift. Yet not so much for his lot do I grieve as for Achilles; for Zeus promised me to make him glorious in the Aeacid halls, in recompense for the bridal I so loathed that into wild wind now I changed me, now to water, now in fashion as a bird I was, now as the blast of flame; nor might a mortal win me for his bride, who seemed all shapes in turn that earth and heaven contain, until the Olympian pledged him to bestow a godlike son on me, a lord of war. Yea, in a manner this did he fulfil faithfully; for my son was mightiest of men. But Zeus made brief his span of life unto my sorrow. Therefore up to heaven will I: to Zeus's mansion will I go and wail my son, and will put Zeus in mind of all my travail for him and his sons in their sore stress, and sting his soul with shame."

So in her wild lament the sea queen cried. But now to Thetis spake Calliope, she in whose heart was steadfast wisdom throned: "From lamentation, Thetis, now forbear, and do not, in the frenzy of thy grief for thy lost son, provoke to wrath the Lord of Gods and men. Lo, even sons of Zeus, the thunder king, have perished, overborne by evil fate. Immortal though I be, mine own son Orpheus died, whose magic song drew all the forest trees to follow him, and every craggy rock and river stream, and blasts of winds shrill-piping stormy breathed, and birds that dart through air on rushing wings. Yet I endured mine heavy sorrow: Gods ought not with anguished grief to vex their souls. Therefore make end of sorrow-stricken wail for thy brave child; for to the sons of earth minstrels shall chant his glory and his might, by mine and by my sisters' inspiration, unto the end of time. Let not thy soul be crushed by dark grief, nor do thou lament like those frail mortal women. Know'st thou not that round all men which dwell upon the earth hovereth irresistible deadly Fate, who recks not even of the gods? Such power she only hath for heritage. Yea, she soon shall destroy gold-wealthy Priam's town, and Trojans many and Argives doom to death, whomso she will. No God can stay her hand."

So in her wisdom spake Calliope. Then plunged the sun down into ocean's stream, and sable-vestured night came floating up over the wide firmament, and brought her boon of sleep to sorrowing mortals. On the sands there slept they, all the Achaean host, with heads bowed beneath the burden of calamity. But upon Thetis sleep laid not his hand: still with the deathless Nereids by the sea she sat; on either side the Muses spake one after other comfortable words to make that sorrowing heart forget its pain.

But when with a triumphant laugh the dawn soared up the sky, and her most radiant light shed over all the Trojans and their king, then, sorrowing sorely for Achilles still, the Danaans woke to weep. Day after day, for many days they wept. Around them moaned far-stretching beaches of the sea, and mourned great Nereus for his daughter Thetis's sake; and mourned with him the other sea gods all for dead Achilles. Then the Argives gave the corpse of great Peleides to the flame. A pyre of countless tree trunks built they up which, all with one mind toiling, from the heights of Ida they brought down; for Atreus's sons sped on the work, and charged them to bring thence wood without measure, that consumed with speed might be Achilles' body.

All around piled they about the pyre much battle gear of strong men slain; and slew and cast thereon full many goodly sons of Trojan men, and snorting steeds and mighty bulls withal, and sheep and fatling swine thereon they cast. And wailing captive maids from coffers brought mantles untold; all cast they on the pyre: gold heaped they there and amber. All their hair the Myrmidons shore, and shrouded with the same the body of their king. Briseis laid her own shorn tresses on the corpse, her gift, her last, unto her lord. Great jars of oil full many poured they out thereon, with jars of honey and of wine, rich blood of the grape that breathed an odour as of nectar, yea, cast incense-breathing perfumes manifold marvellous sweet, the precious things put forth by earth, and treasures of the sea divine.

Then, when all things were set in readiness about the pyre, all, footmen, charioteers, compassed that woeful bale, clashing their arms, while, from the viewless heights Olympian, Zeus rained down ambrosia on dead Aeacus's son. For honour to the goddess, Nereus's child, he sent to Aeolus Hermes, bidding him summon the sacred might of his swift winds, for that the corpse of Aeacus's son must now be burned. With speed he went, and Aeolus refused not: the tempestuous north in haste he summoned, and the wild blast of the west; and to Troy sped they on their whirlwind wings. Fast in mad onrush, fast across the deep they darted; roared beneath them as they flew the sea, the land; above crashed thunder-voiced clouds headlong hurtling through the firmament. Then by decree of Zeus down on the pyre of slain Achilles, like a charging host swooped they; upleapt the fire-god's madding breath: uprose a long wail from the Myrmidons. Then, though with whirlwind rushes toiled the winds, all day, all night, they needs must fan the flames ere that death-pyre burned out. Up to the heavens vast-volumed rolled the smoke. The huge tree trunks groaned, writhing, bursting, in the heat, and dropped the dark grey ash all round. So when the winds had tirelessly fulfilled their mighty task, back to their cave they rode cloud-charioted.

Then, when the fire had last of all consumed that hero-king, when all the steeds, the men slain round the pyre had first been ravined up, with all the costly offerings laid around the mighty dead by Achaia's weeping sons, the glowing embers did the Myrmidons quench with wine. Then clear to be discerned were seen his bones; for nowise like the rest were they, but like an ancient giant's; none beside with these were blent; for bulls and steeds, and sons of Troy, with all that mingled hecatomb, lay in a wide ring round his corpse, and he amidst them, flame-devoured, lay there alone. So his companions groaning gathered up his bones, and in a silver casket laid massy and deep, and banded and bestarred with flashing gold; and Nereus's daughters shed ambrosia over them, and precious ointments for honour to Achilles: fat of cattle and amber honey poured they over all. A golden vase his mother gave, the gift in old time of the wine-god, glorious work of the craft-master fire-god, in the which they laid the casket that enclosed the bones of mighty souled Achilles. All around the Argives heaped a barrow, a giant sign, upon a foreland's uttermost end, beside the Hellespont's deep waters, wailing loud farewells unto the Myrmidons' hero-king.

Nor stayed the immortal steeds of Aeacus's son tearless beside the ships; they also mourned their slain king: sorely loth were they to abide longer mid mortal men or Argive steeds bearing a burden of consuming grief; but fain were they to soar through air, afar from wretched men, over the ocean's streams, over the sea queen's caverns, unto where divine Podarge bare that storm-foot twain begotten of the west wind clarion-voiced. Yea, and they had accomplished their desire, but the gods' purpose held them back, until from Scyros's isle Achilles' fleet-footed son should come. Him waited they to welcome, when he came unto the war-host; for the Fates, daughters of holy Chaos, at their birth had spun the life threads of those deathless foals, even to serve Poseidon first, and next Peleus the dauntless king, Achilles then the invincible, and, after these, the fourth, the mighty hearted Neoptolemus, whom after death to the Elysian Plain they were to bear, unto the Blessed Land, by Zeus's decree. For which cause, though their hearts were pierced with bitter anguish, they abode still by the ships, with spirits sorrowing for their old lord, and yearning for the new.

Then from the surge of heavy plunging seas rose the Earth-shaker. No man saw his feet pace up the strand, but suddenly he stood beside the Nereid goddesses, and spake to Thetis, yet for Achilles bowed with grief: "Refrain from endless mourning for thy son. Not with the dead shall he abide, but dwell with gods, as doth the might of Herakles, and Dionysus ever fair. Not him dread Doom shall prison in darkness evermore, nor Hades keep him. To the light of Zeus soon shall he rise; and I will give to him a holy island for my gift: it lies within the Euxine Sea: there evermore a god thy son shall be. The tribes that dwell around shall as mine own self honour him with incense and with steam of sacrifice. Hush thy laments, vex not thine heart with grief."

Then like a wind breath had he passed away over the sea, when that consoling word was spoken; and a little in her breast revived the spirit of Thetis: and the god brought this to pass thereafter. All the host moved moaning thence, and came unto the ships that brought them over from Hellas. Then returned to Helicon the Muses: beneath the sea, wailing the dear dead, Nereus's daughters sank.

History of the Fall of Troy

Introductory Letter

CORNELIUS NEPOS sends greetings to his Sallustius Crispus. While I was busily engaged in study at Athens, I found the history which Dares the Phrygian wrote about the Greeks and Trojans. As its title indicates, this history was written in Dares'

own hand. I was very delighted to obtain it and immediately made an exact translation into Latin, neither adding nor omitting anything, nor giving any personal touch. Following the straightforward and simple style of the Greek original, I translated word for word.

Thus my readers can know exactly what happened according to this account and judge for themselves whether Dares the Phrygian or Homer wrote the more truthfully – Dares, who lived and fought at the time the Greeks stormed Troy, or Homer, who was born long after the war was over. When the Athenians judged this matter, they found Homer insane for describing gods battling with mortals. But so much for this. Let us now turn to what I have promised.

Section 10

HILE ALEXANDER was on Cythera, Helen, the wife of Menelaus, decided to go there. Thus she went to the shore, to the seaport town of Helaea, intending to worship in the temple of Diana and Apollo. Alexander, on hearing that she had arrived, wanted to see her. Confident in his own good looks, he began to walk within sight of her. When Helen learned that the Alexander who was the son of King Priam had come to Helaea, she also wanted to see him. Thus they met and spent some time just staring, struck by each other's beauty.

Alexander ordered his men to be ready to sail that night. They would seize Helen in the temple and take her home with them.

Thus at a given signal they invaded the temple and carried her off – she was not unwilling – along with some other women they captured. The inhabitants of the own, having learned about the abduction of Helen, tried to prevent Alexander from carrying her off. They fought long and hard, but

Alexander's superior forces defeated them. After despoiling the temple and taking as many captives as his ships would hold, he set sail for home.

On the island of Tenedos, where they landed, he tried to comfort Helen, who was having regrets; and he sent news to his father of his success.

Menelaus, having learned what had happened, left Pylos accompanied by Nestor, and returned to Sparta whither he summoned his brother Agamemnon from Argos.

Section 11

MEANWHILE ALEXANDER arrived home with his booty and gave his father an exact description of everything he had done. Priam was delighted. He hoped that the Greeks would seek to recover Helen, and thus would return his sister Hesione, and the things they had taken from Troy. He consoled Helen, who was having regrets, and gave her to Alexander to marry. When Cassandra saw Helen, she began to prophesy, repeating what she had already said; until Priam ordered her carried away and locked up.

Agamemnon upon his arrival in Sparta, consoled his brother. They decided to send men throughout Greece to gather an army for war against Troy. Among those who assembled at Sparta were Achilles, who came with Patroclus; and Euryalus, Tlepolemus and Diomedes. They swore to avenge the wrongs the Trojans had done and to ready an army and fleet for this purpose. Agamemnon was chosen commander-in-chief, and messengers were sent to summon all the Greeks to the Athenian port with their ships and armies. From there they would set out for Troy together to avenge the wrongs they had suffered.

Castor and Pollux, immediately upon learning of their sister Helen's abduction, had set sail in pursuit. When, however, they landed on the island of Lesbos, a great storm arose and, lo and behold, they were nowhere in sight. That was the story. Later, people thought that they had been made immortal. The Lesbians, taking to the sea and searching even to Troy, had returned to report that they found no trace of Castor or Pollux.

Section 12

DARES THE PHRYGIAN, who wrote this history, says that he did military service until the capture of Troy and saw the people listed below either during times of truce or while he was fighting. As for Castor and Pollux, he learned from the Trojans what they were like and how they looked: they were twins, blond-haired, large-eyed, fair-complexioned and well-built with trim bodies.

Helen resembled Castor and Pollux. She was beautiful, ingenuous and charming. Her legs were the best; her mouth the cutest. There was a beauty mark between her eyebrows.

Priam, the king of the Trojans, had a handsome face and a pleasant voice. He was large and swarthy.

Hector spoke with a slight lisp. His complexion was fair, his hair curly. His eyes would blink attractively. His movements were swift. His face, with its beard, was noble. He was handsome, fierce and high-spirited, merciful to the citizens and deserving of love.

Deiphobus and Helenus both looked like their father, but their characters were not alike. Deiphobus was the man of forceful action; Helenus was the gentle, learned prophet.

Troilus, a large and handsome boy, was strong for his age, brave and eager for glory.

Alexander was fair, tall and brave. His eyes were very beautiful, his hair soft and blond, his mouth charming and his voice pleasant. He was swift, and eager to take command.

Aeneas was auburn-haired, stocky, eloquent, courteous, prudent, pious and charming. His eyes were black and twinkling.

Antenor was tall, graceful, swift, crafty and cautious.

Hecuba was beautiful, her figure large, her complexion dark. She thought like a man and was pious and just.

Andromache was bright-eyed and fair, with a tall and beautiful body. She was modest, wise, chaste and charming.

Cassandra was of moderate stature, round-mouthed and auburn-haired. Her eyes flashed. She knew the future.

Polyxena was fair, tall and beautiful. Her neck was slender, her eyes lovely her hair blond and long, her body well-proportioned, her fingers tapering, her legs straight and her feet the best. Surpassing all the others in beauty, she remained a completely ingenuous and kind-hearted woman.

Section 13

AGAMEMNON WAS BLOND, large and powerful. He was eloquent, wise and noble, a man richly endowed. Menelaus was of moderate stature, auburn-haired and handsome. He had a pleasing personality.

Achilles had a large chest, a fine mouth and powerfully formed arms and legs. His head was covered with long wavy chestnut-coloured hair. Though mild in manner, he was very fierce in battle. His face showed the joy of a man richly endowed.

Patroclus was handsome and powerfully built. His eyes were grey. He was modest, dependable, wise, a man richly endowed.

Ajax, the son of Oileus, was stocky, powerfully built, swarthy, a pleasant person and brave.

Ajax, the son of Telamon, was powerful. His voice was clear, his hair black and curly. He was perfectly single-minded and unrelenting in the onslaught of battle.

Ulysses was tough, crafty, cheerful, of medium height, eloquent and wise.

Diomedes was stocky, brave, dignified and austere. No one was fiercer in battle. He was loud at the war cry, hot-tempered, impatient and daring.

Nestor was large, broad and fair. His nose was long and hooked. He was a wise adviser.

Protesilaus was fair-skinned and dignified. He was swift, self-confident, even rash.

Neoptolemus was large, robust and easily irritated. He lisped slightly, and was good-looking, with hooked nose, round eyes and shaggy eyebrows.

Palamedes was tall and slender, wise, magnanimous and charming.

Podalirius, was sturdy, strong, haughty and moody.

Machaon was large and brave, dependable, prudent, patient and merciful.

Meriones was auburn-haired, of moderate height, with a well-proportioned body. He was robust, swift, unmerciful and easily angered.

Briseis was beautiful. She was small and blond, with soft yellow hair. Her eyebrows were joined above her lovely eyes. Her body was well-proportioned. She was charming, friendly, modest, ingenuous and pious.

Section 14

THE FOLLOWING is a list of Greek leaders and the ships they brought to Athens. Agamemnon came from Mycenae with 100 ships; Menelaus from Sparta with 60...

Arcesilaus and Prothoenor from Boeotia with 50; Ascalaphus and Ialmenus from Orchomenus with 30; Epistrophus and Schedius from Phocis with 40; Ajax the son of Telamon brought along Teucer, his brother, from Salamis, and also Amphimachus, Diores, Thalpius, and Polyxenus from Buprasion, with 40 ships; Nestor came from Pylos with 80; Thoas from Aetolia with 40; Nireus from Syme with 53; Ajax the son of Oileus from Locris with 37; Antiphus and Phidippus from Calydna with 30; Idomeneus and Meriones from Crete with 80; Ulysses from Ithaca with 12; Eumelus from Pherae with 10; Protesilaus and Podarces from Phylaca with 40; Podalirus and Machaon, the sons of Aesculapius, from Tricca with 32; Achilles, accompanied by Patroclus and the Myrmidones, from Phthia with 50; Tlepolemus from Rhodes with nine;

Eurypylus from Ormenion with 40; Antiphus and Amphimachus from Elis with 11; Polypoetes and Leonteus from Argisa with 40; Diomedes, Euryalus, and Sthenelus from Argos with 80; Philoctetes from Meliboea with 7; Guneus from Cyphos with 21; Prothous from Magnesia with 40; Agapenor from Arcadia with 40; and Menestheus from Athens with 50. There were 49 Greek leaders, and they brought a total of 1,130 ships.

Section 15

WHEN THEY HAD arrived at Athens, Agamemnon called the leaders to council. He praised them and urged them to avenge the wrongs they had suffered as quickly as possible. Let each one, he said, tell how he felt. Then he advised that, before setting sail, they should consult the oracle of Apollo at Delphi. The council agreed unanimously and appointed Achilles to be in charge of this mission; and thus he, along with Patroclus, set out to Delphi.

Meanwhile Priam, having learned that the Greeks were preparing for war, sent men throughout Phrygia to enlist the support of the neighbouring armies. He himself zealously readied his forces at home.

When Achilles had come to Delphi, he went to the oracle. The response, which issued from the holiest of holies, said that the Greeks would conquer and capture Troy in the 10th year. Then Achilles performed his religious duties as ordered.

At the same time the seer Calchas, the son of Thestor, had arrived, sent by his people, the Phrygians, to bring gifts to Apollo. When he inquired on behalf of his kingdom and of himself consulted the oracle, the response which issued from the holiest of holies said that the Greeks would sail against Troy and would continue their siege until they had captured it, and that he would go with them and give them advice.

Thus Achilles and Calchas met in the temple and, after comparing responses, rejoiced in each other's friendship and set out for Athens together.

At Athens Achilles made his report to the council. The Greeks were delighted. And they accepted Calchas as one of their own.

Then they set sail. But a storm arose and prevented their progress. Thereupon Calchas, interpreting the omens, said that they must return and go up to Aulis.

On arriving at Aulis, Agamemnon appeased the goddess Diana. Then he commanded his followers to sail onwards to Troy. Philoctetes, who had gone with the Argonauts to Troy, acted as pilot.

Then they landed at a city which was ruled by King Priam. They took it by storm and carried off much booty.

One coming to the island of Tenedos, they killed all the people, and Agamemnon divided the booty.

Section 16

THEN, HAVING CALLED a meeting of the council, he sent envoys to Priam to ask for the return of Helen and the booty Alexander had taken; Diomedes and Ulysses were chosen to go on this mission. At the same time Achilles and Telephus were sent to plunder Mysia, the region ruled by King Teuthras.

They had come to this region and had begun to despoil the country when Teuthras arrived with his army. Thereupon Achilles put the enemy to flight, and also wounded the king. He would have finished him off if Telephus had not stood in his way. Telephus came to Teuthras' aid and protected him under his shield, for he remembered their friendship, the time in his boyhood when Teuthras had been his generous host: Teuthras had felt indebted to Telephus' father, Hercules, for Hercules, so they said, had slain Diomedes, the previous king of Mysia, from whom Teuthras had inherited the kingdom. (Diomedes had met his death while hunting with his wild and powerful horses.) Nevertheless, now Teuthras realized that he was unable to live much longer, and so he appointed Telephus heir to the throne and king of Mysia.

Telephus had a magnificent funeral for Teuthras. Then Achilles urged him to stay behind and take care of his newly gained kingdom. Telephus, he said, would aid the Greeks much more by sending supplies than by going to Troy. Thus Telephus stayed behind in his kingdom, and Achilles, carrying much booty, returned to the army on Tenedos. His report of what had been done won Agamemnon's approval and praise.

Section 17

MEANWHILE the envoys had come to Priam, and Ulysses stated Agamemnon's demands. If Helen and the booty, he said, were returned and proper reparations were made, the Greeks would depart in peace.

Priam answered by reviewing the wrongs the Argonauts had done: the death of his father, the sack of Troy and the capture of his sister Hesione. He ended by describing how contemptuously the Greeks had treated Antenor when sent as his envoy. He, therefore, repudiated peace. He declared war and commanded that the envoys of the Greeks be expelled from his boundaries.

Thus the envoys returned to their camp on Tenedos and reported what Priam had answered. And the council discussed what to do. [...]

Section 19

THE GREEKS DEBATED whether they should make their attack against Troy secretly at night or during the day. Palamedes urged them to land by day, for thus they would draw the enemy forces out of the city. His advice was accepted unanimously. Then they decided to give Agamemnon command; and the envoys

were appointed to gather supplies in Mysia and other places: Anius and the two sons of Theseus, Demophoon and Acamas.

Then Agamemnon, having called the soldiers to assembly, praised them and demanded their immediate and total allegiance.

When the signal was given, the ships set sail and landed at Troy, with the whole fleet widely deployed. The Trojans bravely defended their country. Hector met and slew Protesilaus and caused great confusion among the rest of the Greeks. (Protesilaus had gone inland, wreaking slaughter and putting the Trojans to flight.) But wherever Hector withdrew, the Trojans fled. The losses on both sides were heavy until the arrival of Achilles caused all the Trojans to flee back to Troy. When night brought an end to the battle, Agamemnon led forth all of his army onto the land and set up camp.

On the next day Hector led forth his army out of the city ready for battle. Agamemnon's forces moved opposite, shouting their war cry. The battle that arose was fierce and raging; the bravest of those who fought in the vanguard fell. Hector slew Patroclus; he was trying to strip off his armour when Meriones snatched the body out of the action. Then Hector pursued and cut down Meriones. This time, however, while trying to despoil the body, he was wounded in the leg by Menestheus, who had come to the aid of his comrade. Hector, though wounded, slew a great number of the enemy and would have successfully turned the Greek forces to flight had Ajax the son of Telamon not stood in his way. Immediately upon meeting Ajax, Hector remembered that they were related: Ajax's mother was Priam's sister Hesione. Therefore, he commanded the Trojans to stop setting fire to the ships. And then the two men gave gifts to each other and departed in friendship.

Section 20

ON THE NEXT DAY the Greeks obtained a truce. Achilles mourned for Patroclus, and the Greeks for their dead. Agamemnon held a magnificent funeral for Protesilaus and saw to the proper

burial of the others. And Achilles celebrated the funeral games in honour of Patroclus.

During this truce Palamedes continuously pressed for sedition. Agamemnon, he said, ill-deserved the command of the army. Palamedes openly boasted of his own numerous accomplishments, particularly his tactics on offense, his fortifications of the camp, his regulation of guard duty, his invention of signals and scales and his training of the army for battle. These things were due to him, and it was therefore not right, he said, for Agamemnon, whom only a few had chosen as leader, to command all those who had joined the campaign later. All of them had a right to expect a man who was brilliant and brave in this position.

After two years, during which time the Greeks debated who should command them, the war was resumed. Agamemnon, Achilles, Diomedes and Menelaus led forth their army. The forces of Hector, Troilus and Aeneas moved opposite. A great slaughter arose, and many very brave men fell on both sides. Hector slew Boetes, Arcesilaus and Prothoenor. When night brought an end to the battle, Agamemnon called all the leaders to council and urged them to enter the fray and try to kill Hector especially, for Hector had slain some of their bravest commanders.

Section 21

WITH THE COMING of morning, Hector, Aeneas and Alexander led forth their army. And all the Greek leaders advanced with their forces. A great slaughter arose, and on both sides countless numbers were sent down to Ocrus. Menelaus began to pursue Alexander who, turning around, pierced him in the leg with an arrow. Nevertheless, though pained by his wound, Menelaus continued to pursue, and Locrian Ajax accompanied him. Hector saw what was happening, and immediately he and Aeneas came to the aid of their brother. While Aeneas, using his shield, provided

protection, Hector led Alexander out of the fighting and into the city. Night brought an end to the battle.

On the next day Achilles and Diomedes led forth their army. The forces of Hector and Aeneas came opposite. A great slaughter arose. Hector slew the leaders Orcomeneus, Ialmenus, Epistrophus, Schedius, Elephenor, Diores and Polyxenus. Aeneas slew Amphimachus and Nireus. Achilles slew Euphemus, Hippothous, Pylaeus and Asteropaeus. And Diomedes slew Antiphus and Mesthles. When Agamemnon saw that his bravest leaders had fallen, he called back his forces; and the Trojans returned to their city, rejoicing. Agamemnon was worried. Calling the leaders to council, he urged them to fight on bravely and not to give way. More than half of their forces had fallen, but any day now an army was coming from Mysia.

Section 22

ON THE NEXT DAY Agamemnon ordered the whole army, with all of the leaders, to go forth to battle. The Trojans came opposite. A great slaughter arose, with both sides battling fiercely and losing countless numbers of men, there being no break in the fighting, which raged for 80 consecutive days. Agamemnon, seeing the steadily mounting casualties, felt that time was needed for burying the dead. Therefore, he sent Ulysses and Diomedes as envoys to Priam to seek a truce of three years. During this time the Greeks would also be able to heal their wounded, repair the ships, reinforce the army and gather supplies.

Ulysses and Diomedes, while on their way to Priam by dark, met a Trojan named Dolon. When he asked why they were coming to the city, in arms and at night, they told him that they were envoys from Agamemnon to Priam.

When Priam heard of their coming and knew what they wanted, he called all of his leaders to council. Then he announced that these were envoys

Agamemnon had sent to seek a truce of three years. Hector suspected something was wrong. They wanted, he said, a truce for too long a time. Nevertheless, when Priam ordered the embers of the council to give their opinions, they voted to grant a truce of three years.

During the truce the Trojans repaired their walls, healed their wounded and buried their dead with great honour.

Section 23

AFTER THREE YEARS, the war was resumed. Hector and Troilus led forth their army. Agamemnon, Menelaus, Achilles and Diomedes commanded the Greeks. A great slaughter arose, with Hector killing the leaders of the first rank, Phidippus and Antiphus, and Achilles slaying Lycaon and Phorcys. Countless numbers of others fell on both sides, as the battle raged for 30 consecutive days. Priam, seeing that many of his men were falling, set envoys to seek a truce of six months. This Agamemnon, following the will of his council, conceded.

With the resumption of hostilities, the battle raged for 12 days. On both sides many of the bravest leaders fell; and even more were wounded, a majority of whom died during treatment. Therefore, Agamemnon sent envoys to Priam to seek a 30-day truce for burying the dead. Priam, after consulting his council, agreed.

Section 24

WHEN TIME for fighting returned, Andromache, Hector's wife, had a dream which forbade Hector to enter the fray. He, however, dismissed this vision as due to her wifely

concern. She, being deeply upset, sent word to Priam to keep her husband out of the battle that day.

Priam, therefore, divided the command of his forces between Alexander, Helenus, Troilus and Aeneas. Hector, on learning of this, bitterly blamed Andromache and told her to bring forth his armour; nothing, he said, could keep him from battle. She tried in vain to make him relent, falling at his feet, like a woman in mourning, her hair let down, holding the baby, their son Astyanax, out in her hands. Then, rushing to the palace, her wailing rousing the city as she went, she told King Priam how she had dreamt that Hector would eagerly leap into battle; and, holding Astyanax, she knelt before him and begged him not to allow this. Accordingly, Priam sent all the others to battle, but kept Hector back.

When Agamemnon, Achilles, Diomedes and the Locrian Ajax saw that Hector was not on the field, they fought the more fiercely, slaying many leaders of the Trojans. But Hector, hearing the tumult and knowing that the Trojans were being hard pressed, leaped into battle. Immediately he slew Idomeneus, wounded Iphinous, cut down Leonteus and thrust a spear into Sthenelus' leg. Achilles, seeing these leaders fall and wanting to prevent other Greeks form meeting a similar fate, determined to go against Hector and slay him. But by the time he caught up with Hector, the battle continuing to rage, the latter had already killed Polypoetes, the bravest of leaders, and was trying to strip off the armour. The fight that arose was terrific, as was the clamour from city and armies. Hector wounded Achilles' leg. But Achilles, though pained, pressed on all the harder and kept pressing on until he had won. Hector's death caused the Trojans to turn and flee for their gates, their numbers greatly depleted. Only Memnon resisted. He and Achilles fought fiercely, and neither got off without injuries. When night brought an end to the battle, the wounded Achilles returned to camp. The Trojans lamented for Hector, and the Greeks for their dead.

Section 25

ON THE NEXT DAY Memnon led forth the Trojans against the Greeks. Agamemnon, having called the army to assembly, urged a truce of two months for burying the dead. Thus envoys set out for Troy, and there, having told what they wanted to Priam, received a truce of two months.

Then Priam, following the custom of his people, buried Hector in front of the gates and held funeral games in his honour.

During the truce, Palamedes continued to complain about the Greek leadership, and so Agamemnon yielded to sedition. He said that the Greeks might choose as their general whomever they wished, so far as he cared.

On the next day he called the people to assembly and denied he had ever wanted to command them. He was ready to accept whomever they chose. He willingly yielded. All he desired was to punish the enemy, and it mattered little how this was done. Nevertheless, as he was still king of Mycenae, he commanded them to speak as they wished.

Then Palamedes came forward and, showing his qualifications, won the acclaim of the Greeks. They made him commander-in-chief, a position he gratefully accepted and began to administer. Achilles, however, disparaged the change.

Section 26

WHEN THE TRUCE was over, Palamedes, arranging his forces and urging them on, led forth the army ready for battle. Deiphobus commanded the Trojans, who offered fierce opposition. The Lycian Sarpedon, leading his men, attacked and caused great slaughter and havoc. The Rhodian Tlepolemus met and resisted Sarpedon, but finally fell badly wounded. Then Pheres, the son of Admetus, came up and, after a long hand-to-hand fight with Sarpedon, was killed. But Sarpedon also was wounded and forced from the battle. Thus for several days there was fighting, and many leaders died on both sides. The Trojan casualties, however, were greater. When they sent envoys to seek a respite for burying their dead and healing their wounded, Palamedes granted a truce of one year.

Both sides buried their dead and cared for their wounded. Their agreement allowed them to go to each other's areas; the Trojans went to the camp, the Greeks to the city.

Palamedes sent Agamemnon to Mysia to Acamas and Demophoon, Theseus' sons, whom Agamemnon had put in charge of bringing supplies and grain from Telephus. Upon his arrival in Mysia, Agamemnon told them about Palamedes' sedition. When, however, he saw that they were displeased, he admitted that he had agreed to the change.

Meanwhile Palamedes was readying the ships and fortifying the camp with walls and towers. The Trojans were training their army, repairing their walls, adding a rampart and ditch and diligently getting everything ready.

Section 27

O N THE FIRST anniversary of Hector's funeral, Priam, Hecuba, Polyxena and other Trojans went to the tomb. There they happened to meet Achilles, who, being struck by Polyxena's beauty, fell madly in love. The burning power of his love took all the joy out of life. (His soul was also rankled by the fact that the Greeks had deposed Agamemnon and made Palamedes commander-in-chief instead of himself.) Accordingly, urged by his love, he sent a trusted Phrygian slave to make this proposal

to Hecuba: if she would give him Polyxena to marry, he would go home with his Myrmidons, and thus would set an example which the other leaders would follow. When the slave went to Hecuba and made the proposal, she answered that she would be willing, if Priam agreed, but that she must talk with him first. Then the slave, as Hecuba ordered, returned to Achilles and told him her answer.

Agamemnon, coming from Mysia with a large group of followers, arrived in camp at this time.

When Hecuba talked to Priam about Achilles' proposal, Priam refused to agree. Granted that Achilles would make a good relative, it was not right to marry one's daughter to an enemy; and even if Achilles himself went home, the other Greeks would not follow. Therefore, if Achilles wanted this marriage, he must promise a lasting peace, a treaty with sacred oaths; and the Greek must depart. On these conditions, Priam would willingly give him his daughter in marriage.

The slave of Achilles, according to his understanding with Hecuba, returned to her and learned what Priam had said. Then he reported all he had heard back to his master. Thereupon Achilles complained, to any and everyone, that for the sake of one woman, that is, Helen, all Europe and Greece were in arms, and now, for a very long time, thousands of men had been dying. Their very liberty, he said, was at stake, and this was the reason they ought to make peace and take their army back home.

Section 28

WHEN THE YEAR was over, Palamedes led forth the army and drew it up. And the Trojans came opposite commanded by Deiphobus. (Achilles, however, refused to take part because of his anger.) Palamedes seized an opportunity to attack Deiphobus and slaughtered him.

A fierce battle arose, fiercely fought on both sides; there were countless numbers of casualties. Palamedes, active in the first ranks, urging his men to fight bravely, encountered and slew Lycian Sarpedon. But as he continued to prowl in the vanguard, spurred on by success, exulting and vaunting his prowess, Alexander (Paris) pierced his neck with an arrow; and then the Phrygians, seeing their chance, hurled their spears and finished him off. King Palamedes was dead. Accordingly, all the Trojans attacked. They pursued the Greeks, and the Greeks retreated and fled to the camp. The camp was besieged, the ships set on fire.

Achilles, though told what was happening, chose to pretend that things were all right.

Ajax the son of Telamon bravely led the defence until night brought an end to the battle. Then the Greeks lamented the loss of Palamedes' wisdom, justice, mercy and goodness; and the Trojans bewailed the deaths of Sarpedon and Deiphobus.

Section 29

ALSO DURING THE NIGHT Nestor, since he was the eldest, called the Greek leaders to council and, speaking with tact, urged them to choose a new general. He felt that, if they thought best, Agamemnon's reappointment would cause the least discord. He reminded them that while Agamemnon was general things had gone well and the army had prospered. If, however, anyone had a better idea, he urged him to speak. But all, agreeing with him, made Agamemnon commander-in-chief.

On the next day the Trojans came forth. And Agamemnon led the Greeks opposite. The battle was joined, and the two forces clashed. Towards evening Troilus advanced to the front and, wreaking slaughter and havoc, sent the Greeks flying back to their camp.

On the next day the Trojans led forth their army. And the forces of Agamemnon came opposite. A horrible slaughter arose. Both armies fought fiercely; Troilus slaughtered many Greek leaders, as the battle lasted seven days.

Then Agamemnon, having obtained a truce of two months, held a magnificent funeral in Palamedes' honour. Both sides saw to the burial of all the leaders and soldiers who had died.

Section 30

DURING THE TRUCE, Agamemnon sent Ulysses, Nestor and Diomedes to Achilles to ask him to re-enter the fighting. But Achilles, still moody, refused to budge from his decision to stay out of battle. He told about his promise to Hecuba and said that he would certainly fight rather poorly because of his passionate love for Polyxena. They whom Agamemnon had sent were not welcome. A lasting peace – that was the need. For the sake of one woman, he said, the Greeks were risking their lives, endangering their freedom, and wasting a great deal of time. Thus Achilles demanded peace, and refused to re-enter the fighting.

When Agamemnon learned of Achilles' stubborn refusal, he summoned all the leaders to council and asked them to tell what they thought should be done. Menelaus urged Agamemnon to lead the army to battle and not to worry about the withdrawal of Achilles. He himself would try to win over Achilles, but if he should fail, he would not be dejected. Furthermore, he said, the Trojans now had no one to take Hector's place, no one so brave. Diomedes and Ulysses answered that Troilus was the bravest of men and the equal of Hector. But Menelaus denied this and urged the council to continue the war. Calchas, taking the omens, informed them that they ought to do battle and not be frightened by the Trojans' recent successes.

Section 31

W HEN THE TIMe for fighting returned, Agamemnon, Menelaus and Ajax led forth the army. The Trojans came opposite. A great slaughter arose, a fierce and raging battle on both sides. Troilus, having wounded Menelaus, pressed on, killing many of the enemy and harrying the others. Night brought an end to the battle.

On the next day Troilus and Alexander led forth the Trojans. And all the Greeks came opposite. The battle was fierce. Troilus wounded Diomedes and, in the course of his slaughter, attacked and wounded Agamemnon himself.

For several days the battle raged on. Countless numbers fell on both sides. Then Agamemnon, seeing that he was losing more of his forces each day, and knowing that they were unable to last, sought a truce of six months.

Priam, having called a meeting of his council, reported the desires of the Greeks. Troilus felt that they were asking for too long a time; he urged the Trojans to continue fighting, and fire the ships. When, however, Priam ordered the members of the council to give their opinions, the vote was unanimous in favour the Greek petition, and thus they granted a truce of six months.

Agamemnon buried his dead with honours and saw to the care of the wounded, such as Diomedes and Menelaus. The Trojans also buried their dead.

During the truce Agamemnon, following the advice of his council, went to rouse Achilles to battle. But Achilles, still gloomy, refused to go forth; he felt that the king should be suing for peace. Nevertheless, after complaining that it was impossible to refuse Agamemnon, he said that he would send forth his forces when war was resumed, though he himself would stay back. For this Agamemnon gave him his thanks.

Section 32

WHEN THE TIME for war returned, the Trojans led forth their army. And the forces of the Greeks came opposite. Achilles, having drawn up his Myrmidons, sent them to Agamemnon ready for combat. A great battle arose, fierce and raging. Troilus, fighting in the first ranks, slaughtered the Greeks and put the Myrmidons to flight. He pressed his attack even into the camp, killing many and wounding most who stood in his way until Ajax the son of Telamon stopped him. The Trojans returned to the city victorious.

On the next day Agamemnon led forth his army along with the Myrmidons and all of his leaders. And the Trojans came opposite, eager to fight. The battle was joined. For several days both sides fought fiercely, and countless numbers were lost. Troilus, attacking the Myrmidons and breaking their order, put them to flight.

When Agamemnon saw that many of his men had been killed, he sought a 30-day truce for holding their funerals. This was granted by Priam, and thus the Greeks and Trojans buried their dead.

Section 33

WHEN THE TIME for war returned, the Trojans led forth their army. And Agamemnon came opposite with all of his leaders. The battle was joined. A great slaughter, fierce and raging, arose. When the morning had passed, Troilus advanced to the front, slaying the Greeks and making them flee with loud cries in general confusion. It was then that Achilles, seeing this mad and savage advance – the Greeks being crushed and the Myrmidons being relentlessly slaughtered – re-entered the battle; but almost immediately he had to withdraw, wounded by Troilus. The others continued to fight for six days.

On the seventh, the battle still raging, Achilles (who until then had stayed out of action because of his wound) drew up his Myrmidons and urged them bravely to make an attack against Troilus. Toward the end of the day Troilus advanced on horseback, exulting, and caused the Greeks to flee with loud cries. The Myrmidons, however, came to their rescue and made an attack against Troilus. Troilus slew many men, but, in the midst of the terrible fighting, his horse was wounded and fell, entangling and throwing him off; and swiftly Achilles was there to dispatch him.

Then Achilles tried to drag off the body. But Memnon maintained a successful defence, wounding Achilles and making him yield. When, however, Memnon and his followers began to pursue Achilles, the latter, merely by turning around, brought them to halt.

After Achilles' wound had been dressed and he had fought for some time, he slew Memnon, dealing him many a blow; and then, having been wounded himself, yielded from combat again. The rest of the Trojan forces, knowing that the king of the Persians was dead, fled to the city and bolted the gates. Night brought an end to the battle.

On the next day Priam sent envoys to Agamemnon to seek a 20-day truce. This Agamemnon immediately granted. Accordingly, Priam held a magnificent funeral in honour of Troilus and Memnon. And both sides buried their dead.

Section 34

HECUBA, bewailing the loss of Hector and Troilus, her two bravest sons, both slain by Achilles, devised, like the woman she was, a treacherous vengeance. Summoning her son Alexander, she urgently begged him to kill Achilles, and thus to uphold the honour of himself and his brothers. This he could do

in an ambush, catching his victim off guard. She would summon Achilles, in Priam's name, to come to the temple of the Thymbraean Apollo in front of the gate, to settle an agreement according to which she would give him Polyxena to marry. When Achilles came to this meeting, Alexander could treacherously kill him. Achilles' death would be victory sufficient for her.

Alexander promised to do as she asked. During that night he chose the bravest of the Trojans and stationed them in the temple with instructions to wait for his signal. Hecuba, as she had promised, sent word to Achilles. And Achilles, because of his love for Polyxena, gladly agreed to come to the temple that morning.

Accordingly, on the next day Achilles, along with Antilochus, Nestor's son, came for the meeting. Upon entering the temple, he was treacherously attacked. Spears were hurled from all sides, as Alexander exhorted his men. Achilles and Antilochus counterattacked, with their left arms wrapped in their cloaks for protection, their right hands wielding their swords; and Achilles slew many. But finally Alexander cut down Antilochus and then slaughtered Achilles, dealing him many a blow. Such was the death of this hero, a treacherous death and one ill-suiting his prowess.

Alexander's order to throw the bodies to the dogs and birds was countermanded by that of Helenus to take them out of the temple and hand them over to the Greeks. Thus the Greeks received their dead and carried them back to the camp. Agamemnon gave them magnificent funerals. He obtained a truce from Priam for the purpose of burying Achilles, and then held funeral games in his honour.

Section 35

THEN HE CALLED a meeting of the Greek council, at which he gave an address. It was unanimously decided that Achilles' command should be given to Ajax, who was Achilles' cousin. But Ajax

objected that Neoptolemus, Achilles' son, was still living, and thus had first claim; therefore, they should bring Neoptolemus to Troy and give him command of the Myrmidons and all of his father's prerogatives.

Agamemnon and the rest of the council agreed and chose Menelaus to go on this mission.

When Menelaus had come to the island of Scyros, he urged King Lycomedes (Neoptolemus's grandfather) to send Neoptolemus to battle. The king gladly granted the Greeks this request.

The truce having come to an end, Agamemnon drew up his forces and, urging them on, led them to war. The Trojans came opposite out of the city. The battle was joined, with Ajax fighting up front, but wearing no armour. Great was the clamour that arose, and many died on both sides. Alexander, using his bow with frequent success, pierced the unarmed Ajax' body; Ajax, however, though wounded, pursued and finally killed his assailant. Then, as the wound had exhausted his strength, he was carried back to the camp; and there, though they drew out the arrow, he died.

The Trojans, having rescued Alexander's body, fled back to the city, exhausted, before Diomedes' fierce onslaught. Diomedes pursued right up to the walls. Then Agamemnon, having ordered his forces to encircle the city, spent the whole night ready for battle, his guards always alerted.

On the next day, in the city, Priam buried Alexander. Helen took part in the funeral with loud lamentations. Alexander, she said, had treated her kindly; and thus she had become like a daughter to Priam and Hecuba, who always made her welcome at Troy and never let her remember her homeland.

Section 36

ON THE NEXT DAY Agamemnon drew up his army in front of the gates and challenged the Trojans to come out and fight. But Priam stayed in the city, increasing his fortifications and waiting for Penthesilea to come with her Amazons.

When Penthesilea arrived, she led forth her army against Agamemnon. A huge battle arose. It raged several days, and then the Greeks, being overwhelmed, fled for their camp. Diomedes could hardly prevent Penthesilea from firing the ships and destroying all the Greek forces.

After this battle, Agamemnon kept his forces in camp. Penthesilea, to be sure, came forth each day and, slaughtering the Greeks, tried to provoke him to fight. But he, following the advice of his council, fortified the camp, strengthened the guard, and refused to go out to battle – until Menelaus arrived.

When, on Scyros, Menelaus had given Neoptolemus the arms of his father, Achilles, he brought him to join the Greeks at Troy. And here Neoptolemus wept and lamented above the tomb of his father.

Penthesilea, according to her custom, drew up her army and advanced as far as the camp of the Greeks. Neoptolemus, in command of the Myrmidons, led forth his forces. And Agamemnon drew up his army. Greek and Trojans clashed head-on. Neoptolemus wreaked great slaughter. Penthesilea, having entered the fray, proved her prowess again and again.

For several days they fought fiercely, and many were killed. Finally Penthesilea wounded Neoptolemus, and then fell at his hands; in spite of his wound, he cut her down. The death of Penthesilea, the queen of the Amazons, caused all the Trojans to turn and flee in defeat for their city. And then the Greeks surrounded the walls with their forces and prevented anyone's leaving.

Section 37

WHEN THE TROJANS saw their predicament, Antenor, Polydamas and Aeneas went to Prima and asked him to call a meeting of the council to discuss the future of Troy and the Trojans.

Priam agreed, and so the meeting was called. Antenor spoke first, he and the other two having obtained permission to give their advice. The Trojans, he said, had lost their foremost defenders, Hector and the other sons of the king, along with the leaders from other places; but the Greeks still had their bravest commanders, Agamemnon, Menelaus, Neoptolemus, who was no less brave than his father, Diomedes, the Locrian Ajax, and many others besides, like Nestor and Ulysses, who were very shrewd men. Furthermore, the Trojans were surrounded and worn out with fear. Therefore, he urged the return of Helen and the things Alexander and his men had carried off with her. They must make peace.

After they had discussed making peace at some length, Amphimachus, Priam's son, a very brave youth, arose and, calling down curses upon Antenor and his associates, blamed them for the way they were acting. He felt that the Trojans should lead forth their army and make an attack on the camp and never give up until they had either conquered or died fighting in behalf of their country.

After Amphimachus had spoken, Aeneas arose and tried to refute him. Speaking calmly and gently but with persistence, he urged the Trojans to sue for peace with the Greeks. Then Polydamas urged the same course as Aeneas.

Section 38

AFTER THIS SPEECH Priam arose with great eagerness and hurled many curses at Antenor and Aeneas. They had been the means, he said, by which war had arisen, for they were the envoys who had been sent to Greece; Antenor, who now urged peace, had then urged war when, on returning from Greece, he had told how scornfully he had been treated; and Aeneas had helped Alexander carry off Helen and the booty. In view of these facts, he, Priam, had made up his mind. There would be no peace.

He commanded everyone to be prepared. When the signal was given, they must rush from the gates and either conquer or die. He had made up his mind.

After exhorting them thus at some length, Priam dismissed them. Then, taking Amphimachus along toe the palace, he told him that those who urged peace must be killed. He feared that they would betray the city. Also, they had won much support for their views among the people. Once they were killed, he, Priam, would see to his country's defence and the Greeks' defeat.

Begging Amphimachus to be faithful and true, he told him to gather a band of armed men. This could be done without any suspicion. As for this part, tomorrow after going to the citadel to worship as usual, he would invite those men to dine with him. Then Amphimachus, along with his band, must rush in and kill them.

Amphimachus agreed to this plan and promised to carry it out. And then he departed from Priam.

Section 39

DURING THE SAME DAY, Antenor, Polydamas, Ucalegon and Dolon met in secret. They were amazed at the stubbornness of the king, who, when surrounded by the enemy, preferred to die rather than sue for peace, thus causing the destruction of his country and people. Antenor had a plan for solving their problem, and if the others would swear allegiance, he would reveal it.

When all had sworn as he wished, he first sent word to Aeneas, and then told them his plan. They must, he said, betray their country, and in such a way that they might safeguard themselves and their families. Someone must go – someone that no one could suspect – and tell Agamemnon. They must act quickly. He had noticed that Priam, when leaving the council, was enraged because he had urged him to sue for peace; and he feared that the king was devising some treachery.

All promised their aid and immediately chose Polydamas – he would arouse least suspicion – to go in secret and see Agamemnon.

Thus Polydamas, having gone to the camp of the Greeks, saw Agamemnon and told him the plan.

Section 40

THAT NIGHT Agamemnon called all the leaders to a secret meeting of the council, and gave them the news, and asked their advice. The council decided unanimously to trust the traitors. As for the plan, Ulysses and Nestor said that they were afraid to carry it out; but Neoptolemus spoke in its favour; and thus a disagreement arose, which it was decided by obtaining a password from Polydamas that Sinon might test with Aeneas, Anchises, and Antenor.

Thus Sinon went to Troy and tested the password (Amphimachus had not yet stationed his guards at the gate), and returned and told Agamemnon that Aeneas, Anchises and Antenor had given the correct countersign. Then the members of the council, binding themselves on oath, promised that if Troy were betrayed the next night, no harm would come to Antenor, Ucalegon, Polydamas, Aeneas and Dolon, or to any of their parents, or indeed to their children, wives, relatives, friends, and associates, or to any of their property.

When they had sworn to this promise, Polydamas gave them instructions. At night, he said, they must lead the army to the Scaean gate – the one whose exterior was cared with a horse's head. Antenor and Aeneas would be in charge of the guard at this point, and they would open the bolt and raise a torch as the sign for attack.

Section 41

THEIR AGREEMENT being complete in every detail, Polydamas returned to the city and reported the success of his mission. Antenor, Aeneas and all their associates, he said, must go by

night to the Scaean gate and open the bolt, and raise a torch, and thus welcome the Greeks.

That night Antenor and Aeneas were ready at the gate and let Neoptolemus in. After opening the bolt and raising the torch, they looked to a means of escape for themselves and their people.

Antenor, with Neoptolemus providing protection, led the way to the palace, to the point where the Trojans had posted a guard. Then Neoptolemus, breaking into the palace and slaughtering the Trojans, pursued and cut down Priam at the altar of Jupiter.

Hecuba, fleeing with Polyxena, met with Aeneas and entrusted her daughter to him. He had her concealed at the home of his father Anchises. Andromache and Cassandra hid in the temple of Minerva.

During the whole night the Greeks did not cease wreaking slaughter and carrying off plunder.

Section 42

WITH THE COMING DAY, Agamemnon called all of his leaders to a meeting on the citadel. After giving thanks to the gods, he praised the army and ordered that all the booty be gathered together and fairly divided. At the same time he asked them what they wanted to do with Antenor and Aeneas and those who had helped betray Troy. All of them answered, with a loud shout, that they wanted to honour their promise to these.

Thus Agamemnon, having summoned all of the traitors, confirmed them in all of their rights. Antenor, when Agamemnon had granted him leave to speak, began by thanking the Greeks. Then he bade them to remember how Helenus and Cassandra had always pled with Priam for peace, and how Helenus had successfully urged the return of Achilles' body for burial.

Accordingly, Agamemnon, following the advice of the council, gave Helenus and Cassandra their freedom.

Then Helenus, remembering how Hecuba and Andromache had always loved him, interceded with Agamemnon in their behalf.

And again Agamemnon, by advice of the council, gave these their freedom.

Then he made an equitable division of the booty and rendered thanks to the gods with the sacrifice of a victim.

The council voted that they should return to their homeland on the fifth day.

Section 43

WHEN THE TIME for sailing arrived, a great storm arose and raged several days; Calchas informed them that the spirits of the dead were displeased.

Then Neoptolemus, remembering that Polyxena, the cause of his father's death, had not been found in the palace, voiced his complaint; he blamed the army and demanded that Agamemnon produce her. Agamemnon summoned Antenor and told him to find Polyxena and bring her there.

Accordingly, Antenor went to Aeneas and earnestly begged him to hand over Polyxena, so that the Greeks would set sail. And thus, having found where she had been hidden, he took her to Agamemnon. And Agamemnon gave her to Neoptolemus. And Neoptolemus cut her throat at the grave of his father.

Agamemnon was angry with Aeneas for hiding Polyxena and ordered him and his followers to depart from their country immediately. Thus Aeneas and all of his followers departed.

For several days after Agamemnon set sail, Helen, returning home with Menelaus, her husband, was grieved more deeply than when she had come.

Helenus went to the Chersonese, accompanied by Cassandra, his sister, and Andromache, the wife of his brother Hector, and Hecuba, his mother.

Section 44

So much and no more Dares the Phrygian put into writing, for, as a faithful follower of Antenor, he stayed on at Troy. The war against Troy lasted 10 years, six months, and 12 days.

The number of Greeks who fell, according to the Journal that Dares wrote, was 866,000; the number of the Trojans 676,000.

Aeneas set sail with the 22 ships that Alexander used when going to Greece. He had about 3,400 followers, people of all different ages; Antenor had about 2,500; Andromache and Helenus about 1,200.

Achilles in the Modern Period

In MODERN RETELLINGS, Achilles has remained the hero of myth, but his status as a hero of ritual has faded from his narrative. Yet his story has continued to resonate, inviting opportunities to explore the nature of heroism, what it means to stand up for one's friends, and how far is too far.

A popular nineteenth-century version of his experiences appears in *Life Stories for Young People,* composed by German historian and teacher Karl Friedrich Becker (1777–1806) and translated into English by American journalist George P. Upton (1834–1919). Written for young readers, Achilles' exploits are rendered with pathos and dramatic flair, with an emphasis on the emotional bonds among friends and family members. He (like his counterparts on the Trojan side) is portrayed as an exuberant warrior concerned with honour who throws himself into the fight in pursuit of it. The text demonstrates that Achilles' journey to accept his mortal limits continues to resonate, even as its cultural context remains in the distant past. We join the text at Chapter VII.

Chapter VII
Agamemnon Advises Flight – Council of the Princes – A Deputation is Sent to Achilles

FEAR AND UNREST prevailed in the camp by the ships, and even Agamemnon was no longer confident. He quietly called the chieftains to a council of war. "Friends," he said, "I perceive that Jupiter is not inclined to fulfil the promise of his omens and no longer desires that I take Troy and lead ye home laden with booty. He has already destroyed many of us and our misery grows greater day by day. Surely he is but making sport of us. Therefore let us launch our ships and return home, saving at least those of us who are left."

For a while the princes were silent. Then Diomedes sprang up and spake: "Do not be angry, O King, if I disagree with thee. It seems to me thou art faint-hearted, for none of us has given up hope. Truly the gods do not give everything to one man, and Jupiter has made thee a powerful king; but valor, the flower of manly virtues, he has denied thee. If thou art so anxious to return, very good; then go. The way is open and the ships are ready. But the rest of us will remain until we have destroyed Priam's fortress. And if all others should flee, I would remain with my friend Sthenelus, for it is the gods who have brought us hither."

All the warriors applauded this, and when Nestor had praised Diomedes' words, there was no further talk of retreat. The venerable man now counselled that the walls should be carefully guarded and that watchfires should be lighted everywhere. He signed to Agamemnon to invite the friends into his tent, offer them refreshment, learn each one's opinion, and to follow the best.

Nestor was the first to speak. "Great Atride," he began, "if thou wilt consider when it was the gods began to compass our ruin, thou wilt admit that our misfortunes began on the day when thou didst unjustly insult and abuse, to our great sorrow, that most valiant man whom even the immortals have honored. We were all displeased and thou knowest how I tried to dissuade thee. I think that even now we had better seek to conciliate the angry man with flattering words and gifts."

"Honored Nestor," answered Agamemnon, "I will not deny that I was in the wrong. It is true a single man, if chosen by the gods, is equal in might to an army. But having offended I will gladly make amends and offer him every atonement. I will give him rich gifts and he shall have, besides, the maiden over whom we quarrelled. How glad I would have been to return her as soon as my rage had cooled. If Jupiter will but grant me the good fortune to destroy Priam's mighty fortress, Achilles' vessel shall be heaped up with gold and silver and he may select twenty Trojan women for himself, the fairest after Helen. And when we return to Argos I will refuse him none of my daughters, should he wish to become my son-in-law, and will present him with seven of my most populous cities as a wedding gift. Thus will I honor him if he be willing to forget."

To this Nestor answered: "Son of Atreus, thou dost offer princely gifts which might well propitiate the proudest. Let us send messengers to him. Let them be Ulysses and Ajax and the venerable Phœnix, whom his father Peleus sent hither as his companion and friend. Let the heralds, Hodius and Eurybates, accompany them."

The encampment of the Myrmidons was on the seashore and they found Achilles in his tent, apart from the others, playing the harp and singing of heroic deeds. His good friend and comrade, Patroclus, sat opposite him listening. Ajax and Ulysses entered first and Achilles immediately put down his harp and came towards them. Patroclus also arose to welcome his old comrades.

"Ye are heartily welcome, old friends," began Achilles, "for I am not angry with you. Sit on these cushions and, Patroclus, bring a tankard and mix the wine, for we have honored guests here."

After they had eaten and poured out a libation to the gods, Ulysses took the goblet and drank to Achilles with a hearty handclasp. "Greeting to thee, Pelide," he began. "It is not food and drink we crave. But we are troubled that thou art not on the battlefield. The Trojans have pushed forward to the ships and nothing stops them. Jupiter has sent fiery tokens to encourage them and the invincible Hector is hard upon us with murder in his eye. Already he has threatened to burn the ships. Even at night he does not retire, but encamps on the open field and the whole plain is illumined by his campfires. No doubt he is now eagerly awaiting daybreak to destroy us, for he fears neither gods nor men.

"Hear what Agamemnon offers thee—gifts so costly that they would suffice to make any man rich and powerful. Ten pounds of gold will he give thee, and seven new tripods, with twenty polished basins, besides twelve magnificent horses and seven Lesbian slave women accompanying Briseïs' daughter. And when we shall have conquered Priam's city, thou shalt heap thy ship with gold and bronze and take twenty of Troy's fairest women for thyself. And when we return to blessed Argos thou shalt be his son-in-law and he will honor thee as his own son. But if thy hatred of Atreus' son is so great that thou canst not forgive him, then consider the dire need of the Achaian people, who are ready to pay thee honor like a god. Truly thou shalt earn great glory."

Achilles answered him: "Noble son of Laërtes, let me open my heart to thee frankly. Neither Agamemnon nor any other Greek can move me to fight again for this ungrateful people. The coward and the hero enjoy equal reputation among you. Why should I risk my life for others? As the swallow feeds its young with the morsels which it denies itself, thus I have spent my sweat and blood these many days for the ungrateful Achaian people; have watched through many a restless night, fought brave men, burning their houses and stealing away their women and children. I have destroyed twelve populous cities in Troy by sea and eleven by land and always delivered the spoils up to Agamemnon. He remained quietly at the ships and took my plunder gladly, keeping always the greater part for himself. Although each chieftain received a princely gift, he took mine from me—the lovely woman who was dear to me as a spouse.

"Why did we accompany him hither? Was it not for the sake of beauteous Helen? Do we not love our women even as he? Let him leave me in peace and take counsel with thee, Ulysses, and with the other chieftains. For Hector shall never again meet me in battle. To-morrow

I shall launch my ships, make offerings to the gods, and if thou wilt take notice, friend, thou shalt see my ships at dawn, floating upon the Hellespont. If Neptune favors me I may reach my native Phthia on the third day. There I have riches enough, so that I shall not need the gifts of the haughty king. No, should he offer me twenty times as much, and even a city like unto the Egyptian Thebes, which, it is said, has one hundred gates out of each of which issue two hundred men with horses and chariots in time of war, even then he could not persuade me until he had atoned for his insult.

"Let him find another husband, who is nobler and more powerful than I, for his daughter. Should I reach home safely, my father will choose me a noble consort, for there are many beautiful Achaian maidens who are not wanting in rich dowries. I long for Phthia and already I foretaste the joys of reigning over my father's good subjects and enjoying a life of plentiful ease by the side of a gentle spouse. Life is worth more than all Agamemnon's treasures, and once lost can never be regained.

"Dost know what fate my goddess mother hath revealed to me? Either I die young upon the battlefield and my name shall be imperishable upon earth, or I shall live to a great age without renown. Let it be as I have said, and if ye would have a word of advice from me, it is this: 'Sail away before Hector burns your ships, for ye will never conquer Troy.' Go, friends, and take this message to the Greeks. But, Phœnix, stay and return with me to our native land, if so it pleaseth thee; for I would not compel thee."

They were all silent until the gray-haired Phœnix began to speak. "If thou hast determined to return, noble Achilles, how can I part from thee, my son, for thy father confided thee to my care? Thy splendid deeds have made me proud and happy; but now, forgive me, godlike Achilles, now thy obstinate and unreasonable behavior grieves me. Calm thy rage. A gentle disposition well becomes the hero, and even the anger of the gods can be placated. How often have we seen them appeased by sacrifices and penitential prayers. Yea, woe unto him who listens not to repentant supplication and who hardens his heart against the enemy who is ready to make atonement. Behold what gifts

Agamemnon offers to win thee. What is the wrong thou hast suffered in comparison with this great honor? The ancient heroes of whom our fathers tell certainly were subject to fits of anger, but they also allowed themselves to be conciliated."

"Phœnix, honored sire," answered Achilles, "do not disturb my soul with lamentations; rather as my friend shouldst thou hate him who hath wronged me. But now repose thyself. As soon as dawn appears we will take counsel whether to go or stay." With a secret sign he bade Patroclus prepare a soft couch for Phœnix.

Hastily Ajax arose, saying: "Let us be going, for we can scarce expect to persuade this hard-hearted man, and our friends are awaiting us anxiously. Cruel man, to cause all thy friends to suffer for one. How oft have anger and revenge for a murdered brother been forgotten when the murderer has offered gifts and tokens of repentance. But thou hast a stony and implacable heart in thy bosom, and all this on account of a girl. Oh be persuaded! We have come here as thy old friends."

"Ajax, godlike son of Telamon," answered Achilles, "thou hast read my soul. But my heart is full of bitterness when I think of the man who treated me so vilely before the Argives. Go and bear him the message. I will not take up arms until the firebrands of the Trojans fall upon my own ships. Terrible as he is, I think Hector will not venture near my tents." Perceiving that their eloquence was unavailing, the ambassadors returned to Agamemnon's tent. Phœnix, however, remained with Achilles.

The Greek princes were much cast down at the answer to their mission. Only Diomedes was able to keep up their courage by his unshakable confidence. "Atreus' son," he cried, "would thou hadst never implored help of the Pelide or offered him rich presents. He was proud enough before. Let him go or come; he will take up his lance as soon as his heart speaks. But do thou, King Agamemnon, as soon as Eos' rosy fingers paint the sky, array thine horsemen and thy cohorts in front of the ships and place thyself at the front. Let us now to rest, for it is late and to-morrow we fight for our lives."

All agreed. The goblets were filled once more, a libation poured out to the gods, and then they separated, each one going to his own tent.

Chapter VIII
Agamemnon in Battle – Many of the Greeks are Wounded

MORNING had scarcely dawned when Agamemnon called all to arms, appearing in the foremost ranks clad in his most splendid armor and determined to fight more heroically this day than ever before. The great mass of foot-soldiers pressed forward in long lines shouting their battle cries, the war chariots containing the leaders following after them.

At last the two armies met and whole ranks of men fell like grain before the reaper's scythe. For some hours each side held its own, but toward noon the Achaians broke through the enemy's lines and forced them back. As soon as the ranks were broken and bodies of men began to scatter in little groups over the plain, the charioteers had room for action and dashed forward to terrorize the foot-soldiers.

Agamemnon was among the foremost, hurling his deadly lance continually at the Trojan princes. Two young and beautiful sons of Priam, both in one chariot, fell before him, and he took their accoutrements and horses. Next two sons of Antimachus came his way and received no quarter at his hands. He stood with bloody arm uplifted, swinging his lance, ready to strike down any who approached him. The Trojans fled in multitudes at the sound of his lionlike voice, and amid the wild confusion one could see frightened horses, with empty chariots trailing behind them, galloping back toward the city. Agamemnon and the other chieftains were relentlessly pursuing the flying Trojans, and as a lion following a herd of cattle will fasten his cruel claws into the necks of those which fall behind, thus the Achaians struck down many a fleeing warrior.

It was now Hector's care to stop the rout and bring order into the ranks once more at the city gates. He implored, he admonished, he scolded and threatened, and thus drove them back again after a brief rest. Shamed by his words, the young prince's sought out the most dangerous antagonists to show their valor. Iphidamas, son of Antenor, was even anxious to contend with Agamemnon himself, who, however, saw him coming and was the first to cast his lance. But the youth dodged the missile and ran quickly at him with his own spear and would surely have run him through had the brazen coat not bent the point of the weapon and broken the force of the blow. Agamemnon seized hold of the youth's lance with his powerful left hand and forced both him and it down, while, with a sudden blow of his sword, he cut off the youth's head. A servant soon stripped him and carried off the armor.

Koon, Antenor's second son, who had seen his brother's fall, called some of his companions together to avenge him. They approached Agamemnon unobserved and Koon cast his spear, which struck the hero's arm, wounding him so that the warm blood spurted forth. The youth was triumphant, for although Agamemnon did not fall, he saw him stagger backward. He wished to make use of this moment to carry off his brother's body, but as he was bending over it, Agamemnon's spear entered his side, and before he could recover himself Agamemnon had sprung upon him and cut off his head. The hero then turned away and attacked another body of the enemy, slaying many. As long as the warm blood continued to gush out he did not notice his wound, but when it began to dry, he could no longer endure the pain and was obliged to retire from the field. He mounted his chariot, admonishing the Achaians once more to fight bravely, and then drove rapidly away to his tent to have his wound dressed.

His departure revived the sinking courage of the Trojans. Hector pressed forward and the Achaians, abandoned by their courageous leader, turned to flee, as the Trojans had done before. The young princes sought to measure their strength against Hector, but only paid for their temerity with their lives. Seeing this, Ulysses' heart burned with rage. He called Diomedes and said: "Son of Tydeus, let us fight together against that terrible man. It would be a shame should plumed Hector take our great ships from us."

"Gladly will I tarry here," answered his friend surlily; "but much good will it do us, for Jove, the Thunderer, does not intend the victory for us, but for the Trojans." However, they set forth together and plunged amongst the swarms of soldiers like two raging lions, driving them backward, as waves are whipped by the wind. Hector saw this from afar and quick as a flash he bore down upon them in his chariot, sprang to earth, and met the heroes on foot.

"Look," cried Diomedes to Ulysses when he saw him; "there cometh our destruction. But let us stand firm, we will not flee."

They stood awaiting him with their lances in position, and at the moment when Hector emerged from the crowd Diomedes' spear struck his helmet with such force that he was thrown stunned to the ground. But the weapon had not wounded him, for his iron helmet was not broken, and before Diomedes had time to rush upon him with his sword, Hector had jumped up and plunged back into the crowd. Ulysses' lance had missed the mark, and before the two had recovered their weapons Hector was safely on his chariot. Diomedes stamped his foot with rage. He now set upon the enemy more murderously than ever, and as he drove them back and was nearing the tomb of the old Trojan King Ilus, he was met by Paris, who stayed his mad impetuosity. Hiding behind a pillar of the tomb, he let fly one of his never-failing arrows, which struck Diomedes, pinning his foot to the ground. He saw the hero falter and stand still and sprang from his hiding place crying in triumph: "Ha! it was a good shot. But how gladly would I have pierced a vital part and taken thy life!"

"Miserable coward!" roared Diomedes. "Hadst thou met me in the open thy bow and arrow had helped thee little. And now thou boastest as though thou hadst conquered me, and it is but a scratch. It is as though a mosquito had stung me. Woe unto thee when I catch thee!" However, the wound was troublesome enough, for he could not stand on his foot, and Paris would perhaps have ventured to shoot a second arrow, if Ulysses had not come up in the nick of time. He placed himself in front of his friend and covered him with his shield, while Diomedes sat on the ground and drew the arrow out of his foot, which caused him sharp pain. He then called for his charioteer and drove back to the ships, his heart full of bitterness.

Ulysses remained behind alone, for his companions had retreated in terror, and now he found himself suddenly surrounded by the Trojans. He could not escape and resolved to sell his life dearly with the blood of his enemies. He met their attack like a wild boar at bay, and so savage was his onslaught that the enemy, surprised, stood still and none dared come near him. But when he had stabbed Charops, the noble son of Hippasus, his brother Socus, full of grief and anger, stepped boldly forward to avenge him, crying: "Murderous Ulysses, either thou shalt boast that thou hast slain both of Hippasus' sons or thou shalt die by my hand!" With this he threw himself upon Ulysses with his spear and did actually pierce the shield and coat of mail, tearing the flesh and causing him to start back. But when Ulysses felt that the wound was not mortal, he quickly hurled his own lance, crying: "Miserable man, thou too art destined to fall this day by my hand!" Socus shrieked aloud, for the weapon had pierced clean through his breast.

On the other side of the battlefield the fighting was equally fierce. Hector and Paris were busy with spear and bow. Paris wounded the venerable Machaon, a good soldier and much prized for his surgical skill, for he had saved many lives. Therefore his friends were anxious about him and Nestor lifted him into his chariot and drove quickly away with him to camp. There they dismounted to refresh themselves in the cool breeze from the sea and to dry their damp clothing. Then they entered Nestor's tent, where he bound up his friend's wound and gave him food. While they were eating Patroclus entered the tent. Achilles had sent him to inquire who the wounded man was whom he had seen brought in by Nestor's chariot. For Achilles was accustomed, when the Greeks were fighting, to station himself on the high deck of his vessel to watch the fray, not without regrets that he was condemned to idleness; often his hand would grasp his sword involuntarily. His joy over the overthrow of the Achaians was the sweetest revenge he had for his wounded pride.

"Ah, here is Patroclus," cried Nestor. "Enter, friend, and sit down with us. I have not seen thee for a long time."

"Do not press me, venerable sir," answered Patroclus. "I may not remain, for I must take the tidings to Achilles for which he has sent me, and now that I have seen Machaon I must away. Thou well knowest how impatient he is."

But Nestor continued: "We thought that Achilles was no longer interested in our fate. And hast thou, his friend and companion, no influence with him? Canst thou not win him with persuasive words and tame his proud heart? That was what thy good father expected." Patroclus was moved by his words, and promising to do what he could, took his leave.

Once more the Achaians were obliged to take refuge behind the walls of the camp. Hector, followed by the victorious Trojans, drove all before him.

When the greater part of the Achaians had reached the shelter of the gate, Hector gave orders that all the charioteers should leave their chariots and lead their bands on foot across the moat, for he was determined to climb or tear down the flimsy walls. Hector was successful, although there was a fearful struggle at the wall. The Achaians defended their last stand with desperate courage, while the Trojans were just as determined to accomplish their purpose of driving the enemy from their coasts and burning their ships that day.

Thus far Jupiter seemed to aid the Trojans, for a terrible gale arose which blinded the eyes of the Achaians with dust, though they still fought manfully on and Hector was not able to accomplish his purpose. Two Lycian youths, Sarpedon and Glaucus, met outside the wall, resolved to shed glory upon their people by their bravery and enterprise. They sought to break down the wall at a spot defended by Menestheus, and their first onslaught was so savage that the Greek looked about him for help. He sent a messenger to Ajax and Teucer to come quickly to his aid, and they came running up with spear and bow. Ajax threw a stone which killed Sarpedon's attendant, who was already on top of the wall. Next Glaucus climbed up, but received Teucer's arrow in his arm, which incapacitated him for further fighting. He got down very quietly, so that the Achaians should not observe his misfortune, pausing to cast one more spear, which did its deadly work. Then he drove back to the city.

At last Sarpedon succeeded in making the first breach in the top of the breastworks, and under repeated blows the rest followed. This made the wall so low at this place that the soldiers could shoot over it, and here the hottest fighting now took place. It was impossible to move Sarpedon from his position. After a long struggle Hector came up, saw the breach, and cried joyfully: "Forward, ye Trojan horsemen, break through the Argives' wall and cast burning brands into the ships!" He raised a mighty stone in both arms, and although it was so heavy that two of the strongest men could not have lifted it or even have loaded it on a wagon with crowbars, Hector bore it as easily as a shepherd might carry a bundle of shorn wool, and with feet planted firmly wide apart, he hurled it with such force against the gateway that the bolts cracked, the hinges gave way, and the gate flew wide open. He sprang triumphantly into the intrenchments, followed by the shouting

Trojans. The frightened Achaians hurried away to defend their ships. The cries and confusion were indescribable. The Achaians were in despair. Nothing remained for them but to save their ships, and placing themselves in front of them in long rows with lances set, they thus awaited the final onset of the Trojans.

Each now forgot his own distress and all worked together, and soon a solid chain of armed men surrounded the ships like a wall. Hector himself, like a mighty rock which falls from the mountain top and plunges from ledge to ledge until it rests upon the plain, could get no farther, but was obliged to pause before the wall of lances. He tried to encourage his men by promising them great rewards. Now they believed that the last decisive moment had come and that before night it would be seen whether the gods had determined on the destruction of the Achaians or of Troy. But Jupiter was but favoring the Trojans in order to please Achilles and his mother, Thetis. Fate had already decreed that Troy was to fall, and even the gods could not change this decision, for they too were subject to the laws of iron necessity. As soon as Agamemnon had been sufficiently punished and Achilles could be persuaded to join the ranks of fighting Achaians, the destruction of the mighty city was to be expected.

As soon as the Achaians had intrenched themselves they grew bolder and began a fearless attack. Idomeneus charged the Trojans, followed by his brave Cretans. As the hurricane raises dark clouds of dust between the battle lines, thus the ironclad cohorts moved hurriedly forward and threw themselves on a party of the enemy. Idomeneus himself sought an antagonist among the princes, and now he chanced upon Othryoneus, who had just joined the Trojans with his squadron and had a reputation for great bravery. He had wooed Priam's most beautiful daughter, not with the customary gifts, but instead had promised his aid in driving the Achaians out of Asia. Priam had given his word, and the young hero was just beginning the struggle for the lovely prize when Idomeneus' spear put a sudden end to his life.

The battle raged fiercest on the right side of the camp where Hector was fighting. He was determined, in spite of the heroes who opposed him, to capture and burn the ships. All the fury of war was displayed on this spot—rage, despair, revenge, wild cries, fear, horror, and flight. The ground was slippery with the blood of the fallen; there was now no time to remove the corpses of the slain. The Trojans were the first to lose courage. Even Hector dared not keep his post where Ajax, Ulysses, and Idomeneus stood together like a wall, but sought out weaker adversaries and contented himself by answering the challenge of the two Ajaxes with insults and boasts.

"Why dost thou seek to frighten the common soldiers?" called the elder Ajax to him. "Drive us back if thou canst! Thou wouldst gladly take our ships, wouldst thou not? But I tell thee that thy proud Troy shall sooner sink into ashes than our fleet, and thou shalt sooner turn thy face homeward in flight than triumph over us."

At this moment an eagle flew high over the heads of the Achaians toward the right and, delighted with the omen, they had confidence in Ajax's words. But Hector answered him defiantly: "Miserable boaster, what foolishness is this! Would I were but as certainly a son of Jupiter as that to-day will bring destruction upon ye all. And woe to thee shouldst thou stand before my spear! It would tear thy delicate body and give thy blood to the dogs." He then dashed away with his band to enter the battle at another point. All were intimidated where he appeared, and the battle cries of the Trojans surrounding him rose high into the air.

Chapter IX
Agamemnon Consoled – The Gods Take Part in the Strife and the Trojans are Driven Back

THE GREEK HEROES who had been wounded on the morning of this unlucky day and had been obliged to retire from the fight had remained in their tents in great discouragement, caring for their wounds. Nestor still sat with Machaon, and after he had tended him and given him food and drink he arose restlessly and said to his wounded friend: "My dear fellow, let me go and see what our fortunes are. The shouts of the warriors seem louder at the wall."

He took a shield and lance and went out. Alas, what a sight met his eyes! The wall was half demolished, the gateway shattered, the Trojans inside the intrenchments, and such wild confusion prevailed that one could not tell friend from foe. He sighed deeply and considered for a moment whether he should go down into the turmoil or seek Agamemnon in his tent. He chose the latter course. But as he turned in the direction of the kings' ships, the wounded lords, Tydeus' son Diomedes, Ulysses, and Agamemnon, came toward him with slow steps, leaning on their lances and sick with wounds.

"Nestor, Neleus' son," cried Agamemnon, "whence comest thou and why didst thou leave the field? Alas, I fear that all will come to pass as Hector has threatened; that the Trojans will not rest until our ships are burned and our people destroyed. The Achaians hate and curse me as Achilles hates me, for it is I who have led them into this misery. No doubt they are now deserting or sitting brooding beside the ships."

"What has been, even Jupiter cannot change," answered Nestor. "But let us consider what is still to be done."

"Then let me tell thee what I think," said Agamemnon. "As we are at the end of our resources, my advice is that as soon as it is dark we launch our ships and sail away while the Trojans are asleep. Let them call us cowards! It is better to escape thus than to be destroyed."

"What words are these, O Atride," said Ulysses, frowning. "Thou shouldst have led an army of deserters hither, instead of commanding men like us, who have been taught from early youth to support the hardships of war unto death. What? Dost thou really intend to save thyself by stealing away like a thief in the night? Hush! That no one else may hear such unbecoming words!"

Agamemnon answered him: "Ulysses, I feel thy stern rebuke deeply, and I would not have the Argives launch the ships against their will. If anyone can give better counsel, let us hear it."

Now Diomedes began to speak. "It is not far to seek if thou wilt listen to me. I am indeed the youngest here, but as well born as any, and I think Jupiter hath given me courage and strength for manly deeds. My advice, then, is that we return to the battlefield, not to fight, for our wounds prevent that, but in order to encourage the others."

This speech pleased all and they followed him straight to the place of combat. Just as they arrived there they were met by Poseidon in the figure of an elderly warrior, who grasped the right hand of the ruler and said: "Take courage, brave Atride, the immortal gods will not be angry with thee forever. Thou shalt surely see the day when the Trojans will retreat in defeat to their city and their heroes fall before our lance thrusts."

With these words the old man returned to the fight and with encouraging words spurred on the hesitating soldiers to renewed effort. His voice resounded over the battlefield like the shouting of a thousand men and the Achaians obeyed it. The princes gazed after him in astonishment, for his kingly figure was unknown to them. They suspected that it was a god come to encourage them. Through hatred of the Trojans, Poseidon was secretly aiding the Achaians contrary to the express commands of Jupiter. But it would have gone hard with him if the son of Cronos, who was looking down on the battlefield from Mount Ida, had discovered him at once. Juno contrived a scheme to prevent this for a while at least. She went to Aphrodite and said coaxingly: "Wilt thou grant me a favor, or refuse it because thou art resentful of my aiding the Achaians, whilst thou art for the Trojans?"

Aphrodite graciously answered: "Mighty Juno, speak. What dost thou desire? If I can grant it I will do so."

Then Juno said cunningly: "Give me thy magic girdle of love and longing, which inclines the hearts of gods and men to thee. I wish to visit old grandfather Oceanus, who has quarrelled with his spouse Thetis, and try if I may not reconcile them."

"How could I refuse thee my help?" answered the goddess. "Here, take it, and mayest thou be successful."

Smiling happily, Juno took the magic girdle and hastened to her chamber. She bathed her delicate body, anointed it with ambrosial oil, and arranged her hair in shining ringlets. She then put on the fine long robe which Athena had woven for her, closed it with golden clasps on her breast, and wound the magic girdle about her waist. Beautiful earrings, a shimmering veil, and golden sandals completed the splendid dress. Juno now hastened over the heights of Olympus and across the mountains and streams of earth to Lemnos, where she found Sleep, the brother of Death.

He was indispensable to her in carrying out the trick she had planned, so she took him graciously by the hand and said: "Mighty Sleep, who tamest gods and men, if thou wouldst ever do me a service, do it now and I shall be forever grateful. My son Hephæstus shall fashion thee an indestructible seat, whose cushions are always soft, and it shall be shining with gold and have a comfortable footstool for thy feet."

A smile like a ray of sunshine lit up the god's face. Nothing could have tempted him more. Yawning he asked: "What dost thou want of me, honored goddess?"

"Come with me and put the father of the gods to sleep for a short time," she said. "And to make it easier for thee, I will beguile him with sweet speeches."

"Thou askest a hard thing," answered Sleep. "Anyone else I would dare approach, even ever-flowing old Oceanus; but Jupiter, the Terrible, I cannot venture near unless he calls for me himself. Only remember how he raged the time I deceived him at thy behest, when thou didst pursue his dear son Hercules with storms, with intent to imprison him on the island of Kos. All Olympus trembled at his wrath, and I should have been lost had Night not protected me out of friendship."

Juno replied: "Dost thou suppose the father of the gods cares as much for the Trojans as he did for his dear son? No indeed! As thy reward I promise thee for thy wife the fairest of the Graces, whom thou hast so long desired."

"Then swear it," cried Sleep, overjoyed, "that I may trust thee, and I will do thy bidding instantly."

The goddess touched the earth with one hand and the sea with the other and swore by the River Styx and by the gods of the underworld. Then they both passed over the sea to Phrygia. Juno went straight up Ida, while Sleep, in the form of a nighthawk, slowly circled about the mountain top and hid himself in the branches of a tall pine tree.

When Jupiter saw his consort he was greatly astonished. His dear wife had never appeared so lovely to him before. She had Juno's eyes, but Aphrodite's soulful glance; Juno's voice, but the words seemed to come from the heart of the goddess of love. The masterful, rebellious Juno, become gentle, kind, tender, and modest, so surprised him that he immediately forgot all his past grievances against her and gave himself up to the sweet delusion that this change would last forever. And now Juno became so confiding and affectionate that her lord forgot the Trojans and in looking at her his back was turned to them, so that he could not see his disobedient brother Poseidon. At last she made secret signs to the bird lurking in the pine branches to encompass the happy one with his outspread wings, and he was soon peacefully at rest. Sleep then flew quickly down to Poseidon to tell him that Jupiter was slumbering and that it was now time to aid the Achaians in earnest.

Then the sea god in the shape of an old warrior went up and down the ranks preaching courage. Under his leadership the people charged forward like a hurricane beating against a forest. Many men fell, most of them Trojans. Hector knew not that a god was opposing him, so he did not give way and still expected victory. But he soon met his doom. He had just cast his lance in vain at Ajax, and was about to pick up a stone, when Ajax quickly hurled a great piece of rock, which struck the hero under his shield and he fell back breathless. Shield and stone dropped from his hands and he tumbled over in the sand. Ajax and his friends were about to come up and strip him, but at this moment the bravest Trojan princes, Æneas, Polydamas, Agenor, and the valiant Lycians, Sarpedon and Glaucus, surrounded him, all covering him with their shields at once, until some of the servants lifted him on their shoulders and carried him to his chariot. When the chariot crossed the ford of the little River Scamander or Xanthus, the friends lifted down the moaning and still unconscious hero, laid him on the ground, and sprinkled him with water. He revived, opened his eyes, and wanted to arise, so they took hold of his arms and lifted him to a kneeling position. A stream of dark blood burst from his lips and he sank into unconsciousness again.

The news of Hector's fall was greeted with loud rejoicing in the Achaian army. Their old courage returned and Poseidon's presence worked wonders of heroism. The Trojans retreated farther and farther and few of the leaders fought alone. Victory now inclined toward the side of the Achaians, for Hector lay wounded on the banks of the Xanthus and the gods no longer fought for Troy. Thus the Trojans soon found themselves again near the city walls and even forced behind them.

Chapter X
Jupiter's Message to Poseidon – The Battle
for the Ships

JUPITER AWOKE and rubbed his eyes. His first glance sought the ships. How changed was the situation! "Ha, Juno," he cried angrily, "this is thy work, deceitful, malicious woman! So that was the meaning of thy caresses, thy friendliness and sweet talk, false serpent. Of what use is it to chastise thee? Hast thou already forgotten thy punishment when thou didst send a storm to drive my son Hercules into imprisonment on Kos and I made thee swing on a chain twixt heaven and earth with an anvil fastened to each foot? Suppose that now I were to—"

"Heaven and Earth are my witnesses, and I will even swear it by the Styx, that Poseidon did not go into the battle at my behest," said the affrighted goddess. "I do not know whether the Achaians have persuaded him to it or his own heart. Rather would I counsel him to go whithersoever thou commandest."

The father of gods and men answered, smiling grimly: "If thou wert of my mind, regal Juno, Poseidon would certainly soon change his course. But now call Iris quickly and Apollo of the bow, that they may descend and command Poseidon to leave the battlefield and return to his palace."

The lily-armed Juno willingly obeyed, though she still meditated mischief in her heart. She drove quickly to high Olympus, where she found the immortals in the banquet hall. Craftily she spoke to them. "It is useless to seek to change Jupiter's decrees," she said. "Little he cares for us, for he feels himself high above us all in strength and power. Only just now I saw Ascalaphus, the beloved son of mighty Mars, slain in battle."

"Do not blame me, ye dwellers in Olympus, if I go to avenge the death of my son," wailed Mars; "even though the bolt of the Thunderer strike me down." He rushed from the hall and donned his shining armor, appearing greater and more terrible than ever.

Incalculable mischief would have followed if Athena, concerned for the rest of the gods, had not hurried after him and taken his helmet, shield, and lance from him by force. "Imbecile," she cried, "wouldst thou destroy us all? Woe unto us if he should see thee, the terrible Jupiter! Thy son was but a mortal and other noble warriors have fallen; it is impossible to save them all from death." With these words she forced her angry brother back to the throne and he obediently submitted to her warning.

Apollo and Iris flew quickly down to the green summit of Ida, where Jupiter sat enveloped in dark clouds. Iris he sent with a stern message to Poseidon and his beloved son Apollo to Hector to strengthen him with his divine breath. "Then lead him into the battle once more," said Jupiter, "and aid him thyself to drive the Achaians on board their ships. Take the terrible ægis in thy hand and shake it, that their hearts may quake."

Iris delivered her message to the sea god and he answered it defiantly. "Powerful as he is, I call that tyrannical. To combat my will—mine, who am his equal! For are not he and Pluto and I brothers, and were not the upper and under worlds divided equally between us? We cast lots; air fell to him and water to me, but earth and sky are free to us all, and he shall not stop me here. Let him rule his consort and his sons and daughters. What care I for his threats or commands!"

Then Iris said doubtfully: "What, dark-haired World-power! Shall I take Jupiter thy answer in just those words, or wilt thou not change thy mind? It is well to keep the peace and respect is always due the elder."

"Iris, exquisite goddess," answered the angry king, "thou speakest sensibly and with reason, but it was righteous anger overcame me, for no brother should rule another. Now that I come to think it over, I know I had best obey him. But tell him this—that if, contrary to the wishes of all the other gods, he protects Ilium's fortress and gives not the victory to the Achaians, he may expect our eternal enmity."

He spoke, left the battlefield, and plunged into the sea. Meanwhile Apollo had appeared to Hector, saying: "Be comforted, son of Priam, for Jupiter sends me to save thee. I am Phœbus Apollo, who hath so often protected thee and thine. Follow me, that we may scatter the Achaians." Thus the god encouraged the shepherd of the people, and like a colt which has broken its halter and gallops after the other horses to the pasture, he hastened into the battle turmoil. The reappearance of the hero caused astonishment and consternation among the enemy, and as the invisible Apollo shook the shield of Jupiter, the mighty ægis, fear and horror took complete possession of the people, and turning they fled back to the ships. The battle raged fiercer than before, and many brave men fell there.

Then Hector called aloud: "The time has come, brave Trojans, to board the ships. Let all keep together. Let no one tarry to gather booty, and if one remains behind, he shall die by my own hand." He urged his horses across the moat, and the others followed him with exultant cries. When they reached the ships they paused and prayed aloud to the gods for victory. A long roll of thunder presaged good fortune, and with redoubled courage they charged forward. Hector tried to board a vessel, but in vain. The Achaians, from the deck, thrust back everyone who made the attempt with their long oars, and where Hector fought there were always to be found gathered together the bravest warriors. The Trojans, with their double-edged lances, fought in their chariots, but the Achaians, from the high decks of their dark vessels, used long, ironbound oars.

While the battle raged between the wall and the ships Patroclus was sitting in Eurypylus' tent nursing his wounded friend. But he dared not remain long, for fear of arousing Achilles' anger. He felt that he must see how his friends were faring, and his heart urged him to persuade Achilles to come to the rescue of the Achaians at last. He left the tent and gazed with horror upon the dreadful battleground. He saw Hector rush forward with a flaming torch and try to fire a ship, but the Achaians turned aside the fatal missile. Ajax of Salamis stood upon the deck and thrust down with his lance all who bore a burning brand. Hector aimed his javelin at him, but it struck Lykophron, who stood beside him. Ajax then called upon Teucer: "Look, brother, our friend has fallen by Hector's hand! Where is thy avenging arrow?"

Teucer hastily climbed up with his bow and with the first arrow struck Klitus from his chariot. He then selected a second and sharper arrow for Hector and, as he was quite near to him, would doubtless have pierced him had the cord of his bow not broken just as he was in the act of drawing it. "Woe is me!" he cried. "A god brings all our attempts to naught and must have broken this cord, a newly twisted one, which I put on this morning."

Hector had seen the accident, accepted it as a favorable omen, and cheered on his men. "Let everyone fight with all his might, for the Olympian Jove is with us. And if ye fall it shall be a glorious death for the women and children of Troy, and surely the Trojans shall recompense ye as soon as the Achaians are driven away."

Where Hector rushed in, the troops huddled together like a herd of sheep before a wolf. None dared defend himself, but bowed his head in terror, and trembling, received his deathblow with averted face. The hero's fluttering plumes were like a lion's mane and his eyes flashed fury under his dark brows. Fear and shame kept the Achaians together. They continually encouraged one another. Nestor particularly besought the people to make one last attempt.

Among the Achaian leaders the most notable courage was shown by the Telamonian Ajax. He ran from one ship to another to encourage the soldiers, who could scarcely be forced to make another stand. A Trojan brought Hector a torch, which he threw into the foremost of the deserted ships. The sight drove the Achaians to desperation. They all rushed forward to defend the ship and a horrible struggle took place. Battle axes, swords, and lances hissed through the air and much blood flowed. Hector clung to the ship and shouted: "Bring up the firebrands! Jupiter has given us the day and we shall certainly take the ships." And "fire! fire!" echoed through the entire army, so that all the Achaians trembled. Ajax himself could make no headway, but standing on one of the ships, he threw lance after lance at everyone he saw approaching with fire. His voice was never silent, but rose continually above the din, calling to his people: "Friends, keep up your courage and show yourselves men! Is there any help but in yourselves or is there another wall behind you? Do ye know of other ships, if these are burned, to carry you over the sea? Your deliverance depends solely upon yourselves!"

Fruitless zeal! The rattling spears of the enemy drove them to flight more convincingly than the voice of the lone leader to the attack. Their strength was broken.

Chapter XI
Patroclus Hastens into Battle and Scatters the Trojans – Hector and Patroclus

Profoundly grieved at the sad fate of his comrades, Patroclus turned from the bloody spectacle and hurried to Achilles' tent. Hot tears were rolling down his cheeks as he entered. Achilles, dismayed, forgot to rebuke him and inquired with concern: "Why dost thou weep, Patroclus? Speak, tell me all!"

Sighing deeply, Patroclus replied: "Son of Peleus, thou mighty hero of the Achaians, do not be angry with me if I tell thee that the Achaians are suffering too great misery. All over the field and at the ships their bravest warriors have fallen, and but few of the princes remain unharmed. Diomedes has been shot through the foot and Agamemnon through the arm; Ulysses is wounded in the side and Eurypylus received an arrow in his thigh. The deserted soldiers are panic-stricken and thou, obstinate one, wilt not take pity on them. Cruel man! Thou art so brave and yet thou wilt not raise thy hand to save thy despairing friends. May a god never be angry with me as thou art angry. Surely Peleus is not thy father nor a goddess thy mother. The dark sea depths or adamantine rocks must have brought thee forth, so unfeeling is thy heart. Or is it that thou obeyest some secret command of the gods and darest not take part in the battle? Then, at least, send me and give me thy Myrmidons that I may perchance drive back the Trojans from the ships. Lend me thy armor that the Trojans, deceived, may retreat and the Achaian warriors take fresh courage."

"No behest of the gods restrains me," replied Achilles, "nor is it my purpose to be angry forever. As soon as the Trojans approach my tents and ships, I shall gird on my sword and spear, and woe to him whom I shall meet! But until then, let Agamemnon bitterly repent his outrage and promise expiatory sacrifices to all the gods. But I shall not allow the Trojans the pleasure of destroying the ships. Therefore go, as thou desirest. Lead the Myrmidons into battle, for the danger is great. Diomedes no longer shakes his mighty spear and I do not hear the hated Agamemnon's valiant battle cry; instead, Hector's lionlike voice penetrates my tent, with the loud rejoicing of the Trojans. Take my resplendent armor, but listen well to what I say. Thou mayest drive the Trojans from the ships and back to the intrenchments, but pursue them no farther. Take care not to allow thyself to be enticed into an open battle, nor still less dare to storm Troy's fortress without me, for mine must be the glory, that the Achaians may learn whom they have insulted."

With these words he climbed to the upper deck of his ship to reconnoitre. And how horrified he was to see Protesilaus' ship in flames, Hector still advancing, and the Achaians giving way. "Hurry, hurry, Patroclus!" he cried and smote his thigh with impatience. "The ships are already burning! Put on the armor quickly, while I gather the Myrmidons." There were more than two thousand of them, splendid warriors of great strength and stature. At their leader's call they assembled under arms. Achilles divided them into five companies, to each of which he gave a leader of proven courage and experience. Meanwhile Patroclus bade Automedon bring forth Achilles' chariot and horses, with a second one for emergencies. Then he put on the shining armor, placed on his head the great helmet with its crest of waving horsehair, and took two lances, but not that of Achilles, for no other living mortal could wield that.

Thus armed he sprang into the chariot beside Automedon, who was waiting, whip in hand. Then Achilles went to the chest which his mother had given him, filled with cloths and warm garments, and took out of it a precious golden goblet from which he was accustomed to make sacrifice to the greatest of the gods alone. He dipped it in the sea, washed his hands, then filled the goblet with clear wine, and with it in his hands went to the door of his tent. "Father Jupiter, ruler of the world," he prayed, while he poured the first drops on the ground in honor of the god, "hear me now as thou didst hear me when I was honored before the Achaians. Grant that my friend may return to me covered with glory, and fill his heart and the hearts of his companions with courage, that they may make an end of the Trojans at the ships, and that Hector may learn that Patroclus knows how to order the battle even if I am not with him."

The appearance of Patroclus and his followers was like sunshine after a shower to the Achaians. The Trojans were frightened, for they thought that Achilles had come forth again, and even without him the advent of two thousand fresh warriors was matter enough for concern. When Achilles' band made a dash for Protesilaus' burning ship, not a Trojan stood his ground. The space about the ship was cleared by the Myrmidons and they quenched the fire which had already destroyed half of the ship. But the battle was by no means at an end. The leaders of the Trojans rallied their forces inside the intrenchments and put them in order once more. Patroclus did his friend credit; he was indefatigable and himself slew many of the boldest warriors. The other Achaian leaders joined him and new life and hope filled every breast.

The Trojans could no longer maintain their position inside the intrenchments. Hector was the first to reach the open plain with his chariot, but many another who tried to follow him was crushed in the throng. But the rout would not have been so general had Patroclus remembered Achilles' instructions. But his success, the suddenness of the victory, and particularly his secret desire to kill Hector, misled the zealous man to pursue the fleeing enemy. He jumped from his chariot, which he instructed to have follow him, and hurried after his victims. Now he overthrew Pronous and took his armor; next he slew the charioteer Thestor and took his likewise. With a stone he crushed the head of Euryalus, who was about to attack him, and many others were struck down by his mighty arm. Not a Trojan was able to withstand Patroclus. The foolish man! Had he but remembered Achilles' warning he might have escaped death; but Jupiter's decree is mightier than man.

A few hours earlier the Trojans had broken down the enemy's wall and now the Achaians were seeking to conquer the lofty walls of Troy's fortress, and Patroclus himself was ambitious of being the first to enter the city. But Hector plucked up courage and commanded his charioteer to drive straight at the leader. As soon as he saw him coming, Patroclus left the wall and ran furiously to meet him, holding his lance in his left hand and in the right a stone which he had hastily picked up. This he threw with all his might at the two tall men in the chariot, and behold, it struck the good Kebriones, Priam's son, and crushed his skull, so that his body fell abruptly across the chariot seat. Patroclus cried out maliciously: "See how hasty the man is! There are splendid divers among the Trojans. If he could but have tried his luck in the water, instead of in the sand, he would have caught plenty of oysters to satisfy his hunger."

He sprang upon the wounded man to take his arms, but Hector jumped from his chariot and seized his brother's head. Patroclus took his feet and the two men struggled for the body. A crowd of Trojans and Achaians came to their aid, and spears, shields, and naked swords rattled noisily against one another. The Trojans defended Hector as well as they could, but while he struggled for the body, none could get near him. However, a bold Trojan seized a favorable opportunity, and with a powerful blow of his sword, knocked off Patroclus' helmet, cutting the strap of his shield at the same time, so that it fell to the earth. The hero started back and let go the corpse, but as he turned, Euphorbus stabbed him in the back. He tried to escape, but Hector laid him low with his heavy lance. The Achaians trembled, and even the most courageous of them lost their heads, and none dared interfere as Hector, bracing his foot against the body, drew out his spear, then stripped off the armor. It was now Hector's turn to mock at the dying man and he cried: "Well, Patroclus, dost thou still expect to lay waste our city and carry off our women? One could see thou hadst great deeds in mind. No doubt Achilles bade thee not return without Hector's bloody coat of mail. Now, poor man, thou liest here and givest me thy fine armor, but thee I give to the dogs and birds of prey for food."

Faintly the dying man answered him: "It is a foolish boast, Hector. Thou camest, when I was defenseless and wounded, to rob me. In open conflict I could have slain twenty like thee, but a boy could have done what thou hast done. But vengeance is approaching and when it comes, think of me. The godlike Achilles still lives."

"Spare me thy prophecies and die," replied Hector. "Who knoweth but Achilles, like thee, may give up his soul at the point of my spear?" With these words he left the dying man and carried the splendid armor to a place of safety, then went back into the fray.

Chapter XII
The Fight for Patroclus' Body – Achilles Mourns for His Fallen Friend – Thetis and Vulcan – Achilles' Shield

HECTOR NEXT ROVED about seeking to capture the splendid steeds of Achilles with which Patroclus had entered the field, but he could not come near them, for Patroclus' charioteer, Automedon, was already far distant. Meanwhile the space about Patroclus' body was deserted except for Menelaus, who stood guard beside it, covering it with his shield until some of his comrades should come up to bear it away to the ships. He was spied by Euphorbus, brother of that Hyperenor who had fallen by Menelaus' hand the day before. He approached within a spear's cast and called to him: "Son of Atreus, stand back from the dead! Thou shalt not give honorable burial to this destroyer who hath slain so many of us. Back, before I rob thee of thy sweet life!"

"Great Jupiter," cried Menelaus, "did one ever hear such insolence! Only yesterday thy brother Hyperenor was equally bold, but I believe he has paid the penalty, for he can scarcely have returned to his dear wife and old father on his own feet. The same fate awaiteth thee, if thou approach nearer. I advise thee to escape while thou canst."

"It is for my brother's sake that I would fight with thee," cried Euphorbus. "How delighted shall my father be when I bring him thy bloody armor in token of vengeance. But why do I waste time in talk? Let us try our skill."

As he spoke he ran at Menelaus full tilt with his lance, but the point bent like lead against the shield and did not even scratch it. Then Menelaus ran him through with his own spear and the slender youth fell, as a tender sprout of olive is uprooted by the wind. His long waving hair was bathed in blood and he, who but a moment before had bounded among the ranks of warriors like a deer, lay unrecognizable. Menelaus was about to take his armor when he saw Hector at a distance, and not caring to face him he left Patroclus' body and ran to fetch the elder Ajax, that together they might protect their friend from the thieving hands of the Trojans.

Then Glaucus spoke sullenly to Hector. "Thou art a great boaster, but never have I seen thee at the post of danger, nor attempting to defend or avenge any of thy comrades. The heroic Sarpedon, who sacrificed so much for thee, was left to his fate, and no one knoweth where he fell. Do the Lycians deserve this at thy hands? If thou art so ungrateful and no honor is paid a fallen hero, then mayest thou fight thy battles alone and I will take my Lycians home. If ye Trojans were men of courage and decision, ye would carry off the body of Patroclus to a place of safety. Doubtless the Achaians would then offer the body of Sarpedon and his weapons in exchange and even more. But thou fleest the battle like a coward, fearing Ajax, who is, indeed, quite another sort of man."

Darkly Hector gazed at him and began: "Ah, my friend, I have always taken thee for a man of sense, but now hast thou spoken rashly. When did the enemy or the snorting of horses ever terrify me? No, I fear neither Ajax nor Diomedes nor any of the Achaian heroes, but rather the decree of Jove, who has apparently given victory into the hands of the enemy. What availeth the valor of a mortal against the god of gods? But if thou wilt observe my actions, take heed and see if I am as timid as thou hast said."

Clad in Achilles' magnificent armor he immediately assembled his men with loud battle cries. Calling all the princes together, he spoke to them. "Friends and allies, not to be in the midst of many men have I called ye to Troy, but that ye might aid me in time of danger to protect our wives and children. It is for this that our poor people are laboring to feed and sustain ye with their flocks and the fruits of their fields, and for this I am striving with sword and speech to encourage ye and spur ye on to the combat. Then let us fight to the death! And to him who bears the body of Patroclus into Troy I promise a rich recompense."

All followed him, shouting, to the spot where Menelaus and Ajax stood shielding the body of Patroclus. Their hearts beat wildly when they saw the little band bearing down on them, and Menelaus ran as fast as he could to procure more help. "Come friends," he cried, "there lies Patroclus, whom the Trojans would seize and carry away to become food for Trojan dogs. Do ye not feel the shame of it?"

The younger Ajax was the first to hear and respond; then came Idomeneus and Meriones, each with a band of followers. They arrived beside the corpse just as Hector and his men came up, and the shock of meeting was like the ocean tide at the mouth of some mighty river which empties into the sea, so terrible was the crash of shields and lances.

Then Automedon with Achilles' steeds came dashing along, resolved himself to contend for the corpse. Hector saw him coming and cried, rejoicing, to Æneas: "There come Achilles' splendid horses! Come, if thou wilt aid me, let us take them!" They ran toward the chariot, but Automedon, springing to the ground, called Ajax and Menelaus to his aid. Chromeus and Aretus joined Hector and Æneas and a fresh contest raged about the chariot. Hector aimed well and cast with mighty power, but Automedon dashed quickly aside and the spear flew far over him into the earth, where it quivered for a long time. Automedon was more fortunate, and although Hector dodged the blow, it struck Aretus, who stood behind him. Meanwhile evening was descending and Ajax was anxious to secure the body before night came on. But it was all the Achaians could do to hold back the enemy. Then Ajax said to Menelaus: "If only some good youth would hasten to the ships and take to Achilles the tidings of his friend's death perhaps he would come himself to rescue the body from the enemy's hands. Dost thou see Antilochus, Nestor's son? I think he could reach camp quickest." Menelaus hastened away to seek the youth, where he was fighting at the other side of the battlefield. He was horrified to learn of the hero's death and tears filled his eyes; but he did not tarry and hurried away to Achilles.

Menelaus returned straightway to Ajax, saying: "I have sent him, but I doubt whether Achilles will come without his armor. So let us try once more to secure the body."

"Thou art right," answered Ajax. "Let us make another attempt, and if they retire but a little way, do thou and Meriones seize the corpse while the rest of us keep off the mighty Hector and the other Trojans."

This strategy partially succeeded and Menelaus and Meriones were able to drag the body some distance away. Meanwhile Achilles had been impatiently awaiting his tardy friend. He ascended to his usual post, the high deck of his ship, and saw, approaching through the twilight and clouds of dust, dense crowds which looked like fleeing men. It seemed to him that he could hear Hector's triumphant voice pursuing the Achaians. An uneasy premonition seized him and he was about to send out a messenger when young Antilochus appeared before him and spake, weeping: "Woe is me, son of Peleus, I bring thee sad tidings. Patroclus is slain, and our warriors are fighting desperately for his naked body, for Hector has taken his weapons."

Achilles grew pale as death. He tore his hair with rage, beat his breast, and threw himself upon the ground, covering dress, face, and head with dust. His eyes flashed dangerously, his heart palpitated, and horrible groans escaped his half-open lips. His slaves gathered about him in affright; but when they learned the cause of his boundless sorrow, they all burst out weeping. Antilochus wept also and held the hero's hands, fearing that the passionate man would harm himself. This terrible despair lasted a long time, but at last the overburdened heart found relief in tears and he broke out in loud lamentations.

His mother Thetis heard him and arose from the depths of the sea to seat herself beside her unhappy son. She pressed his head to her bosom and inquired tenderly: "Dear child, what is troubling thee now? Do not conceal anything from me. Speak! Hath Jupiter not fulfilled thy wish and given the victory to the Trojans?"

"What care I for the favor of Jupiter when Patroclus, whom I loved as myself, lies dead! Hector hath slain him and taken the armor, that splendid gift of my valiant father. For what a fate was I born! But, indeed, I will not live if I may not slay Hector and avenge the death of my friend."

"Glorious son," said his mother, weeping, "when thou hast slain him it will be thy doom; for thy death is decreed immediately after Hector's."

"Would that I were already dead," answered Achilles gloomily, "as I was not permitted to save my friend. But I will avenge him and pay him such honor as no mortal has ever received before. Then let Jupiter do with me as he will. Death is the lot of all. Even great Hercules died, the best beloved of all Jupiter's sons. But before Death takes me, many a Trojan woman shall lament that I have slain her son or young spouse. They shall all learn that my long rest is ended."

"I shall not restrain thee," answered the silver-footed Thetis, "for thy grief is righteous and thy resolution to honor the dead and save thy friends from destruction is commendable. But thou hast no weapons and I forbid thee to enter the turmoil of Mars until at dawn thou seest me returning with armor from the hand of the artist Vulcan." She suddenly disappeared and ascended to Olympus to beg the weapons from the god.

Meanwhile the noise of the struggle grew louder as the fortunes of war drove the Achaians to flight. With loud cries the Trojans followed the body of Patroclus in the twilight, and although the two bearers hurried as fast as they could to get it to a place of safety, they were often in danger of losing it. Hector pursued them continually with his men and more than once had seized one of the dead man's feet. The two Ajaxes had no thought of killing Hector, for his gigantic stature appalled them. They only held the corpse tighter, to keep it from being torn from them. Just as they were nearing the moat, they would have lost it, if a swift messenger had not summoned Achilles. "Help! help! Achilles!" he cried. "Hector will soon have taken the body of Patroclus. He threatens to cut off the head and put it on a pike and to throw the trunk to the Trojan dogs. What a disgrace if thy friend's body be taken and misused!"

Like a maniac, without armor or weapons, Achilles rushed out, and in a voice like thunder rolling in the mountains, he roared out most terrible threats, so that both Trojans and Achaians were overcome by fear and Hector, terrified, let go the corpse and quickly retired with his followers, thinking Achilles was already on his track. Thus the two heroes brought the corpse safely into camp. Achilles gazed long upon his friend, speechless, with bowed head, clenched hands, and tears coursing down his cheeks. The Trojans now held council whether they should spend the night in the city or on the battlefield. Polydamas was anxious to retire, for he feared Achilles; but Hector insisted on remaining, for he held that it would be cowardly to allow the enemy to suspect that they were afraid. "Let Achilles come forth to-morrow," he concluded; "he will do so at his own risk. I shall surely not fly before him. I long to meet him, and then Jupiter shall decide which one of us shall be covered with glory. Mars is a vacillating god, who oft destroys the destroyer."

So they encamped on the field for the night. Youths brought forth animals from the city for the sacrifice, together with bread and wine, lit fires, and prepared the evening meal. The Achaians also, after supping, laid down to rest. But Achilles could not sleep. Kneeling beside his dead friend, he laid his hand on his cold breast and sobbed. Overcome with grief he cried: "Before the earth hides me, thou shalt be avenged, my Patroclus. I will lay Hector's weapons at thy feet and Hector's bloody head beside them. I will slay twelve Trojan youths in thine honor. Rest thou here in peace, for the morrow shall shed glory upon thee and me."

Meanwhile Thetis had arrived in Olympus and went straightway to Vulcan's dwelling. Late as it was, she heard him hammering in his workshop, for he was making twenty bronze tripods for the Olympians' hall. He had fastened golden wheels to each foot, so that they could roll to the banquet of themselves. They were all finished except for the handles, and these he wished to complete that night. Aphrodite, the beautiful spouse of the lame fire god, was the first to spy the newcomer at the door. She took her hand, saying: "Welcome, dear friend, what bringeth thee so late from thy sea depths? Thou dost not often visit me." She led her within and called her spouse.

He immediately left his anvil, washed his hands with a sponge, also his sooty face, neck, and powerful chest, threw on his cloak, and leaning on his golden staff, came limping to the door. He took the goddess' hand and bade her welcome. "I always think of thee with gratitude," he said; "for thou didst take me in when I was lamed and my mother would not tolerate me in heaven. Then I lived for a time in thy crystal palace under the sea and fashioned many a pretty piece of work—rings and clasps, pins and chains—until Juno took me into favor again and I left thy dwelling. Therefore, Aphrodite, see that thou entertain our guest worthily."

When Thetis had partaken of the nectar and ambrosia which Aphrodite set before her, she began to recite all her son's troubles, from Agamemnon's injustice down to the fall of Patroclus. Then she begged the god to forge new armor for the unlucky Achilles, so that he might be ready to attack Hector in the morning. Aphrodite was displeased, for she feared for the Trojans, but the god paid no attention to her and promised to fulfil Thetis' desire. He immediately returned to his workshop and began the work.

Before the night was two thirds past the most splendid suit of armor that ever a hero had possessed was completed. The shield especially was a work of art. In the middle the earth was represented with the sea and sky, sun, moon, and stars. There were also two cities; one at peace and the other in the throes of war. In one a wedding was being celebrated with music and dance and there were many pictures of peaceful labor in field and vineyard. The other city was in a state of siege, and one could plainly see the besiegers and the citizens defending themselves. Around the edge of the shield flowed the deep river Oceanus.

Chapter XIII
Achilles and Agamemnon Reconciled –
Achilles Goes into Battle

ROSY-FINGERED EOS was mounting the eastern sky as Thetis arrived at her son's tent with the rich suit of armor. She found him still stretched beside Patroclus' body with the mourning women about him. Achilles accepted Vulcan's wonderful work joyfully, and the sight of the weapons made his eyes flash with a dangerous light. When he had carefully examined and admired the artistic embellishments he said to Thetis: "Mother, these weapons are not the work of a mortal; some god has forged them. Come, I will arm myself, that the Trojans may tremble at the glorious sight."

He then approached the tents and ships of the Achaians, calling to them loudly to come forth. They rejoiced to hear the thunder of that voice, which had been silent so long, and came hastening to the council place. Diomedes was limping painfully and leaning on his lance. Even Agamemnon and Ulysses, both weakened by painful wounds, came dragging themselves along with staves. When they were all seated in their places, Achilles took up the sceptre and spoke. "Son of Atreus, let us be reconciled, as we have long wished to be. I had rather the gods had slain the rosy maiden before ever a quarrel on her account had estranged us and my anger sent so many noble Achaians down to Hades. But let us forget the bitter past. I have moderated my anger, for a generous man should not be implacable, however much he has been wronged. And now let us hasten to lead our people to the combat, for the Trojans must not burn the ships to-day."

He was interrupted by a loud shout of exultation. The tidings that he had relented and would join them in the battle was enough to fill all hearts with joy. In their excitement they did not care to hear more, and not until the thunderous tones of the heralds had commanded silence could Agamemnon's answer be heard. "Jupiter alone knows," said he, "how blind rage could have led me to commit such an injustice, from which my heart now recoils and which I have long bitterly repented. Thou hast already heard from Ulysses of the gifts which I offered thee in reparation, and even now, that thou comest of thyself, I will take nothing back. My servants shall deliver all to thee, if thou wilt but save the Achaians."

Smiling, the warlike Achilles answered him: "I care not whether thou givest or retainest thy treasure. Let us think only of the war and lead the battalions without delay against the enemy, for there is much work to do and great deeds must be accomplished this day."

Now Ulysses spoke up. "Not thus, excellent Achilles; we must not be hasty. Let the soldiers partake of food, for the battle will not be of a few hours' duration only. Thou hast more endurance than all others, but none but thee can hold out through the long day's work without food or drink. Let the people first break their fast, while Agamemnon sends for the promised gifts, that we may all look upon them. Then he shall feast thee in his tent, that thou mayest enjoy all the honor due thee; for even a king should propitiate the man whom he hath wronged."

"I gladly follow thy wise counsel," answered Agamemnon, "and if thou wilt, thou mayest go thyself to my ships, with six picked men, to fetch the promised gifts."

"Son of Atreus," interrupted Achilles, "never mind the gifts. Let us think only of the slain, who are calling to us to avenge them. And ye talk of eating and drinking and of rest! If I were in command the people should be led forth fasting and at night; after the day's work they should feast twice over. For my part, not a drop shall pass my lips until I shall have avenged my friend. I have no thoughts, but of murder, bloodshed, and the death rattle of falling men."

"Great son of Peleus," suggested Ulysses, "though thou art no doubt stronger and braver than I, yet I think I can give thee good counsel, for I have lived longer and seen much. Take my advice this once. Thou canst conquer only with warriors who are rested, refreshed, and eager for the fight; but the hungry and thirsty soldier will follow thee half-heartedly and in the end be overcome by his own weakness."

Without awaiting Achilles' answer, the leaders gave the soldiers the signal to break their fast. Ulysses quickly selected six good comrades and went to fetch the presents from Agamemnon's ships and tents. He selected the basins, ewers, the horses and women, weighed out ten pounds of gold, and then summoned the fair Briseïs to follow him. On their return to the council place Agamemnon sent the gifts immediately to Achilles' encampment.

In vain the noble Achaian heroes surrounded Achilles and begged him to join them at the banquet. He shook his head, saying: "Kind friends, do not trouble me, for I am very sorrowful and I shall fast until the sun sets." The princes retired sadly to their tents to partake of food. Only Atreus' sons and the noble Ulysses, Nestor, Idomeneus, and the gigantic Phœnix remained with him, trying to comfort the mourner. He sat brooding over his sorrow. "Dear, unhappy friend," he said, "how oft hast thou brought me my breakfast and tended me while the others went forth to battle, and now thou liest here dead; but neither food nor drink can refresh me while I mourn for thee. I had always hoped that I alone should die in the Trojan land and that thou shouldst return to Phthia, to bring up my son, dear Neoptolemus. And now thou art gone before me."

Thus he lamented, and all his friends mourned with him. Even Jupiter was touched by his deep sorrow and sent his daughter Athena down secretly to strengthen his heart with heavenly nectar, and thus the hero was able to appear in all his glory when the warriors gathered together. The lust of battle had dried the tears upon his eyelids.

Chapter XIV
Achilles in Battle – The Fight on the River

ALL OLYMPUS was now interested in the combat of mortals since the godlike Achilles had taken up arms again. Many of the divinities promised him victory, but Jupiter was resolved

that he should not yet destroy the splendid city of the Trojans, for fate had not decreed that it should fall by his hand. Therefore he commanded the other gods to stay the zeal of the Pelide should he rage too terribly. The Trojans were already armed and in the field and the swarms of Achaians flew to meet them like a heap of dry leaves driven before the wind. Achilles looked everywhere for Hector, but without discovering him. Instead, he espied two other chieftains, Aeneas and Lykaon.

Aeneas determined to face the hero. He commended his soul to his divine mother and pushed forward shouting fierce threats. Achilles ran toward him without hesitation and then stopping suddenly he called out: "How canst thou venture so far from thy men, Aeneas? What is it impels thee to fight with me? Dost think perchance that if thou shouldst conquer me thou shalt become ruler of the Trojans? Priam has still plenty of sons! Did I not meet thee on Mount Ida, where father Jupiter himself was scarce able to save thee? Thou didst run like a deer, not daring to look behind thee. Thou hadst better fly now, if life is dear to thee, and take care not to get in my way a second time."

"Son of Peleus," answered Aeneas, "do not hope to frighten me with words like a child. My race is as exalted as thine own, for I was fathered by Anchises of Dardanus' family and Aphrodite is my mother. My family is old and powerful. But why do we gossip like women? Come, let us see whether it be Aphrodite or Thetis who shall mourn for her son today."

He was the first to cast his spear, and Achilles held his shield before him at arm's length, so that should it pierce the metal, it might not touch his body. But the swift-flying weapon glanced off harmlessly. Immediately he hurled his own powerful lance, but Aeneas threw himself on the ground and covered himself. The mighty lance crashed through the edge of his shield and buried itself in the ground just behind the crouching man. He arose quickly, seized a great stone and threw it at the head of Achilles, who was rushing upon him with drawn sword in a blind rage, forgetting to shield himself, so that had Vulcan's helmet not been so strong, helmet and skull would doubtless have been crushed. Aeneas was about to exult over his fall, but Achilles only staggered back a step and a god warned Aeneas to escape.

He therefore drew Achilles' heavy spear from his shield, and throwing it down, fled into the crowd of Trojans.

When Achilles came to, he found himself on the ground, supporting himself on one arm, and alone. He was astonished and said to himself: "What miracle is this? Here lies my spear and my adversary is nowhere to be seen. But indeed Aeneas must be beloved of the gods, for no one has ever vanquished me thus. But he did not venture to kill me in my swoon and is, no doubt, happy to have himself escaped. And now I must away to measure myself with other Trojans." He first returned to his Myrmidons and cheered them with loud cries of "Forward, man to man! Let none hold back! I cannot alone conquer the whole Trojan army, even Mars himself could not do that. But my lance shall never rest."

Among the Trojans the gallant Hector was going about encouraging his bands. "Do not fear, ye valiant Trojans, because the enemy has gained a single man today. Grim Achilles has certainly uttered great threats, but words are not deeds. Behold, I go forward to encounter him unafraid, though his hand were a bolt of lightning and his breast of bronze."

Achilles had already broken into the ranks of the Trojans and slain a man here and there. He was like a hungry wolf hasting from one victim to another. His lance was constantly in flight. He pierced the noble Demoleon, then laid his charioteer Hippodamos in the dust, then drawing his spear from the body, he hurled it after Polydorus, Priam's youngest son, whom his father had begged not to enter the fight. But the youth, considered the best runner in the army, was passionate and fiery and would not be restrained. Just as he was flying past, Achilles' terrible spear struck him. He fell, groaning and holding his wounded side. Thus his brother Hector espied him and in a passion of grief he advanced upon Achilles, swinging his lance like flashing lightning.

Seeing him coming thus, Achilles cried: "Ah! there is he who killed my friend! Come, Hector, come, that thou mayest meet thy doom!" He had scarcely spoken when Hector stood before him and answered unabashed: "Do not hope to intimidate me with words, O Achilles! Even if thou art stronger than I, it rests with the gods to decide whether I shall not rob thee of thy life."

He threw the lance with all his might, but it glanced off Achilles' hard-polished shield. He turned about, frightened, and fled like the wind before the hero's hissing spear. "Ah! truly Phoebus must be with thee," cried Achilles. "Destruction was hard upon thee and thou hast escaped. But the next time I meet thee I shall send thee down to Hades." He glanced about angrily for other adversaries.

See, now his chariot pursues a band of Trojans who prefer to flee all together rather than meet this single man. He pressed forward to one side, cutting them off from the rest of the army and driving them all into the river. There they paddled about like swimming poodles until Achilles, leaving his lance on the bank, sprang after them to stab those whom he could reach with his sword. Finally he drove 12 youths into the reeds and there bound their hands behind their backs with his armour straps. He then led them out and gave them into the hands of his charioteer to take back to the Myrmidons. They were destined for a cruel sacrifice to Patroclus.

Achilles turned again to the river and there he recognized with astonishment, among those who were trying in vain to clamber up the steep banks, a youth, son of Priam, named Lykaon, whom he had taken at the beginning of the war and sold for 100 oxen into Lemnos. Some years later a rich Phrygian had purchased him, from whom he had but lately escaped, having returned only eleven days before to the house of his venerable father. "Ha! there is Lykaon!" cried Achilles in surprise. "How comes he here? This time he shall taste the tip of my spear and we shall see if he return from the underworld to cause me trouble again." He went to fetch his spear and Lykaon swam as hard as he could to throw himself at his feet and beg for mercy.

"Fool!" thundered the terrible voice of the hero, "what do I want with ransom money? Before Patroclus fell I was inclined to show mercy and carried away many captives, but now not one who falls into my hands shall survive – least of all one of Priam's sons. Die then, my friend! Thou criest out in vain. Patroclus, too, had to die, who was far mightier than thou. And seest thou not how great and powerful I am? My father was a noble king, a goddess is my mother, and yet my death and doom are drawing near and sooner or later I shall fall by the spear or arrow."

The poor youth's heart and knees trembled. He spread out his arms, shut his eyes and thus received the death stroke. Then Achilles seized him by the feet and flung him far out into the river. "There! Swim among the fish," he cried. "Many a one shall feed on Lykaon. Thus I shall pursue ye all, until ye have atoned for Patroclus' death and the woe of the Achaians."

But the river god who heard this blasphemy was angered. Asteropaeus, son of Pelegon, was still standing in the water and Scamander breathed courage into him. He was practised in casting with both hands and Achilles saw him advancing with two raised spears. He shouted to him: "Who art thou, rash man? Unhappy are the parents of those who contend with me!"

"What wouldst thou know of me, great Pelide?" he answered. "I came from distant Paeonia with a gallant army but eleven days ago. Now let us fight, valiant Achilles."

With these words he let fly both lances at once upon the hero. One of them rebounded harmlessly from the shield, the other brushed his left elbow and buried itself in the sand. And now Achilles swung his bloody staff, but missed aim also, and his lance struck the sandy bank on the other side of the river. Angrily he sprang into the water with drawn sword, and striding powerfully through the waves, he approached the unlucky Asteropaeus, who was trying in vain to secure Achilles' lance. Before he could do so the hero felled him, and he sank down unconscious.

"Ah," he cried joyously, "thou couldst scarcely contend with a man of Jupiter's divine race, although thy ancestor was a river god."

Achilles drew his spear out of the earth and left the dying man gasping at the water's edge. He threw himself next upon a troop of Paeonians and drove them into the stream. Those who would not go of their own accord he thrust down into a watery grave. Then from the depths of the stream he heard the voice of the river god: "O Achilles, thou art superhuman in thy fury and the gods are always with thee. But I warn thee, that if Jupiter hath given the Trojans into thy hand this day, murder where thou wilt, but do not pollute my waters, for my stream is already glutted with the dead, and even now I can scarce flow down into the holy sea. Therefore forbear!"

Achilles heard the warning unmoved and replied: "It shall be as thou sayest, divine Scamander, but I shall never stop destroying the Trojans until I have fought the last decisive battle with Hector."

But when he chanced upon a fresh troop of the enemy, who were astray near the river, he forgot the river god's decree, and when they all jumped into the stream to gain the opposite shore he plunged in after them. Then the invisible god arose in his might, determined to destroy him. He sent wave after wave breaking over him and drew him deeper and deeper down. Struggle as he might he could make no headway against the mighty stream on whose waves he rose and fell, almost losing his balance and being carried away. The bodies of the slain bore against him and he could scarcely hold them back with his shield. He struggled to the shore, but the angry god stirred up a foaming surf which threw him back again.

Almost exhausted he struggled forward once more and grasped a young elm whose branches hung over the stream; but just as he was about to swing himself up by it the roots gave way, so that it lay across the river like a bridge. Upon this the hero reached the bank, although he vainly hoped to escape the river god thus. Furiously Scamander followed him across the fallow fields with breaking waves. He also called to his aid the other streams who generally dash their waters from the mountain heights to destroy the farmer's fields only in springtime. To the Simois, which joins him just before he flows into the sea, he cried: "Come, brother, and help me stem the power of this terrible man, else he will batter down the walls of Priam's fortress today; for none can withstand him. Arise, friend, let thy floods loose; roll down rocks and stones with thundering waves upon him, that we may tame him. For I ween that neither his strength nor beauty nor his resplendent weapons shall save him. They shall be buried deep in mud, and him will I cover with sand and heap a monument of shells and pebbles over him so high that none shall ever find his bones."

The hero was almost overcome and in his despair cried aloud: "Father Jupiter, not a single one of the gods will take pity on me, and I thought ye all loved me! But none has deceived me more than my divine mother, who promised me the glorious death of a hero before Troy. And now, alas, an ignoble end awaits me, and I shall be drowned as ignominiously as any swineherd in a mud puddle."

Then from afar a solemn and consoling voice arose. "Be comforted, Peleus' son, thou shalt not die in the waters. Keep up the struggle until the Trojans have fled the field. But when Hector is vanquished thou shalt return."

This promise filled his heart with courage, for it was the voice of Poseidon, to whom all streams are subject. And now the waters quickly subsided and were drawn into the broad gulf of the sea. Then a south wind arose which sucked up the moisture from the ground and bore it away. The valiant hero soon stood upon firm ground again and hurried away as fast as he could to plunge into the fray. Fired by his example, his people followed him like a consuming flame fanned by the wind. All who could do so fled to the walls, most of them toward the gate. The venerable Priam sat upon the top of the wall, looking mournfully down upon the sad plight of his people. When the crush at the gate became intolerable he descended and called to the guards: "Friends, open the doors and let the men in, for they can no longer withstand the terrible Pelide. When all are inside, shut the gate and put up the bars, that the enemy may not enter also."

In the confusion of flight, where none wished to be lost, Achilles and his band would doubtless have pushed in with them had not Apollo distracted his attention by the sight of Agenor. This bold youth stood concealed behind a beech tree turning over a thousand projects in his anxious mind. "What shall I do?" he said to himself. "I am too far behind to follow the others – he would take me in the back like a coward. If I try to creep along the wall and escape by way of the thickets of Ida, the bushes may hide me; then I could steal up to the gate at night and whisper to them softly to let me in. But what if he should discover me there? Then I should be lost indeed; for who is as strong as he? But his body is not invulnerable and he is a mortal like the others. Therefore I will try my skill with him, that I may save my life with honour."

Meanwhile, Achilles came running up and espied the man hidden behind the tree. Agenor stepped boldly forth and cried: "Madman, dost thou hope to destroy the fortress today? Nevermore! There are still plenty of brave men in the city, and all are fighting for parents, wives and children. On the contrary, thy own sad fate may be upon thee today, thou ungovernable monster."

With these words his flashing sword descended upon Achilles, and not without effect. He struck his shin, and only the impenetrable greaves fashioned by Vulcan prevented the leg from being shattered. Like a wounded boar Achilles pounced upon the youth, who fled through wheat fields and thickets along the river, leading his grim pursuer far away from the city; for he did not give up the chase until the youth was lost to sight. And this never would have occurred had the blow on his leg not sapped his strength. But

Apollo had arranged it thus, so that for this time the Trojans should escape; for when he returned breathless he found them safe behind their walls.

Chapter XV
Hector and Achilles – Hector's Death

THE ACHAIANS, their shields slung over their shoulders, were awaiting Achilles close under the walls of Troy. All the Trojans were within the city except Hector, who had remained outside, resolved to meet Achilles once more in combat; for he believed that he owed it to his fatherland and to his own honour, either to free his people from this dread enemy or to give up his own life for them. His old father looked gloomily down from the wall and signalled for him to come inside, but in vain.

Achilles returned from his pursuit of Agenor, his lance on his shoulder. At the sight old Priam beat his breast in consternation and he trembled, seeing his son without and alone. "Dear son," he entreated, "do not face that cruel man, for he is stronger than thou. Alas, would that the gods hated him as I do and he would soon be food for the dogs! How many of my sons he has already murdered or sold to distant isles! And now, my Hector, thou on whom the Trojan people put their hopes, wilt thou also go to meet him? Come, take pity on me! Already hath Jupiter heaped endless misfortunes upon mine old age, and should he rob me of thee now, I already foresee the enemy breaking into our fortress, carrying off our women, murdering our children, and plundering our treasures. Woe is me! for I shall become food for mine own dogs in the courtyard. Alas, that would be the most lamentable of all destinies!"

But Hector could not be persuaded and remained steadfast at the gate, awaiting Achilles. "Woe is me if I should hide now behind walls and gates!" he said. "Then Polydamas could chide me with reason for sacrificing so many good friends today. I would not follow his advice and retire into the city, but presumed to contend with Achilles alone, and alas, I have not saved a single man from his fury and, I openly avow, have myself avoided him in fear, for he is truly terrible in his might. But now I must challenge fate boldly, that the women of Troy may not denounce me for leading the people to destruction and then fleeing like a coward. But how would it be if I should lay helmet and shield on the ground beside my lance and thus go to meet the hero and offer him a peaceful settlement? Offer him Helen and all their treasure, together with half of all the goods which the houses of the Trojan princes contain? But no! I cannot approach him a suppliant. It would be base and unworthy and he would strike me down unarmed like a weak woman. No! I will fight like a man. Be my fate what it may, I will conquer or die with honour."

Achilles came up looking like Mars himself. When Hector saw him he trembled, and fled like a dove pursued by a hawk. Hector turned first to the left, then to the right, striving to tire out his pursuer; but in vain. Now they ran past the watch tower, now past the fig tree, and now by the hot springs, where were the stone basins of the washerwomen. His pursuer drove him clear round the great city, yea, even three times round the walls, and as often as Hector tried to slip through an open portal, Achilles would drive him out again into the open fields, keeping near the walls himself. But when they passed the place where the Achaians were resting on their spears awaiting the outcome, Achilles forbade anyone to cast a spear at Hector and rob him of the honour of the victory.

As they neared the hot springs for the fourth time, a man ran forward as though to offer Hector aid. It was Athena in the form of Hector's brother Deiphobus, who called to him: "Brother, I saw thy danger and am come forth to help thee. Stop and await him boldly."

"Beloved Deiphobus, how didst thou dare –"

"My soul was wrung and I could no longer look upon the grief of my father and mother."

"So be it, I will fight," said Hector, and made ready to meet the foe. "I will no longer flee before thee, O Pelide," he cried to Achilles. "My heart bids me encounter thee, whether I conquer or fall. But let us first make a compact and swear to it before the all-seeing gods. Should Jupiter give me the victory, I will not misuse thee. Thy armour will I take and leave thy body to the Achaians, that they may give it burial. And thou shalt do the same to me."

But with a furious look Achilles roared his answer. "No compacts, hated Hector! Does the lion make a compact with the cattle, or the wolf with the lambs? One of us must lie stretched upon the ground, that Mars may be satiated with his blood. I hope that thou mayest not escape me, and thus atone at once for all the woe thou hast inflicted on my people."

Thus speaking, he sent his terrible spear flying through the air. But Hector, quickly sinking on one knee, avoided it and the iron missile passed over him. Fresh courage filled him, and springing up joyfully he cried: "Wide of the mark, godlike Achilles! Thou art a good talker and crafty, hoping I should lose strength and courage. Now protect thyself, for my spear shall not strike thee lightly!"

He hurled his lance with tremendous force and did not miss the mark, for the point struck the boss of the shield with a loud crash and would have pierced both shield and breast had the shield not been forged by Vulcan himself. But the lance rebounded like a ball thrown against a wall and Hector stood confounded, for he had but one spear. He quickly looked about for Deiphobus and called loudly for another spear, but there was no answer and his brother was nowhere to be seen. Then he was filled with foreboding. "Woe is me!" he cried. "Some cunning god in Deiphobus' shape hath deceived me, and now, when I hoped he would save me, he has disappeared." In desperation he seized his sword, rushing forward like a soaring eagle swooping down upon its prey. But Achilles had already picked up Hector's spear, and, as they charged each other, the long spear reached its goal sooner than the short sword. Taken in the neck above his breastplate, the hope of Troy sank into the dust, while the cruel victor and all the Achaians loudly rejoiced.

"Ha!" cried Achilles as he drew forth his spear, "only yesterday thou wert so proudly triumphant, as thou didst invade our ships in Patroclus' stolen harness, and today thou liest powerless before the walls of thy proud fortress. Surely thou didst little dream that the slain hero had left a powerful avenger. We shall pay him all the honours of a hero, while thou shalt make a shameful end among the dogs and birds of prey."

Breathing painfully, Hector tried to speak. "I conjure thee by thy life and by thy parents, let me not be torn by Damaean dogs, but accept the bronze and valuable gold which my father and mother shall offer thee. Send my body to Ilios, that the men and women of Troy may pay me the last honours of the funeral pyre." But Achilles shouted: "Silence and die, contemptible one!"

Dying, Hector answered: "Indeed I knew I should not move thee, for thou hast an iron heart. But think of me when the gods avenge me and thou sinkest into the dust felled by the shots of Phoebus Apollo." And Death, the brother of Sleep, bore the hero's soul down to Hades. Many warriors from the Greek army came up and looked with admiration upon the splendid form of the hero. And to one another they said: "It is wonderful how much gentler he is to look on now than there at our ships when he was leading the assault."

Achilles arose among the people and spoke. "Friends, now that the gods have permitted me to subdue the man who has done us greater injury than any other, let us discover whether the Trojans will dare withstand us, without the support of their great hero. But what am I saying? My friend lies still unburied. Therefore let us chant the hymn of victory and take Hector with us as an expiatory offering for my friend."

First the procession passed by the Scaean gate, that the Trojans standing there upon the walls might see it. There sat old Priam and his spouse Hecuba, without any warning of the outcome of the combat. What a horrible sight for the venerable father and loving mother! Their bravest son, the pride and hope of Troy, dragged at the wheels of the victor's chariot! All Troy set up a despairing lament, as though the city were already in ruins and a prey to devouring flames. His mother, almost beside herself with grief, wrung her hands, and shrieking, pulled the veil from her head and tore her grey hair. And his father was scarcely to be restrained from going down to cut his son loose or die across his mutilated body. He called on those by name who stood about it; begged, implored, wept and threw himself on the ground, strewing dust on his grey head. And all those who saw it wept with him.

Hector's faithful wife, Andromache, was the last to learn the sad tidings, for she had been busy in her home attending to household duties among her women. And now, as twilight fell, she sent one of her maids to heat water in a tripod for the hero's bath when he should return. From a distance arose a sound of loud lamentation and wailing of women. The wife trembled and sad foreboding filled her heart. "Follow me," she cried to two of the maids. "My knees are trembling, for I fear the noble Achilles has cut off the valiant

Hector from the city, for he is always before all others and fears no one."

She rushed out, the servants following after her. There was nobody to be seen in the street; the cries came from the walls. The unhappy woman hastened thither. One look revealed the tragedy, and she sank down in a swoon. She lay for long as one dead, and at length, when consciousness returned, she began in a low, broken voice: "Hector! Alas, the unhappy people! Oh, that I had never been born! Now must thou go down to Hades and I remain here a widow, miserable and deserted. And thy young son – trouble and sorrow menace his future now that thou art gone – for others will seek to take his patrimony – and his childhood shall pass without a friend. For an orphaned child has no playmates; and when the other boys take their share of their fathers' feast, none calls the orphan boy to divide with him. The child casts down his eyes ashamed and weeps silently. Then, hungry, he goes about among his father's friends, pulls one by the coat, another by the cloak; and if one of them is kindly inclined, he will perhaps hold the goblet to his lips. But, alas, he does not give him his fill. The other boys, insolent and greedy, do not suffer him at their feasts, but push him away, crying: 'Thy father doth not sit at our feasts.' Then the child goes away and cries in his mother's arms. O ye gods, my Astyanax! How gayly his father used to rock him on his knees! And now, robbed of a tender father, he shall suffer much – our Astyanax, as the Trojans call him."

Thus mourned Andromache, and round about her wept and lamented the women of Troy.

Chapter XVI
Priam and Achilles – Hector's Burial in Troy

It was after sundown when the assembled Achaians dispersed. Each returned to his own ship or tent to partake of the evening meal and then lay down to rest, well content. Only Achilles could not sleep for thinking of his lost friend. In vain he tossed to and fro on his bed; sweet slumber came not nigh him. Thus

he mourned half the night, then suddenly arose, ran out into the darkness, and wandered up and down the shore, his heart full of sorrow. At last he went to Patroclus' grave, then hastened back to yoke his horses to the chariot, to which he bound Hector's corpse once more and dragged him thrice round the grave mound. After this he drove the horses back to the enclosure and threw himself again upon his couch.

Meanwhile the palace of old Priam had become a house of mourning. The afflicted father had taken no food nor drink since the death of his son, and the wailing of the wife and mother had so touched the people that they gathered about the house in crowds. Even the gods looked down pitifully on the unhappy family and Apollo appeared in dreams to Priam to strengthen his heart and encourage him to enter the Greek camp and plead for the body of his son. Jupiter commanded Hermes to accompany the old man, so that no enemy should hinder him or do him an injury by the way. Overjoyed at the divine vision, Priam forgot his complaints and went at once to the chamber where stood the chests in which he kept his treasures. He said to Hecuba, his mourning spouse: "I go to conciliate our terrible enemy with presents, and the god who has given me courage will protect me."

Then the queen burst out weeping, saying reproachfully: "Unhappy man! Hast thou lost thy senses? How canst thou go alone to the ships and meet the man who has slain so many of thy valiant sons! Truly thy heart is made of iron! Ah! if he set eyes upon thee and seize thee, that false and terrible man will have neither mercy nor respect nor reverence for thine age. Oh, do not go! Let us mourn at a distance our lost son, whom the fates at his birth decreed should be vanquished far from his people. Remain with us, dear one, that thou mayest preserve thine own life."

But the old man answered confidently: "I should not go if it were only a priest or seer who sent me, but I saw a god in my dream. He will not deceive me and my own heart impels me to go. Dost thou say the monster would kill me? Oh let him do so, if only he will strike me down upon the breast of my dear son!"

He opened the chest and took out the rich garments which he intended to take with him for a ransom—twelve splendid festal robes, twelve warm covers, and as many tunics and magnificent cloaks. Then from another chest he took ten talents of gold, four polished basins, and two tripods. Even the exquisite goblet presented by the Thracians when he visited them as ambassador from his father he did not withhold. For he did not begrudge giving even his greatest treasure to soften the hard heart of Achilles and ransom his beloved son.

When he had closed the box and turned around, he found himself surrounded by a crowd of idle people, who had come up to stare at the treasures which were to be offered for Hector's ransom. Angrily he cried out: "Out with you! Away, ye idlers! Have ye not trouble enough at home, that ye come to look upon my sorrow? Only think what ye have lost in Hector! Without his support the Achaians will have an easier victory. Then it will be your turn to lament, but I shall doubtless then be dead!"

He drove them out of the courtyard, then called for his sons, reproving them. "Where are ye? Not one is at hand when I need ye! My best sons are dead, only the good-for-nothings remain. Pack these gifts quickly in the hampers, and when it grows dark, harness the horses and summon my old, experienced Idæus."

Abashed, the sons obeyed all these commands and Hecuba began to prepare a strengthening draught for the travellers. Carrying a golden goblet in her right hand, she came out to the chariot, and placing herself in front of the steeds, she said to her husband: "Here, beloved, take this and pour out a libation to Jupiter and petition him for a safe return, as thou goest against my wishes. For I should never let thee go if I could prevent it. And even now I would counsel thee to consult the god and learn whether it is his will to protect thee. Should this prayer remain unanswered then I would say, Remain. For woe to him who goes into danger without divine support!"

The worthy man answered her: "I will obey thy behest. It is always well to lift up our hands to Jupiter." He spake and called upon the stewardess for water, which she brought in a silver dish, sprinkling him with her right hand, while with the left she held a basin beneath. After this he received the wine cup from his spouse, poured out the first drops in honor of Jupiter, and prayed aloud with eyes raised to the sky: "Father Jupiter, almighty ruler, let me approach Achilles as a friend and find favor before him. Grant me a sign that thou wilt protect me, so that I may set out confident and comforted." His wish was fulfilled, for soon afterward one of the eagles which nest high up in the clefts of Mount Ida flew past on his right hand. All who saw this rejoiced and the king and his companion mounted the chariot, full of confidence. His sons accompanied him to the city gates and, weeping, wished him luck.

Now the swift messenger of the gods descended from Olympus to the shores of the Hellespont and wandered along the road which Priam was to take. He had assumed the form of a Greek youth of noble race, whose appearance inspired confidence. Priam had arrived at the grave of Ilus, where the Scamander flows gently along, and there he had stopped to water his horses. Old Idæus saw the godlike youth coming along the river bank in the twilight and said fearfully to the king: "Look! son of Dardanus, there cometh a strange man. He will surely kill us both and make off with our goods. What shall we do? Shall we fly to the city or shall we get down and embrace his knees, begging for mercy?" Priam looked up and saw with dismay that the man was already close to the chariot. Sudden fear paralyzed his limbs, but when he saw the youth's face close by and heard his friendly voice he was reassured.

"Greeting to thee, old man." Thus the youth addressed him. "Whither goest thou so late when all other mortals are asleep? Dost thou not fear the Achaians, who are not far away? And neither thou, nor the old man thy companion, are fit to defend yourselves. But I will not harm thee, for thou art so like my dear father, noble king, that I am drawn to thee."

"Fortune favors me," cried the old man. "Now I see that Jupiter is with me, as he hath sent me such a noble guide through the dark night, of such remarkable stature and strength and of such wisdom. Truly thou hast fortunate parents."

"Tell me, old man," continued the stranger, "where art thou taking these goods? Art trying to carry thy greatest treasures to a place of safety before the destruction of Troy, or art thou flying secretly from the city for fear of the victorious enemy? For indeed thou hast lost thy chief treasure. As long as noble Hector lived, ye could battle on equal terms with the Achaians." This warmed the old father's heart. "Who art thou," he asked, "who speakest so kindly of my poor son?"

"Who does not so?" answered the stranger. "How often I have seen him in the stress of battle driving the Argives in droves before him. We often stood and admired him from a distance when Achilles forbade us to join in the battle; for I am one of his companions and came hither in the same ship with him. My father is a noble Myrmidon called Polyctor. He has property and money, but is an old man like thyself. I am the youngest of seven brothers. When Achilles went to war we cast lots to see which should go with him, and the lot fell to me. I have been wandering about, thinking of the fate of Troy, for to-morrow the Achaians intend to assault the city. They are weary of the long truce and are anxious to end the war."

"If thou art one of Achilles' companions," said Priam, "thou canst doubtless tell me whether my son's body is still lying at the ships or whether the cruel man has already thrown it to the dogs."

The stranger replied: "Not yet have dogs or birds of prey touched it, although it has lain there for twelve days and Achilles drags it round the grave of his friend every morning. Neither has decomposition touched it, and the beautiful limbs are still preserved in remarkable freshness. Seeing him, one would suppose he had but just died. Thus the gods watch over him even in death, for they always loved him."

How happy the old man was at this news. "Oh child," he cried, "how good it is for a man to pay honor to the gods with due offerings. My son never forgot that. He never failed to make sacrifice before he partook of food himself, and now in death he is receiving his reward. Oh what a happy father I am! Here, friend, take this handsome cup in remembrance of Priam. It was intended for Achilles, for I am going to him to ransom my Hector. But I have enough other gifts for him. Take it and guide me to his tent. Thou knowest the way."

"Wilt thou tempt me, old man?" answered the stranger. "I will not yield to it. I cannot take a gift from thee without Achilles' knowledge and rob him of it. No, I am too much in awe of him. Some harm might befall me. But I will accompany thee, notwithstanding, and no plunderer shall come nigh thee unpunished."

With these words he swung himself on to the chariot and placed himself between the two old men, taking the whip and reins from the herald. The horses trotted along boldly and confidently through the fields and soon brought the travellers to the walls of the camp. From a distance they saw the servants busied with the remains of the evening meal, but the god waved his staff and they all sank into a deep slumber. Then he unbarred the gates, drove inside and in the direction of the enclosure in which the tents and ships of the Myrmidons stood. There he took leave of Priam and disappeared; but before he went he pointed out Achilles' tent and encouraged the trembling old man. "Go boldly in," said he, "and embrace his knees. The sight of thee will certainly move him, for his soul is filled with melancholy. Adjure him by his father and by his divine mother, whom he loves tenderly. Thou wilt certainly touch his heart if thou speak of her."

Much comforted the king got down, leaving the chariots and the presents outside in the care of his old companion. His heart beat faster as he crossed the threshold of the tent, but after a moment of indecision he entered. He found Achilles still sitting at the table where he had supped. Beside him stood his two favorite companions, the excellent driver Automedon and the skilful spearsman Alkimos. The great hero was leaning on his elbows, sunk deep in moody thought, and was not aware of the entrance of the old man until he had fallen at his feet, clasped his knees, and kissed his hands—those horrible hands which had murdered so many of his sons. Achilles was amazed, for he had been taken completely by surprise. For a moment they gazed into each other's faces, Achilles puzzled and agitated, Priam imploring and anxious. At length a flood of tears relieved the oppressed heart of the venerable man and in a trembling voice he uttered these beseeching words:

"Remember thy father, godlike Achilles, who languishes at home, old and helpless like myself. Ah, perhaps his neighbors are even now oppressing him and there is none to protect him. But he knows that he has a good and faithful son, even though far away, who will make an end of all his troubles when he returns. The old man is full of hope and every day he cherishes sweet thoughts of thee. But woe is me! I was the happiest of fathers. I had raised fifty sons, nineteen of them born of one mother. They were my pride and joy. Then ye came to invest my city and the unhappy war took one of them after the other until but few were left. But among them all, the best one still remained—he who had protected me and all of us thus far; but now he also is no more. Alas, I can no longer beg for his life, but we long to see the dead once more and pay him the honors due my son. At home sisters, wife, and mother mourn for him, and see, here lies his unhappy father at thy feet. Give him back to me. I have brought thee rich gifts. Fear the gods! Bethink thee and imagine thy old father kneeling thus to a younger man. But I suffer as no mortal ere has done before me and press my lips to the hand which slew my children."

The heart of the invincible hero could not withstand these words and tears. He was deeply moved. The picture of his own gray-haired father rose before him and a sad longing for his embrace filled his heart. He wept aloud and bent gently down to raise the old man up, but Priam still clasped his knees tightly. Thus they both sobbed, each conscious of his own fate through the sorrow of the other. At last, when they had wept for some time, Achilles spoke. "In truth, unhappy man, thou hast been much afflicted. And yet thou hast dared to come alone and by night to the Achaian ships and to the man who has slain thy bravest sons. Thy heart is certainly strong and courageous. But come, forget thy sorrow and let me see no more of thy tears. Arise and sit here and let us calm ourselves. The gods have decreed that miserable mankind should live in sorrow, while they know naught of trouble. For many they have mixed the sad lots with the happy ones, but some receive only ill fortune, so that his whole life is a miserable failure and he is favored neither by gods nor men. Alas! neither is my father fortunate. Although the gods have bestowed worldly goods and power upon him, and although a goddess became his spouse, it is ordained that there shall be no heir to his kingdom; for alas! he shall never look upon me again, though his heart longs for me. I am not fated to return home a peaceful ruler, to enjoy a happy old age. Thus has fate robbed thee, also, of thy good son. But he is dead; therefore lament no more. Thou canst not bring him back to life. Who can do aught against the all-powerful gods?"

"Bid me not sit," sobbed the old man. "I will lie here until thou hast given me back my only beloved son, that my tears may fall upon him. But take the gifts and enjoy them in peace when thou returnest to thy native land, because thou sendest me away filled with gratitude and love."

At these words Achilles frowned and said: "Do not agitate me further, old man! Arise, for I have already determined to give thee back thy son. Do not insult me with fears and mistrust!"

Silently the old man obeyed this earnest behest and rising seated himself. Meanwhile the hero, mighty as a lion, arose and went out, followed by his two friends. Before the tent they unyoked the horses and conducted the herald inside. They then took the valuable gifts out of the hamper, except two soft garments, in which they were to wrap the body of Hector. Then, unseen by the father, Achilles caused two female slaves to wash the body and to cleanse, arrange, and anoint the hair. Next the servants wrapped the body in the fine robes and Achilles himself lifted it onto the chariot and laid it on a bier prepared for it. Then he stood still a moment and said: "Do not be angry with me, Patroclus, if thou shouldst learn, perchance, in Hades' dwelling, that I have returned Hector's body to his unhappy father. Look, he brings me a not unworthy ransom and a share of it shall be consecrated to thee."

He reëntered the tent and seated himself opposite his two guests. "Now thou canst rest content, old man," he said. "Thy son is ransomed and lies on thy chariot wrapped in fine garments. Now let us partake of food and comfort our hearts. Even Niobe did not forget to eat, although her heart was torn by bitter sorrow when Artemis had slain her six blooming daughters in one day and Apollo her six splendid sons. So let us feast. Thou canst mourn for thy son at home, for he is doubtless worthy of thy tears."

With these words Achilles got up quickly, fetched a sheep and killed it. His companions cut up the meat and roasted it carefully on spits. Then they sat down at table, Automedon passed bread in a basket, but Achilles himself served the meat, and they all ate and drank their fill. The old man admired and wondered at the splendid proportions of the great hero, his godlike mien, and his bold and fiery glance. But Achilles too was amazed at heart when he noted the awe-inspiring, majestic demeanor and the dignified countenance of the king and heard his words of wisdom. When they had finished eating, Priam said: "Now, godlike host, take me to a place, I beg thee, where we may refresh ourselves with slumber; for I have not closed my eyes since my son sank down among the dead, and this is the first food and drink that have passed my lips."

Achilles commanded his comrades to prepare a couch for Priam and his companion in the porch. The maids brought soft cushions and warm blankets, arranged them all, and lighted the strangers out with their torches. Achilles accompanied the king to the door and pressed his hand at parting. A few hours' sleep sufficed for the old man. Then he arose to awaken Achilles, for he was anxious to start before daybreak.

"Restless old man," said Achilles kindly, "depart then. But first tell me something. How soon dost thou intend to bury thy son? For until then I will keep the peace and restrain my people from battle."

"O Achilles," answered the old man, much moved, "if thou wilt grant us this favor, give us nine days to mourn the dead and prepare for his burial. On the tenth day we will burn him, on the eleventh erect the grave mound, and on the twelfth, if it must be, we will resume the war."

"Let this, too, be as thou desirest," replied Achilles. "I will hold the army in check for as long as thou hast demanded."

He clasped the old man's wrist to assure him of good faith, then accompanied the chariot as far as the gate in the wall, taking care that none of the Achaians should harm the old man. Priam drove once more through the well-known fields, past the ford of the flowing Scamander, where yesterday the friendly youth had appeared. And now, just as he was watering his horses there, the sun rose. Cassandra, Priam's favorite daughter, who had been standing on the watch tower since dawn awaiting the return of her father with beating heart, recognized the travellers. She waited until she could discern all plainly, even the covered body of her brother on the chariot. Then she ran down the stairs to the palace, calling her mother and sisters loudly. "Only look, they are coming! Hasten, Trojans, to look upon the body of Hector, if ye have ever rejoiced over him alive as he returned from the battlefield. For he was the pride of the city and of all the people!"

All who heard her voice hurried forth, men and women, all hearts filled with boundless sorrow. But first of all came the old mother and Andromache. They went out to meet the chariot and stopped it at the city gate with loud cries. Mother and wife threw themselves on the body and wet it with their tears, tore their hair, touched his head, and lifted up the cloths to look upon his wounds. The crowd gathered, weeping, about them. But the king cried: "Stand back and let the horses pass! Ye may weep your fill when I have carried him into the house."

They all stood aside and the king entered the city, the crowd following him to the palace. When the corpse was lifted from the chariot the universal lament began afresh. Singers were brought to chant the hymn of mourning and round about the women sobbed, especially Andromache, the beautiful princess. She held the dead man's head in her hands and moaned: "Beloved, thou hast lost thy life, but the widow, alas, is left behind and thy young son. How shall he grow to manhood? For before that Troy will fall, as thou art dead, who didst defend the walls, the women, and lisping children. Soon they will be carried away to bondage, myself among them. And thou, my dear son, wilt go hence to endure ignominy with thy mother, if indeed some cruel Achaian entering the conquered city does not seize thee by thy tender neck and hurl thee down from the tiles into the streets below. Thy valiant father hath slain many Achaians; therefore the people mourn. O Hector, what unspeakable sorrow thou hast caused thy parents, but I am unhappy above all others! Dying, thou couldst not give me thy hand nor speak words of wisdom which I might have cherished." Thus she spake, weeping, fathomless sorrow in her heart.

The old mother also could not be torn from her beloved son. First she caressed his head, then the cold hands, as though she hoped to call him back to life. Helen too lamented over the dead. "Hector dearest," she cried, "thou didst love me more than any of my husband's brothers. What insults I have suffered since the hero brought me to Troy! Thou alone hadst never an unkind word for me. Yea often, when thy mother or one of my sisters-in-law or even their husbands heaped abuse upon me, thou didst mollify the angry ones and make peace. How thy friendly encouragement comforted me! Ah, I shall never hear that dear voice again, and I have no longer a friend in this house, where all turn from me with loathing."

Thus she lamented, and all the women mourned with her. But the venerable Priam now raised his commanding voice and spake. "Ye Trojans, fetch wood into the city and go without fear that the Danæans are lying in wait for you. For Peleus' son promised with a sacred vow not to raise his hand against us until the twelfth day."

Quickly they yoked oxen and horses to the carts, and on the tenth day, when golden Eos arose, the people all assembled for the funeral obsequies of Hector. With loud lamentations they carried out the corpse and laid it on the high scaffolding, which they set on fire. When the pyre had burnt itself out, they quenched the gleaming embers with red wine. His brothers and the comrades of the hero gathered together the white bones out of the ashes and deposited them in a golden urn, which was placed in the grave and gigantic blocks of stone heaped upon it. The grave mound was raised above it and sentinels were stationed about the place so that the Greeks should not surprise and attack them. After this all the people returned into the city and the solemn funeral feast was held in Priam's palace. Thus the Trojans paid honor to the body of great Hector.